Last Train to Happiness

E. R. Bendrihem

Last Train to Happiness

Published by Lainemar Publishing

Printed by KDP

Formatting by Rik-Wild Seas Formatting (http://www.WildSeasFormatting.com)

Cover Design by Germancreative

The Library of Congress has established a Cataloguing-in-Publication record for the contents of this book.

ISBN: 978-1-7338684-4-0

Acknowledgements

This is my third book. In my first book, *Believing in Second Chances*, I was very fortunate to have the support of my family: my lovely wife, *Elaine*, our daughter, *Danielle*, and my brother *Maurice*. Elaine and Danielle have spent countless hours reading and re-reading various versions of the manuscript—each time coming up with great recommendations to ensure the continuity of time and content matter. My brother Maurice, although dealing with medical issues, has also contributed valuable changes to the book.

List of Characters

Andy Fitzpatrick	Police officer and Randall's friend
Darlene	Marcus' assistant
Dr. Prescott	Tom's client and friend
Harvey	Rachel's pug
Jacob	Jeweler, Joseph's partner
Jason	Randall's buyer of stolen goods
Jim Stevens	Tom's brother
Joseph	Jeweler, Jacob's partner
Joshua	Jeweler & Marlene's partner-in-crime
Marcus Jefferson	Tom's boss
Marlene	Jacob's assistant
Max	Susan's late husband
Michelle Jefferson	Marcus' wife
Rachel	Susan's sister
Randall Lapointe	Jewel thief
Rebecca	Jacob's wife
Samuel	Diamond dealer
Susan Anderson	Tom's girlfriend, Max's wife
Tom Stevens	Main character

Chapter 1

*T*he clock struck seven as it had done for the last thirty-five years, but this time Tom didn't have to get out of bed. It's amazing how hard it is to break some habits in life after so many years. The one major difference today is that Tom was not going to make the 8:05 to Providence-maybe a thing of the past for him.

Today, Tom planned to take a train ride across the country to slow his pace down—he's led a very fast pace up to this point, and he was not aware of the different adventures that lay ahead of him: different places to see and different people to meet along the way. For health reasons and on advice by his doctor, he needed to slow his pace down and enjoy life for once. *How did I let all those years get by me?* he continuously asked himself.

As was promised, the Uber driver arrived on time. To Tom's surprise, a black limo came to take him to the train station—he felt like a VIP. "Good morning, sir. Thank you so much for picking me up and on time," Tom informed the driver. "Not a problem, sir. It's our pleasure," the driver responded in a surprised way, not used to being appreciated nor, for that matter, being thanked for picking up a passenger.

The train had already arrived on gate thirteen, and passengers were in the process of boarding in an orderly fashion. Tom got out of the vehicle and joined the others in line. The conductor took Tom's ticket and signaled him to go to the left to car number one. Tom found it to be a bit strange as there was no one else boarding that car.

As he entered, he realized it was totally empty except for one individual who sat across from his assigned seat. Tom felt inclined to introduce himself. "Hello Miss, my name is Tom Stevens. It looks like you and I are the only ones in this car so far." Tom cordially introduced himself with a welcoming smile. "Hello, Mr. Stevens. My name is Susan. I think we're going to be riding together."

Susan had short auburn hair with a medium-sized frame. Her facial expressions reflected she may have had a hard life — stress had a way of leaving its footprint on her. Tom could see from Susan's reaction that she wanted to be left alone and he respected her privacy accordingly.

Chapter 2

Tom has been a workaholic all of his life. Driven by his job to continuously be at the top of his game, he won top awards every year along with the big bonuses that went along with those accolades. Socializing was not in his vocabulary as one day rolled into another for him. He looked forward to the weekends to be able to go to the office where it was very quiet, and he would be able to get a lot of work done. His family consistently begged Tom to stop and smell the roses once in a while. In one ear and out the other went all the life-improving recommendations given to him. He was set in his ways, and he was not about to change easily.

Tom thought he had it all figured out until one day when he tried to get out of bed, and his legs were no longer able to keep him on his feet. As he sat on the floor to catch his breath, he continuously asked himself if he was dreaming. *This cannot be happening to me*, he muttered to himself. After a while, Tom realized he was very much awake contrary to the lack of sensation in his legs. No matter how many times he talked and rationalized to himself to get up from the floor, his legs did not listen to a word he said—his legs were more stubborn than he was.

Tom stretched and reached for his cell phone on his night stand and decided to call one of his clients who was in the medical profession—Dr. Prescott, a neurologist. "Dr. Prescott, my apologies for calling so early in the morning," Tom apologized profusely to his client of over twenty-five years. "No problem, Tom. I don't know how many times I've called you on weekends and holidays and you were always very gracious to take my calls. What can I do for you?" the doctor asked. Tom explained, hoping his doctor/client would prescribe a magic pill to make everything go away.

Instead, Dr. Prescott opted to pay Tom a visit as he lived nearby—a practice he was not accustomed to doing for most of his patients. Tom and Dr. Prescott have had a very close relationship over the years so the doctor didn't think twice about making the house call. Tom had been his consultant and friend for many years, and he was very grateful for all the money-saving advice Tom had provided him in the past. As far as Dr. Prescott was concerned, there weren't many Tom Stevens around— he was very fortunate to have him in his life—both as his friend and consultant.

After performing various tests on Tom's legs, Dr. Prescott unofficially concluded, with the limited tests he was able to perform, that he needed to slow down and get some rest. The stress was beginning to take its toll tightening all of his muscles and nerves. The doctor gave him some muscle relaxers along with a prescription to obtain more if Tom felt he needed them.

Tom worked from home for a few days since he was not able to drive himself to the office. Since Tom didn't know how to relax, working from home gave him a sense of purpose and made him feel productive. Working was one of those things he was very good at.

At times, he had to close his eyes when the medicine kicked in—it made him feel very sluggish. He felt very much at ease and lethargic following his short naps. It gave him time to reflect on his life and consider what might have been: what if he had gotten married, what if he had children, what if he had done this or done that? *Was life sending me a wake-up call?* he thought at times. Tom needed to pay more attention this time.

Tom was in his mid-fifties and both his family and Mother Nature were sending him messages *to slow down or else*! He was financially secure to stop working if he chose to do so—he didn't have to work for the rest of his life should he decide to come to a full stop. Money was not an issue for Tom; he just didn't know how to stop working. He was driven to work twenty-four hours a day if his body didn't ask for some downtime.

Tom's cell phone rang waking him from his deep sleep. "Tom, this is Dr. Prescott, did I wake you? How are you feeling? You sound like you just woke up. I just wanted to let you know you that I have analyzed your tests and blood work." Suddenly, Tom quickly felt alert and honed in on every word his client said.

"I highly recommend you take it easy for a while. You were extremely lucky this time, but I don't know if you're going to be as lucky next time. You had acute stress which could lead to cardiovascular disease. If you value your life, you *have to* reduce your stress level—you need to slow down from 100 mph to 30 mph—you cannot continue the way you've been going. Are you listening to me, Tom?" Dr. Prescott raised his voice a bit towards the end of his quasi-lecture for Tom to realize that he was serious.

"Thanks, Doc. I hear you loud and clear. It was very scary to find myself sitting helplessly on the floor. I know what I have to do," Tom replied very somberly, with a very earnest acknowledgment.

Contrary to his past work ethics, Tom decided to listen to his inner voice. He planned to stop working for — at least — a month and then evaluate how he felt. He decided to book a trip from Providence to San Diego by train. Not a specific destination, he simply needed to be in a quiet environment to be with his thoughts and have his body catch up on life.

Everyone in his office applauded his decision and wished him well during his vacation. Vacation was something very unfamiliar for Tom as he hardly ever took one. As a matter of fact, Tom must have had weeks or even months of unused vacation time he hadn't taken.

Chapter 3

Tom took the opportunity to sit back in his seat and begin a conversation with his newly found passenger/companion. "If I may ask, Miss, where are you headed?" Tom inquired, as he attempted to strike a conversation. It was getting too quiet for him. The passenger sitting across from him, Susan, appeared to be in her own little world. As she did not appear to be very present, Tom did not want to bother her, as he could see she was in deep thought and he didn't want to disturb her—she appeared to be in her own little world. Since he wished to respect her space and privacy, he did not repeat his question.

"I'm sorry, Mr. Stevens, did you say something?" All of a sudden, Susan spoke out from her trance. "It appears, we're going to be passengers for a while, and I can see you would like to be left alone and not be disturbed. My apologies for disturbing you."

"I've been through a great deal lately, sir, and I'm just trying to come to grips with my life," Susan informed Tom politely, with a look of sadness about her. Tom could see she had the world on her shoulders. "I know what you mean. I'm trying to do the same, but please don't let me disturb you. I will be mindful of that in the future," Tom said, as he took out a book out from his case. "May I ask why you are going to San Diego, Mr. Stevens, if I may have the liberty of asking?" Susan decided to start a conversation. "Please, Susan, call me Tom."

Suddenly, Susan felt a bit more comfortable with her newly found passenger and began to share with Tom some of the events in her life that had led her to this train to San Diego where she could get away from it all. She explained how her husband mistreated her, and how he lost his life in a tragic automobile accident.

She paused and somberly looked outside at all of the passing countryside. The peaceful setting gave her a sense of comfort to open up to Tom. He could see she was in deep thought and began feeling very sympathetic towards her. He could also see she was hurting, and he was very surprised she — unexpectedly — volunteered a great deal of personal information — as if the passing countryside calmed her down and made her feel more at ease. He knew he had a long ride ahead of him, so he did not mind listening and perhaps, attempt to make her feel better.

"It seems to me, Susan, you are trying to get away from it all — leaving your past behind. You are aware that you can go from one end of the country to the other, and you would still be carrying all of your burdens with you. Getting away may give you a break to step back and get a fresh perspective on life." Susan stopped to process everything Tom, a total stranger, said to her.

"Are you carrying all of your burdens as well, Mr. Stev…, sorry, Tom," Susan asked, as she decided to give Tom a bit of his own advice. "Actually, I'm trying to catch up on my health. I've been working too much in my life, and nature has decided to give me a wake-up call to slow down," Tom relayed. He decided it was his turn to share the reason that brought him to this point as well; however, Tom noticed Susan went back into her shell and closed her eyes.

Tom decided to close his eyes as well and join her in an afternoon nap. It was very strange for Tom to sit back and relax—a new concept for him. From the little information Susan had shared before her nap, it appeared that she needed to get away as much as he did.

Prior to closing his eyes, Tom decided to turn around and again marveled that no other passengers were in the car with them. *Maybe I'll ask the conductor when he comes by*, he thought.

Chapter 4

Susan grew up in a very religious home and her mom and dad worshipped the ground they each walked on. They all helped and respected each other. Susan had a sister, Rachel, with whom she regarded as her best friend. They shared their toys growing up, as well as being each other's confidants as they grew up. They all went to church together on Sundays and they were very thankful for the little they had. No one ever complained for the things they didn't have—always thankful and blessed for the things they *did* have.

Susan's mom was a seamstress to help put food on the table, and her dad was a worker in the local steel mill. They didn't have much as far as material things were concerned, but they had each other and they were always happy—something that money couldn't buy. Love and family made them the wealthiest people in the area. These values were passed down to both Rachel and Susan—they were both better off for these attributes.

Susan met Max, her childhood sweetheart, in grammar school. They stayed together all through high school. Max treated her with respect and he enjoyed getting together with her family. He felt very much loved and at home with her family; more so than with his own family. Susan's family noticed how well Max treated her, and they were very happy she had found someone who cared for her. Her parents felt the respect and admiration Max had for her was far more important than material things.

Max reminded Susan very much of her own dad — strong work ethics and loved the family life very much. During the middle of their senior year in high school, Max decided to join the Marines after he graduated. He felt the need and drive to serve his country. His enlisting in the armed forces reminded Susan when her dad had joined the Army during the Korean conflict.

At first, she was uncomfortable with the idea, but then she recalled how her dad had joined the Army after high school, and he had turned out to become a great husband and father. All of this made Susan feel more comfortable and very much at ease with Max joining the Marines.

After graduation, Max joined the Marines and was sent to Germany followed by a tour in Vietnam. Susan was devastated when she heard the news, as Vietnam had made the nightly news seven days a week. It was very much *in her face* so to speak. Every time body bags were shown on TV to be shipped back to the states, she envisioned Max occupying one of them. She was not going to feel comfortable until she saw Max come back home. This was a very rough time for Susan.

Susan was notified by Max's family that he had been injured in Vietnam and was being sent back home. Susan was devastated for his injuries but thrilled she would soon be in his arms. When he came home, he needed both physical and mental attention. Unfortunately, the mental injuries took more of a toll on both Max and Susan.

Susan was very patient with Max when he got back and she made sure he went through all the medical treatments at the local VA hospital. In no time, Max was able to walk and run again — the physical therapies were a success. The psychological treatments, on the other hand, were not as successful, but Susan's love for Max helped him along the way.

At times, Susan stared at him looking to see if she could find the old Max she once knew. He was there somewhere, but she had to really peel back the many layers to see if she could get a glimpse of the old Max. The war did a great deal of mental damage to Max, as well as to many young men and women who came back from the war.

Susan did not give up on Max. Her family was very proud of how devoted she was to a person who had fought for his country. Within a year, Susan and Max got married. She worked in a local bank as a teller, and he got a job in the local post office in the backroom operations. Because of his war injuries, management felt they should limit his interactions with customers.

Susan could see Max was not the same old Max she once knew in high school, but she prayed and worked with him every day. She had the patience of a saint. Her faith gave her the strength to go from day to day. Her parents continued to support her; she was a devoted wife who lived her wedding vows word by word—*in sickness and in health.*

Chapter 5

*T*om sat back in his seat and occasionally glanced at Susan who peacefully sat in her seat. He opened his book and wondered when he sat down last with a book. This was a new experience for him — to relax and enjoy a good book. On occasion, his mind would digress to his office, wondering who took over his duties to handle and manage his accounts he had worked long and hard to develop.

He treated his clients like family, and he worked very closely with them. Prior to taking a leave of absence, he contacted his major clients to let them know he was going on vacation. They all applauded him for getting away from it all. His clients assured him he was doing the right thing which made him feel more comfortable for the decision he had made — a long overdue one at that.

Tom continued to steal glances at Susan. She looked very angelic as she sat in her seat with her eyes closed. From the small chat they recently had, Tom sensed she had a lot on her mind that weighed heavily on her shoulders. He wished he could help her with the cross she appeared to carry. At times, he noticed her twitch as if she were having a bad dream. *Maybe fate put me on this train to help her*, he thought.

Tom always thought that things in life happened for a reason. Just as he couldn't get up from the floor several weeks ago, he felt it was a sign for him to stop and slow down. He now made it a point to listen to the signs that life was throwing his way.

As Susan slowly woke from her catnap, she looked up at Tom and decided to start a conversation with him. "Tom, if I may ask, how far are you going on this train?" Tom looked up from the book he was trying to get into. He was very thankful for Susan's interruption from a book he was very close to stop reading anyway.

Tom was not used to either sitting down nor having the patience to read a book. He very much welcomed the opportunity to start a conversation with Susan, no matter what the subject may have been. Personal interaction was a rare treat for him, and he looked forward to entertaining it. His full-time job was to talk with clients about business twenty-four hours a day. He was not accustomed to being quiet for any period of time.

"Oh, I have no specific destination, Susan. I just decided to take a ride across the country to try to relax and allow my body to catch up on life. How about yourself?" "My sister lives in San Diego, and she's been hounding me for months to pay her a visit. She felt a change in scenery would do me some good."

"Do you have any other siblings?" Tom inquired. "No, just my sister, Rachel. It's been a while since I last saw her. I've been very busy trying to get my life back in order after my husband, Max, passed away." "So sorry to hear about your husband." "It's been a blessing in disguise. Maybe I'll tell you about it one day," Susan decided to open her heart a bit and give Tom a sneak peek.

"Tom, do you have any siblings?" "Yes, I have a brother, Jim, who lives in Providence. I was there with him when his wife passed away from a long illness."

"Sorry to hear, I'm sure you must have been a great help to him."

Since Max passed away, Susan did not have many opportunities to talk one-on-one; especially, with a total stranger. From the short time they knew each other, Tom gave her the impression that he cared. She did find it refreshing to talk with someone who was not there to judge her, but to possibly help her—just by being there to listen.

Small conversations continued between Susan and Tom to pass the time, but neither one wanted to fully open up; more so for Susan as her life had more twists and turns than Tom's. They had just met and neither one of them had established a comfort factor with the other. Deep inside they both wanted to get to know each other better, but they were very hesitant to embark on that ship.

It was going to be a long train ride to San Diego, and there were going to be plenty of opportunities for deeper conversations. This was definitely a new experience for Tom—talking to a woman on a personal basis. He did not have much experience in the area of human development; however, Tom surprised himself that he felt comfortable striking a conversation with Susan.

Chapter 6

"Next stop, Hope Junction. Ladies and gentlemen, we will be stopping in the next ten minutes. We will be parked at the station for about an hour on gate thirteen. Please feel free to disembark and stretch your legs. Make sure you take your boarding pass to get back on the train along with any valuables you may have," the conductor announced over the public address system.

"Were you planning to get off, Tom?" "Yeah, I've been sitting for too long. I need to get off and stretch my legs—get my circulation going. My doctor recommended I go for a walk whenever possible. You?" "Sure, why not; it would do me a world of good. Would you like some company? We can walk around town for a few minutes and do some window shopping if you like? Who knows what we'll come across!" Susan suggested.

Tom and Susan walked down the steps of the train towards the platform. "Susan, did you notice anything strange?" Tom asked, while looking around and noticing an empty platform. As Tom asked, Susan observed the platform as well. "Are we the only ones around?" "That's exactly what I was thinking," Tom noted, while she attempted to look for any other signs of life.

"Oh, well, maybe the others got off before us." They paid no attention and continued to walk. They just had that strange feeling that something wasn't right as there was no one else in the entire train except for them.

When the whistle blew, they walked back to the train and, again, noticed no one else was around. "I saw a lot of people in line when I got on the train. It doesn't make any sense that no one is here now," Tom replied. The train pulled out of the station from gate thirteen, and both Tom and Susan sat in their assigned seats. Tom felt he wanted to get to know Susan better.

Tom didn't have much of personal interaction with women other than the women he worked with in the office. Either he didn't have the opportunity, or he just didn't have the time — a bona fide workaholic. He was in the midst of crossing unchartered waters with Susan. He wanted to take a chance to do so, but he was a bit hesitant to start a friendship with a female companion with whom he had no prior experience. He felt lost and Susan noticed he wasn't an individual who planned on taking advantage of her. She found his air of innocence very welcoming. This was a new experience for her as well compared to the marriage she had with Max.

Shortly after Max died, Susan noticed that men started knocking on her door to begin a new relationship — something she was not very interested in pursuing. Her mind was not ready to accept any budding relationships; at least, for the foreseeable future. The last couple of years had been very debilitating for her. Max had a very bad drinking problem in addition to exhibiting abusive behavior — she was not ready for a relationship with anyone at the moment. She needed to get her life in order first — both physically and mentally. Tom appeared to be a very decent person who made an attempt to be friendly with her.

Tom found the interaction with a non-business-related female interesting and intriguing. He did not know how to react to it—he was like a fish out of water. Susan picked up on those vibes immediately. She noticed he had trouble making eye contact with her. They found themselves in a precarious position.

Tom was a neophyte when it came to women, and Susan was a widow who was not ready for any relationship. Neither one had any expectations of the other—a perfect situation for the both of them.

They both felt and sensed they were just going to be casual acquaintances who shared a train ride together. Most likely, once they reached their respective destinations, they would each go their separate ways and not see each other ever again. In this manner, they could talk freely with each other, and all will be forgotten once they parted ways, or so they thought.

The train rolled down to the next town. There was very little chit-chat between Tom and Susan. They each assumed the other didn't want to be disturbed—each one made an effort to be as courteous as possible with each other. At times, they hoped the other would kick off a conversation. Suddenly, the train began to screech as it applied its brakes. In looking out of the window to see why the train stopped so abruptly, a herd of cows began crossing the tracks. A voice came over the speaker apologizing for the sudden braking. "Sorry, folks, we didn't see the cow crossing sign," the conductor attempted to make humor out of the situation.

This emergency braking gave Susan and Tom an opportunity to start a conversation. "Can you imagine those cows," were comments they both expressed. "What were they thinking?" Tom asked. This broke the ice between the both of them. Susan began to get comfortable—a new experience for her. She found this situation a breath of fresh air that was long overdue.

Chapter 7

As the train rolled from one town to the other, Tom and Susan began to get a little more comfortable with each other. Their conversations were more personal in nature as their comfort level with each other began to slowly increase. Sitting across from each other for a long period of time over a long distance has had a positive effect on both of them.

"How long do you plan to stay with your sister?" Tom asked, as he tried to break the lull in conversation. "I'm planning on staying with Rachel for as long as she'll have me. We haven't really talked about it. Knowing my sister, she would love to have me move in with her." "Would that be a bad thing, Susan?"

"No, it wouldn't, but she has her life in San Diego, and I have some roots back in Providence. We'll see what happens when I get there. For now, I haven't made any decisions. What about you?" Susan asked. Tom informed her he did not have any plans in mind as well, other than to get his health back and get back to work.

"To tell you the truth, Susan, I don't know what I'm going to do. For now, I might go back to work. Or, if I really enjoy my time off, I might just retire. I'm going to see what fate has in store for me." "So, you're going to play it by ear, so to speak?" "Yes, so far," Tom informed her, as he enjoyed the interaction he was having with Susan.

"Tom, life is strange and unpredictable. We go through life thinking we're on the right path at the time only to realize later on we should have zigged instead of zagged." "What would you have done differently if you had the opportunity to go back in time?" Tom asked, feeling very philosophical.

"I can give you all sorts of *what-ifs,* but you and I both know that whatever options there are, they would just be pie-in-the-sky dreams that may or may not have been possible in reality." "Very true, but such discussions might affect where you go from here, and they may just give you fresh perspectives or alternatives to move in a different direction."

"I never thought of it that way, Tom. Do you think your life might take a different approach?" "Susan, I honestly hope so as I don't wish to relive the life that I've had." Neither had an idea how life was going to be for each other, but they found it therapeutic to talk about it.

Both Susan and Tom sat back in their seats and looked very intently out the window thinking about the advice they had each given to one another. What could have been might very well be what it is. "I had a dream not too long ago that I was invited to a gathering by a friend in my neighborhood. I dreamt I met someone who was going to change my life for the better," Susan relayed, as she appeared to have been transported back to a make-believe world. Both her eyes and her body language reflected a very euphoric state of mind.

"If I may ask, where else did this dream take you?" "Well, from what I recall, I met someone who had recently lost his spouse as well — a common bond between us. We dated for a while and we took trips together. Something like that." "It sounds like you found yourself in a good place?" "Yes, Tom, I did, and I felt very much at peace and happy. In fact, I was very disappointed when I woke up only to find myself caught in an illusion. For a split moment, I wanted to go back to sleep to continue my dream."

Tom could see Susan was very comfortable sharing her dream with him. It was a place where she found herself to be safe and happy. She needed this safe-haven in her life contrary to the pain and agony she must have felt in her real life — an escape from reality.

Tom listened attentively and was very content she was in a happy place. When Susan realized she had relayed a very personal dream to a total stranger, tears began to roll down her face — a sense of sadness overtook her make-believe world. Tom, realized that her metamorphic transportation back to reality had a negative effect on her. He leaned over and gently touched her hand. Susan had not felt this sense of warmth and caring in a very long time — it momentarily took her back to the feelings she had in her dream.

"Thank you, Tom," Susan relayed, with a very innocent and genuine smile. "For what?" "For sharing my pain with me." "You're welcome. I'm glad I was able to be of some help. You looked like you were really hurting, and you needed someone by your side." "For a brief moment, Tom, you took me back to my make-believe world, and you made me feel at peace and happy again."

"We all need a happy place to go to once in a while. As a matter of fact, I had a similar dream a couple of weeks ago that I also met someone at my brother's house who happened to be a do-it-yourselfer. We went to Home Depot together and purchased supplies to paint my brother's house. I was very surprised when I woke up as I neither had any experience with painting nor with women, for that matter," Tom shared, realizing he had that same good feeling Susan had when she shared her dream.

They both shared their respective dreams which took them to a place where they found themselves to be very happy and content—a make believe world where they were the only two inhabitants.

"Tom, I have an idea. Why don't we go back to that dream together?" For a brief moment, Tom felt Susan had asked him out on a date, and he liked how that felt. In the past, Tom didn't have the nerve nor the will to ask anyone on a date. Most likely, because he didn't make the time.

Now, however, he found himself with all the time in the world, and he also found himself in an empty train car with an attractive woman. *Did life bring us together?* he briefly thought. In reality, Tom had no idea or comprehension what that meant, but he liked the way it felt. He wanted to freeze this moment in time and preserve it forever as in a snapshot of a camera.

Chapter 8

Tom has one brother, Jim, who is four years younger than he is. Growing up they shared everything. Jim was far more outgoing than his older brother and, on many occasions, he tried to set his older brother up with blind dates, but Tom consistently came up with excuses to avoid going out with his brother and a stranger. Tom preferred to stay at home to study. Time for dating, according to Tom, was not in his social calendar. As a matter of fact, Tom had no social calendar at all.

When Jim got married, he felt bad Tom was going to be left all alone. There were many instances where Jim invited Tom over for dinner. Jim's wife, Betty, understood what both Jim and Tom were going through without each other's company. When Betty passed away, Tom and Jim resumed their coffee get-togethers at Starbucks. They frequented one location so often, a booth should have been named after them. When his wife passed away, Jim leaned a great deal on his older brother. Jim was very depressed as he was by Betty's side for every moment—she battled a deadly disease.

Tom was also there for his younger brother whenever he needed him, and Jim was very appreciative to have a shoulder to cry on. Tom wanted to keep his brother company and helped him get through the day. He got together with his brother often to get him out of the house that was filled with so many great memories of Betty. He also distracted Jim by sharing the news of the day with him—mostly about sports and politics.

They were good for each other.

A couple of years had passed, and Jim began to date again. Many attempts were made by Jim to double date with his brother again, but Tom continued to come with a myriad of excuses to stay at home instead. After a while, Jim gave up; he just came to the conclusion that either his brother was too shy, or he was just plain scared. Tom was a loner and that was that; however, Jim did not totally give up on his older brother. All Jim wanted for his brother was for him to be happy. He didn't want him to be alone.

Tom was very thankful he was able to meet with his brother on an ongoing basis. He felt very sad for Jim when his wife passed away, and he did all he could to keep him occupied. Jim, in turn, constantly reminded his older brother that there was life after work, and he shouldn't make work his life. Jim never gave up on his older brother; he kept him involved as much as possible. In retrospect, Tom knew his brother was right; he only had the best of intentions for him.

Chapter 9

Tom continued to watch Susan sleep, and, after having had various conversations with her, he felt the need to take the hurt away from her. For some reason, he felt a sense of responsibility to make her smile and be happy again. Occasionally, Tom watched her move from side to side while she slept, as if she were searching for a comfortable position.

Tom slowly got up from his seat, and, unbeknownst to her, sat next to her and leaned his body towards her to catch her head the next time she swayed her body to one side. As his shoulder prevented her body from swaying, her body came to a full rest. He felt her head slowly sink onto his shoulder. Tom felt good that he was able to provide some level of comfort for her.

Tom could feel Susan peacefully sleep on his shoulder. Her short auburn hair glistened every time the sun shone through the window. The floral essence that emanated from her hair was a very strange and welcoming feeling for Tom—a feeling he was starting to get comfortable with. *How can anyone mistreat an angelic individual like this*? Tom pondered. He wanted this moment to last forever. He felt very much at peace. If only he could give that feeling to her on a silver platter. Maybe he could?

Susan began to wake up and realized Tom was sitting next to her, and she had used his shoulder as a pillow. When Tom noticed the weight of her head lift from his shoulder, he informed her of her restlessness while she slept. "Thank you, Tom, that was very nice of you. Actually, you felt very comfortable and I felt I had a very restful sleep." "That's great, maybe that's what you needed." A feeling of being wanted overtook Tom—a feeling he began to like.

"If I may ask, why didn't you ever marry?" Susan, from nowhere, decided to ask Tom. "I don't know. Maybe I was too engrossed in my work, or I was just afraid." "Afraid of what, Tom?" "I truly don't know, Susan. I can't put my finger on it. Time just passed and I didn't realize that years or, for that matter, life had a way of passing me by. I guess I didn't have my priorities in order. I can give you a thousand reasons, and I would not be able to come up with the correct one. It could have been a combination of many things. The thought did cross my mind, at times, and I wondered what it would have been like."

Suddenly, Susan caught herself and realized she had just crossed unchartered waters herself—getting more personal with Tom than she wanted to get. She wished she could have taken back her last question—it was too late. It just came out. She started to feel very comfortable with him being by her side. When Tom was ready to get up to go back to his seat, Susan turned towards him and asked, "you are welcomed to sit here, if you like?" A feeling of elation came over Tom—a feeling he had not felt before. *Am I dreaming all this?* he asked himself.

Tom found himself having personal conversations about his life with a total stranger. He never had the opportunity to do so in the past until now. Life had brought Susan and him together. For years, Jim attempted to orchestrate a similar situation for Tom with different people, but Tom was not ready until now.

There was a chemistry that began to surface between Tom and Susan, subtle, but with a great deal of potential. They were both very cautious of this newly found relationship they both found themselves in — both being very careful not to come to any conclusions. *Were we meant to meet on this train and ride in an empty train car?* Susan asked herself. She found herself very fortunate that a total stranger had just walked into her life and became a very nice and pleasant riding companion. She was very thankful for the moments she shared with Tom. *We'll see where this train ride takes us,* she thought to herself.

Chapter 10

The train traveled through the countryside of Iowa where dairy farms were widespread as far as the eye could see. Both Susan and Tom commented on the various farms and farm animals — small chit-chat that helped them pass the time. Every so often, the conductor would announce the approaching town, but neither Tom nor Susan paid any attention — they were in their own little world. They were focused on each other's conversation.

Neither Tom nor Susan looked at their cell phones to check on their emails or texts. They were in their own real life face-to-face chat room. Technology didn't have any room for the moments they shared. They liked being disconnected from the rest of the world — a first for the both of them. They found their company more interesting than what the internet had to offer. New conversations were more stimulating than anything they had encountered for a long time.

Tom had spoken to a few women in his life — mostly professional and family; however, he had not encountered this type of relationship before. Although he had trouble dealing with it, he was intrigued by it. He felt a desire to explore it further. Susan was medium in frame, and he found her to be very pleasant in appearance — something he had problems in processing as well. He tried not to read too much into it — he was enjoying the moment with a very lovely and pleasant individual.

Suddenly, Susan noticed Tom staring at her. "Is everything OK, Tom? You look like you're staring into oblivion." "No, no, I had a few things on my mind. I have to stop thinking about work and enjoy where I am at the moment." "I know I'm enjoying the moment and I have to thank you for being here with me. I was very depressed when I got on the train, and you have been a great help." Tom honed in on every word she said. They began to get more personal than either one had done in the past, at least, for Tom. Tom had a hard time comprehending the whole situation, but, nevertheless, he liked it. He did not want the moment to end.

"Susan, I'm going to get a snack and a beverage. Would you like me to get you anything?" As Tom got up from his seat, he temporarily lost his balance; most likely, from sitting down for a long period of time. As he tried to get his footing, his body went forward, and he managed to break his fall by instinctively holding on to the first thing to break his fall—Susan's knee.

"Susan, I'm so sorry. I lost my balance…" Tom said embarrassed when Susan interrupted him, "No problem, Tom. I'm glad you didn't fall on the floor. Would you mind getting me a cup of coffee if you don't mind?" she asked, to change the subject.

As Tom left, he replayed in his mind how he had lost his balance and held on to Susan's knee to break his fall. This was the first time Tom found himself in such an awkward and embarrassing situation with a woman. He became flushed when he realized he had held on to her knee.

When Tom got back to his seat, he noticed Susan had a pleasant air about her: she had freshened up, combed her hair, sprayed a fine mist of perfume and touched up her make-up. "Susan, here's your coffee, and I also found this pastry if you would like to share it with me. Oh, by the way, I do want to apologize again for losing my balance and falling on you when I left."

"Tom, it's quite alright—it was an accident." Tom's face turned red again with embarrassment as he apologized to her. Susan found his reaction to be genuine and innocent.

Susan folded down the table in between their seats to set the coffee and pastry upon it. Tom took a knife from the folded napkins he brought, and proceeded to cut the pastry in half to share with Susan. "I see, Tom, you have a sweet tooth." "You concluded this from one pastry?" Tom asked surprised. "Remember, Tom, when you got on the train, you were munching on a candy bar."

"I have to say, Susan, you are very observant." "Well, you are not alone in that department. Fortunately, I recently lost a lot of the weight. I had been eating a great deal of sweets after Max had died. I realized how he had affected me after he passed away. So, I started jogging and watching everything I ate. When I lost most of the weight, I decided I was going to get away to visit my sister."

"Well Susan, I'm so glad you did." "That I lost the weight?" "No, no, that you decided to get away from it all; otherwise, I wouldn't have had the opportunity to have met you." This comment brought a smile to Susan's face—a much needed one for her. Not realizing his comment was going to have a pleasant effect on Susan, Tom noticed that he felt very much at ease with her and was happy he was able to paint a smile on her porcelain-like face.

Tom found the train ride to be very pleasant, and did not feel as lonely had he been by himself. Susan made all the difference, and he felt very fortunate she was there. Conversations between the two were more relaxed and the barriers they both had when they first met, were slowly coming down. Tom and Susan had so much to ask each other. Thankfully, there were still many miles to go before reaching their destination. They were both savoring the moments they had with each other.

Chapter 11

"Please, Susan, if you don't mind sharing, tell me more about the dream you had about being invited to a neighbor's gathering. Somehow, that dream made you feel very much at ease and content; so much so, that you were disappointed for being awakened," Tom requested, wanting to know as much as possible about the person who had just walked into his life.

"It just seemed so real as if I were really there, Tom. As I mentioned before, my neighbor invited a few neighbors to help him paint his house," Susan relayed so vividly as if she were really there. "Did your neighbor have the usual pizza and beer as a reward for painting his house?" Tom asked jokingly, to keep the conversation going.

"What I vaguely recall is that his brother brought in many trays of finger foods." "Susan, that is pretty detailed for you to recall the food that was brought in." "I just cannot believe how real that dream was, Tom—I really didn't want to wake up from it."

"Then what happened?" "Well, I met my neighbor's brother who was a real gentleman, and we both decided to go to Home Depot to buy supplies to paint my neighbor's house, similar to your dream." Susan relayed her dream so vividly, Tom felt she was really there. He had not recalled when someone related a dream with so many details.

"It's possible that painting may not have been the sole purpose of your dream unless you were Leonardo or Michelangelo." "You're a funny guy, Tom," Susan pointed out, with a very pleasant and genuine smile. "It's just that your dream sounded so life-like and vivid let alone very detailed in nature, similar to the one I had."

"I believe, that, subconsciously, my mind may have taken me to a peaceful place where I was safe and comfortable. My life had been turned upside down. For many years before my husband passed away, I was mistreated and abused..." Susan paused, as she was momentarily taken back to the state prior to her husband's death. All those emotions seemed to have been reawakened, and her whole demeanor began to change. Tom felt that facing all those emotions that were trapped inside her, would help her deal with them. She brought them out rather than to have them aggravate her any further.

"Susan, my sincere apologies. I did not mean for you to relive those moments — you sounded as if you've been through enough in your life, and you didn't need to relieve those ordeals again." Tom apologized, as he held her hand while he attempted to be as sympathetic as possible. While she wiped her tears and tried to recapture her composure, Susan looked down and noticed Tom gently held on to her hand.

Susan gently gave Tom's hand a gentle squeeze as a form of appreciating his efforts for helping her. For a brief moment, she felt very close to him for understanding what she had gone through. It was a good and warm feeling that she had not felt in a very long time and she did not want them to leave.

"Tom, I have all these thoughts and anger I need to get off my shoulders — they are weighing me down,"

Susan divulged, as she continued to look down and sob. "Please, Susan, I'm here for you. I know you hardly know me, but I'm a good listener and I can; somehow, feel what you have been through.

This trip to visit your sister may just be the therapy you need. It may not resolve all of your problems, but it's possible it may get you on to the road to recovery. It's going to take time, Susan. Please be patient with yourself." Unbeknownst to Tom, he continued to hold Susan's hand while he attempted to comfort her.

Chapter 12

"Next stop, Lincoln. Please be advised ladies and gentlemen, the train will be at the station for a couple of hours. Please feel free to disembark to stretch your legs. Also make sure to take your boarding pass and valuables with you as you will need your boarding pass to get back on the train," the conductor announced over the speaker.

"Susan, would you like to go into town and take a walk?" Tom turned towards her and asked with an inviting smile. "That sounds great. I can surely use some fresh air." As Tom stepped out, he handed Susan his hand to help her out of her seat. When Susan handed him her hand, Tom felt a sensation he was not able to explain to himself. All he knew, was that he wanted this feeling to continue. Tom felt like a new person when he was with Susan. He did not recall ever feeling this way before.

Tom and Susan stepped off the train. As they both stepped onto the platform, Susan reached out to hold on to Tom's hand. He gently held on to her soft, warm hand being mindful not to hold her too tightly. This was a new experience for him—an experience he had trouble explaining to himself.

Susan also realized Tom held on to her hand very gently—a new sensation for her as well. She was also very concerned she was getting close to someone new; something she promised herself she wouldn't do at the moment. Her grueling experience with her late husband had left a deep-rooted scar in her soul.

At one time, she had promised herself that any future relationship with a man would be very superficial. For as much as her late husband had physically and mentally abused her, Susan's faith taught her to forgive him—a continuing plea she included in her daily prayers. Her prayers provided the strength she needed to get through the tough times she had gone through.

As Tom and Susan walked hand-in-hand through town, they both found the quaint shops very interesting. In front of one of the shops they were about to go into, they noticed a homeless person who sat on the floor. Tom took out several bills from his wallet and handed them to him. Susan took note of Tom's generosity to a person he had never met before. She noticed she was slowly peeling the layers of Tom's true self; she was very happy what she had seen so far.

"That was very nice of you, Tom," Susan thanked Tom, while she got closer to him. "Who knows what that poor guy has been through in his life to get him to this point? It's possible that at one time he may have had a family, a job, and a home—who knows what else? Susan, we have to be thankful for what we have—we are very blessed," Tom uttered these words very solemnly and earnestly which Susan carefully took note of as she looked down. She truly appreciated and understood what Tom had professed. We sometimes take the little things in life for granted that later on become big things when we don't have them anymore.

Susan and Tom entered the antique shop where the homeless person sat by on the floor. They browsed through the artifacts in the shop making subtle comments every now and then how certain pieces reminded them of different events in their lives. They were both sharing a pleasant experience together — moments in life that memories are made up of.

Susan and Tom decided to purchase a few small pieces to take back home as souvenirs. When they left the shop and began to walk, Tom decided to go back to the shop and made up an excuse he had left his phone on one of the shelves. Susan stopped in front of a shop while she waited for Tom to return. As she glanced inside the shop through the window, she noticed her reflection on the window. This made her pause and give some thought to where she was in life. She saw only herself, but she was not alone.

From the side of her head, Susan noticed that Tom was on his way back. "Tom did you find your phone?" "Yes, I did. I had left it on one of the shelves when I was looking at one of the pieces in the store. Here Susan, this is for you." "What is it, Tom?" Susan took the little box Tom had gotten for her and began to carefully remove the wrapping. He looked intently and anxiously as Susan unwrapped the gift.

"Tom, what is this? You didn't have to get me anything," Susan said, as she looked at Tom, while she opened the box. She took out a little figurine with a saying on its base: *So nice to have you enter my life.* Susan was speechless — she did not know how to react to such a kind gesture.

Susan did not know what to make of Tom's gift, but she was very pleased he had gotten her such a touching gift. She had not felt this way in a long time; nevertheless, she liked it and was very pleased someone had thought of her — she was touched by his gift. She approached him and gave him a small hug. Tom was caught off guard that someone thanked him for a small gesture of gratitude.

Suddenly, Tom and Susan were interrupted by the homeless individual they had previously encountered. "Sir, are you Thomas J. Stevens?" Tom turned around to address the individual. "Yes, sir, I am. How do you know my name?" Tom asked, puzzled that the stranger knew who he was. Susan looked at the stranger with a puzzling look as well.

"Well, Mr. Thomas, you dropped this when you left the antique shop—it must have fallen out of your pocket." The stranger handed Tom his wallet. Both Susan and Tom were surprised with the honesty of this individual who, most likely, did not have a penny to his name. Despite his financial status, the homeless gentleman was very wealthy with integrity and honesty.

Tom proceeded to give all of the money from his wallet to the honest stranger as a reward for returning his lost wallet. "Thank you, Mr. Stevens, but I cannot accept a reward for what I'm supposed to do. This is your money, you earned it, and you should keep it." Both Tom and Susan were stunned and pleasantly surprised that there were good and honest people still left in the world.

"Would you, at least, let us take you to lunch?" Susan offered. "That's very generous of you, ma'am, but I have already eaten. God bless you both," the stranger replied, as he walked away. For a split moment they both stood stunned and amazed at this perfect stranger who had just walked into their lives and touched them in a way they had not expected—a divine gesture indeed.

Tom looked at Susan solemnly and relayed, "throughout our lives many individuals make surprise appearances with acts of generosity and kindness. What can one conclude from these visits, Susan? Are they coincidences or are they just divine interventions? This can only be answered by the affected individuals. In either case, it leaves it up to each and every one of us to make that determination. There is no correct answer!"

Susan was stunned at Tom's philosophical outlook on life. She could not believe this total stranger had just walked into her life, and she wanted him to stay there forever.

Chapter 13

The train began to slow down when it approached a tunnel. The sun shone radiantly, and the clouds appeared as if an artist had stroked them with a brush on a wide canvas. Conversations between Susan and Tom became more natural—they became more comfortable with each other. The conductor had just announced the train would be making another stop where the passengers could disembark to stretch their legs again.

"Let's hope the next stop has quaint little shops like the other one. That was fun, I really enjoyed it!" exclaimed Susan, with a positive and cheering demeanor. Tom took note of how Susan appeared to be more comfortable—her body language made it very obvious. Tom also noticed how comfortable and at ease he felt in her presence. He did not want this train ride to end. He felt he was living in the dream that Susan constantly alluded to.

Tom and Susan disembarked the train, looking around at their new surroundings. Antique shops were nowhere to be found. Just a small mining town with a few shops, one gas station and one small coffee shop. "Do you feel like a cup of coffee where we can sit down and chat?"

"Sure, I can go for one. The sign of pecan pies on that window makes it very welcoming. Pecan pies are one of my favorites, Tom. I wonder if they put ice cream on top," Susan asked, as she sounded like a small child in a candy store.

Tom took note of the excitement in her voice when she saw the pecan pies. "I see you're a lover of pies?" "Yes, it's one of my weaknesses. Although I'll tell you, Tom, it's much cheaper than retail therapy!"

"Retail therapy? What's that?" Tom asked, with a very strange look about him. "You mean to tell me you've never heard about retail therapy? Well Tom you're in for a treat. Let's say when a woman is stressed, she goes on a shopping spree and all that shopping somehow relieves a great deal of stress," Susan explained.

Tom attempted to comprehend all the excitement in Susan's voice. "And, since I don't have the means to go shopping for expensive things, I go to the supermarket and buy as many desserts, pies and ice cream that I can load in my shopping cart."

"Did that do the trick for you?" "Yes, Tom, it certainly did, but it still wound up to be very costly — I don't mean in dollars and cents, but in putting on the extra weight. As I said, when Max died, I went all out on sugar, and I wound up being even more depressed when my clothes didn't fit anymore. Retail therapy makes your wallet empty and binging on desserts fills you up with extra pounds." "Thanks, Susan, for that descriptive analysis. You probably saved me a great deal of money to see a therapist one day."

Both Susan and Tom entered the small-town coffee shop taking in the aroma of freshly brewed coffee and waited to be seated. "Please folks, sit anywhere you like, no reservations needed here. We're happy you came in. You're both in luck, you just missed the lunch crowd — all six of them." At the onset, they took note of the waitress who had a very enthusiastic attitude. She reminded them of the character Flo in one of the sitcoms they had seen a while ago.

They walked inside the coffee shop and, instinctively, approached the small white and red checkerboard-clothed table in the corner where they felt it would be more private. As they sat, they both commented how small the coffee shop was. Kathy, the waitress, approached them to see if they wanted coffee.

"Yes please, what kind of coffee do you have?" "Our coffee specials for the day are: black coffee and coffee with milk and sugar, if you like," Kathy informed them, with a very serious disposition. "Black for the both of us is fine, thanks." Lattes from Starbucks were nowhere to be found in the small coffee shop they found themselves in.

In looking around the small establishment, they noticed two individuals clad in black from head to toe with very heavy white beards. "Tom, do you think they're Amish?" "No, the way they are dressed they look like their Yiddish." "Yiddish?" "Yes, I think they are Orthodox Jews. There are certain parts of New York City where you would find many individuals dressed like that." "Thanks, Tom, you're such a world traveler. I did not know that."

The pies arrived with half a scoop of melted vanilla ice cream cascading on both sides of the recently warmed pecan pies. Susan's eyes were akin to a small child opening gifts on Christmas day. Tom could see the joy in her eyes when the dish containing a decadent treat was put in front of her. Tom also noticed his piece was a bit larger than hers.

"Susan, may I ask you a favor? Would you mind if

we switched plates? I'm not that hungry and I would hate to see such a delicious piece of pie go to waste." Susan gladly accepted to swap the pies with Tom being very mindful not to be over thrilled with the swap. Tom could readily see Susan was very excited to have traded desserts with him.

"Tom, do you mind going for a walk before going back to the train? That pie, as delicious as it was, is sitting in my stomach like a lump of lead." "That's a great idea. I can use the walk myself. I do have to say, Susan, the pie was delicious and sinful. It's not often I indulge myself with such a decadent treat."

Tom noticed Susan was very coyishly holding on to his hand as they walked through the small one-horse town. His heartbeat raced. This was a feeling he did not know how to handle, but he didn't make any effort to let go of her hand. It felt good, and he was very comfortable holding on to her hand. He changed his soft grip to a more medium grip. Susan noticed the change immediately, and also noticed Tom, in turn, was more comfortable holding her hand.

Susan and Tom walked hand-in-hand back to the train where it was scheduled to depart shortly. Again, they noticed that no one else got on the train. *Maybe they already got on*, he thought. As they walked through the aisle towards their seats, they noticed the two black clad individuals they had seen in the coffee shop. As they sat down, Tom and Susan nodded to the both of them. "I guess we're not alone anymore in this car," Susan remarked. "No, I guess we're not."

"Did you folks just get on?" asked one of the men in black. "No, we got on back in Providence," replied Tom. "And where are you folks headed?" Susan took a turn to cross examine. "*Ve* are going to San Diego." "That's where we are going as well," Tom got into the act.

"My name is *Yacob*, and this is my partner, *Yoseph*." "My name is Tom and this is my friend, Susan. We are going there as well. Are you traveling on business or are you both on vacation?" "No, *ve* are on business," Jacob replied, without providing any details to the nature of their business. They kept their conversation short and sweet.

"Tom, do you mind if I put my head on your shoulder again so I can take a little nap? I got very tired all of a sudden. I think the pie is working overtime." "Of course, Susan. I'll make sure I don't move around so I don't disturb you." Tom occasionally took a gander at the two newly found passengers and wondered what business they might be in.

Tom knew it was none of his business as the men in black had an opportunity to volunteer that information when he inquired whether their trip was personal or business. At the moment, Tom's thoughts centered around Susan peacefully sleeping on his shoulder. She felt warm and very comfortable and he enjoyed that his shoulder became a pillow. In turn, he leaned his head gently on her head, and he took a catnap himself. He felt very much at peace and comfortable with Susan by his side. *What did I do to deserve this?* he asked himself.

Chapter 14

Tom thought of all the opportunities he's had in his life to pursue a female companion. He sat back and pondered all the possible reasons why he hadn't: too shy, too busy at work, lots of commitments and getting tied down, to name a few. For the brief encounter he's had with Susan, he liked it and felt very comfortable. *Was all this going to end when we get to San Diego?* he asked himself. *And this is why a relationship never went anywhere. Enjoy the moment, and see where life takes me,* he further thought to himself.

One of the passengers, Jacob, quietly approached Tom speaking in a broken English. "Sorry to bother you, sir. Do you have a phone charger I can borrow?" Jacob asked very quietly, conscious of the sleeping woman beside Tom. Tom pointed to the charger that was attached to his phone, and motioned him to take it.

"My phone is already charged," Tom whispered to his passenger/companion. Jacob gently pulled out the connection from the phone and the outlet and proceeded back to his seat. Tom followed Jacob back to his seat and noticed that his partner, Joseph, was glad to get reunited with the world wide web. He wondered about those two who recently joined them in an empty car.

After a while, Susan began to wake up. "Did you have a nice nap, Susan?" Tom asked, as she looked up. "Again, Tom, thank you for letting me use your shoulder as a pillow. I have to say, it was very comfortable and warm." "Anytime." Susan gave Tom a small kiss on his

cheek which made Tom look like a deer in headlights—
he did not know what to make of it or how to react.

"What was that for?" Tom asked surprisingly. "Not
every question has an answer, my dear. Don't you know
that?" "No, I guess not. I must have been out that day
when that was taught." This brought a little smile from
Susan.

While Susan and Tom chatted, Susan noticed
something odd in Joseph. He had a black bag by his side
that had not moved from the moment he sat down. It
looked like it was glued to the side of his body. They also
noticed the sun reflecting a circular metal object by his
hand which aroused their curiosity even more.

"I wonder what that is?" Tom asked, while he
affixed his eyes on the black bag. As Jacob moved his
hand, it became very obvious what it was—handcuffs.
They were carrying something in the bag which was
apparently very valuable. "What do you think could be
in that bag?" whispered Susan, as she looked at Tom
with a very curious and puzzling look.

"I have absolutely no idea," Tom replied, while he
whispered back as well. "It has to be something very
valuable to have him handcuffed to the bag," Susan
interjected, as she shrugged her shoulders. "My guess,
and it's only a guess, is that they may have diamonds in
that bag." "What makes you say that, Tom?" "Well, if
these folks are from New York City, they probably work
in the diamond district."

"You mean there's an area in New York called the
diamond district?" "Yes, and all you see in that area are
guys dressed like that, and they buy and sell diamonds
all day long." "Tom, you are exaggerating. Why would
they be traveling in a train with diamonds handcuffed to

themselves?"

"Because it would be very inconspicuous for them to be on a train. Someone carrying all those valuable gems would most likely be flying rather than taking a slow train across the country." "I guess we'll never know. Why don't you go and ask them?" "Susan, I'm going to leave well enough alone." Susan sat back in her seat and didn't wish to address that anymore.

"Tom, I forgot to tell you about the dream I just had while I slept on your shoulder. I dreamt we went to Disney World." "Disney World? Really? Another dream?" "Yes, we went with a couple of friends and we acted like children all day long." "Sounds like fun." "Yes, it was Tom. I felt happy and content, but most of all, it was with someone I was falling in love with."

Tom realized that Susan made mention of many dreams she's had so far. Given her past with her husband, she probably has relied on dreams to get her away from reality—to a place she felt safe and happy. As far as Tom was concerned, dreams were a place where Susan gravitated to feel safe. Who was he to tell her to stop dreaming? From the many conversations Tom has had with Susan about her past, he was not about to tell her otherwise.

Chapter 15

"Do you realize, Susan, you've lived your life and I've lived mine, and we both have taken different paths along the way. Life has taken each one of us on different paths with many curves and bumps along the way," Tom philosophized again, as he appeared to look out into space.

"Tom, where are you going with all of this, or are you just getting very Aristotle on me?" "I'm just sitting here, Susan, on this train uninterrupted by outside forces, sitting with you and very much enjoying your company, not knowing where this relationship is headed to." "Do you get moments like these often?"

"No, Susan, not really. I'm always busy working so hard that I've been swept up by the tide of work. I just didn't realize there was a life out there until I met you. Suddenly, nature, time or some outside forces just made me collapse on the floor when my legs gave out—a wake-up call so to speak." "And had your legs not given out on you, we wouldn't be here talking to each other." "Exactly, that is correct."

"Had my husband not died, and had he not made my life a living hell, I wouldn't be going away to visit my sister in San Diego." "Well, I'm happy all roads have led us here," Tom said with a smile, while gently reaching out to hold Susan's hand. Susan then gave Tom's hand a gentle squeeze and replied, "Me too, Tom. This train ride has certainly taken me away from it all, and I don't want it to end." "Neither do I, Susan." And they had just proven to themselves where life has taken them to this point in their lives.

Tom snapped back to reality and began to wonder how those guys dressed in black wound up on the same train as theirs. Tom motioned with his head to look towards the two gentlemen quietly sitting with their eyes closed. Susan looked at both of them in a different way.

"I wonder if they are part of our journey, and we have not yet been made aware of their purpose," Susan interrupted. "I guess that remains to be seen. Susan, I'm going to get a cup of coffee. Would you like me to get you one?" "Yes, that sounds like a good idea. Why don't you ask them if they would like a cup as well?" "Good idea. That would be very neighborly of us."

"Gentlemen, I'm going to get a cup of coffee. Would you like for me to get you one?" Tom asked, as they appeared to be half asleep. Tom noticed one of them had a gun tucked under his coat. Both Jacob and Joseph immediately closed their jackets as they realized Tom was close to them.

"That's very nice of you, mister. *Ve vould* definitely like some coffee. Black for the both of us, please," Jacob requested, as he attempted to go into his jacket to get his wallet to pay for it. "That's quite alright, gentlemen. Coffees are on me." "Very nice of you, sir," Jacob replied.

Noticing they were open to coffee, Susan decided to get up to help Tom carry back four cups of coffee. "Thanks, Susan. I wondered how I was going to bring them back all by myself." One could see that Tom and Susan felt more comfortable with each other.

Susan and Tom went together to get coffee for themselves and their newly found passengers. Anyone seeing them for the first time would assume they're a couple. One of the benefits of the long ride to San Diego, so far, was that they had more time to feel more relaxed with each other compared to when they first met back in Providence.

"Susan, there is something strange about those two characters and I can't put my finger on it," Tom informed Susan, as they walked towards the cafeteria car. "Tom, what makes you say that?" Susan turned towards Tom as she commented. "It is strange for the two Hassidic-type men to be here with a bag handcuffed to their wrist, and one of them, we know, has a hand gun. Who knows, maybe both of them are armed? We need to keep our eyes opened."

Chapter 16

While Susan and Tom were away getting coffee, Jacob and Joseph decided to chat without concern that anyone would overhear their conversation; although they could have spoken in Yiddish, and no one would have understood them. "Now, that *vas* a very nice gesture by that gentleman." "Yes, it *vas, Yacob*." "Do you think that guy can be trusted? They both look like nice people. You don't see people like that these days. *Ve* need to talk to Susan alone. *Ve* didn't know she was going to be *vith anyvone*."

"You have to relax, my friend. Not *everyvone* in this *vorld* is out to get us. *Ven ve* get to San Diego *ve* need to get out of these clothes and shave to blend in *vith* everyone else." "I still feel *ve* should have changed our look before *ve* left…" "Shh, they're on the *vay* back *vith* our coffee," Jacob motioned to Joseph.

"Thank you very much for getting us coffee—you are very kind. Are you sure *ve* can't pay you for it?" "Positive. Enjoy your coffee, you are our neighbors," Susan said, as she and Tom proceeded back to their seats. Jacob and Joseph looked at each other surprised to see such nice people.

Such acts of kindness are rarely seen in their home in New York City. People there are always on the go, and hardly ever stop to smell the roses. It's a very fast paced city, and, according to Jacob and Joseph, it's very rare to see such acts of kindness.

"Tom, did you notice those two? They sat firmly in

their seats without moving a muscle?" "Susan, we should just mind our own business and let them be." "Tom, I just have this uncomfortable feeling in my stomach that's all." "Hopefully, the coffee should help clear your stomach." Tom felt the same thing about the two gentlemen from New York City, but he didn't want to show any signs of concern to Susan, since she seemed to calm down and feel relaxed.

Susan sat back in her seat, occasionally turning around and taking inconspicuous ganders at the two gentlemen dressed in black. *Why did Tom not feel what I felt*, Susan pondered. Too many mystery movies were coming to the forefront of her mind. In addition, she was aware of things Tom was not aware of, and she was not about to say anything.

Tom peacefully sipped his coffee and contemplated how happy he was feeling at the moment. He was riding in a train with a beautiful and wonderful woman—a companion of the opposite sex he thought he would never have a relationship with. In his mind, he began to quote Lou Gehrig of the New York Yankees when he retired from baseball: *I'm the luckiest person on the face of this world.*

Work, a life-long passion of Tom's, had not even crossed his mind since he boarded the train; he didn't even check his emails. For the moment, life was good for Tom, and he didn't want to interrupt that feeling of elation.

"Tom, wake up. You're going to spill your coffee all over yourself," Susan said, gently putting her hand on his arm to wake him up. "Sorry, I must have dozed off for a few minutes," Tom noted, while he took a deep breath and slowly shook his head to wake up. "A few minutes? You've been out for about half an hour." "No!" "Yes."

Suddenly, there seemed to be a loud discussion from the two men dressed in black who suddenly made an effort to lower their voices, but it didn't make any difference as no one around them understood what they were saying—they were talking in Yiddish.

The loud chatter caught Tom's attention which caused his head to turn slightly towards them. "I wonder what those two are arguing over?" Tom asked, while he turned back towards Susan. "Probably nothing. Who knows, they might be discussing what they're going to do next when they get to their destination."

"All of a sudden, Susan, you understand Yiddish?" "Really Tom? Tell me you are kidding." Tom pondered for a fleeting moment how certain Susan sounded when she attempted to decipher the conversation the two mysterious passengers were having.

Chapter 17

"Good morning, Marlene. Do you happen to remember when *Yoseph* is coming?" Jacob asked, while checking his phone. "Yes, he said he was coming at 10:15 so you guys can go out to lunch afterwards. May I ask why you're not flying to San Diego instead of traveling by rail," Marlene asked, as she always wanted to make it easier for Jacob.

"It's a long story, my dear. I *vill* explain it to you some day." Marlene decided she didn't want to ask any more questions. She just found it odd and unusual that Jacob wouldn't go into more detail as he was always in the habit of going overboard with details.

Marlene worked with Jacob for over twenty years and knows more of his comings and goings in his life than his wife, Rebecca. She was taken aback that he hadn't elaborated any further on his upcoming trip with Joseph. She wasn't even made aware of the purpose of the trip across the country either, let alone why he chose to travel by train instead of flying.

Working with Jacob has been a labor of love for Marlene; she never looked at the clock when it was time for her to leave for the day. He has been a great person to work with. He always gave her the latitude to run the office, and she came and went as she pleased. Jacob was very much aware she didn't take advantage of her position; however, she sensed something didn't feel right this time. Marlene's instincts told her there was more to the story than Jacob let on. She was determined to find out more.

"Jacob, is there something I need to prepare for you for your upcoming trip?" Marlene asked, wondering whether the back-door approach would work instead. "Many thanks, my dear, but I *vill* definitely let you know." "Would you like me to order a car or a hotel when you get there?" Marlene's persistence continued.

"Not a problem, *ve're* staying *vith* family *vhen ve* get there. You're *alvays* looking out for me, my dear. *Vhat vould* I do *vithout* you?" "I just want to make sure, Jacob, you are comfortable and I can take care of the little things for you." Marlene sounded as if she were pleading with him.

Marlene felt she hit a dead end. *If he wants this to be a private trip, it's OK with me,* she thought to herself. Suddenly, Jacob stuck his head in her office and asked her, "if you hear from a *voman* by the name of Susan, please let me know as soon as possible." "OK, will do. Is she a new client?" "Perhaps."

Chapter 18

Every new town brought out new facets of Susan's and Tom's personalities—they each got the opportunity to see a new side of the other. "Tom, I was just thinking that most people who meet for the first time do not spend as much time with each other as we have." "That's a good point, Susan. It's like speed dating but at an accelerated pace."

"We've been riding together on this train for a few days now, and I find it very strange that there are only four passengers in this car, and the rest of the other cars are full," Susan pointed out. "It's one of those mysteries of life I am not going to question." "In a way, it's been very quiet here except for those two," Susan noted, as she slowly raised her finger from her hand that rested on her knee.

"No, I can't complain either, and, for the most part, those two have been very civil. If I only understood what they were saying, Susan." "Then you would be eavesdropping, wouldn't you, Tom?" "I guess when you put it that way, I would be intruding on their privacy. I just don't know how these guys wear the same thing every day and never have to shave every day."

"It's a Hassidic custom, Tom, that dates back to thousands of years. They may ask you as well how you can shave and wear a different outfit every day." "I guess you have a point, Susan." Tom noticed Susan was very astute on certain things. Tom elaborated further, "You sound, Susan, as if you know their culture." Tom noticed a little snicker from Susan. "Tom, you just have to interpret their body language, that's all." Tom was very impressed how she was able to understand them.

"Tom, I have an interesting question to ask you," Susan queried, with a very serious look about her. "What would you do if you had the opportunity to become extremely wealthy?" Tom sat back and gave a great deal of thought to Susan's out-of-the-ordinary question.

"Interesting question, Susan. I guess, you reach a stage in your life where material possessions do not mean that much anymore. When you're younger you want to build up a nest egg for your family, house, college, retirement and things like that. When you get older and you have satisfied all the basic necessities of life, companionship, friends, health and time become the most important things in one's life. Again, Susan, this is my interpretation of life's values," Tom offered, as he continued to philosophize. "Tom, that makes a lot of sense, and I truly appreciate your sharing your values. I think what I meant to ask was what would you do if you were to become mega-wealthy?"

"I can see this subject is very important to you for you to continue to dwell on it." "Well, Tom, I find this to be a very interesting topic as it gives one a perspective of an individual's values." "Are you psychoanalyzing me, Susan?" "No, silly. We're just having a conversation in this long train ride, and the subject just popped into my mind. But getting back to it, what would you do if you had that opportunity?"

"OK, Susan, I see this subject has some measure of importance to you so I will play along with your query." He put his head back on the headrest to give Susan's question more thought. "Well, Susan, what comes across my mind was that I would love to help needy families without taking any credit for it—just total anonymity." Susan was pleasantly surprised at Tom's reply. "What would you do if you found yourself in a similar position?" Tom decided to play Susan's game and volley the question back to her.

Susan did not expect for Tom to echo back the same question she posed to him. Tom could see she was taken off guard and she had trouble giving Tom an answer after his philanthropic response. "Tom, I really don't know. I guess I have to find myself in that position first." "You mean you asked me a question for which you didn't have an answer for if you were to find yourself in a similar position?" Tom was surprised Susan had asked a question she had not considered what she would do in a similar position.

"I have a proposition for you, Tom." Tom sat on the edge of his seat waiting to hear the surprise Susan had up her sleeve. "Let's say when we arrive in San Diego you were presented with a lot of money." Susan decided she was going to take a different approach. "I see, Susan, we are still playing this game. OK, I'll go along with it." Tom could see this was a subject that mattered very much to her.

"First, I would make inquiries to ascertain if the money you referred to was legitimate—that it is, in fact, real. Was it stolen? And, second, why would someone arbitrarily give me that amount of money?" "Putting all that aside. Assume it's legit, and that someone wanted you to have it because you're a good person." Tom could see, again, this was a very important subject for Susan, so he wanted to continue to play along.

"Susan, fortunately, I am blessed for the many things I have because I have worked very hard all of my life to achieve them. Be that as it may, if a very generous person were to endow me with more money than I could ever use, I would establish a fund to help the many unfortunate individuals in this world who are not as blessed as I am," Tom informed Susan, hoping the possibility of his becoming very wealthy overnight would quell Susan's curiosity.

Susan appeared to be giving Tom's assumption of becoming wealthy overnight a bit more thought. She felt it was very magnanimous of Tom to put himself in a position to be able to help the multitude of people who are not as blessed as he was.

Chapter 19

The train approached the next town which gave Susan and Tom another opportunity to stretch their legs again. Jacob and Joseph decided to stay in the train to plan their next move. As Tom and Susan left the train, they noticed the two had remained in their seats, and they looked at each other while they shrugged their shoulders.

"You know, *Yoseph*, Susan is a fantastic actress. That chap she's with has no idea how dangerous that *voman* is." "*Yacob*, he's an innocent bystander who appears to be a nice guy, and he has no idea about that *voman. Ve* don't know how he *vound* up in this car. I thought *ve* paid for the whole car *vithout* any other passengers, but this *vone* must have slipped through."

"I *vonder* how far Susan told this gentleman she *vas* going to travel." "Don't know *Yoseph*." "*Ve* have to confirm *vith* her *vhere ve* are going to leave the train and *vhen ve* are going to meet *vith* Samuel. Oh *vell*, it's neither our problem nor our business. *Ve* need to get rid of these diamonds *vhen ve* get them." "For sure!"

Tom and Susan continued their stroll through another small town when she heard the beep of a text on her phone. Tom paid no mind to it as he continued to window shop. Susan was very careful to open her bag and peek at the newly sent message from Jacob: *We have to talk*! Susan knew what the boys wanted to talk about, and she had to be careful not to get Tom involved.

Susan was very well aware of Jacob's message: *the next step*. She found herself in a very difficult and uncomfortable position as she did not expect to meet Tom and develop feelings for him. *Business is business,* she thought to herself. She felt very uncomfortable with the position she found herself in. She needed to have a one-on-one with Jacob and not have Tom become suspicious of her double agent role. The furthest thing on her mind when she boarded the train was the possibility of meeting someone with whom she was going to have feelings for. Susan just wanted this caper to be over with, so she could get on with her life—more so now that Tom had entered her life.

"Was that a text you got Susan?" "No, it was my timer that we should be getting back to the train." Susan realized she had just lied to a wonderful person who had just come into her life. Thoughts crossed her mind of not only going through with the heist she was about to undertake, but to come clean with Tom. *What is Tom going to think of me when he finds out the truth? What is Tom going to think if he were to find out about the diamonds?* she asked herself, as she continued to think of all sorts of possibilities to get herself out of the current predicament that she found herself in.

Chapter 20

"*Ok* Marlene. I'll be back in a couple of weeks," Jacob said, in passing Marlene's office. "Jacob, do you have a minute before you leave?" "I have to run or I'm going to miss my train." "Jacob, this is important. I've known you for over twenty years and I know for a fact when you have to catch a train, a plane or a bus, that you like to be there with plenty of time." Marlene knew his habits very well, and he couldn't back out of this one. She was very concerned why Jacob didn't confide in her; he always made it a point to inform Marlene about every little detail of his trips. *It must really be serious for him not to tell me what was going on*, she pondered.

"Marlene, my dear, I have some personal things I have to take care of, and I can't make you part of it for your own protection." Marlene suddenly noticed from Jacob's body language that something wasn't kosher. "Are you in some kind of trouble?" Marlene knew him well enough that his body language told her otherwise — she didn't like what she saw.

"Look, *boobela*, there are things I have to take care of and I don't *vant* to share them *vith* you for your own good and because I don't *vant* to make you part of it." "You're in trouble, Jacob, and you're running away? When will you be back? Is there anything I can do? You know you can trust me."

"Please, Marlene, it's because I trust and care for you that I can't make you part of it this time." Marlene felt she had gone as far as she could. She knew Jacob well enough and could see he made every effort to protect her.

"OK, Jacob, please take care of yourself. If you need *anything*, I mean anything, please let me know. You know I'm here for you." Marlene could see Jacob was uncomfortable not telling her about his trip. And because he cared for her deeply, he didn't want to share his upcoming adventure with her.

Marlene got very close to Jacob over the past twenty years they worked together. She got to see him more than his own wife did. She probably had more conversations as well.

Marlene had been with Jacob during many difficult times in the past, and he had always been upfront with her. She felt the situation he was presently in must be a really tough one for him not to confide in her. She also felt very helpless she wasn't in a position to do anything for him. She had a sinking gut feeling that she was not going to see him again—a feeling she didn't want to think about.

"Jacob, I have one more question I need to ask you before you go, and I promise this will be the last one: does Rebecca know?" "No, I couldn't even let her know for the same reasons I can't let you know." Marlene felt a bit better she was not the only one who was not aware of Jacob's travels. *It must really be serious for Jacob not to inform her and his wife*, Marlene thought.

Chapter 21

*J*acob sat in the train in a trance while looking at the passing countryside, recollecting the last conversation he had with Marlene. He felt bad he could not make her part of his latest escapade. He didn't because he cared for her so much that he wanted to protect her from any possible harm. He didn't want her to be part of anything that might go in the wrong direction because of her association with him. It was very hard to leave her out of the loop and what he was about to do. *Maybe I'll call or text her later to let her know I am alright*, Jacob thought for a brief moment.

"*Yacob*, are you here?" "Sorry, *Yoseph*, I must have dozed off." "You scared me, my friend. Look, *ve* have to confirm *vith* Susan that everything's going according to plan." "I have a plan, *Yoseph*, to confirm this." "Oh? And *vhat* is that?"

Tom and Susan got back to their seats, taking a quick look at the other passengers dressed in black. As they sat down, Jacob came over and put a couple of dollars in Susan's palm while he looked at her. "Please, miss, you *vould* make me feel better if you took this for the coffee you so kindly got for us before. Just put it in your bag for the next time you go for coffee." Again, Jacob gave her a look that what he put in her hand was for more than reimbursement for the coffee.

For the little time Susan had known Jacob, she knew him well enough it was not just coffee money. "Thanks, Jacob. It really wasn't necessary, but I'll use it to get coffee again." Susan pretended Jacob had put several dollars in her hand. She wondered when there was going to be some form of communication between Jacob and her.

At this, Susan excused herself. "Excuse me, Tom, I have to go to the ladies' room." Susan got up from her seat with the money Jacob gave her clutched in her hand. When she got into the ladies' room, she noticed there was a note from Jacob within the dollar bills: *Joseph and I need to get off at the next stop. Get off the next stop also and we will pick you up. Jacob.* Susan had not planned to get off the train, especially since she just got to know Tom.

Susan noticed the plan was in place and she had to face the moment of truth. She had to make an excuse to get off at the next stop without Tom noticing. Once she got off the train, and the plan was underway, she planned to call Tom to reconnect. Although Tom got to know Susan pretty well, or so he thought, he knew something was up once she was no longer on the train. Also, what would go through Tom's mind when Susan called him to reconnect? *Bad idea,* crossed her mind.

If only she had the ability to walk away from it all and start a new life with Tom—a genuine and down-to-earth person. *This was not supposed to happen,* she was angry at herself. Something had changed, and she was getting deeper and deeper in a no-win situation; there was no way to undo the predicament she found herself in. What would Tom think if she were to come clean with him?

Chapter 22

When Susan got back to her seat, Tom noticed there was something different about her. He hadn't known her for that long, but he felt something was not right—he couldn't exactly put his finger on it. "Is everything OK, Susan?" Tom asked, with a real concern in his voice. "Sorry, Tom, I just don't feel well." Tom felt helpless he wasn't able to help her.

"Is there anything at all I can do to make you feel better?" Susan noticed a genuine sense of concern on Tom's part, but she couldn't make him part of her involvement with Jacob. "I just need to close my eyes for a bit, and hope this headache goes away," Susan informed him, as she leaned her head back on the headrest.

As Susan closed her eyes, she recalled how it all began, and how she got involved. She recalled how Max got home from the post office one day with a small box under his arm. He walked sideways in an attempt to hide the box. She also noticed he had taken the box to the upstairs bedroom—the bedroom that had an annoying squeak whenever its door was opened.

Susan also recalled how Max used to say, *I'll get to that squeak; I'm busy now.* Needless to say, that squeak never went away—a constant reminder of his constant procrastination to take care of things. *I wonder what's in that box*, she used to say to herself every now and then.

Max never informed her he had brought a box home from the post office let alone what it contained, if he even knew. She was tempted at times to go and look for the box, but she never got around to it. Time had gone by and the thought of that box became a distant memory until one day.

Max had a serious drinking problem and his addiction came to a screeching halt when Susan received a fateful call one night. Max had too much to drink when he was out with his friends after work. She recalled the many times he used to complain about the stressful environment he and his friends worked in—everyone shared the same sentiment. Going out to the bar after work became the norm every day except when fate decided to step in and end it.

Not only did Max take his own life, but he also took the life of another person during that rainy and windy night. The end of his life was also the end of his constant mental and physical abuse to Susan. She was both sad and relieved at the same time. She also recalled feeling guilty for having the feeling of relief she sensed. She consoled herself that Max was no longer in pain. More importantly, she was no longer in pain as well.

Everything had come to a head, and it was a lot for Susan to come to terms with. She had faith in herself, and her family was always there for her to lean on; especially, her sister Rachel.

Months had passed and Susan finally got the courage to dispose of Max's things. Goodwill was the recipient of many bags of his clothing and personal effects. In the process, she came across the box that Max had sneaked into the house that had remained hidden in the closet.

The box had remained sealed, and there was no physical evidence it had been tampered with. Susan looked at the box, and it brought back memories of that night when Max attempted to sneak it into the house. Susan looked at the return address and it had Jacob Horowitz's name with a New York City address, and it was mailed to a private individual in town. She was at a crossroads to either open the box or attempt to contact Jacob to inform him the box had been mysteriously found.

The addressee was nowhere to be found. *Is this why it was not delivered?* she thought. At the post office, Max worked in the department of undeliverable items. *Should I take it back to the post office?* she pondered. This, most likely, would have generated all sorts of inquiries as to why she was in possession of the box. Susan thought of all the reasons to hold on to the box for a few weeks until a better idea surfaced; after all, it had been in the closet for a very long time.

One day, Susan realized she needed to do the right thing. She went online and procured the phone number of the office that appeared on the return address. At first, she decided to look up Jacob Horowitz's name on the internet in NYC, but it was like searching for the name O'Reilly in the Dublin phone book—there were too many of them.

Susan felt the right thing to do was to return the box to its rightful owner. This is the way she was brought up by her family. *Return what is not yours to its owner*, was one of the many mantras her parents brought her up with. Susan was raised with values and she was happy that she had—it made her a better person. She kept the box on her dresser for a couple of weeks until she had the nerve to follow up with her premise to call the person on the return address who appeared on the box.

Chapter 23

"Is this the office of Jacob Horowitz?" Susan asked. 'Yes, whom am I speaking with?" Jacob's personal assistant, Marlene, asked. "This is Susan, may I please speak with Mr. Horowitz. It's very personal, and I need to speak with him directly. I believe I have something that belongs to him." "Miss, I'm afraid he's not in at the moment. Is there anything I can assist you with?" Marlene asked very professionally. "No, Miss Marlene, I need to speak with him directly—it's personal."

"OK, Miss, please give me your number and I'll have him give you a call when he gets in. Is there a message you can leave with me?" "Yes, please inform Mr. Horowitz I have a box that belongs to him." "Will do, Miss. I'll pass that message on to him." *I wonder what's in that box?* Marlene thought to herself. At the moment, nothing came to mind, but she was curious to see what it was.

No sooner than Marlene hung up the phone with Susan, Jacob walked in with shopping bags in both hands. "Perfect timing, Jacob. You just missed a call. Does a girl by the name of Susan ring a bell?" By Jacob's body language and by the look on his face, Marlene knew Jacob knew of no one by that name.

"OK, Jacob, let me try something else. Does a missing box you sent out in the mail ring a bell?" *Ah, this question raised a few eyebrows*, Marlene thought to herself. "No, I don't *sink* so. Did she, by any chance, leave a number for me to find out more information?" Jacob asked very nonchalantly. "Yes, I left her name and number on your desk."

Marlene noticed Jacob made a concerted effort not to rush back to his office. Shortly, she noticed Jacob had closed his office door. "Is this Miss Susan? My name is *Yacob*. My assistant mentioned that you called. She said you had a box for me. Did you happen to open it?" "No, Mr. Jacob, I didn't open it."

"How is it that you are in possession of that box? Are you *vith* the post office?" Susan felt the interrogation had begun. Why is he asking me all those questions as if I had done something wrong? Maybe he had put a formal missing shipment request with the post office and he thinks the post office is getting back to him, she thought.

"No, Mr. Jacob, I am not with the post office, and I'm not at liberty to divulge how I became in possession of the box. The fact of the matter is I found a box with your name on it and it's in my possession at the moment." "Then *vhat* do you *vant* in exchange for the box?" "Mr. Jacob, I called you because I found your box. Where I found it doesn't matter, and I don't want anything for it." "Are you sure you didn't open it?" Jacob asked, as he raised his voice a bit.

"Mr. Jacob, I called you because I found your box, and I wanted to return it to you. Would you like me to open it because I can do it right now as I'm talking with you on the phone. Let me see. I can pull this tape…" "No, no, Miss Susan, please do not open it." Suddenly, Susan concluded the contents of the box could be very valuable and Jacob did not wish for Susan to be made privy to its contents.

Susan did not like the direction the conversation

took, and decided to end the conversation. "Sorry, Mr. Jacob, my phone is losing its charge." Susan abruptly hung up the phone. She felt very uncomfortable with the conversation she had with Jacob. After all, she went out of her way to call Jacob and inform him she had something that belonged to him. In turn, he took a rude and obnoxious attitude and began interrogating her as if she had done something wrong.

Jacob noticed Susan's telephone area code was 401. "Marlene, *vould* you please find out *vhat* area code is 401?" "Will do." Within a couple of minutes Marlene informed Jacob that 401 was the area code for Providence, Rhode Island. Jacob decided to ask Marlene to find out which orders were mailed recently with the area code 401.

Within a short period of time, Marlene came back with a list of clients the office had mailed shipments to Providence. "Jacob, in the past year we made three shipments to Providence. Two of them had confirmed receipts of the shipments. One of them did not receive the box we sent them. After many phone calls to the post office, they could not locate the tracking number we had.

Everyone concluded the box had been lost in the mail. As you recall, we put in a claim to our insurance carrier and within four months, we were reimbursed for the lost shipment. Is it possible, Jacob, this Susan person may have found the lost box?" Jacob stood by her office door, perplexed at how this person could have recovered the lost box.

Chapter 24

Tom noticed Susan was waking up, and hoped she felt much better. "How are you doing? Do you feel better after your nap?" Tom asked gingerly, as Susan appeared to be in that morning fog between being asleep and being awake. "Yes, I do, thanks." Tom was thankful her nap helped her, but he did not want to pry why she was acting the way she was before her nap.

Susan gave a great deal of thought to the predicament she found herself in. She also felt she had known Tom well enough in the short time they knew each other that it was time for her to be honest with him.

Susan leaned over to him and whispered, "Tom, we need to talk." Realizing it was important from her tone of voice, Tom whispered back, "OK, when we get off at the next stop and we go for a walk. Is that, OK?" Susan was thankful Tom was discreet in his tone of voice.

The next stop came by faster than either Tom or Susan had anticipated. Susan sat back and went over in her mind the approach she was going to take with Tom. *If you care enough for this person, be honest with him*, she thought.

Tom also wondered what the hush-hush was all about when she leaned over and requested they talk privately. He also felt in a relationship each person had to be honest with each other. More importantly, they needed to respect each other as well.

"Jamestown next stop. We'll be there for a couple of hours ladies and gentlemen. Please take your boarding pass before disembarking," the voice over the P.A. system announced.

Susan and Tom carefully stepped off the train holding each other's hands. Tom was very anxious to hear what Susan had to say, and the reason why she had to whisper on the train for the need to talk. He wanted to ensure her privacy by not asking too many questions when she spoke to him.

After walking for about ten minutes and confirming no one was in earshot of their conversation, Susan began to explain another reason why she was on the way to San Diego, other than getting together with her sister. She informed Tom of the mystery box she had found when cleaning out Max's things. "So, did you ever find out what was in the box?" Tom queried. "I'll get to that some other time." Tom, noticing she did not readily volunteer that information, held back any further questions relating to the contents of the box.

Susan was very cautious of her surroundings and who might be listening. "So, you're going to hand the box you found over to this Jacob guy once you see him in San Diego?" "Yes, so I can be done with this box." "Is it also a coincidence the gentleman in the train is also named Jacob?" "No, Tom, it isn't." "So, you have known this guy all along?" "No, not exactly; only when I made attempts to inquire on the origin of the box over the phone."

"OK, Susan, I'll pretend when we get back to the train you don't know either one of them. When were you planning to hand over this mystery box to Jacob? Oh, by the way, did you ever try to contact the person who the box was meant to go to?" "Yes, I did on various occasions, but the person did not seem to exist. The address was a post office box, and when I queried the post office, they didn't recognize the name."

"That is odd. So why didn't you just leave the box with the post office?" "That did cross my mind, but then that would have just opened Pandora's box. I would have been asked all sorts of questions on how I obtained the box. For example, they may think I may have stolen it."

"So, you are just going to give the box to Jacob without knowing what's inside?" "Yes, as he is the one who sent it and his name appears on the return address. When we get back to the train, I am just going to give Jacob the box and be done with it." "That's great, Susan, just put it behind you," Tom recommended to Susan.

Tom looked at his watch and realized it was time to walk back to the train. As they approached the car, Susan turned around and thanked Tom for listening and for being there for her. Tom nodded his head signifying that it was no problem. He was glad she confided in him and thought of various possibilities on how Susan was going to handle the matter at hand. As they walked to their seats, they noticed that neither Jacob nor Joseph was in their seats. "Maybe they're still out walking." "Perhaps."

"Ladies and gentlemen, we will be departing in five minutes," the conductor announced. Both Tom and Susan simultaneously looked at the door to see if either Jacob and Joseph were coming in. The train began to move and there were no signs of either one of them. Either they were in another car or they missed the train altogether. *They wouldn't have left without the box I have for them*, crossed Susan's mind.

They both looked over their seats and noticed their

bags were missing. "They must have thought I left the box in my bag, so to play it safe they took both bags. I guess they took the box after all," Susan pointed out to Tom.

After half an hour, Tom and Susan concluded the men in black must have left the train and they were no longer to be found. When the conductor came by to check their tickets, they queried him on the whereabouts of the two gentlemen. "I'm sorry ma'am, I didn't see either one of them. They're really not hard to miss, if you catch my drift."

Both Tom and Susan knew exactly what the conductor meant by that comment and they nodded accordingly. "So, somehow, Susan, the boys got their box," Tom concluded from Susan's missing bags. "Yes, Tom, they did with one exception—they'll soon find out the box is empty!" *That was brilliant on Susan's part*, Tom thought.

Chapter 25

"Thank you, Samuel, for picking us up. I guess it pays to know *somevone* who owns a plane. I have to ask, *vhy* did it take you so long to get in touch *vith* me? I've been *vaiting* for your call for days!" "Samuel, *ve* had a little complication." "Did this girl, Susan, not have your box?"

"Yes, she did, but there *vas* another passenger in the train that *vas* not supposed to be there." "I thought you said you paid for the whole car?" "I did, but, somehow, there *vas* somebody else and *ve* couldn't retrieve the box; *anyvay*, *ve* got the box." "And, she didn't ask for any *revard*?"

"Look, I found that very surprising as *vell*," Joseph chimed in. "She didn't know *vhat vas* in the box." "Are you sure?" Samuel asked, surprised the box was missing for so many months, and it still hadn't been opened. "Positive, I wrapped it up myself *vith* my tape and there *vere* no signs of it being tampered or opened."

"*Vhat* time are *ve* meeting *vith* the buyer, Sam?" "We're scheduled for nine tonight, Jacob." "You stressed *vith* the buyer that it's a cash deal?" "Yes, yes. Let's have a nice dinner first. I've made reservations at a fine restaurant—then *ve'll* meet *vith* the buyer at nine. I still cannot believe that *voman* didn't ask for a *revard*."

"Me too. So *vhat* are *ve* going to do? All she asked *vas* to pay for her train fare to San Diego." Jacob shrugged his shoulders in total disbelief as well. "That's a bargain!" "That's *vhat* I said." They were all pleased that they managed to get a hold of the box without having to pay any reward.

"OK, gentlemen, let's get down to business. *Ve* agreed on $2 million for *twenty*-eight grade D diamonds." "Listen, Jacob, this *vas* over nine months ago *vhen* the market *vas* different. I'm ready to offer you $1.5 million in today's market."

"Samuel, Samuel, you are going to tell me about market values? If *ve* are going to go on market values, then it should be $2.5 million. Now, if you don't *vant* to do business, *ve'll* go *somevhere* else. Have a good day, Samuel, call us *vhen* you change your mind. *Ve* have other buyers *vaiting* for my call."

"Look, Jacob, *ve* know each other for a very long time, and because *ve* know each other for a very long time, this is *vhat ve* are going to do. Let's settle for $1.75 million and *ve* can all go home richer."

Jacob began packing up the box and was ready to leave. "Jacob, Jacob, *vhat* are you doing? I *sought ve vere* close in having a deal?" "Samuel, you thought *Yoseph* and I were going to fall for that? I tell you *vhat*. Let's close this deal at $1.9 million because you caught me on a good day. How does that sound? *Ve* got a deal?" Samuel hemmed and hawed and began to open his bag to show Jacob and Joseph the cash.

Joseph volunteered to count the money while Jacob and Samuel examined the diamonds. Samuel took out his Swiss army knife and began to cut the top of the tape that sealed the box. They all waited with bated breath to see the reflection of the colors from the D-grade diamonds that lay hidden for months. While Jacob began to open the box, he turned over to Samuel and commented again, "you're lucky, you got me on a good day…"

Samuel stepped back and said in total disappointment, "*vhat* kind of *meshuggeneh* do you *sink* I am, Jacob?" Jacob was startled at Samuel's reaction, but it all made sense when he opened the other flap of the box and noticed the D-grade diamonds were not to be found—only river rocks. Jacob's and Joseph's expressions said it all.

"Samuel, I don't understand. I taped the box myself—I cannot explain it." "Jacob, this is *vhere ve* part friends and business associates. I never *vant* to deal *vith* you again." "Samuel, do you *sink* I'm going to travel across the country to sell you rocks?" Jacob pleaded with him, while at the same time he was taken for a fool by Susan.

Samuel and his partner got into their car and left Jacob and Joseph along with the river rocks stranded in the middle of nowhere. Jacob put his hands on his sides, took a deep breath and shook his head. "*Yoseph*, I don't understand *vhat* just happened. I'm at a loss for *vords*." Joseph turned towards Jacob and jokingly said, "*vouldn't* it be funny if that Susan lady took your diamonds."

Jacob did not, for one minute, think that comment was a joke, but as a real possibility. "*Ve* have to find that lady. *Ve* should fly to San Diego and meet her at the train station!" Jacob was furious as this had not happened to him in all the years he's been in the business.

Jacob and Joseph caught their breath and considered several possibilities to get the diamonds back that the insurance company had already reimbursed them for.

Chapter 26

"Susan, what did you mean when you said the box was empty?" "Well, not exactly empty, Tom. I took out the contents of the box and replaced them with rocks." "What exactly was in the box, if I may ask?" Susan paused and hesitated to share the contents of the box with him. Tom took note of her hesitation, and he didn't want to impose on their budding relationship.

"Susan, I totally understand. For all practical purposes, I am a stranger to you. You don't have to tell me anything," Tom informed her, as he wanted to respect her privacy. He did not feel it was his place to request the contents of the box.

Susan appreciated that Tom respected her privacy, and he didn't want to cross that imaginary line in the sand. "Tom, I've been giving it a lot of thought, and I feel we should go our separate ways when the train comes to the next town." This took Tom by a total surprise and Susan noticed it immediately in his eyes.

"You know, Susan, I was starting to see and feel what it was like to fall in love, but if this is what you want, I don't want to get in your way." He went over to her, held her hand, and gave her a warm hug. As he hugged her, she felt a tear fall on the base of her neck. She was touched by his sensitivity towards her and she knew that Tom would respect whatever decision she came up with. Susan decided she did not want to lose this person who had just crossed her path in life.

"Tom, we need to talk. I could potentially be in a

great deal of trouble, and I'm afraid you could be as well if we were to stay together," Susan informed Tom, with a great deal of compassion in her voice. "Susan, I've been waiting all my life to find someone like you, and now that you've entered my life, you're going to leave?" Tom held her hand while he poured his heart out to her.

"Tom, I'm going to be honest with you. In the very short time we've known each other, I have fallen in love with you as well—something I was not going to allow myself to do after Max died. And because I have, I want to protect you from any danger that may be facing me."

"I understand you might be in danger because it has to do with whatever was in that box, but I don't want you to face that potential danger all by yourself." Susan saw in his eyes the true warmth he had for her. She had not seen that in anyone for a very long time.

"Susan, I'm now recalling the hypothetical question that you asked me regarding what I would do if I were to find myself mega-wealthy. I think those were the words you used. Were you referring to the contents of the box that Jacob took?"

"Yes, and I know he will be coming after me with a vengeance to reclaim what was in that box. I don't want him to come after you as well—you had nothing to do with it, and I don't want to be responsible if something were to happen to you as well."

"Susan, you came into my life, and I came into yours. We didn't plan this—it just happened. We were both in the same place at the same time. I don't want to leave you. If it means they'll be some bumps along the way, then let's get on that road together. Let's put our heads together and figure out how we're going to get out of this mess." "Tom, you have no idea what mess we could be in. We could be dealing with dangerous people. You saw the gun that one of them had in his pocket."

"All I know, Susan, is that it involves you, and I would like to be with you. First thing we have to do is to get off this train. I'm sure Jacob is aware of all the stops this train makes along the way from here to San Diego, and he could be waiting for us at any one of those stops." "He also knows we are in the first car...alone."

"So, we need to not only get off the next stop, but we should also go into another car where he wouldn't be expecting to find us." "I see you've given this some thought." "We have to outsmart them, Susan. We should also change our clothes, get baseball hats and sunglasses." "I see you're really getting into this." Susan realized how far Tom was willing to go to protect her.

"The other avenue we can take, Susan, is to get in touch with Jacob, and see how we can give him back what belongs to him which brings me back to an interesting question: why did you empty the box in the first place?"

"Tom, when I found the box in the house, I made every effort to return it to Jacob. When I finally connected with him, he was both rude and obnoxious— he reminded me of Max all over again." "Sorry to hear. I guess he hit a nerve." "Big time. In retrospect, I should have mailed the box back to him, but that doesn't change the position we find ourselves in at the moment."

"What doesn't make sense, Susan, is why didn't the post office mail the box back to the sender if the recipient was unknown." "Tom, I truly don't know—all I know is that I found that box in my home when I was cleaning out Max's things. Why Max brought it home in the first place is a completely different story, and one I can't even venture to guess, Tom."

"I have no doubt that not only did Jacob put a tracer on that box when it went missing, but he must have also insured it to the hilt." "So, if he in fact insured it, he must have collected its value from the insurance company. On top of this, he now wants to double-dip by selling its contents." "You're probably right, Susan. The guy sounds like a sneaky snake in the grass."

"Susan, our number one priority is to get out of harm's way and to totally avoid those men in black. We then have to figure out a way to dispose the contents of that box." "I noticed, Tom, you still are not aware of what was in that box." "Susan, I'm respecting your privacy when you hesitated to tell me a few minutes ago."

"Aren't you bit curious though?" Susan asked, wondering why Tom didn't inquire on the contents of the box. "No, not really, Susan. If you wanted me to know, you would have already made me aware of it. Also, whatever it is, you're going to give it back anyway, aren't you?" "I may," Susan said, with a doubtful look about her.

Chapter 27

"Yacob, how did that box go missing? Did you happen to put the wrong address on it?" "Yoseph, vhen I got that box that vas the first thing I checked." "And?" "The address vas correct—I double checked it." "Then vhy did it go missing and how did that voman get a hold of it?" "The only thing I can sink is she must vork in the post office and she managed to steal it."

"If she stole it, Yacob, I don't understand vhy she vent to all that trouble to go on the train to meet you, and then empty the box before she put it in her bag." "She could have just emptied the box and thrown it avay. Vhat vas the point of getting on the train to give you the box?" "A mystery, my dear friend! I truly don't know vhat vas on her mind."

"Yoseph, ve need to see vhere the train is going so ve can get the diamonds from her." "And you sink she has the diamonds vith her?" "She could have put them in a safety deposit box or have them in her closet somevhere?" Jacob speculated all the possible places the diamonds could be.

"Yoseph, I called Samuel and explained the situation to him." "You sink he's going to believe you or vould even vant to help you find them?" "Vell, I offered him a very good price if he helps us find the diamonds." "And he agreed?" "Yes, he vill use his plane to intercept the train and ve'll get her vith the diamonds. Once ve have her, ve'll use force if ve have to, but ve vill get our diamonds back from her one way or the other."

"*Yacob, ve* have to be smart about this. *Ve* don't *vant* to have problems *vith* the law." "That *vill,* my friend, be up to her." "Nothing is *vorth* going to jail for, my friend." "Look, *ve* have $2 million *vorth* of diamonds that *ve're* going after. That's a lot of shekels." "Also, *Yacob,* the insurance company already paid us *vhen* they got lost in the mail, so *vhy* are *ve* going to go after them?" "Because *ve* have an opportunity to make more money!" "*Yacob,* my long-time friend, I don't *vant* to get into trouble."

Jacob was determined to get the lost diamonds from Susan even though he was handsomely reimbursed by the insurance company. He found this to be an avaricious opportunity that was very close to his fingertips, and he didn't want to let it go. On the other hand, his partner, Joseph, was more realistic about the whole situation; he did not want to get in trouble by being greedy. He and Jacob made a nice living, and he was very surprised Jacob was pursuing stolen goods. For Jacob, the diamonds were so close to getting them he could even taste them.

Jacob and Joseph have worked together for many years and have made a lot of money in the diamond industry. Joseph could not understand his partner's desire to pursue diamonds for which they were already reimbursed. Greed was the only thing that came to his mind.

Chapter 28

"Susan, is this you? Can't wait to see you. I'll be at the train station tomorrow at 3:00 PM if the train is still on time?" Rachel inquired, anxious to see her older sister again. "Rachel, it's so good to hear from you. How are you? A lot of things are going on, and we don't think we'll be at the train station tomorrow at three."

"Who is *we*? Was there a problem with your train?" Rachel asked about the connotation of *we*. "Look, Rachel, first, I met someone on the train—a real nice down-to-earth guy; I can't wait for you to meet him. Second, there are a lot of things going on that I am not at liberty to talk about on the phone; I'll explain when I see you."

Rachel and Susan have always been two peas in a pod since they were children growing up. She has been holding on to Susan's hand all through her marriage to Max. She even hosted a party when Max died. When Susan introduced Max to Rachel, he was a totally different person before he joined the Marines.

Rachel gave a lot of credit to her sister for hanging in there with him; she wouldn't have been able to have done what she did. She considered her sister an angel for doing so, for only an angel would have had the strength to do what she had done. Rachel always looked up to her older sister and knew her better than her parents did.

Susan and Rachel always double-dated when they were in school—a condition from mom and dad so each one would look out for the other. Rachel always had the highest respect for Max when they dated, but he was not the same person when he got back from Vietnam.

The war changed many lives, and Max was no exception. In a way, she felt sorry for Susan, but she had the greatest admiration for doing what she did. In Rachel's opinion, Susan met all the qualifications for sainthood.

To this date, Rachel admits that Susan had more patience than she had. The endless therapy sessions she took Max to were more than the average person could have handled, but according to Susan, *love conquers all*.

Rachel recalled the many nights Susan ran to her house crying for refuge. She would witness Susan crying hysterically with bruises on her arms and face. No one should go through life like that, but Susan reassured her sister that his fits of anger were temporary as Max was expected to get better after therapy.

Rachel informed Susan not to put all her faith in therapy as Rachel noticed that Max had gotten worse, and therapy was beyond the help he needed. Working in the post office and going to bars after work, were the recipe for disaster. That should have been Susan's first clue that he was not on the path of recovery, but her faith taught her not to give up.

Fortunately for Susan, she had her young sister available whenever she needed her. Susan recalled the countless times Rachel recommended she leave Max, but Rachel knew her older sister was true to her faith and she was not about to change. When Max died, Rachel felt her prayers had been answered. At times, Rachel felt guilty for praying for someone to die when, in fact, she was praying for her sister to be safe no matter what form that took.

Rachel looked forward to getting together with

Susan, as well as spending quality time with her. She knew her sister went through a great deal emotionally and needed someone to be there for her. Rachel was pleasantly surprised that Susan had met someone on the train — she couldn't wait to hear all about it.

Rachel sensed from Susan's tone of voice over the phone that she sounded a bit happier than when they had spoken the week before. *Was it a bit too soon for her?* Rachel asked herself at times.

Rachel had to see for herself what relationship her sister was about to embark on. All she wanted was for her sister to be happy and have some stability in her life. Her life had been on a roller coaster ride for the past three years, and she needed a well-deserved break. *Maybe the person she met on the train was the answer to her prayers*, Rachel thought and hoped.

Chapter 29

"From the train schedule, Susan and Tom had a few more stops before arriving in San Diego," Jacob informed Joseph and Samuel. "*Yacob*, if you *vere* a smart man, you *vould* have offered this *voman* a big reward—it *vould* have been an incentive for her to have given you the diamonds." "I offered to pay for her train ride." "You call that an incentive, my friend? *Vhat* kind of incentive is that? You should have offered her a first-class airplane ticket to San Diego."

"Samuel, *ve* could spend all day arguing *vhat* incentive I should have given her, but at the moment, it's not going to change anything. *Ve* have to find her." "Did you try to call her to offer her an incentive to return the diamonds?" "No, I did not. That did not cross my mind." "*Vell* maybe it should have. Come on, don't be a *schmuck.* Give her a call; it might save you a lot of money and aggravation." "Do you *sink* she *vants* to talk to me—I stole her box." "First, it *vas* your box, not hers, and second, you *vant* back *vhat's* yours." "OK, OK, I'll give her a call." Jacob conceded to Samuel's approach to offer Susan a more deserving incentive.

As Samuel strongly recommended, Jacob called Susan. The phone rang and rang repeatedly, and Jacob's call went directly to voice-mail: "Susan, this is *Yacob.* I *vant* to give you a big *revard* for the diamonds you stole from me. Please call me back."

"*Yacob*, you have convinced me you are a class act *schmuck*. First, you don't tell her *vhat* the *revard* is, and then you tell her about the diamonds she stole from you. There is a saying in America that you can catch more flies *vith* honey than *vith* vinegar."

"Are you making this up? Who said that?" "Some guy a long time ago in the colonial days named Benjamin, something or other." "Oh, one of us? Did he deal *vith* diamonds as *vell*?"

"Call her back, *Yacob*, and offer her some money if you *vant* to see your diamonds again so you can sell them to me." Samuel could see that tact and diplomacy were not in Jacob's vocabulary. He had to remember that in the future.

Joseph brought the train schedule he downloaded from the internet. "There are two stops before San Diego: one in New Mexico and one in Arizona." "*Ve* can fly to both stops, and go look for her." "Gentlemen, gentlemen, *ve* are not dealing *vith* a stupid person. Look how she repacked the box that I packed—I couldn't tell that she repacked it. She definitely knows *vhat* she is doing." "*Vhat* do you suggest then?"

"I *sink ve* need to talk *vith* her first and reason *vith* her." "Do you know *vhat* her last name is at least?" "No, I don't. All I know is that her name is Susan. She never revealed *vhat* her last name *vas*." "That's very helpful, *Yacob*." "So, *vhat* are *ve* going to do now?" "*Vhat ve* should do is for you to call her back and offer her a big *revard*, like $100,000. And go one step further and give her one of the diamonds as *vell*." "Are you crazy?"

"Do you *vant* to see two million dollars' *vorth* of diamonds again?" Jacob realized that Samuel made a great deal of sense. "Samuel, I'm going to start *vith* a $100,000 *revard* first. If that doesn't *vork*, I might try offering her one of the diamonds," Jacob suggested.

"Jacob, now you have come to your senses. Had you done this before, *ve* may already have the diamonds in our hands."

"OK, Samuel, let's move and see if she goes for your plan. You know I don't like to give money away." "So, *vhat* else is new?" Samuel informed him, while he shrugged his shoulders.

Chapter 30

"Hey, Tom, I just received a voice mail from Jacob offering me $100,000 for the return of the contents of the box. I have a funny feeling they are not going to come after us because it would be like finding a needle in a haystack," Susan eagerly informed Tom of her big reward.

"Is that something you would consider?" Tom asked, anxiously waiting for Susan's response. "Well, $100,000 is a lot of money, but not in comparison to the contents of the box." "You mean to tell me you know the value of the contents?" Tom asked, wondering how she had arrived at that conclusion.

"Yes, Tom, I've done extensive research, and I have come up with a value of almost two million dollars." "Susan, that's a *helluva* lot of money. What was in that box, diamonds?" Tom asked facetiously. Susan just stared at Tom in total disbelief that he had come up with the contents of the box on his first guess. "You mean to tell me you have two million dollars' worth of stones in your possession?" Tom was flabbergasted and speechless.

"Can you see, Tom, why I might be in danger?" "You mean the both of us? I am not going to have you face this all by yourself—we are both in danger." Tom took her in his arms to convince her this was not just her dilemma.

"If I may ask, Susan, are these diamonds with you as we speak?" Susan hesitated again. "I put them away before getting on the train." "OK, great. Let's figure out a way to get to your sister's house when we get off this train. Is your sister aware of the diamonds?" Tom asked, wondering how many people were aware of Susan's latest escapade. "No, I didn't want anyone to be part of my heist." Susan looked in Tom's eyes indicating she hesitated to even tell him.

"Heist? You mean, hoard? I do have to say, Susan, you did a great job to keep all of this very secretive." "I know what it feels like to be hurt, so I didn't want anyone to be part of it. Now you have become part of it, Tom," Susan regretfully informed Tom.

"I would like to think that I have become part of your life." Susan held on to Tom's hand, and put her head on his shoulder. "Tom, what am I going to do with you?" "Susan, please get some rest—we have a bumpy road ahead of us, but we have to face this head on; it's not going to go away by itself."

"I have to confess, Tom, that I'm very lucky not to face all this by myself," Susan said, as she felt relieved that she wasn't alone anymore. She also appeared that part of her burden had momentarily been lifted.

Tom and Susan managed to find two empty seats near the last car. The conductor didn't mind as the seats had been empty for a while, and the train was not too far from their destination. Susan noticed, again, that Tom did not inquire for the location of the diamonds. She appreciated the space he gave her and respected her privacy.

Tom sat back in his seat and recollected how he and his brother, Jim, used to meet frequently at Starbucks to discuss sports, world events, and politics. Those days, though lonely for the both of them, were simple in comparison to the predicament he found himself at the moment. *What future do I have with Susan?* he pondered over and over in his mind.

He didn't want her to be by herself with the diamonds and Jacob. She had gone through a great deal in her life to have another anchor placed over her neck. For sure, he didn't want her to be alone during this difficult and dangerous time in her life—he cared too much for her.

"I'm really looking forward to seeing Rachel again—it's been a while," Susan informed Tom. "You didn't say why Rachel moved across the country, Susan." "She had a job opportunity she couldn't pass up—even if it meant moving across the country. This was a recent move for her—several months after Max had died. I don't know if she would have taken the job had Max been alive—she was very protective of me; especially, in the condition I was in."

"Tom, aren't you a bit curious as to the whereabouts of the diamonds?" Susan wondered why Tom had not asked. "Is there a reason I need to know that? My most important concern is where you are and how you are, not the diamonds. And, more importantly, that you are safe."

Susan found this to be odd as Tom had not shown any interest whatsoever in the diamonds. Tom felt the diamonds, most likely, had been stolen by Susan's ex-husband, Max, and she probably felt they should be returned to their rightful owners. How this was going to be achieved without anyone getting hurt was another story.

"Susan, do you know if Jacob is the rightful owner of the diamonds?" Tom asked, as this was the first interest he had expressed in the diamonds. "I suppose they are. His name appeared on the return address on the box." "If that's the case, why don't you just mail them back to his office and be done with it?" Susan stopped to think about the validity of Tom's inquiry.

Tom continued, "is there a reason why you replaced the diamonds with the rocks?" "I truly don't know, Tom. As I said, I was just annoyed at the way Jacob interrogated me about the box." "Or, could it be the box was the last link between you and Max?" Susan paused to come to grips with Tom's latest inquiry about the diamonds; she felt speechless that he had made a connection between the diamonds and Max.

The train approached the next stop with screeching brakes — the stop Susan and Tom planned to get off. They both gathered their belongings and sat until the train came to a full stop. As they disembarked, Tom and Susan held on to each other's hand. They looked down the length of the train towards the first car to see if there were any signs of Jacob, as their appearance would not have been too hard to miss. Fortunately, none was seen. Tom and Susan felt their journey to escape Jacob and his cronies had begun.

Chapter 31

As Jacob and Joseph were on their way to the next stop before San Diego, Jacob's telephone dinged—a text from Susan: I'm ready to send your diamonds back for the reward you offered. For your information, the diamonds are not in my possession. I'm currently in Denver. I decided to get off the train and fly to Denver to see my aunt." Jacob turned towards Joseph and Samuel to show them the good news he had received about the diamonds.

"*Mazel Tov, ve're* getting our diamonds back." The excitement they showed was similar to hitting the jackpot—two million dollars' worth. "Gentlemen, *ve* have to be very careful *vith* this *voman*. Remember how she packed the box *vith* those stones. She even fooled me, and I packed the box," Jacob's comments got Joseph and Samuel thinking.

Prior to sending the text to Jacob, Susan opted to pass it by Tom to see what he thought of it. "That's great, Susan. You might have thrown them off their tracks by informing them you were in Denver—nicely done! I just realized what I said. My apologies for the pun *tracks*."

"No apologies required. I'm starting to understand a bit more about you each day. I guess the next step is to coordinate the reward with the shipping of the diamonds. Any thoughts?" Susan asked, seeking Tom's opinion.

"Well, Susan, the reward may be easier to receive if you were to give them the banking information for them to wire the money directly into your account; although, I don't recommend giving them your mailing address for fear they may show up at your doorsteps. I'm sure you would not want that!" "That makes sense, Tom." Susan took note of the recommendation that Tom suggested.

"You now have to go back to where you hid the diamonds so you can ship them back to them." Susan coyishly took out her toiletry case she kept in her handbag and slowly unzipped it—a plethora of colors emanated from inside that stunned Tom. He was amazed at the different colors the diamonds gave off. "On second thought, Susan, let's open a post office box and have them mail you the $100,000 in cash by overnight mail."

Tom could not believe the brilliance of the diamonds. A quick thought passed through his mind that he was in the company of a fugitive who had absconded with valuable gems, and now he, for all practical purposes, had become an accomplice. *It's amazing how love makes one do crazy things one never would have done otherwise*, Tom thought to himself. "Susan, I cannot believe what you have gotten yourself into—you have a fortune in gems in your possession," Tom pointed out, as he continued to shake his head in disbelief.

"I wonder if Max knew the contents of the box that he had brought from the post office. I guess I'll never know the reason he took the box in the first place, and then decided to hide the box somewhere in our house." "Susan, I'm wondering if there are any more boxes hidden in your house," Tom asked, prompting Susan to think if that were a possibility to consider.

Tom also could not believe the position he found himself in. Who would have believed, once I boarded the train to San Diego, that I would find myself falling in love with a woman who had absconded with millions of dollars' worth of diamonds? he asked himself.

Chapter 32

"Gentlemen, gentlemen, I just received a text from Miss Susan that she has reconsidered our offer, and she *vill* take it in exchange for the diamonds," Jacob informed his cronies, as he almost jumped for joy. "Are you really going through *vith* it? You are really going to give her $100,000?" Joseph queried Jacob.

"I'm going to answer your question *vith* a question, *Yoseph*. Do you *vant* to see the diamonds again? As far as I am concerned, I have no idea *vhere* this *voman* is let alone *vhere* the diamonds are at the moment. If you gentlemen have a better idea how to get our diamonds back, I'm all ears," Jacob pointed out, seeking suggestions from Samuel and Joseph. Jacob was also very hesitant about paying any reward for the diamonds in the first place, but then he realized it was the only way to see them again.

"Gentlemen, I just received another text from Miss Susan. She sent us the post office box information for us to send her the money in cash by overnight mail. I gave this information to Marlene for her to take care of. Marlene also requested we give Miss Susan the address for her to mail us the diamonds back."

"*Yacob*, I have an idea. I don't *vant* to take any chances to have them lost in the mail again. Do you? *Vhy* don't *ve* fly and pick them up ourselves at the Albuquerque airport?" "Great idea, Samuel. I *vant* to make sure I have them in my hands."

"Another text from Miss Susan *vith* the address for

us to pick up the diamonds once she receives the box with the *revard* money." "This *voman* sounds like a professional. I *vonder* if she's done this before?" "You're a funny man, *Yoseph.*"

"Another text has come in *vith* a picture of a store *vhere* the diamonds *vill* be located." "She's good!" "I hope, *Yacob*, she's not playing us for fools. You know she did it to us once before." "Yes, but she didn't have an incentive this large before to give up the diamonds." "True."

"I don't trust this *voman;* she's too detailed with her instructions." "So, *vhat's* wrong *vith* that? I don't *vant* to be left in the dark *vhen* we have so much at stake. Instead, let her know to meet us at the Albuquerque airport and we can do the exchange there."

Susan received instructions from Jacob to meet at the Albuquerque airport to make the exchange. When Susan received the instructions, Tom and she felt that was doable and agreed to meet him at the Albuquerque airport in a couple of days.

"It'll take us an hour to fly to Albuquerque airport *vhere* she is. *Ve'll* pick up the diamonds and *ve'll* all go home. Everybody *vins. Yacob*, please text her back and instruct her to meet us at the Hertz rental counter at Albuquerque. It *vould* be much easier for us to pick up the stones and get right back on the plane." "This is strange, Samuel. *Ve* are giving her instructions." "Not an unreasonable request for the $100,000 *ve* are going to give her, don't you *sink*?"

Chapter 33

"Tom, I just received a text from Jacob giving us the location to drop off the diamonds — at the Hertz rental counter at the Albuquerque airport," Susan informed Tom, as she showed him the text from Jacob on her phone. "Do you feel comfortable with that, Susan?" "Sure, we can be at a distance from the counter, and they should be easy to spot as they'll all be dressed in black with white beards." "What time did they say they'll be at the airport?" "Between nine and nine-thirty tonight."

"OK, we can go out to dinner and relax before we go out to the airport and surrender the diamonds. Are you OK with all this, Susan? You are aware, we are dealing with people who may be armed," Tom informed her, as he noticed that Susan's mind was somewhere else.

"Susan, are you OK? Are you here?" "Yes, I am," Susan responded, as if she had come out of a trance. "If you would like, I can take the diamonds for you tonight," Tom recommended to ease Susan's anxieties. "Thank you, Tom, but I can't let you do that. What happens if you get hurt?" "What happens if you get hurt, Susan?" "I appreciate the offer, but we can both go together and drop off the stones. Then we can go and see Rachel and put all this behind us." "OK, Susan, let's do this together." *What a way to start off a relationship*, Tom thought.

Susan and Tom went out to dinner and Susan offered to treat Tom as she was about to retrieve $100,000 that was on its way to her post office box. "Thanks,

Susan, that's very nice of you. I've never been treated by a wealthy woman before." "Tom, I'm by no means wealthy. My checking account will just get a little fatter. You know, Tom, I should really give you half for being here with me and risking your own life."

"You're being very generous, Susan." Tom was very surprised at Susan's offer. "Susan, you're going to need that money should you decide to move to San Diego to be close to your sister," Tom unselfishly suggested to Susan. Susan could not believe the extent her newly found beau had gone to put her first.

Tom realized that all of the activity with the diamonds had brought them closer together. For his first meaningful relationship, this was one for the books. No one would ever believe the adventure they both were about to undertake. *I would have to spend a couple of days at Starbucks to explain all this to Jim, and he still would not believe me*, Tom thought.

Tom and Susan sat at a nice restaurant sipping their favorite Cabernet and enjoying each other's company. "Tom, I don't know how to thank you for being by my side. How did we manage to sit across from each other on an empty rail car?" "Susan, fate is a funny thing and it has a mind of its own." Tom attempted to get philosophical with Susan again. "You should have been a philosopher, Tom," Susan suggested, as she stared at him.

"Sitting here with you and sharing dinner are gifts I never expected to receive," Tom held her hand passionately, while the words just naturally flowed from his lips. "Thanks, Tom. I have an interesting question for you; what plans do you have once we get to San Diego?"

"Until I met you, Susan, I had none. I don't want to

be presumptuous, but I would like, if it's OK with you, to continue our relationship to see where life takes us." "Not being presumptuous at all, but neither one of us knows what tonight will bring after we free ourselves of the diamonds..."

"Sorry to interrupt you, but speaking of the diamonds, we are to meet the boys in black in half an hour—they said between nine and nine-thirty." "Tom, you know they are not going to leave without the rocks in my bag," Susan informed him, as she looked down at her bag.

"OK, we'll finish our dessert, and we'll head off to the Hertz rental counter. This is why we opted to have dinner at the airport, so we wouldn't have to rush. Are you ready to part with them?" "Yes, it's not only parting with the stones, but also my last link to Max—I'm ready to move on, Tom."

"That's very healthy for you to say, Susan; you're on your way." "Again, Tom, thank you for everything you've done for me." "Please thank me later after we leave the men in black for the last time. Susan, did you hear that? Was that thunder?" Tom turned around seeking where the big bang had come from. "I don't know, it sounded more like an explosion. I wonder what happened."

Tom and Susan left the restaurant and headed to the Hertz rental counter to part with the diamonds. They both arrived at the counter ten minutes early so they would not miss them. They were both over anxious to see the end of this adventure. They both sat in the airport seating area to catch the men in black. Nine-thirty came around, and there was no sign of them. An hour later, the same—no one had showed up. They gave themselves till eleven before attempting to call or text them. At ten after eleven they both decided to leave and check in at the nearest hotel and wait for further instructions from the boys.

The following morning Tom checked in with Susan to see if she had heard from Jacob. "No, Tom, I didn't get a text or a call." "That's really odd. You would have thought there would have been some form of contact" "You would think."

They went to the nearest coffee shop for breakfast. While sitting at a table waiting for their coffee, they overheard a conversation from a nearby table: *did you hear about the crash last night? Those guys did not know what hit them…* Susan, taking note of their conversation, asked Tom, "Tom, do you suppose…?"

"I don't know, Susan. Do you have his assistant's number in New York just to make sure?" "Yes, it's the only number in my list of recent calls that begins with 212." "Do you think you should give her a call and check in with his office?" "Good idea. Let me call her now."

"Mr. Jacob's office, may I help you," Marlene answered the phone with a very somber tone. "Yes, I'm returning Mr. Jacob's call." "I'm sorry, when did he call you?" "He called me a few days ago, and I'm just getting around to returning all my calls."

"I'm sorry, Miss, Mr. Horowitz has been in an accident and we don't know when he'll be back," Marlene informed Susan, sniffling every now and then. Susan noted the tone of her voice over the phone. "Thanks. I'll try again later, and I hope he's OK."

"I guess, Tom, you heard the conversation with his assistant." "Yes, I'm going to Google *airplane accident in Albuquerque.*" They were both shocked to see the headlines that three men from New York City perished in a Lear jet the night before. "Susan, I cannot believe what I'm seeing …" Susan was stunned and in a daze.

"Oh no, those poor men. They were so close to getting the diamonds they were longing to get. What am I going to do with these diamonds now?" Tom just stared at her in a daze as well, and could not believe all the things they've been through. The saga of the diamonds continued.

Chapter 34

"Tommy, how are you? I haven't heard from you in a while. I'm just checking in with you to see how you are doing—the booth at Starbucks is empty without you." Tom's brother, Jim, called to inquire how Tom was doing. "Hi Jim, great to hear from you, bro. You are not going to believe what I have been through in the past week."

"Good news, I hope?" Jim expected to hear great news from his brother. "Yes and no. It'll have to wait till I get back." "When is that, Tom?" "I truly don't know, but the good news is that I met someone—someone really special." "That's great, Tom. Take your time and we'll talk when you get back." Jim was so happy to hear there was someone in his brother's life—something he's been trying to do for a very long time.

"That was my brother, Jim. He called to check in on me." "That's great, Tom. He must have been concerned about you as he hadn't heard from you in a while. Have you kept him up to date?" Susan queried to see how much information Tom had relayed to his brother.

"Absolutely not. First, he wouldn't believe me, and, second, he wouldn't believe me. Certain things, Susan, are best to be left unsaid. I did tell him; however, that I had met a fantastic gal. What do you say we book a flight to San Diego? I would like to give trains a break. Have you had enough of them as well?" "Sounds like a great idea. And, yes, I've had my share of trains as well."

As they left the restaurant on their way to the

airport, they picked up a newspaper. On the front page there was an article about the three men from New York City who perished in a corporate jet the night before. Reality had set in for Tom and Susan. They could not believe they knew the victims of the crash.

It was just a few days ago they had chatted and planned on where they were scheduled to meet to surrender the diamonds. Who would have known? As far as Tom was concerned, this was just another event of many that Susan and he have gone through since they met. Tom got to the point that nothing else would surprise him, and he thought he had seen it all. *What else could happen?* Tom asked himself.

Chapter 35

"*R*achel, it's so good to see you, it's been too long. Come and give your sister a big hug." Susan approached her sister with open arms and affection. "Susan, it really hasn't been that long—about a year." Rachel was overwhelmed with Susan's joy to see her again. "Has it been that long when we used to see each other practically every day?"

"What happened to your train? You should have been here a few days ago. And why did you get off the train and decide to take a flight home? I thought you wanted to take your time to gather your thoughts?" Rachel fired one question after another, as she tried to figure out why Susan flew home instead of taking the train as she had planned.

"It's a long story, sis. I'll explain it to you one day over a few drinks." Susan changed the subject by introducing Rachel to Tom. "Here, let me introduce you to my friend, Tom, who I met on the train."

"Rachel, it's so nice to finally meet you. Your sister has told me so much about you—I feel as though I practically know you. If you guys want to go somewhere to catch up, please go ahead. I'll stay here and play with your dog. What's his name by the way?"

"That's OK, Tom, thanks. We'll have plenty of time to catch up. It really is very nice to meet you. Thank you very much for keeping my sister company all the way from Providence. My dog's name is Harvey. If you pet him on his head and scratch his tummy, he'll be your friend for life. What's going on with you?" Rachel asked, looking to find more information about Tom.

"My apologies, what kind of host am I? Can I get you guys something to drink? I'm sure they didn't give you much on the plane," asked Rachel, trying to be a good hostess. "Thanks, Rach, we can save happy hour for when we go out later. It's been a helluva train ride, one which will probably take many drinks to explain," Susan repeated, as she glanced and smiled at Tom for mental confirmation. Tom snickered a bit and shook his head and smiled. *She can say that again*, thought Tom.

"Well, you're both here and I'm ecstatic you finally got here. Tom, if I may ask, what do you do?" Rachel asked, turning towards Tom in an effort to find out more about the gentleman who appeared to have made her older sister very happy. "I'm in financial planning. I like to help people manage their finances." Tom attempted to provide a quick answer to let the sisters continue and dominate the conversation while he petted Harvey, the pug.

"Can you help me diversify my portfolio, Tom," Rachel asked facetiously, generating a laugh from Susan, who knew all too well her sister didn't have a *pot to piss in*. Rachel made an attempt to get to know a bit more about the beau who made her sister smile.

"Rach, what's going on in your life since you moved out here?" Susan asked, as she turned towards to her sister to hear all about her life. The sisters were in the habit of chatting every day on the phone. Tom got the hint that the sisters needed some alone time to talk about everything—including him.

Tom sat back and observed the chemistry of the two sisters, and was happy they finally got together after their harrowing experience they had during the past week. Tom couldn't even believe the trip they had let alone explaining it to Rachel.

After Rachel graduated from high school, she went to college on a scholarship. She had the grades and the SAT scores to merit the various scholarships she received. Susan always thought of her as the brains of the family and was very happy for her younger sister.

Rachel was also very philanthropic with her time helping the underprivileged, but kept it very quiet from everyone. She spent time during the week assisting in the neighborhood soup kitchens. Susan was also very proud of this side of Rachel—her sister had a heart of gold. She knew this a long time ago when Rachel took care of her through many of Max's rants.

"Excuse me, Susan, but I'm scheduled to help in the soup kitchen tonight, but I'll be back as soon as I'm done." "Look, Rachel, I don't mind going with you, if you folks need an extra hand in the kitchen," Tom offered. Already Tom had earned a gold star with Rachel as Susan took note of his generosity to help Rachel in the soup kitchen. Susan was also very proud of Tom for impressing her sister.

Rachel could see in Susan's eyes how proud she looked when Tom offered to help. "That's very nice of you, Tom, thanks. One of the shortages we have besides food, are helping hands. Susan, would you like to come along as well?" Susan felt she had no choice in the matter, and decided to join Tom and Rachel.

Tom was glad Susan was going to join them, as this might distract her from the recent events with Jacob and his cronies. *I wonder if Susan remembers the diamonds that are in her toiletry case*, Tom thought, as he recollected the events of the prior week. At this point, he didn't think Susan gave the diamonds a second thought. She was with her sister and the camaraderie was worth more to her than the diamonds in her possession.

Once they arrived at the soup kitchen, Rachel helped Susan and Tom put on aprons. They were both glad to help Rachel and the diners. As they served the passing trays, Tom and Susan managed to look at the poor people they served. *How blessed we are for what we have*, Tom pondered in his mind.

Tom could see in Susan's eyes that her thoughts were not far from his own, and she was glad he was able to share this experience with her—another moment Tom and Susan were building together in their cache of memories.

Rachel turned towards Susan and sadly remarked how hard it's been lately to obtain donations to supply the food pantry at the soup kitchen. Tom overheard Rachel inform Susan of the needs of the kitchen. At the same time, Susan and Tom turned towards each other, and their eyes appeared to have had a conversation of their own: *how can we assist Rachel and her crew at the kitchen*. They felt they needed to do something.

Tom couldn't wait to get Susan alone to discuss some options to help Rachel and the needs of the soup kitchen. If only the look in the eyes of the homeless could talk—the stories they would tell: *how did they get here, what happened in their lives, and so on.*

At various times when they placed food on their trays, they imagined themselves in that food line. As they shook those thoughts from their minds, they were thankful and blessed for everything they had. *How fortunate and blessed we are,* Tom stopped to reflect.

After cleaning up, the three went to a small café in town to get a bite to eat. Both Susan and Tom sat in their seats almost speechless at what they had just observed. "Are you guys, OK?" Rachel asked, while she attempted to shake them from their trance. "It's just sad to see those folks of all ages stand in line to be fed," Tom broke the sound of silence that overwhelmed the three of them.

"Tom, I see this every week. I continually attempt to imagine what events led them to this point in their lives—something drastic must have happened to them." "It just makes you really appreciate and realize how blessed we are for the roof we have over our heads and for the things we have," Susan uttered, as she shared the same sentiments of the other two. A tear of joy flowed down her cheek reflecting the intense feeling she had inside. It was a very emotional experience for Susan and Tom.

"Rachel, I would like to write a check to help those folks out," Tom offered, as he took out his checkbook and wrote a check to the soup kitchen. "Tom, that's very generous of you to do so. Thank you, but you don't need to do that," Rachel thanked Tom, while she placed her hand on his arm.

Susan felt very fortunate her newly found friend was very generous to her sister's cause. Susan wanted to mirror Tom's generosity, but she was not in the same financial circles as Tom, or was she? "Rachel, I'm not doing this because I need to—I'm doing it because I want to." Slowly, Susan noted the type of person she just happened to cross paths with on the train.

Chapter 36

Susan looked at her phone and noticed she had received a voice mail from a phone with a 212-area code—New York City: Hi Susan, this is Marlene, Jacob's assistant. We need to talk. I believe you are in possession of something that belonged to Jacob. Susan just stared at her phone and handed it to Tom so he could hear the voice mail she had just received from Marlene.

"Susan, what are we going to do? Are you going to call Marlene back?" "I don't know, Tom. She might want us to send the diamonds back to her." "How does she know we have the diamonds as Jacob and his crew perished in that accident? For all she knows, Jacob had the diamonds in his possession when the plane crashed."

"Tom, that is a very realistic possibility. We could have given them the diamonds just before they crashed—the plane could have been in the process of taking off when they crashed." "Susan, are you implying, if Marlene were to buy your story, that you plan on keeping the diamonds?" "Yes and no, Tom. I definitely would not want to keep them for myself. I would give them all to charity."

Tom did not know what to make of Susan's reaction towards the diamonds. Was she planning to keep the diamonds that were in the box she had found in her home that Max had stolen? Does that put her in the same position as Max? If so, does that mean she's a thief? These were some of the thoughts that went rampant through Tom's mind.

If he were to go along with Susan's way of thinking, would that make Tom an accessory to the stolen goods? Tom was at a crossroads in his relationship with Susan and he didn't know what to do—he was at a quandary. He needed Susan to help him resolve some critical questions that could determine his future relationship with her.

Tom had only known Susan for a short while— sometimes sufficient to know someone and sometimes not. He needed the situation with the diamonds and Susan to play itself out. He did not want to over-react, but the trend was not going in the right direction for him. Tom just needed an indication from Susan to erase all the doubts that were bouncing all over his mind—he needed to find this out quickly!

Chapter 37

*M*arlene sat in Jacob's office trying to figure out what she was going to do with all of Jacob's belongings. For all practical purposes, the business had come to a screeching halt once Jacob and Joseph perished in the airplane accident. Ever since she heard the report of the crash, she has been in a state of shock—at a total loss. His personal effects will be sent to his wife, Rebecca, and everything else would be donated to charity except for the computers and printers which would be donated to the nearest school.

Undoing over twenty years of a business was not going to be easy. Anything of value in the company safe will be sold to pay off the creditors. Marlene was faced with the arduous task of shutting down a business. She was more qualified to do so than Jacob—she was the one who ran the business like a well-oiled machine.

While sitting on Jacob's worn-out classical leather chair (large enough to occupy two of her), Marlene recalled the multitude of conversations they had over the years. When Marlene first joined Jacob's business, she had trouble with the smoke-filled air from Jacob's illegally gotten Cuban cigars.

She had her doubts whether she would be able to cope and work with the cigar smoke ten hours a day. She gave herself a couple of weeks of probation to see if she were able to cope with the smoke. She was young when she started, and no one paid the wages that Jacob had offered. The couple of weeks turned out to be a couple of decades — time flew by in the blink of an eye for her.

Rebecca, Jacob's wife, had authorized Marlene to liquidate the contents of the office. She had as much faith in Marlene as Jacob had in her. Marlene had obtained several Bankers' Boxes to pack Jacob's personal effects to take to his wife. Marlene had already called various schools in the area to donate the computer equipment from the office. A used office furniture equipment company was also scheduled to come to pick up the: office desk, chairs, and file cabinets.

Prior to erasing and shutting down the server, Marlene planned on answering whatever emails either Jacob or she received. She also planned on sending a general email to all of Jacob's contacts and vendors. She wanted to let them know that Jacob's office had closed and thanked them for all the many years of service they had given to Jacob.

One email that caught Marlene's eye was from Jacob five minutes before the fatal crash that took his life: hello, Marlene, we are on our way to pick up the diamonds from Miss Susan. I want to thank you again for sending her the reward money. I should be in the office the day after tomorrow. See you when I get back. Jacob. Marlene copied this email with the date and time it was sent and texted it to Susan.

Upon receiving the text from Marlene, Susan had a blank stare on her face and slowly turned over her phone to Tom. *She knows I still have the diamonds*, Susan thought to herself. Tom and Susan had a lot to talk about being careful not to jump to any conclusions, but Marlene had solid proof that Jacob had not picked up the diamonds.

"Susan, there is no doubt in Marlene's mind you still have the diamonds in your possession. She has proof from the date and time on the email that Jacob sent her shortly before the crash that Jacob had not picked up the diamonds from you. We have a decision to make."

Susan and Tom discussed Marlene's text for hours coming up with all sorts of options of what to do next. It was back to square one for the both of them. All of this appeared like a bad dream they both had a hard time waking up from. What was going to be their next move?

Chapter 38

Marlene stood by the empty office while she looked around and relived many of the memories that were made in the office. The bagels that occupied the office numbered in the thousands. The constant bickering between Jacob and Joseph were as numerous. Marlene was aware of the fact that was the way business was done in the diamond district—it happened every day of the week. After a while, it became a way of life for her.

Marlene also realized there was unfinished business she had to take care of. She couldn't let Miss Susan get away with a couple of million dollars' worth of diamonds after she was rewarded handsomely to return them. She asked herself what she planned to do with the diamonds should they wind up in her lap.

The diamonds, as far as Marlene was concerned, were the property of Jacob's office, and now they are gone. In reality, the diamonds were the property of the insurance company that insured them. Each of their respective families was entitled to a portion of them. From Marlene's recollection, Jacob was a 65% partner and Joseph was a 35% partner, and; thus, their respective families were entitled to their share of the proceeds of the sale.

For Marlene, the first order of business was to get the diamonds back. Since Marlene had not heard from Susan, she decided it was time for a follow-up call with a little more emphasis on returning the diamonds. As with the last time Marlene called, her call went directly to voice mail so she left another lengthy message: *hi Susan, it is very obvious that either you didn't get my first voice mail message, or you are intentionally avoiding my calls. I have proof that Mr. Horowitz never collected the diamonds from you for which you were handsomely rewarded. I have no doubt they remain in your possession. It's in your best interest to contact me as soon as possible so we can work out an arrangement for you to return the diamonds. If you insist on…*(beep) *the voice mail box you are attempting to use is now full*, a message was heard prior to Marlene's ultimatum.

Rather than bearing the burden of retrieving the diamonds totally on herself, Marlene decided to pay a visit to Jacob's wife, Rebecca. "Mrs. Horowitz, I am so sorry for the loss of your husband—he was like a father to me. He took me in as a young girl, and I was very appreciative for everything he did for me."

"Marlene, *ve* have known each other for a very long time. Please call me Rebecca. It's a real *mitzvah* that you came all the *vay* to Brooklyn to visit me and pay your respects. I know my Jacob loved you very much; he never stopped talking about you—Marlene did this, Marlene did that. He knew diamonds very *vell*, but he did not know the operations of an office. Fortunately, you were there, my dear, and you spoiled him," Rebecca shared with Marlene while holding her hand.

"Mrs. Horowitz, sorry, Rebecca, I have some unfinished business I need your assistance in." "*Vhat* is it, my dear?" "You are going through a difficult time at the moment, and I don't mean to bother you with business while you are in mourning for Jacob."

"Marlene, as I said, I've known you for a very long time—you are like family, my dear. I know you haven't come all this *vay* just to visit. *Vhat* is the problem that you need my help in?"

"As you know, Rebecca, your husband was a 65% partner in the business so what I'm about to tell you could have a big financial impact on your family." This raised a few eyebrows with Rebecca, and she was very interested in what Marlene had to say. "Go on, my dear, I'm listening," Rebecca acknowledged, very anxious to hear the big financial impact Marlene was to have on her family.

"Rebecca, as you may recall, Jacob and Joseph went out of town to resolve some unfinished business. Unfortunately, the plane accident prevented them from finishing it. They were on their way to retrieve $2 million worth of diamonds that were stolen by a woman named Susan." Marlene started to relate the situation she was in. "This *voman* still has Jacob's diamonds?" Rebecca asked with interest. "Yes, she does. I have made two attempts to call her to get them back with no luck — she doesn't return my calls."

"*Vhy* don't you call the police then?" "Rebecca, all I have is her first name and a telephone number. That's all. I don't know where she lives, let alone where she is at the moment." "I *sink ve* have a real problem, don't *ve*?" "Yes, we certainly do which is why I came to talk with you — I don't know what to do." "Are these diamonds tagged with serial numbers?" "No, I don't believe they are."

"Marlene, how did this *voman* steal Jacob's diamonds?" "They were mailed to a customer a while ago, and the customer never received them. Of course, we had them insured when we mailed them." "Did the insurance company pay you for the loss?" "Yes, they did." "So *vhat's* the problem, my dear?"

"The problem is that we have an opportunity to get them back." "And, *vonce* you get them back, you're going to give the diamonds to the insurance company, right? *Vhat vas* Jacob and his partner going to do *vith* the diamonds that this *voman* stole?" Marlene paused to think of the response she was going to give to Rebecca.

"I don't know Mrs. Horowitz." Marlene knew Rebecca made sense, and she tried to think of a way to respond to her. "I have an idea, Marlene, but I'm going to keep it to myself. My Jacob, may God rest his soul, *vas* a good man, and I believe he *vould* have done the right thing in the end. I really don't *sink ve* have a problem, my dear," Rebecca informed her, while she put her hand on Marlene's hand.

Marlene felt she had gone as far as she could with Rebecca. She left her without a game plan. She was at a loss and didn't know what to do with the missing diamonds. Marlene did agree with her that Jacob was reimbursed by the insurance company, and, in turn, the diamonds did belong to the insurance company.

How was she going to handle the diamonds in Susan's possession? Greed slowly crept into Marlene. To get the diamonds back would make her a very rich woman where she wouldn't have to work the rest of her life. *How can I get a hold of those diamonds without getting into trouble*, she contemplated?

Chapter 39

"Isn't it strange, Susan, that you haven't heard from Marlene in a week after she left you those two friendly voice mail messages? She made it clear in her text she knows you have the diamonds. She also has proof Jacob didn't get them from you, but nothing—not a word from her at all," Tom informed Susan.

"That thought crossed my mind lately. Being here with Rachel has been a big distraction for me, a good one at that. I've even forgotten for a little while Max and Marlene," Susan paused to reflect on her life at the moment.

"Susan, I have really enjoyed being here with you and Rachel, but I don't want to overstay my welcome. Maybe it's time to leave you two alone and head back home," Tom suggested.

"Is that what you would like to do, Tom?" Susan asked, with a little concern in her voice that the person she fell in love with was about to leave her. "Of course not, I would rather stay here with you," Tom informed her, as he approached and held her in his arms.

"And the diamonds?" "Susan, I'll pretend you didn't ask me that question. The diamonds do not mean anything to me. If you would like my opinion, go to the bank and put them in a safety deposit box and forget about them for a while—they've been nothing but trouble in your life."

"That's a great suggestion, Tom. Would you mind going to the bank with me?" "Of course not. Let me know when you want to go, and I'll go with you." "How about this afternoon?" "Great, Susan. The faster we get them out of your sight, the better off you'll be." "Just curious, Susan. Does Rachel know about the diamonds? Did you happen to mention them to her?" "No, I didn't. It's enough you and I are involved; there's no sense getting her mixed up with them as well." Tom was pleased Susan did not make any more people aware of the diamonds. It was a dead-end subject as far as he was concerned.

"Now, Tom, can we get back to your original thought of your going back home. Is there something pressing for you to get back? Your job for example?" "Nothing urgent. I've been away for a couple of weeks and I hadn't planned on being here that long, but since I've met you, things have changed—you have entered my life, and I like it. As I said, I fell in love with you."

"It's amazing, Tom, we've been together for a couple of weeks, and I feel as if I've known you for a long time." "We certainly have been through a lot, haven't we? Yes, Susan, I agree with you. It does feel like we've known each other for a long time, but this is supposed to be your alone time with your sister, and I seem to be the third wheel. This is also supposed to be your healing time with Rachel."

"Tom, please don't leave. I love having you in my life." "Susan, since we've met on the train, we really haven't been alone, but I totally understand what you and I have been through." "I have an idea, but I would like to pass it by Rachel first."

"Tom, I've talked to Rachel and asked if she would mind if you and I were to go away for a couple of days— just you and I alone," Susan suggested to Tom, hoping for him to accept her offer and not go back to Providence."

"That sounds like a great idea, Susan, but I have to be honest with you. I haven't gone away with a woman before," Tom informed her, with a bit of trepidation in his voice. This was not something Susan expected to hear from him. Susan didn't know how to react to Tom's honesty.

"Tom, that's OK, I won't bite," Susan informed Tom, while she attempted to bring a little humor into the conversation as well as to ease the tension in the air. "OK, Susan, that sounds great. I feel 100% better that you don't bite either," Tom returned the compliment. He then approached her, put his arms around her, and gave her an endearing kiss. Susan stepped back and informed Tom she had not been with anyone since Max had died either.

Chapter 40

"Joshua, is this you?" "Marlene, I'm so sorry to hear about *Yacob*—it was so sudden and unexpected. After the box you mailed my client in Providence disappeared, I didn't know *vhat* to expect," Joshua sounded very surprised to hear from Marlene.

"I think I've solved the mystery why your client didn't receive the box we sent him. Someone at the post office must have taken it and we recently were made aware where the missing diamonds wound up." "Really? They finally showed up? We thought they *vere* lost? Thank goodness the insurance company settled *vith* us so quickly."

"Yes, that was a relief for us as well. Joshua, is it possible for us to meet sometime today? I have a business proposition you might be interested in." "Yes, of course. I'm a couple of blocks from your place—I can come over. Just let me know *vhen*."

"That's great. As you are aware, we're dissolving the business, and we gave all the furniture away. Can I come over to your place instead, if you don't mind? Would it also be possible to chat privately without having anyone around?" "Definitely, come on over *vhen* you can. I'll put a pot of coffee on," Joshua suggested, and wondered what Marlene had up her sleeve.

While on her way to meet with Joshua, Marlene rehearsed in her mind how she planned to approach Joshua on a potential business venture. Joshua and Marlene have worked together on many transactions in the past fifteen years. She knew Joshua well enough for him to jump at any possibility to make a buck—no matter what he had to do. He was, in Marlene's opinion, the perfect individual who would be interested in Marlene's nefarious plan.

"Marlene, how are you? Again, my condolences for our dear *Yacob*—he *vas* a good man," Joshua approached Marlene with open arms, pretending he had any compassion for her and Jacob. He was money driven and Marlene had his number for many years. Give him an opportunity to take a lollipop from a baby to make a buck, and you will hear a baby cry—nothing would get in his way. Marlene hoped Joshua would jump at the idea to go after the diamonds with her. She knew she couldn't do it on her own. She was astute enough that this was beyond her pay grade.

Joshua showed Marlene to his conference room filled with pictures of various gems—mostly diamonds. The aroma of freshly brewed coffee permeated the air. They both sat down at one end of the conference room table, and Joshua wasted no time to get to the heart of the matter. Conversations of condolences were brief, and they were ready to move on.

"*Vell*, my dear, you said you had a business proposition? I'm very curious. How did the missing box all of a sudden show up?" "Joshua, I cannot answer that—it's a mystery to all of us. All I know is that this woman called us saying she had the box. Why she didn't call earlier, I truly don't know—I can't explain it. Be that as it may, I have a pretty good idea who is in possession of the diamonds."

"How sure are you, Marlene, that this *voman* has them?" Joshua's interest and curiosity were very obvious to Marlene, and she knew the fish was close to biting the bait.

"She sent us a picture of one of them, so we are pretty confident she has all twenty-eight of them. We also sent her $100,000 as a reward for returning them. There was supposed to be an exchange on the train, but there was an unforeseen person on the train who prevented the exchange from occurring. To make a long story short, Jacob was to fly to Albuquerque to personally retrieve the diamonds from this woman...well, you know the rest."

"When I was in the process of closing down the office and getting rid of everything, I decided to email all of our contacts that we were closing the office. This is when I came across Jacob's email sent literally minutes before the crash. Poor guy, he didn't know what hit him. Anyway, Jacob was on his way to pick up the stones from this Susan person. So, I know she is still in possession of the diamonds."

"Did you try to call her?" Joshua got excited the more Marlene spoke. "Yes, I did and I left several messages on her voice mail, but she never returned my calls." Marlene updated Joshua on the status of the diamonds, as she hoped he would jump at the possibility of going diamond hunting with her.

Marlene and Joshua discussed various possibilities to retrieve the diamonds from Susan, whose location and address were both unknown at the moment. "Marlene, I've given your dilemma some thought, and I believe *ve* have to make it more enticing for this Susan person to return the diamonds."

"Joshua, we already gave her $100,000. Are you suggesting we give her more?" Marlene asked with a surprised look in her face that Joshua opted to increase the reward.

"Marlene, this person does not sound stupid—she knows *vhat* she is doing." Joshua attempted to paint a picture about Susan's personae. "But Joshua, she was ready to surrender the stones to Jacob at the airport when the plane crashed." "Maybe she has reassessed her position and felt she can get more. I don't know this *voman*, Marlene; otherwise, she *vould* have already answered your messages," Joshua opined why Susan had not gotten back to Marlene.

"What do you propose we do to get the stones back? Do you have any suggestions, Joshua?" Marlene asked, hoping Joshua had some devious recommendation for her. "You just said, Marlene, *ve*? As I said, this person is not stupid. As a matter of fact, she is pretty sharp. She must know she has millions of dollars' worth in stones for which she has already received $100,000, and she might *sink* she can get more. Maybe she has an accomplice who is *vorking with* her and is giving her ideas. Just like you and I are trying to get the diamonds back. I don't know, Marlene—I'm just guessing."

"Are you suggesting we offer her more?" Marlene asked, concerned she would have to come up with more reward money. "Look at it this *vay*. She has the stones, and *ve* don't. Do you see the direction *ve* are going *vith* this?"

"As I asked before, are you suggesting, Joshua, we increase the reward?" "Exactly. I don't believe $100,000 *vas* enough for her to give the diamonds back; especially, if she happens to be *avare* how much they are *vorth*."

"What do you suggest we give her then?" Marlene asked, with a confused look about her. "At least $250,000 more," Joshua suggested, while shrugging his shoulders and taking a sip of his coffee. "Wow, Joshua, that's a lot of money," Marlene remarked, with a very concerned look about her. "So are $2 million *vorth* of diamonds, my dear. If you have any other options to get those stones back, I'm all ears," Joshua said.

"Look, Jacob already gave her $100,000 for the diamonds she originally stole, or so we think. In reality, I don't know who stole the diamonds. All I know, is that she is in possession of them at the moment. I don't think we should give her anymore," Marlene suggested, hoping Joshua would agree with her position. "Marlene, as I said my dear, she has the stones and you don't have them, and she is not returning your calls. *Vhat* do you think she's going to do with them?"

"Joshua, you are probably right. OK, let's give her $250,000 more, but it's coming out of your pocket." "OK, I'll gladly pay $250,000 for $2 million *vorth* of diamonds. I *vould* do this every day of the week, my dear."

"OK, then I'll send her another message that we have reconsidered and will offer her an additional reward." This was something Marlene did not expect, but realized that Joshua made a good point to get the diamonds back.

Chapter 41

$\mathcal{T}$om and Susan went away for a few days to get away from it all. Susan recalled a conversation she had with Tom when they were on the train: *whenever you go away you take your problems with you.* Hopefully, sharing quiet moments together would help them manage some of the issues they were both confronted with lately—the diamonds Susan still had in her possession were on top of their list. They both hoped having the diamonds in a safety deposit box and being out of sight, would make that issue go away. It was like a bad penny—it kept on coming back.

Intimacy was something that neither Tom nor Susan had experienced recently; especially, in Tom's case. While away, they both decided to take it slow with their relationship. Staying in separate rooms was a choice they both agreed without any argument. They both opted to get to know each other better first—they were both very comfortable with that decision.

Susan and Tom were alone. They were not in the company of anyone they knew. Things had to be discussed, and they agreed Rachel did not need not to be involved. Susan found the opportunity to sit down with Tom and share the voice message she recently received from Marlene. Unfortunately, the subject of the diamonds continued to come back.

"Susan, I cannot believe Marlene wants to increase the reward by $250,000," Tom said, surprised Marlene would go that high after she already paid $100,000.

Susan was still in shock over the large amount that was offered to get the diamonds back. She's never been confronted with this amount of money in her life, and she had trouble processing it.

"Tom, let's go for a walk and leave all this behind us for a while. This is too much to process at the moment." Susan needed to change the subject and not dwell on the diamonds for a while.

Susan continued, "I was very happy to see that Rachel is doing well, and she's settling in nicely—I love her dearly." "There's no doubt in my mind that you are sisters with a life-long bond. Have you given any consideration to staying with her and moving down here permanently?" "I have definitely given that some thought, but I didn't expect certain unforeseen curve balls to be thrown at me."

"You mean the diamonds?" "That too but, more importantly, you came into my life." "Susan, you've only known me for a couple of weeks, and do you think that's sufficient time to know someone?" "Tom, it's not the quantity of time that makes a difference in a relationship—it's the quality of time you spend together with someone. But, generally, no, two weeks may not be sufficient time to know someone; however, you and I have been together night and day for a couple of weeks and we have gone through various land mines and survived."

"Tom, would you like to stay here with me in San Diego? Would you like our relationship to grow?" "Susan, I would like that more than anything in the world," Tom replied, with passion in his eyes that was very evident to Susan. She turned and approached him and gave him a big hug and a kiss.

"Tom, I don't believe I have said this in decades: *I love you.*" "Susan, I love you very much as well!" Tom did not recall ever saying those words to anyone in his life, but he had no doubt in his mind he wished to explore them further with Susan.

Chapter 42

" *Joshua*, I received a reply from Susan." Marlene was very excited to share this news with Joshua. "Good news, I hope?" "Yes and no. Yes, she is willing to part with the diamonds, but not for $250,000." "*Vhat*? I'll kill that bitch," Joshua reacted, as he raised his voice.

"Joshua, let's think about this. I remember distinctively what you said recently: *she is in possession of the diamonds and we are not.* We can counter-offer with $400,000: half from you and half from me. How does that sound?"

"Marlene, I love the *vay* you talk and negotiate. *Vould* you like to *vork vith* me after this is all over?" "Joshua, let's get the diamonds first, and then we can talk." Marlene was not in the position of thinking that far ahead—she needed to put the diamonds behind her first. A new business partnership was in the making— Marlene and Joshua both fed from each other's greed. A partnership-in-crime was also in the making.

"Joshua, once Susan agrees to our counter-offer, we have to work out the arrangement on how we are to going to get the diamonds from her. Also, have you given any thought how we're going to dispose of the diamonds once they are in our possession?" Marlene has always been organized, and she needed to know all of the planning steps up front. "Marlene, you leave that up to me; I have many contacts all over the place."

"That's great, Joshua, but we also need to discuss how we are going to split the money after we sell the stones." "I give you 20%. That sounds more than fair, I believe." "Joshua, be realistic. You wouldn't be in the position to sell the diamonds had I not approached you—she happens to be my contact." "That's very true, Marlene. How about 30%? That's 50% more than I originally offered you."

"Joshua, it's going to be 50-50—take it or leave it. It would be the easiest million you ever made." "OK, Marlene, you drive a hard bargain." "Joshua, how many years have I worked with Jacob? Don't you think a few things rubbed off on me?" Marlene was proud of the way she handled herself with Joshua. *Thanks, Jacob, wherever you may be*, Marlene thought, as she looked up and thought of the next steps that needed to be taken to get the diamonds back from Susan.

Chapter 43

The weather in San Diego was a comfortable seventy-eight degrees with little or no humidity. The birds were singing and Susan and Tom were absorbing all the beautiful aspects of nature — they were in their own little world, and they both wanted the moments they shared to be frozen in time.

"Why can't every day be like this? It's so peaceful in this park, and the air smells so clean and fresh," Susan shared, while she looked around and absorbed all of nature's beauty. "Walking and holding hands in this park just adds the icing on the cake, Susan." "Tom, you really have a sweet tooth." Susan looked at him, smiled and snuggled next to him while they walked through the park.

The perfect setting they shared was suddenly interrupted by another phone call with a 212-area code. As usual, they let the call go to voice mail followed by a ding that a message was left. "Gee, Susan, I wonder who that could be?" Tom asked facetiously.

As much as they didn't want anything to interrupt their moment, they both decided to listen to the voice message: Susan, this is Marlene. We are prepared to make you a final additional offer of $400,000 instead of the previous offer of $250,000. This is our final offer which we feel is very generous. This would bring the overall reward to you to $500,000 when you include the $100,000 which you previously received. Please text or call me back that you are in agreement so we can make the necessary arrangements to close this deal. Looking forward to hearing from you. Marlene.

"Susan, did you catch in her message that she said *we* several times? It seems Marlene has gotten herself a partner to raise that kind of money." "Yes, I caught that, and I would like to agree to her final offer, and put all this behind me."

"That makes a lot of sense, Susan—you need to get on with your life. We need to come up with a plan of our own on how we're going to arrange the swap. May I recommend that she give you a bank certified check at the same time the diamonds are surrendered?" "Tom, it makes sense, but my gut tells me this could be very dangerous. Who is to say they won't gun us down and get the diamonds before paying us that kind of money?"

"That's a good possibility as well, Susan. You make a very good point." "And because it is, Tom, we need to prepare for that possibility. Maybe we should have an intermediary on both sides who will accept the money from our side, and one from their side who will pay the money and accept the stones." "Susan, Marlene doesn't know what you look like, and you can pretend to be the intermediary from our side," Tom suggested.

"Not a bad idea, Tom. We need to give that some thought. More importantly, I'm just concerned about safety—I don't want anyone to get hurt." "Maybe I can go in your place, and verify the bank check, or maybe have them wire the funds?" "How about an attaché case filled with $400,000 in it? You do realize we're bringing up options because we don't trust them. Sad, isn't it?"

Tom and Susan spent hours contriving all sorts of options on how to exchange the diamonds for the reward money. Suddenly, Susan came up with an option. "I'm going to text Marlene back and inform her we are ready to accept her offer, and I'm ready to turn over the stones for $400,000 in cash—in 50's and 100's." "Good luck. Let's see what they suggest."

Susan and Tom felt more comfortable there was a plan in place to finally end the saga of the diamonds once and for all.

Chapter 44

"Joshua, have you given any thought how we're going to sell the diamonds once we have them in our hands?" Marlene continued to explore the next steps that needed to be taken once they had their hands on the diamonds. "As I said, I've got plenty of contacts who, I believe, *vill* buy a few of them."

"I also have a few contacts of my own, so when we get the stones, you can have half of them and I'll take the other half. Does that work for you?" Joshua hesitated, and gave Marlene's suggestion some thought. "Let me *sink* about it. *Ve* might have a quicker turnaround if *ve* sell the whole lot all at *vonce*." Although Joshua's option made a lot of sense to Marlene to dispose of the diamonds all at once, there was still the trust issue she had with him.

One thing Marlene learned over the years working with Jacob, was that Joshua was not to be trusted. Thoughts came to mind about accepting the diamonds from Susan and not informing Joshua of the exact date of the swap. Then, she would give him half, as she didn't, for one minute, think that Joshua would give her half.

At that moment, her train of thought was interrupted by an acceptance text from Susan—inquiring instructions on how to swap the diamonds. She further clarified the reward money be in cash which is to be put in an attaché case broken down in 50's and 100's. The drop was scheduled to be in a week.

"I tell you, Marlene, this *voman* sounds like a pro."
"She certainly knows what she is doing—I'll give her that." Marlene and Joshua were very impressed with Susan's ability to delineate the switch, and looked forward to receiving the diamonds from her.

"Joshua, we have a week to come up with $400,000 in 50's and 100's to swap for the diamonds." "You really trust this *voman* after everything you've been through, and *Yoseph* and *Yacob* lost their lives?" "Please fill me in, Joshua. What other options do we have?" "You know, Marlene, these people could be amateurs, and could be taking advantage of us?"

"Joshua, be realistic. We are paying them $400,000 to make a couple of million dollars. I think this is the best deal you will ever make in your life." "I know, I know, but *somesing* doesn't smell so good—this is too good to be true." "Look, Joshua, if you don't want any part of this, please let me know now who you would recommend to make a quick buck—I don't have that kind of money to do it by myself. I do; however, have someone else in mind." Marlene got the feeling Joshua was getting cold feet, and was having second thoughts.

"Joshua, we are losing time. Are you in or are you not? I need to know in the next five minutes, so I can get someone else involved. Time is of the essence!" Marlene felt very assertive with Joshua.

"You've got *somevone* else?" "Yes, I have two others from my contacts, who I have a pretty good idea would jump at the thought of getting involved. I'm going to ask you one more time: in or out?" "Yes, yes, I'm in. Let's get the money."

Tom, Susan, Marlene and Joshua planned to meet somewhere in the middle where they wouldn't have to fly — they did not wish to expose the diamonds or, for that matter, the attaché case full of cash when they got back to San Diego.

For Tom and Susan to drive to Denver would be considered a romantic getaway by car. As they both had their personal vehicles back home, they opted to rent a car, and spend some quality time with each other on the road. Another adventure was in the offing for the both of them.

"Susan, what are you planning to tell Rachel the reason we are going to rent a car to drive to Denver?" "I'll just let her know we are going to take a romantic trip to Denver and go sightseeing while we're there. Rachel will be ecstatic her older sister/widow is planning a romantic trip with her new beau." "Well, if you think that is how Rachel might see it, I'm interested to hear how you see it." "Well, Tom, didn't I tell you that Rachel and I agree on almost everything?"

"That's good to know, Susan. I just cannot believe that I've gone most of my life without meeting someone like you." "That's sweet of you, Tom. Life is definitely funny and God does have a sense of humor. You just cannot predict where life is going to take you next." "Besides, Susan, you wouldn't want to know in advance where life is going to take you; otherwise, you wouldn't have anything to look forward to."

Another road trip was planned for Tom and Susan. Marlene and Joshua planned to charter a private plane to Denver to pick up the diamonds, as neither had the time nor desire to sit with each other for countless hours on the road. Their objective was to pick up the diamonds, get back on the plane, and go back home. Their financial objectives were very different as well.

Marlene and Joshua's objectives were to enrich their bank accounts. Tom and Susan's objectives were philanthropic in nature—to donate all of the reward money to Rachel's soup kitchen.

"Tom, I'm really looking forward to getting away with you on this trip. As a matter of fact, Rachel is also very excited we're getting away. Of course, she is not aware what our real purpose is—there's no need to involve her in this escapade. One day I might just let her know, but for now let's just make it our little secret."

"You mean *big secret*, Susan."

"Do you guys know what your final destination is when you get on the road?" Rachel asked, as she entered the room. "We don't know at the moment—it might be Denver," Susan responded, while looking at Tom. "I can see you guys have done a great deal of traveling since you both met." Rachel wanted to keep the conversation going in an attempt to get to know Tom a little better. She already had a good feeling about him.

"Tom, have you always done a lot of traveling?" Rachel asked. "As a matter of fact, Rachel, quite the contrary. I have spent most of my time working from my office in Providence. You can say I've been a workaholic all of my life, and I decided, or I should say, my health decided for me to slow down and make me take it easy." "Are you OK, Tom? How are you now?" "Oh, yes, nothing serious. I just needed to slow my pace down which is, as you know, how I met your sister. I took a long train ride to relax."

"You two have been the world travelers lately. Do you think you guys might settle down one day in San Diego?" Rachel continued her ongoing quest to see if her sister would live near her. "I don't know, Rachel. I still have my job in Rhode Island, and I haven't officially retired—still a bit young to do so." "How about you Susan? Do you see yourself moving down here one day with all this sunshine and warm weather? And, more importantly, no snow."

"I have to say, it really is very nice down here." "Do you think you'll miss all those cold winters up north, sis?" Tom sat back and took mental notes about the back-and-forth deliberations between both sisters. He could see them both living close to one another, if not living under one roof. Tom had a great deal to think about, but, at the moment, his priority was to help Susan get rid of the diamonds that have been a great burden to her; hence, the main reason for the road trip—getting to know Susan better was an added bonus.

"Tom, we need to sit and plan our trip to Denver and we also need to rent a car." "What is your thought we do this tomorrow morning after breakfast? Rachel, do you mind driving us to the nearest car rental office?" "Not a problem, Tom—I would love to."

One could see in Rachel's eyes she was very happy to see her older sister be more at peace with herself. She also recalled when Susan dreaded the life she led when Max was alive who created a living hell for her. *I guess it's something she had to go through by herself,* Rachel thought at times, but she was glad she was there for her sister when she needed her.

"Susan, do you feel you're doing something behind your sister's back?" Tom asked, after they picked up the rental car. "Tom, I love my sister very much, and one thing I don't want to do is to get her involved in what we are doing. I even feel terrible that you are involved. For this, my dear, I am terribly sorry I've made you part of this adventure," Susan said very earnestly.

"Susan, you have made me part of your life, and I absolutely have no regrets—I would do it all over again." "You're so sweet, Tom. This is why I fell in love with you." Tom just stared at her, and felt a sense of euphoria that she was part of his life.

"Tom, I noticed you insisted on putting your name on the rental agreement?" "Yes, I wanted to keep your name out of it just in case." "Just in case, why?" "I don't know, Susan, just in case things go the wrong way." "Do you have that feeling as well?" "Yes, I do, Susan. We are dealing with very dangerous people when money is involved. Money has a way of changing people, and I don't know what to expect with Marlene and her partner when we make the exchange."

Chapter 45

"Marlene, the car *vill* be picking us up in half an hour. Are your ready to pick up the diamonds?" Joshua called Marlene to coordinate going to the airport. "Yes, Joshua, that has a nice ring to it. I can't wait for this to be all over." "Me too—I'll see you shortly."

The limo picked up Marlene first and then proceeded crosstown to pick up Joshua in Brooklyn. Joshua stood by the curb waiting for the limo to go to the airport. "Good morning, Marlene. *Ve* hope *ve* have better luck than *Yacob* and *Yoseph.*"

"That was a freak accident, Joshua. We don't know, as of yet, why the plane crashed so close to the airport." "And they *vere* so close to picking up the diamonds," Joshua pointed out, as he looked out the window in deep thought. *Vere the diamonds an omen?* Joshua pondered while he stared out the window.

"Joshua, how are we paying for this plane ride?" Marlene asked Joshua, whose mind appeared to be somewhere else. "Oh, the plane ride. Yes, I have a very *vealthy* client who offered us to use his plane as a favor." "It must have been a fantastic favor he owed you." "Yes, it *vas*. I *vas* covering for him…"

"No need to say anymore, Joshua. I get the picture." The less Marlene knew about Joshua the better. She didn't feel there was any need to know too much about her interim partner. Getting the diamonds and disposing of them were Marlene's goals—knowing Joshua better was not an option she wished to entertain.

"*Ve* should be at the airport shortly and we can go and get our diamonds. *Ve* can then get back on the plane and take off right away. Did you inform Susan the approximate time *ve'll* be at the airport?" "Yes, I did, and I also informed her I would text her the exact time we are scheduled to take off." "Good, I just *vant* to pick up the diamonds and leave as quickly as possible."

Joshua shared the same goals and objectives as Marlene's. "You mean you don't want to go sightseeing with me afterwards?" Marlene asked Joshua in jest to get his mind off the diamonds. "You're very funny, my dear. You *sink* this is a pleasure trip?" Marlene was glad to see they were both on the same page.

The plane to Denver took off as scheduled and both Joshua and Marlene were very anxious to relieve Susan of the diamonds she held on to. On occasion, Marlene took a peek at the attaché case containing the $400,000 for the diamonds. She almost wanted to count it again to ensure all the money was there. She did not appear as calm as Joshua — the situation was very stressful for her. In the back of her mind, the diamonds belonged to the insurance company.

Marlene felt Joshua, on the other hand, had more experience in such nefarious activities than she did. Marlene hoped the pit she had in her stomach would go away; she was very uncomfortable with the whole situation.

Marlene's share of the $400,000 came out of the funds from Jacob's business. Once the diamonds were sold, she planned on putting the $200,000 back in the business' checking account as it belonged to Jacob's and Joseph's families. Jacob's wife, Rebecca, had put all her faith and trust in Marlene to dissolve the assets of the business.

Marlene had no intentions of asking Joshua what he was going to with his share of the diamonds. All she wanted was to get her share of the diamonds and be finished with him. She did not wish to pursue any future relationship with Joshua—definitely not something in the horizon for her.

Upon landing at the Denver airport, Marlene was instructed to go to the Hertz rental counter and look for a woman carrying a red umbrella. Susan would be waiting for her. Marlene could feel her heartbeat race, and almost had a fleeting moment of calling the exchange off; however, it was not totally her decision to make.

Tom sat in the waiting area within eyeshot of Susan and her red umbrella. Tom wanted to be with her to hold her hand, as he felt her heart would be racing as well. Marlene also had a red umbrella to identify who she was. Once they made contact, they were to go to the nearest ladies' room to make the exchange.

They even had an *Out of Order* sign to put on the door once they ensured no one else was in the ladies' room to protect their privacy. Joshua did not need any umbrella to signify who he was. The long white beard, black hat and long black coat were clear giveaways. He also continued to wait in the lounge area.

Once the out of order sign was placed on the door of the ladies' room, the girls began their exchange. They both felt introductions were not required—the red umbrellas were sufficient.

Marlene put the attaché case on the bathroom vanity, and Susan turned over her toiletry case containing the diamonds. Marlene slowly opened the toiletry case and recognized the colors real diamond made. The fluorescent lights generated a prism of colors that radiated a rainbow of colors.

While Marlene carefully examined the diamonds, Susan made a cursory flip of the 50's and 100's of each pack to satisfy herself the funds were all there. Not much conversation ensued between the two of them. One came for the diamonds and the other for the reward; hopefully, never to see each other again. They both nodded with a make-believe smile and each went in different directions.

Tom got up once the girls left the ladies' room and connected with Susan. Similarly, Marlene connected with Joshua walking at a pace to keep up with the wave of airport passengers. Both couples disappeared amongst the passengers. Time for all to go home with more than they came with.

Chapter 46

Tom and Susan got back after their airport swap along with the $400,000 reward in the brown attaché case. On occasion, they gave each other a special look asking each other how they were going to give Rachel the money for the soup kitchen.

Prior to doing so, they decided to go to the bank to open a safety deposit box to deposit the money—it was too much money to have lying around. Even though the money belonged to Susan, they opened a safe deposit box in joint names at Susan's recommendation.

Susan had enough trust in Tom to open the safety deposit box in joint names. She felt it was the right thing to do just in case something happened to either one of them. Susan could have included Rachel in the account, but that would have opened many doors that, in Susan's opinion, should remain closed. Protecting her sister was of the utmost importance to Susan. It was enough Tom was already an accomplice to Susan's escapades.

"Well guys, you've been here for a little over a week. What's your next move? Are you planning to stay here?" Rachel directly asked Tom and Susan to see if they were planning to stay in San Diego—she got right to the point. Rachel was known to speak her mind. Nothing would have surprised Susan.

Susan jumped in to address Rachel's concern. "As much as I would like to stay here with you in sunny San Diego, I still have my home in the northeast. It would be very tempting to live here, but, for now, I have to get back. Rachel, thank you very much for your hospitality and for letting us stay in your home," Susan thanked Rachel.

Tom then piped in, "I also have a home back north, as well as a job to go back to." "You are both welcomed to stay here anytime you want. *Mi casa es su casa*," Rachel informed Susan and Tom. "Thank you, my dear. Love ya dearly," Susan said, as she walked over to Rachel and gave her a big hug. She also knelt down and patted Harvey on the head. "Now, you take care of my sister, you hear?" A slight bark was heard from Harvey.

"I have to say, Susan, you two make a lovely couple, and you've only known each other for barely a month. You both are very fortunate to have found each other," Rachel looked at both Susan and Tom with a big heartwarming smile.

For their last night with Rachel, Tom and Susan took Rachel out to dinner, and treated her to the best restaurant around. They talked for hours, and almost closed the place down for the evening. One would have thought that by watching them, they had known each other for a long time.

Tom and Susan decided to make the long drive back home to Providence and make the trip an extended vacation. "Susan, I have an idea I would like to pass by you. Since the ride is about three thousand miles long, we can make the trip both rewarding and memorable." Tom suggested. Susan followed every word Tom said, and was very anxious to hear Tom's proposal.

Tom continued, "before we head out on our trip, why don't we go to the bank and take out some money in one thousand dollars increments and put them in small envelopes." Susan continued to carefully listen to what Tom had up his sleeves. "Go on," she said, with interest on what Tom planned to say.

"Whenever we get to a small town, we can go to the local soup kitchen, churches, and orphanages and anonymously drop an envelope to each one of them." Susan stood there with her mouth opened at Tom's recommendation.

"Tom, you never cease to amaze me. That sounds like a great idea, but I would like to leave $5,000 for Rachel's soup kitchen before we leave." "I know we said we were going to leave the soup kitchen here the whole $400,000, but I believe by traveling across the country and making anonymous donations, we can do good for many families. Also, I think, Rachel would ask many questions and be suspicious if we were to give her the whole $400,000." "That sounds wonderful! We can also make additional contributions to Rachel's cause later on."

The day came for Susan and Tom to leave and Rachel was already feeling sad to see them go. "You guys know you can stay here as long as you want," Rachel did not give up on her recommendation for both of them to stay with her. "Thanks, Rach, you are a very gracious host, and we thank you for everything. Before we leave, we need to ask you a favor, if you don't mind." "Sure, what is it—just name it."

Susan went over to Rachel, and placed an envelope in the palm of her hand. "What is this?" Rachel asked, puzzled to receive an envelope from her sister. "Rachel, Tom and I would like to give you this for your soup kitchen. It's not much, but we put together our traveling money so you can help the needy families at the soup kitchen."

Neither Susan nor Tom mentioned the amount of cash inside the envelope—neither wanted high praises nor thanks for the donation they made. Rachel took a peek inside the envelope, and noticed there were many 50's and 100's.

"I don't know what to say," Rachel said, as tears rolled down her cheek. "You guys are too much. Are you sure you want to donate this much? Tom already gave me a big check for the soup kitchen." "Our pleasure, dear," Susan said, as she held her in her arms and gave her a big hug. Tom was close to shedding a tear or two himself as he witnessed both sisters cry on each other's shoulders.

They all stood by the car giving each other well wishes before parting off on their missionary trip up north. Susan won the coin toss so she drove first—Tom played navigator by keying their addresses on the GPS. "Tom, it was nice to see my sister again, and it was nice that you got the opportunity to meet her—she's a wonderful gal."

"She's good people, Susan. I was glad you introduced me to her. I can't wait to introduce you to my brother, Jim." "Looking forward to meeting him, Tom." Tom noticed Susan was sincere and meant every word about getting together with Jim.

"Tom, did you get a chance to book a motel for tonight yet?" "No, I didn't. I was thinking, if it's OK with you, we could stop in the first small town we come across so we can play Mr. and Mrs. Santa Claus," Tom suggested.

"Mr. and Mrs. Claus, Tom? Are you trying to tell me something?" "Susan, do you wish to be Mrs. Claus?"

Tom wanted to throw some humor into the conversation knowing full well the direction Susan was headed.

Tom and Susan had been through a great deal since they got on the train back in Providence. It turned out to be an accelerated course in getting to know each other. In addition, the diamonds added another dimension that tested their wills and their ability to work together. Under normal circumstances, neither Tom nor anyone else for that matter, would have wanted any part of the trials and tribulations Susan and Tom had found themselves in.

The train ride across the country not only brought them together, but it also united their hearts. Although Tom and Susan had only known each other for about a month, the time and experience they shared would have compared to years for others.

"Tom, I see a sign for a town called Yuma about eighteen miles from here. Let's see what that town has to offer and what we can offer it. I find this exciting; we're jointly doing something for folks in need." "I couldn't agree with you more, Susan—it's really very rewarding. FYI, I went online and found three orphanages in Yuma." "Let's pick one and make a drop off." Susan drove up to the nearest orphanage and parked the car. On one of the envelopes, she wrote the name of the orphanage.

They both walked into the orphanage and followed the signs to the office. Upon entering the office, an older person with small spectacles and half a cigarette hanging out of her mouth approached the counter where Tom and Susan stood. "How can I help you folks?" she asked, while bringing up a cough or two.

"Ma'am, we're a delivery service, and we were

requested to give this envelope to the director of the orphanage," Tom said, as he handed her the envelope. "Mrs. Harrison is making her rounds at the moment, but I can give her the envelope when she gets back, if that's OK." "Sure, that's fine. Have a good day, Miss," Susan expressed, as they were ready to leave. Tom and Susan turned around and left the building.

Back in the office of the orphanage, Mrs. Peters held the envelope that Tom and Susan had dropped off, and placed it on Mrs. Harrison's desk, the director of the orphanage.

Tom and Susan got back on the road and planned to drive to Tucson for the night. Prior to getting on the highway, they decided to drive around Yuma to see what other acts of charity they could perform while they were in town.

One church they drove by was called Oasis Church—a catchy name that made them stop. They went into the church, and came across the janitor who was in the process of washing the floors. Tom asked him where they could find the rectory.

Upon entering the rectory, Susan requested to see the pastor. "Who shall I say is asking, Miss?" the office assistant asked. "Miss, I'm just a messenger to deliver a contribution to the pastor." "I'll get him right now." The pastor came out of his office with a meerschaum pipe in his hand.

"Hello, Miss, my name is Father Gaugin. My assistant informed me you would like to make a contribution to the church." "Thanks, Father, for seeing me. I have an envelope that I was requested to personally deliver to you." "Thank you, my child, but who is this donation from?" "I don't know, Father. The individual wished to remain anonymous, so I'm just doing my job."

Back at the orphanage, the director, Mrs. Harrison, opened the envelope Tom and Susan had left and was flabbergasted at the money she found inside. "Mrs. Peters, did you get the name of the person who dropped off this envelope?" Mrs. Peters could see a wad of bills from the opened envelope Mrs. Harrison had in her hand.

"Someone just left you an envelope filled with money?" "Yes, I just wanted to send them a thank-you note to show our appreciation." "Sorry, they left after they gave me the envelope—I didn't know there was money in it." "Well, may God bless them for their generosity," Mrs. Harrison informed Mrs. Peters.

"Well, how are you feeling after giving away thousands of dollars, Susan?" Tom turned to Susan to hear her response. "Tom, it's a very good feeling this money is going to good use… Excuse me, Tom, my sister, Rachel is on the phone. I'll put her on speaker."

"Susan, Tom, are you guys out of your mind?" Rachel sounded very excited and surprised on the phone. "What's wrong, Rachel? Are you OK?" both Tom and Susan asked in unison. "There was $5,000 in the envelope you left me for the soup kitchen," Rachel blurted out, with total surprise and excitement in her voice. "Is that OK?" asked Tom. "If you would like more, we can scrape some more to send to you." "Guys, you are both unbelievable—you left me speechless! I don't know what to say; the soup kitchen will be very appreciative."

"Rachel, we do have one request to make, please." "Anything, Susan. What is it? Just name it." "You have to inform the soup kitchen the donation came from an anonymous donor. Please, we don't want any recognition for it—we just want to make a difference in the lives of those who go to your place. Please, it's important to us." Tom was pleased that Susan had said: *it's important to us.*

When Rachel hung up the phone, Tom turned towards Susan and informed her: "did I ever tell you how much I love you?" "No, Tom. I cannot recall the number of times you mentioned that to me in the past month since I have known you. Honestly, Tom, it feels like longer." "Now, Susan, how many people do you know who have done all the things we've done in a month?" "No regrets, my dear. Absolutely, no regrets at all." "Hopefully, we'll do more."

Chapter 47

"*Is* this Joshua Rabinowitz?" "Yes, it is." "My name is Aaron Shapiro. I don't know if you remember me or not, but I purchased some diamonds from you a few weeks back." "Oh, yes, I do remember you *vell*. I hope you're happy *vith* them. If I recall, *ve* gave you a good deal. *Vhat* can I do for you, Aaron? Do you need them polished?" "No, nothing like that, sir. I just *vanted* to let you know the diamonds I bought from you *vere* stolen!"

"That cannot be—I bought them from a very reputable dealer," Joshua calmly replied. "I don't know *vhat* to say, Mr. Rabinowitz, the diamonds had serial numbers on them and they *vere* taken from me *vhen* I had them insured. I *vant* my money back, sir, and I *vant* it now!" Aaron raised his voice a bit.

Joshua's mouth fell to the floor. He did not know what to think or do, but he had to turn over the $96,500 back to Aaron or face the consequences. Joshua did not want to entertain the possible consequences Aaron might have in mind.

"Marlene, this is Joshua, *ve* have to talk. This is an emergency." Marlene, noticing the panic in his voice, did not know what to think—she's always known Joshua to be calm and collective. "Joshua, calm down, what is it?"

In all the years Marlene has worked with Joshua, he's always appeared to be on an even keel—shrewd and cunning but always calm. "Marlene, did you know the diamonds *ve* got from this Susan person had serial numbers on them, and one client I just sold diamonds to, just called me."

"And?" "He *vants* his money back because when he *vent* to have them insured, the insurance company kept them, and they did not *vant* to return the diamonds back to him."

"Oh, shit!" Marlene cried out. "So, if whoever we sold diamonds to has them insured, the insurance company will, most likely, keep them?" "Yes, *vhich* means *ve* have to give them back their money." "Joshua, what are we going to do?" A slight panic was heard in Marlene's voice.

"Has anyone contacted you about the serial numbers on the diamonds?" "No, no one as of yet," Marlene replied, trying to keep her composure about her. So far, Marlene has sold half of her share of the diamonds — more than enough to recoup her share of the reward money she gave to Susan. She also felt once the insurance company contacted Joshua, he would be more than glad to inform the insurance company that he had purchased them from her, and pretend he was not aware the diamonds had been stolen.

From Marlene's side, she did not have the follow-up contact information for Susan to place the blame on, other than her cell phone number. Susan left no last name and no address. For all practical purposes, the buck stopped with Marlene.

Chapter 48

Tom and Susan drove from state to state handing out envelopes anonymously with thousands of dollars to soup kitchens, places of worship, and orphanages. They felt like they were giving out candy canes and presents on Christmas—not any different from what Santa Claus does.

"Tom, handing out money to the needy does not get old; it's a great feeling to help people who really need it," Susan opined, as she expressed a very good feeling inside her. "Susan, I really feel we've been very blessed to be given this opportunity to help the poor. Would you have thought when we first met on the train, we were going to be in this situation?"

"When I first met you, sitting across from me, I never expected to be in this position at all. I was sad and depressed, and all I wanted was to be left alone. I certainly did not expect I was going to be very happy overnight. Not only am I happy to be giving out all this money, but I also did not think I was going to meet someone who was going to change my life for the better."

"I share your sentiments exactly, Susan. I, as well, wanted to be left alone to catch up on life. I felt I was in such a whirlwind I couldn't stop. Suddenly, my legs gave me a wake-up call to slow down and take it easy." "Do you really think, Tom, we've been taking it easy lately?"

"Come to think of it, Susan, you are absolutely right,

we've been on the go ever since we met. Who would have thought we would be traveling across the country giving away thousands of dollars to poor people?" "Speaking of needy people, I got tired all of a sudden, and I think we should stop soon. How about you?" Susan asked, as she stretched and yawned.

Susan and Tom took turns driving and playing navigator to find a place to take a break for the night. "Tom, I found a place an hour from here where we can stop, have dinner, and call it a day." "Thanks, I feel like I'm getting tired as well."

They pulled up to a Hampton Inn, and decided to check in before going out to dinner. "Look, Tom, you go park the car, and I'll go inside and check in." "Sounds good. I'll be right back." As Tom drove to park the car, he went over in his mind all the good things that have happened to him since he got on the train in Providence. He felt very blessed for all the good things that have happened in his life lately.

Tom walked into the hotel with their bags, and handed out his hand for Susan to give him the key to his room. "Sorry, Tom, they were all booked—only one room was available." Tom found this to be a bit unusual as they had been staying in two separate rooms wherever they stopped.

"You mean we're going to share a room?" Tom hesitated a bit, and then nodded signifying it would be OK to do so. This was another experience he was not prepared for.

At dinner, Tom was a bit preoccupied and less talkative than usual. It didn't take long for Susan to pick up on this, as they've been together every day for almost a month. She felt she knew him well enough to sense when something was different.

"Tom, is there something wrong?" Susan sensed his mind was somewhere else. "Oh, no, Susan, just a bit tired from all the driving and giving money away," Tom replied, but he did not make eye contact with Susan which she found to be a bit strange. "Tom, I think I know you a little better than that. Are you concerned about staying in the same room with me?"

"A bit, it's a new world for me, and I don't know how to process it." "Remember, it's a new world for me as well," Susan informed Tom, while she attempted to make Tom not feel alone in that regard. "Look, Tom, as we're both in the same world, why don't we both attempt to help each other discover a new world together."

Tom seemed to be more at ease with Susan's approach. This put a smile on Susan's face which made both of them feel more comfortable with each other—they both appeared to be leaning on each other. *She must feel more uncomfortable than I since she has lost a husband*, Tom thought. Tom decided to change the subject.

"Susan, I'm thinking back to the diamonds you found in your house. How long do you think they were there before you stumbled upon them?" Tom could see Susan gave that question some serious thought. "I cannot tell for sure, but it could be six to twelve months, or even longer—that's a rough approximation. Also, Tom, I went through a rough patch with Max's abusive behavior and drinking…"

Tom could see he hit a nerve, and wanted to quickly do an about-face, and pretend he didn't ask that question. "Susan, I'm so sorry, my dear, I should have been more sensitive—I didn't mean to open up old wounds." Tom felt bad he had even broached that delicate subject with her. The last thing he wanted to do was to hurt her feelings.

"Tom, in a way, talking about it has been a little therapeutic. That's one part of my life I would like to unearth and get rid of," Susan expressed her feelings to Tom. "I hope, Susan, I can be that shovel for you." That comment painted a little smile on her face. She put her hand on his and gave it a gentle squeeze.

"Thank you, Tom, for coming into my life—you are just what I needed. I don't know how I would have done it by myself with those diamonds. I'm glad you were there for me. I have to say, it was a bit scary dealing with those characters and the diamonds which brings up an interesting point I have not shared with you." Susan could see this perked Tom's interest.

"Go on." "I was supposed to turn over the diamonds to Jacob and Joseph on the train. They were supposed to get off the train once they had the diamonds in their possession." "What happened?" "Once they noticed you were on the train, they changed their minds—they didn't want you to be a witness to the exchange."

"What was the purpose of the handcuffs then?" "They were supposed to carry the diamonds in their bag once I turned over the stones to them." "So, they handcuffed themselves to an empty attaché case?" Tom asked. "I really don't know what else was in that case." "And then the guns that were in their possession…" "Yes, yes, all the makings of a mystery novel."

"So, I wasn't supposed to be in that car?" Tom asked a bit perplexed. "I believe they had purchased all the seats in the first car for privacy, and, suddenly, you showed up." Tom gave that some thought. "I must have purchased that seat just before they purchased all the other seats. And, your reward for giving the diamonds back was a round trip train ride across the country?" This did not make sense to Tom. "I guess."

"When you found the box in your house, were you tempted to open it?" Tom was curious about the mystery of the box. "I was, but it had a label on it with Jacob's return address. When I first attempted to locate the addressee, I kept on getting roadblocks. When I researched the person who was meant to receive the box in the first place, I had no luck—*address unknown*. The person was no longer at that address. This is when I contacted Jacob's office and I spoke to Marlene. I was so close to opening the box, but I changed my mind when I spoke to her. As I said, Tom, I didn't open the box as it had a return address; otherwise, I would have opened it."

"Then what would you have done with the diamonds had you opened the box?" "I don't know. Most likely, I would have taken them to the police." "And, we wouldn't have had this drama plus I wouldn't have met you. I didn't go to the police because I felt I would have been interrogated extensively on how I came across the box, and I didn't want to subject myself to all the questioning." Tom picked up his wine glass and toasted, "to the diamonds!"

Chapter 49

"Joshua, this is Marlene. Have you heard anymore from any other buyers claiming their diamonds were stolen?" Marlene asked, concerned she may be visited by a dissatisfied client any moment due to the authenticity of their purchase. "No, *vhy*? Have you had any clients come to you?" "No, I haven't. Did you reimburse that guy who had his diamonds insured?"

"Yes, I did. I had to pay him back to keep his mouth shut. I didn't *vant* to be thrown in jail for selling stolen stones. This just means I have to discount them in the future." "Think about it, Joshua, you are still coming out ahead for what you paid for the diamonds. Consider it as a cost of doing business."

"I'm really concerned and scared, Joshua; I had no idea the stones had serial numbers etched on them. I wonder if Susan was aware of it." "It *vouldn't* hurt for you to drop her a line and see, and, besides, what difference would it make to her?" "I guess you're right, it wouldn't matter to her at all."

Marlene sent Susan another text: Hi Susan, sorry we didn't have time to chat at the airport when you gave me the diamonds; everything happened so quickly. By any chance, were you aware the diamonds had serial numbers etched on them?

"Tom, look at the text I just received from Marlene." Tom took Susan's phone and read Marlene's text. "Interesting. May I recommend you text her back and let her know you weren't there to personally surrender the diamonds—you sent someone else on your behalf." "And, your reason for this?" "This way, Susan, she doesn't know what you look like—she'll think it was someone else." "Clever, Tom. Good idea, I like it. Are you sure you weren't a spy in your prior life?"

Susan texted Marlene back: Hi Marlene, first I wasn't at the airport when you received the diamonds. I sent someone else on my behalf. Second, I haven't the vaguest idea what serial numbers etched in diamonds even means. Sorry. Susan.

"Again, Tom, thanks for protecting my identity. That was a good strategy on your part. You don't know who might have taken my picture thinking it was me." "You are quite welcomed, Susan. Sometimes you have to be one step ahead." "Tom, I don't know why we have to live like this—playing the spy game." "Because we are dealing with stolen diamonds, and second, we are dealing with devious people."

"Joshua, Susan got back to me. First, that wasn't Susan at the airport who I received the diamonds from— she had sent someone else in her place. I guess she was concerned for her safety—not that I blame her. Also, she knows nothing about the serial numbers. I think we hit a dead end."

"Thanks, Marlene. I guess it's up to us how *ve* handle the diamonds from here. Anyway, *vhy vould* she know anything about serial numbers—she is not in the diamonds business. This *voman* is very crafty. *Ve* could learn a lot from her."

Chapter 50

"Tom, I think we make a great team," Susan held his arm while applauding him for his assistance in swapping the diamonds at the airport. "Susan, do you have any more diamonds you want to get rid of?" Tom asked facetiously. "No, silly. I don't want to see diamonds ever again." Susan quickly realized what she had said after saying it, and Tom noticed her hesitation. After she realized the words that came out of her mouth about not seeing diamonds again, she wished she could have taken them back.

After dinner, they got back into the car to head back to the hotel. It was getting late and they couldn't wait to call it a day—it was a long day for the both of them. "Tom, do you have any preference which side of the bed you would like?" Susan asked very nonchalantly. "The right side, if you don't mind," Tom answered very cautiously. "That works for me; I prefer the left side. See, Tom, we're more compatible than you thought." Tom let those words percolate in his mind.

Susan went to the bathroom to wash up first; Tom went in afterwards. As they both laid down in bed, exhausted from the day's travel, they turned off the lights, held hands, and they both quickly fell asleep. Their bodies had gone through a nonstop treadmill all day long.

They woke up the next day in the same position they fell asleep. It was a beautiful sunny morning. They were both extremely exhausted from the day before. Tom turned over and gave her a passionate good morning kiss. Tom was very pleasantly surprised how comfortable and happy he felt holding Susan in his arms. Susan held him back, snuggled, and she didn't want to let go.

They laid in bed for a little while and chatted about everything that had happened to them since they met. They were both relaxed, and they didn't feel any need to rush to get up—they had no train to catch—no place to be. They felt thankful and blessed they had each other and, together, they performed good deeds by helping the needy. They both asked each other if this is the pace it was going to be for the both of them, as they both felt they were getting too old for it.

Susan and Tom still had several envelopes with money to make donations along the way to Providence. This was a very exciting experience for the both of them. Rachel had opened their eyes to charitable giving when she introduced them to the soup kitchen. They both found it to be a very rewarding experience and they wished to continue performing such good deeds wherever they went. If only they could share their experience with their loved ones. Unfortunately, it had to continue to remain their secret.

Chapter 51

Tom and Susan got up and decided to go out for breakfast before getting back on the road. This was a new day for the both of them. They stayed together in the same room overnight which brought down a few barriers for them. For Tom, this was a first. For Susan it was the first time since Max died that she was in the same bed with another person.

Susan and Tom appeared to be more relaxed with each other. The escapades with the diamonds; hopefully, were behind them. They were both pleased with the philanthropic stops they made along their way. They were both very thankful they were helping people in need; especially, Rachel's soup kitchen. Seeing the poor families pass their trays before them, gave Tom and Susan a different perspective on life.

There are people in life who have nothing—each one having his or her own story that has led them to this point in their lives. The experience made Susan and Tom appreciate what they had; so much so, they wanted to continue to help those in need. They established a common bond between themselves to help those that were less fortunate than they were.

"Susan, you seem very quiet at the moment. Are you OK?" Tom looked over to Susan, as she appeared to be in a daze. "Sorry, Tom, did you say something? Oh, you asked me if I was OK. Yes, yes, I just got caught up with everything that has happened since we met." "What a roller coaster ride, wouldn't you say? We've had our ups and downs."

"Yup, a theme park I would not like to revisit. Doesn't that sound ironic?" "If I recall correctly, you said you had a dream about going to Disney World. For everything we've been through, was it anything like that?"

"Absolutely not, Tom! It would have helped if we had cotton candy along the way," Susan made light of their experience. Disney World is a place she actually would very much like to visit along the way; especially, with Tom.

"Susan, when we get back home, I would like to continue our relationship, if that's OK with you." "Tom, I hoped you would feel the same way because that is the way I feel. Maybe our lives will be more relaxed, and we can get to know each other a little better under more relaxed conditions. I think I've had enough excitement for a while."

"I'll drink to that, sweetheart." Susan did a double take when Tom called her *sweetheart* without even thinking which generated an endearing smile on Susan's face. She noticed Tom did not realize what he had said. It didn't really matter as far as Susan was concerned. The fact of the matter was, he said it, and it looked like he meant it.

"Susan, do you expect to hear from those guys dressed in black again?" "Tom, I certainly hope not – I don't have the diamonds anymore. Why would I hear from them again?" Susan was surprised Tom even asked her that question. "Maybe there's another box filled with diamonds hidden in your house?"

"Please, Tom, don't even joke about that. I would like to put all this behind me, if you catch my drift. In a way, I have to be thankful for this experience as we got to know each other better. I got to see my sister, and we got to help Rachel financially with her soup kitchen—the silver lining, so to speak…" Susan was interrupted by a phone call.

"Excuse me, Tom, I have a call from area code 619 which is from San Diego. That's strange cause I have Rachel's cell phone number in my phone; maybe she has a land line I wasn't aware of. Hello, Rachel, is this you?" Susan asked, surprised to hear from her. It's been a few days since they last saw each other.

"No, ma'am, this is not Rachel, but I am calling about her. This is Doctor Sean Murphy from the Saint Bonaventure Hospital in San Diego. I regret to inform you that your sister has been in an accident. We found your name and number in her wallet when we attempted to identify her…"

"Is my sister OK, doctor?" Susan asked, in a state of panic. Tom immediately pulled over so Susan wouldn't lose the connection. From the way Susan sounded on the phone, it seemed to sound very important for her not to have lost the call.

"Miss, your sister, Rachel, has been in an accident and she is in a coma. She was hit broadside by a vehicle that ran a light." "Doctor, please, how is my sister? I'm far from where she is, and I need to know, please." "Miss Susan, your sister was pretty badly banged up, but she is breathing on her own; however, she remains in a coma."

"Do you have any idea, doctor, how long she's going to be in a coma?" "Sorry, Miss, we can't tell that at the moment. We have performed various tests, and we are monitoring her vitals every hour, but it's too early to tell if…" "Too early for what doctor?"

Susan was very close to becoming hysterical. "We'll just have to see how she progresses with our treatments," the doctor informed her. "Thank you, doctor. I'll be there shortly so we can chat in person," Susan sat stunned at the phone call she had just received about Rachel.

While Susan was on the phone, Tom was able to overhear the conversation she had with the doctor and he was very concerned for both Rachel and Susan. "Susan, what's going on? Is Rachel, OK?" "I don't know, Tom. She's been in an accident, and I have to get back to San Diego to be with her," Susan informed Tom, relaying everything Dr. Murphy had said about Rachel's condition.

"Susan, let's go to the nearest airport, and take a flight back to San Diego — driving back will take a few days, and we can't afford the time. Rachel's in the hospital and we need to get there as soon as possible," Tom informed Susan. He could see Susan tried to process everything — she was in a state of shock. "Tom, you don't have to come back with me; you have your job and your life back home."

"Susan, do you think, for one minute, I'm going to let you face this crisis all by yourself? We'll go to the nearest airport, we'll return the rental, and we'll both fly back to San Diego as fast as we can. Let's pull over to the nearest rest stop, and see if we can find the nearest airport and see what flights are available to San Diego."

"Tom, you don't have to come with me." "You are absolutely right, Susan, I don't have to go back with you to San Diego — I want to, but if you'd rather go alone, please let me know and I'll respect your wishes." "On the contrary, Tom, I'm glad you offered and, yes, I would like you to come with me. I need you by my side to face this — I don't think I can do this alone."

Chapter 52

Tom and Susan took a flight from Memphis to San Diego. They were anxious to get to the hospital as quickly as possible to see Rachel. "Susan, why don't you go in and check in on your sister. I'll see you shortly after I park the car."

"Tom, thanks so much for everything. You've been by my side, literally, since we met on the train," Susan tearfully informed Tom, as she leaned over and gave Tom a big hug and a kiss, while she attempted to hold her tears back. Unfortunately, those tears had a mind of their own and they came flowing out. "See you shortly, my love." Tom took note of Susan's parting words *my love*, as he pulled away to park the car.

Susan rushed into the hospital to check with the receptionist about the location of her sister. The receptionist informed her that Rachel was in ICU and she would advise her doctor that her sister had arrived. "Miss, you may go right up. Your sister is in room 213." "Thank you, nurse." While in the elevator, Susan texted Tom Rachel's room number for him to meet her there.

When she arrived at Rachel's room, her doctor was present. "Doctor, my name is Susan, and I believe I spoke with you on the phone about my sister Rachel. How is she?" "Miss, as I mentioned on the phone earlier this morning, she's still in a coma, but we're seeing her vitals are headed in the right direction, but it's still too soon." "Thank God!" whispered Susan.

"Under similar cases, Miss, patients in your sister's

condition require life support assistance right away, but your sister is breathing on her own. This is definitely good news, but we have to keep an eye on her condition. If she doesn't come out of her coma shortly, we need to protect her airways so they don't aspirate. In other words, we don't want anything to enter her lungs by accident. It could be liquid, or some other material as this can cause serious health problems like pneumonia."

Dr. Murphy attempted to provide Susan the reason why supplemental oxygen would be required. Susan felt comfortable with Dr. Murphy's assessment of Rachel's condition.

Tom quickly arrived to Rachel's room. "Hi, Tom, the doctor just left and gave me a run-down of Rachel's condition," Susan informed Tom as soon as he arrived. "How does it look?" Tom asked, while he held her to calm her down. "It's going to be touch-and-go for the next couple of days," Susan informed Tom, as she appeared to be mentally exhausted.

"The doctor also said that aside from the coma, there were no major damages to her brain as far as he could see. She will, most likely, have an MRI to confirm this. He informed me her head hit the window hard when the car hit her. He also said her body was banged up badly with no broken bones or major internal bleeding that they have been able to assess so far."

"Poor thing, we'll pray for her to have a speedy recovery," Tom offered, while he held Susan in his arms and offered comfort for her sister. They both stayed with Rachel all day hoping to hear good news from her doctor.

"Susan, as it's getting late, please stay here while I go out and check on hotels in the surrounding area."

Tom kissed her on her cheek and was ready to leave. "Tom, we can stay at Rachel's house — I have a key to her house." "Sorry, I didn't know that." "Yes, we have each other's keys for situations like these." "Let's just hope and pray we won't have to use her key for very long." "Amen to that, Tom."

Susan and Tom stayed by Rachel's side until the hospital chased them away for the evening. They both kissed Rachel on her forehead before they left. Susan noticed Tom had whispered a few words in Rachel's ear before leaving.

"May I ask, Tom, what you whispered in her ear?" Susan asked, as she held his arm and walked away from Rachel's room. Tom did not answer her right away. One of the nurses passing them bade them good night and thanked them for being by Rachel's bedside.

"I just whispered in Rachel's ear that we'll be praying for her to get better and to have a good night. I also let her know we'll be back in the morning to keep her company." "You said all that in just a few seconds?" Susan asked very surprised. "Actually, Susan, I paraphrased what I said." "You're too much, Tom! I don't know what I'm going to do with you."

When they got to Rachel's house, her dog, Harvey, ran towards them begging to be taken outside. After the dog came in, they decided to sit in the living room with a glass of wine to calm down a bit and talk about Rachel — hoping and praying for her to get better soon.

"Susan, I noticed Rachel had a calendar on her fridge." "And?" "Well, according to the calendar, she has soup kitchen duties tomorrow. Why don't we go in her absence; I'm certain her gang will be looking for her." "That's a great idea, Tom. I'm sure Rachel will be very happy we will be filling in for her. By the way, did you forget you have a job back home?"

"No, I didn't forget about my job, but we have more important things to attend to at the moment. As a matter of fact, I check in with my office every day when I have a few minutes, and the crew at the office knows I have my hands full here. I'm also emailing and texting my clients while I'm here as well."

"I have to say, Tom, you are a very busy person! Did you also happen to tell them about the ordeal with the diamonds?" "Susan, do you really think they would believe me if I were to tell them that?" "Tom, I was there with you, and even *I* don't believe it."

"Susan, I noticed when I came in that Rachel had a spare bedroom in the back," Tom pointed to the back of the house. As he was in the process of walking towards to the spare bedroom, he was interrupted by Susan. "Were you planning on staying there? Because if you were planning on it, get it out of your head."

"OK, I'll take Rachel's room then." "No, we're both going to stay in the spare bedroom. Excuse me, the three of us will be staying there. I don't think the poor dog wants to stay by himself. He must be missing his mommy terribly. I'm sure he can sense something is going on.

Don't underestimate the ability for dogs to sense things. Rachel's room is hers, and it'll be there until she gets back; hopefully, sooner rather than later." Tom realized it was no longer an issue the last hotel they stayed in had only one room left.

Susan and Tom got up early and decided to go down the street and have breakfast at the local family restaurant before heading to the hospital. "Susan, I would like to stop by at the neighborhood florist and pick up some flowers for Rachel." "Tom, that's very sweet of you, but she won't be able to see them nor appreciate them while she's in a coma."

"You are right. In Rachel's condition, she will not be able to see them, but she may be able to smell them. A bouquet of fresh flowers may give her hope she's not alone, and, possibly, make her feel like there's some life in the room." "Tom, Tom, what am I going to do with you? You are definitely a piece of work!" Susan exclaimed, while she slowly shook her head from side to side.

Susan and Tom walked into Rachel's room at the hospital with a beautiful bouquet of flowers to place by Rachel's bedside. She was in the same position as they had left her the night before. After a few hours, Dr. Murphy came in to check on Rachel. "Good morning, doctor. We hope you have good news for us today. We noticed you placed an oxygen mask on her," Susan noted.

"We didn't want to take any chances with her," Dr. Murphy informed her. "We understand. It makes a lot of sense after what you told us yesterday. How's our patient doing today? Have you noticed any improvements?" "Well, earlier this morning, we had an MRI and an EEG done on her brain, and we didn't notice any brain damage. Your sister did receive a severe blow to her head which caused her to be in a coma. We've put her on various antibiotics just in case, but her prognosis is good. We'll continue to monitor your sister."

"Thanks, doctor, for everything you've done for Rachel." Both Tom and Susan felt more at ease after they chatted with the doctor and being advised things were headed in the right direction. They each took turns sitting by Rachel to read to her. They spoke to her about the weather and her favorite subject—the soup kitchen. Susan and Tom continued to pray for her speedy recovery.

Chapter 53

Tom and Susan put on their aprons and prepped for the evening crowd at the soup kitchen. On occasion, they looked at each other while they prepared dinner. Tom set out utensils, napkins and made coffee. Susan opened the various cans that were on the menu to be served. They were stepping in for Rachel while she was in the hospital.

One by one each of the diners entered in an orderly fashion. It didn't take long for the diners to notice Rachel's presence and smiling face were missing. "Is Rachel, OK? She never misses Tuesday night," one of the homeless women asked while she looked around to see if she could get a glimpse of Rachel.

"Thanks for asking, ma'am. She'll be out for a little while, and we're hoping she'll be back soon to see your smiling faces again," Susan informed her. "She's sick, isn't she? Please let us know. We've all gotten very fond of her over the years." *Over the years*, thought Tom. *She's been doing this for a long while*, he continued to ponder. *Why didn't Rachel ever mention this part of her life?* Susan thought.

Tom and Susan wanted to be upfront with the people who loved her. "Rachel's been in an accident and she's in a coma, but the doctors are very optimistic she'll return shortly," Susan informed one of the diners. It didn't take long for word to spread about Rachel's condition. After everyone was served, an elderly gentleman dressed in frayed clothing with snow white hair stood up.

"Everyone, may I have your attention, please." Everyone must have considered him one of the respected elders in the group as everyone stopped what he or she was doing to hear what he had to say. "Folks, our dear Rachel is very sick, and we should all bow are heads, hold each other's hands, and pray to God that He brings her back to us real soon. She not only fed our bellies and kept us warm, but her eyes and her smiles fed our spirits." In unison, they all bowed their heads, held hands, and recited the Lord's Prayer: *Our Father who art…"*

Tom and Susan stood there behind the counter in total awe, and noticed the effect the needy people had on them — words could not describe what they felt. The room was filled with grace, beauty and prayer which totally mystified both of them — they stood frozen while tears rolled down their faces. Susan and Tom witnessed the overwhelming effect Rachel has had on the people who came to the soup kitchen — more than just being fed.

"Susan, I cannot believe the effect your sister has had on these people," Tom informed Susan, as he looked around in awe. "Can you see why she has been so attached to the soup kitchen? This is her family, and they all make her feel she's part of theirs. I would not have believed it had I not seen it with my own eyes," Susan said, totally touched with what she had witnessed.

"Has your sister always done charity work like this?" Tom asked, while he felt the same feelings as Susan felt. "If she did, she never mentioned it to me. I guess it's one of those things she has kept to herself," Susan informed Tom, while she shook her head slowly in total disbelief.

Before going home, Tom and Susan decided to visit Rachel in the hospital and get an update on her, hoping every time they paid her a visit, she would be sitting up on her bed. "Hi, Betty, how's my sister doing today? Has she been giving you a hard time?" Betty was one of the nurses assigned to Rachel who Susan and Tom had taken a liking to.

"You folks are so nice to bring her flowers every time you come to visit," Betty said to Susan and Tom with a motherly-looking smile. "We figure any little thing we can do to help Rachel feel more comfortable, we will be more than happy to do." "That's really nice of you. By the way, how long have you two been married?" Betty asked. Tom and Susan looked at each other totally surprised and taken aback with that question.

"No, Betty, we're not married. Rachel's my sister, and I recently met Tom a little over a month ago." Susan shared with Betty, who had a surprised look on her face. "You don't say. My apologies, you look like you've known each other for a long time?" Susan liked Betty more and more.

"What did you think of Betty's question?" Tom asked, quite surprised as well that Betty had assumed they were married. "Tom, she just commented on what she observed."

"Do you think we look like a married couple? Really? I've never been married so I'm not a good judge of that." "Maybe one day you will," Susan informed Tom with an inviting smile.

Chapter 54

Staying long hours at the hospital, and spending half as much time at the soup kitchen, Tom's and Susan's days went by very quickly. Members of the soup kitchen, as well as Tom and Susan, prayed every day for Rachel to get better. Tom continued to whisper words of encouragement to Rachel everyday which Susan took notice of.

In between, Tom found time to service his clients, and keep in touch with his office staff. Everyone back in his office appreciated what Tom was doing in San Diego with Susan's sister. A new lifestyle had begun for Tom and Susan.

One evening after having dinner at the hospital cafeteria, they went up to stay a few hours with Rachel before going back to the house for the evening. When they arrived at her room, they noticed Rachel was not in her bed. Both Tom and Susan panicked not knowing what had happened to her. Tom's first reaction was to go to the floor receptionist and inquire on Rachel's whereabouts.

"She should be in her room, sir," said the burly desk nurse with black-rimmed glasses. Tom ran back to the room to let Susan know that they didn't know either—she should be in her room he was informed.

When Tom got back to the room, Susan was chatting with Rachel a mile-a-minute. "Rachel, so glad to see you up," Tom said, in a very jubilant and earnest voice, as he approached Rachel to give her a hug. As Tom hugged

Rachel, she whispered into his ear, *thank you so much for your prayers — they got me through the day.*" Susan noticed her sister whisper a few words into Tom's ear.

Hours went by and all three chatted as if though they hadn't seen each other for a very long time. Rachel was very pleased and ecstatic the soup kitchen duties were attended to while she was away; especially, when Matthew got everyone into prayer for her to get better — a touching moment for Rachel, to say the least.

"Rachel, do you have any idea how much longer you'll be here?" Tom asked. "The doctor recommended to keep me here for a few more days to see if I'm back to normal. His main concern is that I may relapse and go into a coma again. They want to check if I am able to keep my eyes open for longer periods of time, and awakened from sleep easier — at first by a pinch, then by a gentle shaking of my shoulders, and finally by a sound like calling my name." "That makes sense. It would be pretty scary to go back into a coma while you're at home."

"Susan, are you and Tom behaving in my house?" "Rachel, you know me — I'm an angel at heart," Susan replied, while looking at Tom coyishly. "Can you guys bring me some of my favorite foods when you come back?" Susan was thankful that Rachel quickly changed the subject by requesting some normal food. "Don't they feed you here?" "Would *you* like to be fed intravenously?" Rachel asked.

"When you get out of here, we're going to take you to your favorite restaurant, Rachel," Tom offered. "You're going to take me to Kentucky Fried Chicken — my favorite restaurant?" Rachel asked, with such excitement in her voice.

"You mean to tell me KFC is your favorite restaurant?" asked Tom, in total surprise. "You don't mean that?" Susan asked, with a strange look of disgust in her face. "What's wrong with it—it's finger licking good!" Rachel was surprised they didn't feel the same way about KFC the way she did.

They all gave Rachel a good night hug and promised to see her in the morning. "Susan, our prayers have been answered—thank God!" Tom said, while he kissed Rachel goodbye. "Tom, I feel like a new person after seeing my sister wake up from a coma. You really appreciate things when they are gone. Please don't leave me Tom," Susan requested, filled with emotions and glassy looking eyes.

"What makes you think I am going to leave you? Are you OK?" "I guess I've been through some tough times lately with Max's death, Rachel not too far behind, and the ordeal we just went through with the diamonds." Susan appeared as if she was ready to break down.

"I guess it's hitting you all at once, Susan. The only difference now compared to when Max died is that I hope you don't feel you are alone. I'm not going to leave you alone in anything you go through unless you decide otherwise."

"Tom, you've been by my side ever since we met on the train to San Diego, and I don't know what I would have done had I been by myself," Susan approached Tom, as he held her dearly to his chest. "I have to say, Susan, you certainly have made my life more interesting and exciting. I never would have known what the warm embrace of a woman felt like. I never would have known what $400,000 in cash looked like in an attaché case. More importantly, I also would never have known what it felt like to wake up next to a beautiful and loving woman. If you let me, I would like to continue to get to know you better."

Susan stood in front of Tom dumbfounded, as he expressed his endearing feelings to her. "Tom, I have a very interesting question which I believe I may have asked you before: *why haven't you ever married?*" Susan asked, as she looked up at him. "Because I hadn't found the right woman, and now I find myself standing in front of her."

Chapter 55

"Tom, I have an idea. The doctors have said that Rachel could leave the hospital in a couple of days. Isn't that fantastic? I would like to stay with her for a little while before I return back to Providence. I want to make sure she's OK and strong on her own," Susan informed Tom, while standing close to him with her hands on his shoulders.

"Susan, that makes a lot of sense. You girls also need some alone time." "I'll miss you while you're gone." "For the sake of your sister, you need to be here with her right now—we can catch up when you get back home." "Thanks for being so understanding. I love you very much." "And I love you very much as well." There definitely was a strong connection between Susan and Tom.

Tom flew back home to get back to his life—a life which needed a few minor changes from the prior one he had. He needed to slow his pace and his stress level. As his doctor directed for the sake of his life, he needed to get away from it all and catch up on life before *it was too late*. Tom did not expect to be confronted with the various adventures he had encountered with Susan; mainly, meeting Susan and falling in love.

It was not certain whether fate had stepped in with all the excitement and danger he had run into. He did get to see and feel what love was all about—thinking of someone else first before thinking of himself. As he sat in his living room, he realized what a void was created without having Susan around—she really left a lasting impression on him. He looked forward to getting together with Jim to fill him in on his relationship with Susan, as well as a few other things.

As usual, Tom sat in their favorite booth at Starbucks waiting for Jim. As soon as he saw his brother walk in, he stood up and couldn't wait to give him a warm hug. "Tom, it's so good to see you again," Jim said, as he noticed something different about his brother. "I can't put my finger on it, bro, but there's definitely something different about you." Jim continued to stare at Tom looking for one thing in particular.

"Is that a good thing, Jim?" "Most definitely! You have a great air about you. Was it that gal Susan you met on the train to San Diego?" Jim asked point blank. "Yes, it is, but I don't know where to begin; I feel Susan has changed my life completely." "That's very obvious. Are you going to introduce me to her one day?" Jim asked very eagerly.

"Well, at the moment, Jim, she's in San Diego taking care of her sister. As I may have mentioned in one of my emails, her sister, Rachel, was in a car accident and was in a coma for a couple of weeks." "Is she OK?" Jim asked.

"Thank God she survived the accident and came out of her coma within a couple of weeks. Her sister, Susan, the girl I told you a great deal about, is with her at the moment taking care of her while she recuperates at home."

"Tommy, it sounds like you may have fallen for this person—a first for you, I'm sure. I guess this trip is what you really needed in your life." "Jim, I don't know how to explain it. Things happened so fast, and we were doing everything together." Tom felt he could go on for hours and hours talking about Susan. "I know exactly what you are saying—you guys just clicked." "But we've only known each other for a little over a month."

"Tommy, do you think love has a germination period? It really is great to see you like this. It's a side of you which I don't ever recall ever seeing before, and I like it. She might be your soul mate, Tom." "What exactly do you mean by soul mate?" "No one knows, I just hear about it every now and then."

"Susan and I have been through so much together—I don't know where to begin." As Tom shared his adventures with his brother, Jim could see, for the first time in his life, his brother was alive. Tom, for obvious reasons, chose not to delve into the diamond situations. This was reserved just for Susan and him—no one would believe it anyway. He still doesn't believe it either.

"Tom, let's start with you. How are you feeling? It was scary when you called to tell me that you had collapsed when you got out of bed," Jim leaned forward to hear more about his brother. "Thanks for asking. I'm doing much better, thanks. When I found myself on the floor, I was totally helpless—I couldn't get up. Jim, I didn't know what to do—I was really scared! When the doctor called me later in the day and gave me an ultimatum to take care of myself or else, that did it for me. I decided to take, as you know, a train ride to California where I could relax, read, and catch up on my health. Then, I met a fellow passenger, Susan, and everything changed from there. I mean everything; I totally forgot about my health situation."

"Hopefully, Tom, for the better?" "Oh, without a doubt, Susan changed my outlook on life—I can't wait to see her again." "You may not realize it, but this short time away from each other is going to do wonders for both of you. This is going to make both of you miss each other more. You know how the saying goes: *absence makes the heart grow fonder.*" "Well, believe it or not, I'm feeling it already. I really miss Susan; I can't stop thinking about her—night or day."

"That's a good sign—even better if she feels the same way." "Jim, I don't have much experience in this area. I just wish I could have felt it earlier in life." "Tom, it was not your time. Not to change the subject on you, but what else did you guys do out there?"

"We volunteered at a soup kitchen—it was a wonderful experience for the both of us. It made me appreciate where I live—that I have a roof over my head, and I that I don't have to beg for food. It's a humbling experience!" Jim could see this was a subject his brother felt very passionate about. He was glad that his passion didn't just stop at his desk at work.

"It's amazing how life changes when you least expect it. Something just comes from left field and turns your whole life upside down. In the beginning, Susan and I just shared a train ride to San Diego and sat across from each other. We thought when we arrived in San Diego, we were just going to go our separate ways, but life had other plans for us. It put us in different situations: we got chatting, we went for walks together when the train stopped, and we got to know each other better. Her husband died not too long ago, so she was in a very fragile state of mind. Knowing this, I tried to be as comforting as possible."

"Tom, it looks like you were in the right place at the right time. You may have done her a world of good."

"Jim, I did not intend to fall in love with her..." "Oh, love?" "Yes, I know what I said because it's exactly what I'm feeling at the moment for her." "Tommy, this is how Cupid works. When you least expect it, he shoots an arrow at you." "Cupid, huh? Since when have you gotten so romantic my dear brother?"

"If you recall, Tommy, you never wanted to double date, nor did you wish to be set up with anybody. What I'm trying to say, my dear brother, is that you never got yourself in the position to feel that way. Suddenly, you take a train ride across the country and you get shot with an arrow. Well, I'm so happy you got to feel Cupid's arrow. Isn't it wonderful?"

"I just didn't expect to feel this way this fast. I thought it would have taken more time, but I guess I was wrong." "Tom, I have a friend who got engaged six weeks after they met, and they got married eight months later." "Wow, that was fast!"

"What I'm trying to say is there's no set time to fall in love — it's different for everybody. And for all practical purposes, you were with this girl twenty-four-seven which most people do not have the opportunity to share when they first meet. You didn't just go on dates on weekends. You were with her all the time, so you could say you had an accelerated date." "I see what you mean, Jim." "That's right and, the best part is that you have no idea what is going to happen next. Stay tuned brother — more to come."

Chapter 56

"Good morning, Tom. How are things going back east?" Susan asked, looking forward to hearing Tom's voice again. "Good morning, sweetheart. It's almost lunch time here." "I totally forgot there are three hours difference. I'm so sorry. Would you like me to call you later?" "No, that's fine. How's Rachel feeling?"

"Well, Tom, she's doing remarkably well. You could never tell she was in a coma for a couple of weeks. Before I forget, and if you have time, can you please go to my house when you get a chance and water my plants that I have in my back porch. I'm sure they are thirsty for water. My neighbor who's been taking care of my plants, just went out of town for a while."

"No problem, I'll stop by today. FYI, I've been having coffee with Jim practically every other day, and he can't wait to meet you. As a matter of fact, I will be seeing him after I water your plants today." "How is he? I'm sure he missed your being away for such a long time. Have you kept him up to date with all of our adventures?" Susan asked, wondering how much information Tom had shared with his brother.

"Mostly everything. Of course, I didn't dare let him know about the two wonderful gentlemen who were dressed in black." "Tom, you are aware, they'll be our secret forever and ever." "One thing for sure, it would definitely make an interesting read if we were to write a mystery novel about it."

"I'm sure it would, but please leave me out of it. I

don't want to relive that incident with the red umbrella." "You are aware, that every time you see a red umbrella, you are going to be reminded of that incident at the airport." "I know. I will never own a red umbrella again. By the way, Rachel says hello. Did you hear her in the background?"

"Yes, I heard her. Please give her a big hug for me." "Would you also like me to whisper a few words into her ear for you?" "Susan, you do know that was between her and me." "I know, Tom. You guys had this bond going at the hospital. I really believe she heard every word of wisdom you whispered." "That's great—they were only meant to give her hope and raise her spirits." "Tom, should I be worried?" Susan asked facetiously.

"Worried? Worried about what? Susan, what happened in the hospital while Rachel was in a coma, stayed in that hospital." "All, I know, is that you watched over my baby sister, and I love you dearly for it." "Susan, a thought just crossed my mind." "What?" "Wouldn't it be nice to get my brother together with your sister?"

"Are you now playing matchmaker, Tom? Are you interested in getting into another adventure? Haven't you had enough excitement in your life? You know that you and I were very lucky in the last adventure we had."

"It was just a thought—I've never set anyone up before. Jim was the one who tried many times to play matchmaker, but I was never interested." "Great idea, Tom, but I would like to meet Jim before setting him up with Rachel." "That works. I'll give you his Starbucks schedule and maybe we can set something up?"

Chapter 57

"Hi Tom, I just want to confirm our get-together today at four at Starbucks," Jim reminded Tom about their rendezvous later on in the day. "See ya then. Oh, I forgot to mention, Jim, I'm making a pit stop at Susan's house to water her plants first." "You mean to tell me that she's got you doing chores already and she gave you a key to her house?" "It's no bother, bro. It's on my way to Starbucks anyway. She gave me a key to her house just in case." "Only kidding, Tom—that's very nice of you to do that for her. See you shortly."

Tom had not been to Susan's house before, so he followed the GPS directions. *Your destination is on the right in five hundred feet*, the GPS instructed Tom. As Tom approached Susan's house, he noticed several police cars parked in her driveway. *I wonder if there was a robbery in her house*, Tom thought. Tom decided to approach the officers at her front door and inquire what was going on. As he got closer to the house, one police officer beckoned him to stop.

"Sir, is this your home?" one of the police officers asked Tom. "No officer, this is my girlfriend's house. I'm just here to water her plants. What seems to be the problem, officer?" Tom asked, concerned with all the police activity. "Do you know if there's anybody home? We have a search warrant to search the premises."

"Officer, please let me call the owner of the house, and let her know about this situation." "Sir, may I have your name." "Sure, officer, my name is Tom Stevens, and here's my driver's license if you would like to see it." "No, that's not necessary, but we'll take it as you have it out." "OK, I'll give Susan a call and you can chat with her if you like." Tom had absolutely no idea what was going on, but was startled to see several police cars at Susan's house.

"Susan, I don't mean to alarm you, but there are three police cars in your driveway. I was on my way to water your plants when I ran into the cavalry at your house. One of the officers who has a search warrant would like to chat with you." "OK, Tom, thanks. Please put them on speaker so you can listen as well."

"Sure, no problem, Susan. Officer, here's the owner of the house, Susan Anderson," Tom said, as he handed his phone to one of the police officers. "Is this Susan Anderson?"

"Yes, officer, what seems to be the problem? What can I do for you? Has there been a break-in at my house? Did my alarm go off?" "No, ma'am, we would like to chat with your husband, Max Anderson."

"That will not be possible, officer," Susan replied, wondering why the police requested to see her late husband. "Is he out of town?" "No officer, I'm afraid he's not. You can find him a couple of miles from here in Fairlawn Cemetery." "Is that where he works now, ma'am? I thought he worked at the post office?" "Officer, he doesn't work at the cemetery—he's buried there," Susan said, as she made all attempts to keep her cool.

"Excuse me, ma'am, did you say he's buried there?" "Yes, officer, he died eight months ago when he hit another vehicle broadside." "Oh, I'm so sorry, my condolences." "Thank you, officer—it was a shock to all of us," Susan said, as she appeared to sound depressed about Max's death. "Officer, what's this all about? Did he do something wrong?" Susan sounded as if she were crying.

"I'm so sorry for your loss, but we're on official business." "Officer, I've already informed you my husband has passed away." "No, ma'am, we have a search warrant to search your premises." "Search my premises? Officer, may I ask what you expect to find when you search my home? What are you looking for?" Susan sounded very concerned, although she had a hunch what they were looking for.

"Ma'am, we have a video surveillance of your husband taking a box from the post office." The officer was careful not to disclose the contents of the box. Meanwhile, Tom had a good idea what the police officers were looking for as well. "Officer, my boyfriend has a key to my house. I'm sure he doesn't mind letting you in so you can do whatever search you need to do. Also, as my husband died eight months ago, why are you now searching for this box that he may have taken from the post office? Tom, would you kindly let these officers into my house." "Will do, Susan. I'll call you when they're done."

"Mr. Stevens, may we ask you how long you've known Susan and Max Anderson?" "Officer, I've only known Susan for a little over a month. I've never had the pleasure of meeting her husband since he passed away about eight months ago, long before I met Susan." "If we may ask, how did you meet Susan?" "Susan took a train ride to San Diego to visit her sister, and I happen to be a passenger sitting across from her. May I ask officer what this has to do with me?"

"Just preliminary questions, sir—you don't have to answer any of our questions. We're here to search Miss Anderson's house. We're trying to establish a timeline of Mr. Anderson's whereabouts." "Oh, OK. Let me let you in." "Thanks, sir. We really appreciate any assistance you can provide." "Just to make you aware, officer, this is the first time I'm in this house." "Thanks, sir."

Tom watched the police officers go from room to room scouring every square inch. "Sir, do you know if there's an attic in this house?" "Officer, as I mentioned before, this is the first time I'm here—I have no idea." Tom was astute enough to see what the police officers attempted to do—verify the facts. Tom felt the best way to handle the situation was to stick with the facts. Neither Susan nor Tom did anything that was illegal. Susan did find the box in the house, but she returned it to whomever sent it. How was she to know it was stolen?

Tom sat by the kitchen counter and responded to various emails until the police officers had finished their search. As they prepared to leave, Tom asked, "did you folks find what you were looking for?" "Yes, Mr. Stevens, we did. We can't thank you enough for your assistance." "Well, that's great officer. Hope you guys have a nice day." *Did they really find what they were looking for?* crossed Tom's mind.

After the police left, Tom couldn't wait to call Susan and let her know of his experience with the police officers. He called Jim to reschedule their get-together. "Jim, I'm sorry, I got tied up with a few things. I'll be there shortly." "Tom, why don't we make it another time—I've got a few errands I need to run. How about tomorrow morning, if that works for you?" "Sounds great, Jim. My apologies again."

Tom decided to go back to his house to call Susan on his land line for fear that his phone may be bugged.

Chapter 58

"Hi Tom, why are you calling me on Rachel's land line?" "Susan, my apologies, but the police went through your house with a fine-toothed comb. I'll probably go back to your house later this week to straighten it out." "Tom, that's not necessary; I can take care of it when I get back. Tell me, what happened?"

Susan could not imagine why her house was turned upside down. "Well, wait till you hear this. As the police were in the process of leaving, I asked one of them if they found what they were looking for." "And?" "They informed me that they did. Again, I don't know if they were looking for a reaction from me or not. Is it possible that Max brought home something else?" "Anything's possible. Maybe there was another box of diamonds. I wouldn't be surprised since I found the first one."

"In my opinion, Susan, I think the police are going to continue to watch you and your house. Somehow, I have this gut feeling that they suspect something." "That's very possible. Why now though after so many months? Max has been gone for eight months and they are now looking for things he may have stolen?" "What do you suggest I do, Tom?"

"I have three options for you: 1) we totally stay away from that subject, and never bring it up again while we're in your house; 2) we use the land lines; or, 3) we get burner phones." "Tom, why don't we continue to use our cell phones? We don't need to talk about the stones anymore—they are sold and it's a thing of the past as far as I am concerned."

"Are you trying to write about this experience in a mystery novel, Tom?" "I don't know. This whole situation with the diamonds has a lot of mystiques to it. Don't you think? This is very similar to our relationship—it has all sorts of twists and turns." "Are you getting carried away with all this? Maybe it was a one-time thing?"

"Susan, before I met you, my life was pretty dull—one day was the same as the next. Well, as you can see, our lives have been pretty interesting since we met. Neither you nor I are aware of what is going to happen next. For now, I don't believe we've heard nor seen the last of the police. Nothing's been normal lately."

Tom continued, "they also mentioned they had a video surveillance of Max taking a box when he worked at the post office. Now, you and I made the assumption he took the box from the post office when you were disposing all of his belongings. It's possible he may have taken another box we are not aware of—that's another possibility." "Yes, I suppose. Anything is possible."

"More importantly, how is Rachel doing? I don't want to dwell or come up with options of what Max may or may not have done." "I agree with you. I think we've had enough. Rachel's doing fine, but I'm having trouble getting her to take it easy. She wants to continue with her life as if she was never in an accident. She is totally disregarding the fact she was in a coma and almost died. She even wants to go back to the soup kitchen a few days a week."

"Susan, would you like me to come to San Diego to give you a hand?" "I can't ask you to do that. You have done more than your share. Besides, you have your job and your life back home." "Susan, I thought you were my life. I don't know what I would do without you. I'll see you in a couple of days; maybe we can go to the soup kitchen and help Rachel out."

Susan was stunned to hear that Tom *would not be able to live without her*. For Susan, Tom kept on surprising her. *I wonder if I'm dreaming all this*? Susan stared out of the window and pondered after she hung up the phone with Tom.

Chapter 59

Tom informed his office that he planned to leave for San Diego again to help Susan with her sister. His office was ecstatic he was getting out more often and doing something different with his life other than work. It would take months for Tom to use up his unused vacation time.

"Hi Tom, it's really great to finally see you take time off," his boss, Marcus, said as he stuck his head into Tom's office. "As long as I've been with this company, Tom, you've never taken a day off. As a matter of fact, there have been countless weekends I've seen you here. Care to share what's changed?" Marcus asked with curiosity in his voice.

"Hi Marcus. You see, I met this woman..." "I knew it. It had to be a woman who swept you off your feet. Is it serious, Tom?" "I just don't know how it happened. As you are aware, my doctor recommended I take some time off to catch up on my health. So, I took his advice and I took this train to nowhere which ended in San Diego—I just picked a random destination—just to go *somewhere*. The passenger who sat across from me was a girl who was traveling to see her sister in San Diego. Long story short, we got to know each other and we wound up doing things along the way. Well, one thing led to another..."

"No need to say any more, Tom—I get it. You go and have a good time. Most likely, we'll be texting, emailing or talking on the phone as we did when you left the last time." "Thanks, Marcus, for being so understanding. Just so you know, I'm not going on vacation." Tom explained to Marcus the reason he planned to travel to San Diego—to help Susan with her sister who had been in an accident.

Tom's ride to the airport was on time, and he looked forward to seeing Susan again. He could not believe how much he missed her in such a short period of time. Suddenly, this stranger became part of his life. He found it hard to believe the large void that was created when she was away from him. *Is this what love is all about*? He began to question himself. Tom found the whole relationship concept with Susan to be a novelty, as he had not experienced anything like that before. To put it in Tom's terminology, it was like on-the-job training for him.

As he sat on the airplane, he began to think of all the things he and Susan had been through in the less than two months since they've known each other—too much drama in such a short period of time. The elderly woman seated next to him noticed Tom's mind was somewhere else as he smiled every now and then. She decided to break the silence and begin chatting with him.

"Sir, my apologies for interrupting your train of thought, but you look very content. Either you've won the lottery or you're in love?" She asked, but did not appear to mind that she broke Tom's train of thought. "Since you asked, ma'am, I won the lottery by falling in love," Tom metaphorically replied.

"My goodness, sonny, it looks like Cupid really shot you right in the ass!" the octogenarian decided to cash in on her age and speak her mind—she had no limits to what came out of her thin lips. "Yes, ma'am, I think I got it bad. She is all I think about, night and day," Tom decided to engage in a conversation with her. "Have you been married before?" She continued to pry even further.

"No, ma'am, I haven't. As a matter of fact, I never really had a true relationship—this is my first. The fact of the matter is that we've been through so much in such a short period of time." "I can see, sonny, you light up whenever you talk about her. Has your friend been married before?"

Tom realized this granny-like passenger was either very interested in Tom's life, or she was just plain nosy. He also realized they were to be roommates for the duration of the flight and the time was going to go by faster by having a conversation with someone else.

"Yes, my girlfriend was married before, but her husband died in a tragic car accident," Tom informed her. He did not want to delve into Max's issues—it's enough he just scratched the surface of Susan's prior marriage. "So sorry to hear. Life can be very cruel at times." *If she only knew*, Tom thought. She also appeared to be lonely so he thought it would be nice for him to have a conversation with her.

"Well, sonny, I was married for sixty-three years, and all those years went by extremely fast—if I only had one more day. Enjoy the moments you have with this girl. Thank God, I was very fortunate to have been given all those wonderful and memorable years with my husband that I will cherish every day until the day I die," she shared with Tom, as she sighed and looked down with sadness.

Tom was very polite to his roommate. He appreciated everything she said to him, as he could feel vicariously the references of happiness that emanated from her. In the short period of time he had known Susan, he could feel the sentiments of some of the memories granny shared with him. She was blessed to have had all those years of happiness in her marriage. He had only known Susan barely two months, and he was already very appreciative of the time he had spent with her. He couldn't wait to relay his flight experience to Susan.

"Are you planning to marry this gal you so highly speak of?" "Miss, you are the second person in the last couple of weeks who has made the reference of marriage." "Well, sonny, maybe these are signs sent your way." She spoke to Tom with one hand on his arm, as her eyes of wisdom pierced through his soul. *I can't wait to tell Susan about this,* he thought. *On the other hand, it may not be such a good idea—she might get ideas that I'm not ready for at the moment,* he further contemplated.

Tom's passenger turned towards him and offered more advice, "you know, sonny, speaking from personal experience, you do not get many opportunities to find happiness in life. When you find it, grab it and don't let go!" She left Tom with a great deal to think about.

Chapter 60

Susan waited for Tom outside the baggage area. When she got a glimpse of him, she got out and waved to catch his attention. When Tom saw her, he ran towards her as if he hadn't seen her in ages. "Tom, it's so good to see you. How was your flight?" Susan asked, as the expression in her face was so sincere. "Rachel and I really missed you," Susan said, giving him a big welcome-home hug and kiss.

"Susan, it's great to see you as well—I've missed you terribly. How is Rachel doing these days?" "She's doing much better since she came home from the hospital. At times, I feel like I'm taking care of a child, but she is very appreciative I'm here for her. She is very excited you've come back as well. Tom, seriously, you didn't have to leave your home and your job, but I'm glad you did. You were dearly missed."

"Thanks, but I haven't been away that long, and I felt you could use some help." "What am I going to do with you, Tom?" Tom just shrugged his shoulders. "I guess you are stuck with me!"

"Before I forget, Tom, thanks for being there when the police decided to pay a visit to my home. I'm really surprised they thought Max was still alive; I guess they didn't get the memo. You would think the police would be up to date on matters like that. It is strange they paid me a visit after all these months since Max has been gone."

"I wonder if Max had other hidden gems around the

house. My apologies, I did not mean that to be a pun." "That's OK. I've gotten to know your sense of humor by now. Did the police say what they were looking for exactly?" "No, they didn't — they just came with a search warrant, and they proceeded with their search. They turned your house upside down. When I get back, I will straighten it out for you before you return home."

"Tom, that won't be necessary. I've been meaning to get new furniture after Max died. I might even get the house ready to sell, and start fresh somewhere else — maybe here in San Diego." "That may not be a bad idea. Selling your house might help you get a fresh start on life. I'm sure your house brings back a lot of bad memories for you that, I'm sure, you'd rather put behind you. You might wish to stay at my house while you get your house ready to sell." *I wonder if Tom realized what he just offered me,* she thought.

When they got home, Rachel gave Tom a hero's welcome. "Rachel, it's so great to see you on your feet. Your sister's a great nurse, I see," Tom said. "Tom, your girlfriend thinks I'm still a child — she watches everything I do — takes care of me as if I were a child, and refuses to let me do things on my own." "Rachel, you know it's because she loves you very much," Tom informed her, as he turned and looked at Susan while she rolled her eyes. "This guy's good, sis." "Didn't I tell you?"

"You must be hungry after your long trip. What do they give you these days on the airplane, peanuts?" "Something like that. Rachel, what smells so good? Are you cooking? Shouldn't you be resting?" "You see, my dear Rachel, what have I been telling you — don't push yourself. You are still in the process of recovering,"

Susan chimed in.

"I know, I know, but I have to do something and today is the first time I'm cooking. Tom, your girlfriend has been feeding me frozen fish sticks every day—I'm going to start growing gills." "Now Rachel, please do not exaggerate. I only made you fish sticks three times last week." Susan corrected her. "Wow, you know how to cook fish sticks? You must share that recipe with me or is it a family secret?" "You're a funny guy, Tom. I see you haven't changed a bit since you've been gone." Rachel was amused to watch her sister and Tom go back and forth. *That must be love*, Rachel thought.

"Rachel, since your car was destroyed in the accident, have you given any thought to what kind of car you would like to get? I guess we have to go shopping for a new car for you. Do you have any particular one in mind?" "No, not really. The Teslas look nice and the best part is they don't need gas. You see a lot of them in California." "I considered getting the same car as well when my old clunker decides to roll over and die." Susan stood by while Rachel and Tom had a conversation about cars.

"Now, Rachel, how is it you've been very quiet when we were by ourselves but you're talking up a storm now?" "Come on, Susan, I haven't seen Tom in a while, and I missed him." "Well, I missed him as well!" "Yeah, but when you go back home, you'll have him all to yourself."

Rachel changed the subject and motioned everyone to go into the dining room. "My world-famous tuna noodle casserole is getting cold." They all strolled into the dining room where a nice table setting for three awaited them. To top it off, they were all going to dine by candlelight.

"This looks so romantic," Tom pointed out, while pulling Susan's chair out for her to sit down. "Susan, this guy is very chivalrous. Does he do this all the time?" "Yes, he does. He even opens the door of the car for me." "Now, how come you didn't mention these little things to me before?" "As a matter of fact, I did mention them to you and more, but you were in a coma, Rachel." "Well played, sis."

"I can't wait to try your world-famous tuna noodle casserole, Rachel. Your sister talks about it all the time. Is this a recipe handed down from generation to generation?" Susan put her hand on her mouth and almost chuckled at Tom's comment. "No, silly. I found the recipe on the back of a can of cream of mushroom soup." "Oh?" interjected Tom.

"You had to ask," Susan offered. "Well, it smells fantastic! Can't wait to try it. Can I bother you for some Parmesan cheese?" "What for? My casserole?" "Would I be insulting you if I did?" Rachel hesitated a bit, and before she responded, Tom stepped in. "That's OK, Rachel, I thought it was spaghetti, but I see they're noodles."

Susan noticed how Tom back peddled. She went over to him and whispered, "nice save, my love." Tom looked at the ceiling annoyed at himself for asking for cheese when Rachel went to the kitchen to get a spatula. "Close call," he leaned over and whispered to Susan.

"Rachel, this is absolutely delicious," Tom smiled at Rachel and thanked her for making it. "Do you think it could use some more Parmesan cheese—I only added a little." Tom did not know how to respond, and Susan almost bit her lip in an effort to avoid laughing. "Rachel,

I think you added just the right amount—no more is needed."

After dinner was over, Tom got up and picked up the dishes. "Please guys, you cooked so it's my turn to clean up." "Susan, is this guy for real?" "Yup." "Susan, this guy's a keeper." Susan put her hand by her mouth to avoid Tom from hearing. "I know."

"Rachel where's your Tupperware so I can put away the left-over tuna noodle casserole?" Tom requested, as he rinsed the dishes before inserting them into the dishwasher. "In the first cabinet by the stove." Susan looked at Rachel with a proud smile that Tom knew his way around the kitchen.

"Susan, if you ever get tired of this guy, please send him over my way." Susan was very proud that Rachel approved of her boyfriend. When Tom got back from cleaning up, he brought a pot of coffee. "Tom, you can stay with me as long as you want—in fact, I insist that you do," Rachel suggested.

"Hey, Rachel. Are you forgetting he's my guy and you can't have him?" Tom made a concerted effort not to eavesdrop and get in between the two sisters. After everyone had coffee and dessert, they proceeded into the living room to chat a bit before calling it a day.

"Tom, would you like an after-dinner drink?" "No thanks, Rachel. Remember, I'm running on eastern time. It may be seven here, but it's ten for me back east. I might just crash in a little while. Please stay up and chat, if you like." "We noticed you made coffee, but we didn't see you have any?" "If I were to drink coffee after four in the afternoon, it would keep me up all night," Tom informed Rachel.

Somehow the three got chatting, and the hours

passed before their eyes. "Tom, Susan said there's a possibility we might be going to the soup kitchen tomorrow. Oh, and speaking of the soup kitchen, they were ecstatic with your contribution." "It was our pleasure, Rachel—we know it was for a very worthy cause. Now getting back to the soup kitchen, are you sure you're up to going?" Tom leaned over to Rachel and asked.

"They're my family—I miss them terribly." "We know, but they would want you to get better first." "I have an idea," Rachel proposed. "Why don't we all go tomorrow, and you guys can help out while I sit with my group—I promise, I won't do any work. Deal?" Susan and Tom looked at each other, and they both agreed with Rachel's suggestion. It might do her good to see her old friends again.

Chapter 61

As everyone entered the soup kitchen and saw Rachel sitting down, they each went towards her, one by one, to see her and give her a big hug. Rachel was treated like a celebrity. Tom and Susan now realized why Rachel felt she had to go back. Tom could see in Susan's eyes how very proud she was of her sister and totally understood Rachel's need to go back to the soup kitchen—she was very much part of their family.

After everyone had gone for the evening, Rachel approached Tom and Susan and thanked them very much for not only volunteering to serve dinner, but also for taking her to be with her adopted family—it meant a lot to her. She was very appreciative for everything her sister and Tom had done for her.

"Rachel, if I may ask, how long have you volunteered here?" Tom asked, as he felt that she had been there for a long time for the reception she was given. "Oh, I would say for about a year and a half, I think." Rachel looked as if she gave Tom's question some thought. "If I may ask you one more question. How did you get interested in this very noble project?"

"A little while ago, I ran into a longtime friend I hadn't seen in a while begging on the streets. I could not believe my eyes how this glamorous person who always wore designer clothing, wound up on the streets. To make a long story short, she and her husband fell on hard times, and he left her with a mountain of debt. She literally was left on the streets with nothing but the clothes on her back. When I offered to help her, her pride got in the way. She wouldn't let anyone help her. I made it a point to look for her every week until one day I spotted her walking into the soup kitchen. That's when I started volunteering. Something just took over and I was driven to help. Don't ask me why — you had to be in my shoes to feel it for yourself."

Tom was in awe hearing Rachel's story, and he was able to feel not only what Rachel so vividly portrayed about her friend, but also totally understood why she became a volunteer. "I can see clearly why you volunteer here. You are to be commended for your service. It takes a special person to do what you do — I'm very proud of you."

"I do this, Tom, because there are many unfortunate people in this world who are not as fortunate as I am — I am blessed and thankful for what I have." Tom and Susan stood in total silence, with pride written all over their faces.

Susan noticed Rachel's outing to the soup kitchen had taken its toll on her; she pushed herself and she needed to get home, take her medicine, and call it a day. All in all, Susan felt the trip to the soup kitchen was very therapeutic for Rachel, more so than any prescription drug would have been able to do for her.

After Rachel was put to bed, Tom and Susan sat in her kitchen and discussed the activities of the day, with the soup kitchen being the highlight of their day. "I can see why your sister is driven to volunteer there. She has a calling." "She is a very special person, Tom. I wonder why she never mentioned this to me before."

After chatting for a while, Tom and Susan decided to call it a day. For Tom, it was much later than it was for

Susan, as his body was still on eastern time—traveling had taken its toll on him as well. Susan went to the bathroom and washed up first, followed by Tom. Tom noticed the room was dark and assumed Susan had gone to sleep while Tom washed up.

He slowly crawled into bed trying to be as quiet as possible. Suddenly, Susan turned over to give him a goodnight kiss. As he put his arm around her to reciprocate, he noticed she wasn't wearing anything. All he felt was the warm velvet-like skin next to his arms. He could not believe how soft and beautiful she felt.

His heartbeat raced with emotions—each one taking turns leading the other. This was a feeling and sensation he never had felt before. Amidst this cloak of sensation, his love for her was the icing on the cake. Passion had entered the room, and it was not about to leave.

Morning came and the aroma of coffee permeated throughout the house. After they washed up, they followed the aroma to the kitchen where Rachel had made quite the spread: fresh coffee, toast, pancakes, bacon and scrambled eggs. Susan noticed her sister had cooked up a storm.

"What do we have here, Rachel? You made all this?" Susan was surprised her sister had gotten up early and cooked an abundance of food. "Well, sis, it certainly wasn't the breakfast fairy," Rachel always had the habit of saying what was on her mind—she didn't pull any punches.

"I figured you both would probably be starving this morning." Susan and Tom exchanged eye contact with each other and squinted wondering what Rachel meant by that comment. *Did she hear us last night.? Did we make that much noise?* Susan asked herself.

"Did you guys sleep well?" Rachel asked, with a slight smirk intended for only Tom to notice. Tom felt a little guilty they may have woken Rachel. "Oh my, it's nine-o'clock—we must have been very tired. I don't recall sleeping till nine in a long time," Susan said, while she stretched.

"I'm glad you did, sis. You've been working very hard taking care of me lately from morning till night." "Rachel, you know I don't mind taking care of you— you're my sister." "I love you for that, sis," Rachel said with sincerity. "How do you feel, Rachel? Did you overdo it at the soup kitchen last night?" Tom asked, concerned Rachel may have pushed herself.

"If you would like to go car shopping today, I would be more than happy to go with you," Tom suggested. "Thanks, Tom, very much appreciated. If I choose to get the Tesla, I can go shopping for it on line," Rachel informed Tom. "I'm sorry, Rachel, I don't follow you."

"When you are looking to buy a Tesla, you just go on line, click on the car and buy it?" "Really?" Tom was very surprised that cars could be purchased that easily without having to go to a dealer. "Yes, and when you finally choose your model, you click on it and put a minimum down payment, like $250. Within a short period of time, you need to go to a Tesla center to pick up your car.

As a matter of fact, Tesla sends an Uber to pick you up. They can either go to your home or your office and then they take you to a Tesla center to pick up your car. Mind you, Tom, you can still go and test drive a vehicle before you decide to purchase it. I know a friend who was lent a Tesla for twenty-four hours before she decided to purchase it." Susan took note of the camaraderie between Tom and her sister. She felt good her sister got along with Tom—having your family's approval is sometimes half the battle.

Chapter 62

Tom noticed Susan needed a change of pace. "I have a suggestion for you. If you need a change of pace from your sister, we can go and visit other charitable organizations and play Mr. and Mrs. Santa Claus again." "I see you like to use that analogy of Mr. and Mrs. Claus every now and then, but, yes, that's a good idea. Rachel will be very happy to be left alone in the house for a little while."

"Rachel, do you mind if Tom and I go out for a bit to run some errands?" Susan asked, knowing full well Rachel would be ecstatic to be left alone. "You mean, you're going to leave me here all by myself—unsupervised?" Rachel asked facetiously. "Would that be, OK?" "Duh, yeah. Please take your time; I don't want you to rush and think you have to come back quickly to take care of me," Rachel's smile said it all.

"And, if you're good, we might bring back a bucket of chicken later for you." "You see, Susan, now you've given me an incentive to be good," Rachel replied sarcastically. Rachel added, "also, please make it extra crispy—no dark meat." "Tom, did you hear that. Rachel just put an order for KFC." "That's great. That just means she's getting better."

The area of San Diego was new to both Susan and Tom. They drove around for a while until they found an opportunity to be charitable. One place of worship had a very large thermometer outside on its front lawn showing the progress of their fund drive to-date.

Susan and Tom walked in and inquired where the rectory was located. When they finally found the office, they both walked in and informed the office manager they wished to increase the thermometer a few degrees. "Sorry, sir, I don't follow you."

"Miss, you have a big thermometer on your front lawn showing your donations are up to 60%. We would like to make a contribution to increase the red bar on your thermometer." "I'm sorry, sir, I must have, as the younger generation say today, *spaced out*. We can take the contributions here, if you like." Susan presented her with an envelope filled with fifties and hundreds.

"That's very generous of you. Let me get the pastor; I'm sure he would personally like to thank you for your generosity. We don't get many walk-ins with so much money in an envelope." "Miss, that's quite alright — that won't be necessary," Susan informed her, as she was on her way out the door. "OK then, let me give you a receipt for your contribution." "That won't be necessary either." Susan and Tom smiled as they walked out. "You are both very kind. God bless you both!" "Thanks, ma'am. You have a good day."

"Didn't that feel good, Tom?" Susan asked, feeling very good about herself. "It most certainly did!" Tom said, as his body language mirrored Susan's. "There's something I would like to discuss with you," Tom recommended, with a serious look. "OK, what's on your mind?" Susan asked, as she did not know what to expect from Tom's serious demeanor.

"How would you like to help Rachel get a new car with whatever her insurance company doesn't cover? My apologies, I don't know why I proposed this to you when all of the reward money in the safe deposit box belongs to you." "Tom, do you recall what I said to you when we received the case filled with $400,000?"

"No, I really don't, there was too much excitement going on that day when you got the money." Tom looked at her puzzled, as he didn't know what Susan alluded to. "I said, we will split the reward fifty-fifty." "Oh, yes, now I remember, and, if I recall correctly, I said it was not necessary." "Anyway, as far as I am concerned, it's half yours and half mine," Susan said it in such a way there was no more discussion to be had.

"I'd like to get back to what I previously started to propose," Tom continued, "that we help Rachel get a new car once she receives the insurance money for her car. In other words, we should help her get a new car. Whatever the insurance doesn't cover, we would like to make up the difference." "I think that's great. That's very generous of you." "Correction, Susan. Very generous of *us*."

After dropping off several envelopes to various organizations around town, Susan remembered to stop by the nearest KFC to pick up dinner for Rachel. "I can't believe Rachel would take a bucket of chicken over a fancy restaurant," Tom interjected, as he shook his head and did not understand Rachel's choice of restaurant. "This is what she likes, and we have to respect her wishes." "OK, I'd like to also stop by a drug store before going home." "What for?" "Tums!" Susan smiled.

"Hi guys, would you believe I could smell the chicken from the moment you got out of the car in the driveway?" Rachel noted, as Tom and Susan walked into the house. "Rachel, you have a keen sense of smell." "Thank you very much for getting the chicken; I thought you were going to forget."

"Forget? Absolutely not! When my favorite sister requests a bucket of chicken to get better, how can I forget." "Favorite sister, sis? Really?" "Well, you *are* my favorite sister!" "Do you see any other sister around?" Rachel asked, as she turned her head and looked from one place to another.

Tom unpacked the bag from KFC. "Here are: the biscuits, fries, coleslaw, potato salad and gravy." Rachel could see they went overboard. "Tom, you're the best! I can't believe you got all of my favorite things," Rachel said and thanked Tom, as she gave him a big hug and a kiss.

"Rachel, it was your favorite sister who reminded me to pick up the chicken for you," Tom stepped in, as he felt Susan was the one who remembered to get the chicken from KFC. "That's OK, Tom. I know who rates here. Should I be watching my back, Rachel?" Susan pointed out to her sister who was busy eyeing all the goodies from KFC.

"Whatever do you mean, sis?" "You know very well what I mean?" Tom stood by while the sisters volleyed back and forth when he decided to step in. "OK, guys. Let's stop and dig in. The smell in the car drove me crazy," Tom noted, as he decided to break up the back and forth bickering between the sisters. "Tom, are you exaggerating a bit? If you recall, we stopped at the drug store to get you some Tums."

"Also, Rachel, we got you their cherry pie for dessert. And, before you say anything, please thank Susan. After all, that was also her idea. She remembered how much you liked their cherry pie." "I don't know what to say. You've given me the royal treatment tonight. Maybe I should be in more accidents."

"Please sis, don't even joke about that. Just remember, if you're in more accidents, I will be staying with you more." "OK, sis, I have to be careful what I say in the future. You do make a very good point."

Tom could see there was a special bond between Rachel and Susan, one that reminded him of the bond he has with his brother. He realized that since he went on the train ride and met Susan, his get-togethers with his brother had come to a halt. He made a note to resume his Starbucks dates with his brother once he got home.

At the moment, he did not know how much longer Susan planned on staying in San Diego with Rachel. One thing he was very certain of — he wanted Susan to be part of his life. *Maybe I should have a talk with Susan to see if she feels the same way*, Tom thought.

"Susan, do you mind going for a walk? There are a few things I would like to discuss with you," Tom asked. "Sounds serious, Tom. Rachel, Tom and I are going for a walk — we'll be back soon. We want to walk off some of the dinner we had." "Not a problem, sis. Take your time," Rachel sounded more and more like she wanted her space back, but she did not want to insult her sister who had been more than accommodating to her.

"Tom, I'm a bit concerned why you wished to chat privately," Susan noted, as they started to walk. "Susan, I love you dearly, but there are certain things that are meant to be shared privately between you and me. As you know, I love you very much, and I would go to all corners of the world with you." Susan focused on every word Tom said, yet waited patiently for the *punch line*.

"Yes, go on." "Well, you've been giving me hints you would consider selling your house in Providence and moving here to San Diego to be near to your sister.

Also, I'm at the stage of my life where I can retire and live any place I would like—preferably with you." Susan continued to listen to every word Tom said and patiently waited to hear where Tom was headed with his conversation.

"Susan, I'd like to know if you share the same feelings I do. I don't want to assume anything." "Tom, in the short period of time I have known you, I've grown very fond of you, and now I'm getting hints from my sister that she loves you very much as well…" Tom interrupted Susan, as he didn't like the direction the conversation was headed.

"Susan, do you, for one minute, think there's anything to her hints?" "As far as you're concerned, I hope not, but as far as she is concerned, that's another story—she's getting attached to you, Tom." Susan did not wish to continue with her assertions and decided to proceed.

"Getting back to your original premise, yes, it's true. I would like to sell my house which is filled with bad memories I would like to erase from my mind—I just want to put that part of my life behind me, Tom. Whatever I do with my house has nothing to do with my feelings toward you. As a matter of fact, I would love to spend the rest of my life with you."

Tom did not expect to hear that from Susan, and was pleasantly surprised she shared her feelings with him. Susan continued, "as you know, the weather in the northeast is unbearable in the winter. Here in San Diego, the weather is always nice so this is another added feature. Needless to say, my sister lives here. As much as she loves me, she will definitely want her own space back—she has made this crystal clear to me lately." "I can see you're leaning towards living here, and I can see all the merits for doing so. I would also like to move here and live with you, if it's OK with you?"

"Tom, you've made my day; I would love to live here with you as well." "Why don't we see how much longer your sister needs us to stay with her." "Tom, if it were up to her, she would prefer I leave tomorrow." "I think you need to fill her in on our plans." "Yes, that makes sense as our decision could affect her."

"Then once Rachel is given the green light by the doctor that she's OK to live on her own, we can go back and get our homes ready to put on the market." "Tom, have you always been a planner?" "It's what I do, Susan. Whenever you have a goal in mind, there are steps you have to take to get to your goal, and timing is a big factor in reaching your goal."

"I also have my job that I may retire from. It's been on my mind lately as well." "How will your office react to your retirement?" "I don't know—I hope they'll be happy for me. Since I've been down here with you and your sister, I've been able to work remotely, and I may continue to do so. I don't think I'll have a problem working from here. As long as I can hold my clients' hands, as I'm doing at the moment, I don't believe it should be an issue wherever I may live. As a matter of fact, a large percentage of my client base resides all over the country. No, I don't see my job as an issue, at the moment. When I get back to Providence, I need to have a chat with Marcus on what my future plans with the company will be."

"Do you think it's time to go back to Rachel's? I hope she's not worried about us." "Are you kidding? She's very happy to be by herself! She probably doesn't even realize we're gone." "When is her next doctor's appointment? I think that will determine how quickly we move with our plans." "I think her next appointment is in a couple of days, but I'm not sure. I need to confirm that with her when we get back." Tom and Susan made their way back home.

"Hi guys, did you have a nice walk?" Rachel asked. "Yes, it was good to stretch our legs." "You should do it more often, sis." "And leave you all alone?" "I know, sis, but I'll manage." "Rachel, when is your next doctor's appointment?" "Tomorrow morning, why?" "Time has a way of flying by, doesn't it? We really hope your doctor gives you a clean bill of health." "Me too."

"Rachel, have you decided what car you would like to get?" Tom asked. "I've been researching a variety of cars on line, and I've decided on a Tesla. I would like to make an appointment to test drive one." "We can do that in a couple of days, if you like," Tom suggested.

"Sounds good to me—the sooner the better. Cause once you guys leave, I'm going to be left without a car." "You can also rent one until your car comes in," Susan recommended. "That's true. I should be hearing from the insurance company in a couple of days."

"Speaking of the insurance company, there's something Susan and I would like to discuss with you." Rachel did not know what to make of that comment. *Are they getting engaged*? was one of her thoughts. *Are they moving in together*? Little did Rachel know that any other thoughts she may come up with, would not even come close to what Susan and Tom had up their sleeves.

"Rachel, has the insurance company determined a settlement amount for your car?" asked Susan, to set Tom and her for the next topic of conversation. "Yes, they're going to give me $30,000 for the BMW—it's a shame as it was only four years old and I really liked that car." Tom proceeded. "What do you estimate the Tesla is going to cost you?" "Oh, roughly $50,000. I've already spoken to the bank and they have informed me they will finance the difference."

"Sounds like you have done your homework. Tom and I have decided to give you an early Christmas present. We would like to give you the difference of $20,000, so you can buy your new car," Susan proposed to Rachel. "Is this a joke? I know it's not April Fool's Day. You guys can't be serious!"

"Very serious, sis. We love you dearly, and we would very much like to do this for you." "Not that I'm being ungrateful, I thank you very much for your generosity, but how are you guys able to do this?" Rachel asked, trying to catch her breath from hearing about Tom's and Susan's generous gift.

"Rachel, I received Max's insurance and Tom had a great year in his job. We're very fortunate we're in a position to do this for you. We are also very fortunate you had a solid vehicle that protected you from being hurt even more. Had you had a smaller car with less protection around you to absorb the vehicle that hit you, you might not be here for us to be a pain in the ass and baby you." Rachel smiled a little and moved her head to the side acknowledging Susan's comment.

"I know, Rachel, I may have gone a bit overboard, but we took care of you because you are family and we love you very much." "I know, sis, but sometimes you can be a bit much."

Tom had no doubt the love that existed between the two sisters was much like his love for his brother, Jim.

"Again guys, thank you very much for your generosity—this was a totally unexpected surprise. I don't know what to say. You have left me totally speechless."

"That's what families are for," Susan exclaimed, and approached her sister with a big loving and sincere hug. Tom also came to the realization that this is where Susan belonged—to be near her sister. Witnessing this interaction did it for Tom. *I am ready to leave the northeast to be in San Diego with Susan*, Tom confidently concluded.

Chapter 63

*T*om decided that moving to San Diego with Susan was what he truly wanted to do, and was already working on a plan to execute his decision. He had given this a great deal of thought, and he looked forward to moving there to be with Susan. Thoughts of buying a house with Susan had also crossed his mind, but it would be linking a bridge to a future with Susan—a chat for another day to have with her. He did not have any reservation about having a future with her; however, he wasn't sure she wanted the same.

Tom's first order of business was to sit with Jim when he got back to Providence. He planned to go over his decision to move to San Diego. In the past, they counseled each other, and in many situations, they each came up with a recommendation the other had not considered. Tom was very much aware it was, ultimately, going to be his decision, but he always valued his brother's insight. *Who knows, Jim might move to San Diego as well*, Tom tossed around in his mind.

"Susan, what time will you be taking Rachel to the doctor tomorrow?" "Her appointment is at nine, so we'll leave here around eight." "I'll keep my fingers crossed that everything will be OK." "Thanks, and Rachel will have her fingers crossed as well. I can't believe, in just a very short period of time, we have adopted you as part of our family." "Thanks, Susan. Have you taken care of all my shots? Only kidding. You do know how to open the flood gates of tears—tears of happiness, that is," Tom said teary eyed. Tom felt very wanted and loved.

Susan set the alarm on her phone to prevent her from getting up late the following day; especially, since she had to take Rachel to the doctor. This was a very important appointment as Rachel could taste the freedom to have both her house and life back.

As Susan and Tom laid in bed holding hands while sleep was slowly taking both of them away for the night, they both chatted about their future together. Suddenly, Tom had a thought he wanted to share with Susan. "I can't believe we're lying next to each other here in bed. Who would have believed when we first met on that train ride, that within a couple of months we would be sleeping together?" "That does seem out there, doesn't it?" Susan shook her head in disbelief. "Well, it does seem way out there for me that we've gone through so much in such a short period of time, but I'm very glad the forces of nature brought us together." "God does have a sense of humor, doesn't He?"

Chapter 64

Rachel was ecstatic she was given a clean bill of health—her prayers had been answered; however, she was advised by her doctor to take it easy and not to push herself. As soon as the doctor informed her of this great news, she turned towards Susan and Susan gave her one of those *I-told-you-so* looks. Rachel knew exactly what that meant.

Rachel had gone through a serious life-threatening accident, and she had bruises all over her body to prove it, and, to top it off, she went into a coma for several weeks. She was very appreciative she had her sister to provide the care she needed while she recuperated.

For as much as Rachel complained that Susan may have been overbearing, she knew in her heart that her sister did it because of the love she had for her. She also knew that she couldn't have done it without her.

"This is a cause to celebrate, Rachel," Tom offered. "You don't need to tell us how you would like to celebrate the great news you received today—we know that all too well. Susan and I have already reserved the finest booth at KFC. Tonight, you are not going to dine on paper plates and plastic utensils. We will be taking fancy China and silverware to celebrate the occasion."

Rachel beamed from ear to ear to hear how thoughtful her sister and Tom were. Even Susan got a kick out of Tom's celebratory recommendations. She shook her head at his suggestions. Rachel couldn't wait to celebrate with a bucket of extra crispy chicken with all the fixins.

After Tom and Susan took Rachel home, they went out to run some errands. Rachel wanted to rest a bit. Going to the doctor took a lot out of her—she needed to lie down. Lying down didn't last too long. Now that she had received a clean bill of health, she needed to get up and do things around her house.

Although Susan dusted and vacuumed and did a great job at that, Rachel felt she needed to go back to doing chores around her house. She knew if Susan were home, her sister would not have let her do them by herself. *Freedom*, she thought, *time to go back and take charge of myself and my house.*

Rachel proceeded to straighten up and vacuum the room Tom and Susan stayed in. While she vacuumed, she noticed the cord that was plugged into the outlet in the other room was stretched as far as it could. All she needed was a couple of inches more to reach the corner of the room with the vacuum, and she would be finished. She tugged a bit more to see if she could get those extra couple of inches of the cord to finish the room.

In the process, the cord knocked over a book that sat on the dresser. When the book fell on the floor, it opened and exposed a couple of envelopes filled with fifties and hundreds that Susan and Tom held to donate to charity.

Rachel looked at all the money that was spread out on the floor and stood speechless. *Where did they get all this money?* Rachel asked herself, not knowing what to think. The thought of Susan and Tom's conversation to help her out to purchase her car surfaced, and she began to have all sorts of doubts on the origin of the money. *Is this money legal?* Thoughts of doubt continued to surface in her mind.

Within a short while, Tom and Susan had returned and found Rachel sitting in the kitchen with a dumbfounded look. "Are you OK, Rachel? You look like you've lost your best friend." "Susan, I need you to be honest with me. By accident, the cord on the vacuum cleaner knocked the book you had on the dresser onto the floor." Immediately, Tom and Susan knew the direction the conversation was headed.

"Yes, and?" Susan asked. Rachel attempted to remain cool and collected when she spoke. "Well, when the book fell on the floor, a couple of envelopes with 50's and 100's came out and the money spread all over the carpet. Where did you get all this money? I am very concerned and worried." Tom volunteered to address Rachel's concerns.

"Rachel, when Susan and I first met on the train from Providence to San Diego, one of the things that she and I had in common was to help those unfortunate individuals who are worse off than we are. We felt blessed we had a roof over our heads and we didn't have to beg for food — very similar to you and your soup kitchen. We then decided we were going to pool a certain amount of money from our bank accounts and give it away.

As your sister mentioned before, she did well from Max's insurance policy, and I had a great year at work. We wanted to share our good fortunes with those who are less fortunate." Both Rachel and Susan listened intently to every word Tom said. *Did Tom just pull a rabbit out of a hat?* Susan asked herself. Tom continued, "and just as you kept your soup kitchen activities to yourself, we did the same. We didn't want to tell the world about it.

All the money we have given out so far has been given anonymously. This is what Susan and I have been doing all along when we said we were going out to run errands. So, Rachel, you didn't know you and your sister had so much in common—the apple didn't fall far from the tree."

Rachel sat quietly and processed everything Tom had said, and Susan was no different. She hoped Rachel understood everything Tom so eloquently laid out. "Tom, I don't know why my imagination ran away from me. Everything you said makes sense to me now." Susan sat and listened to Rachel, and thanked Tom for putting Rachel's mind at ease. She agreed to everything Tom had said without having to disclose that the money had come from the reward in surrendering the diamonds.

Neither Susan nor Tom would ever disclose the origin of the money in the safety deposit box which would take volumes and plenty of liquor to fully comprehend. Tom was honest with Rachel in their ability to anonymously donate money to charity. They could very well have done it with their own money which, in fact, the reward money was.

After Rachel went to bed, Tom and Susan decided to take Harvey for a walk before turning in for the night. The evenings in San Diego were warm enough for a walk contrary to the evenings in Providence. The walk also gave them an opportunity to rehash the conversation they just had with Rachel.

"Tom, I don't know what to say. You handled Rachel's concerns and worries brilliantly. Thank you so much for stepping in and putting her fears to rest." "Susan, you would have done the same." "Apparently, you don't know me very well." "I know you well enough to have fallen in love with you." Susan threw Tom a kiss.

"We live three thousand miles away from Rachel. What do you think of going away for a few days to see how she does on her own?" "You know, that may not be a bad idea to see how she does on her own before we go back to Providence."

"Hey Rachel, got a minute? I have some bad news I would like to share with you." Rachel immediately rushed to hear what bad news Susan had to share. "Sis, are you OK? What's the bad news?" Rachel asked with a very concerned look. "Tom and I were thinking of driving up to one of the vineyards for a few days." "And?" "Well, that would mean leaving you here all by yourself with Harvey." Rachel did all she could to not appear overjoyed at being left alone.

"Susan, you are right. I'm really very sad you're going to leave me here all alone with Harvey." "Poor Harvey, he missed you so much when you were in the hospital. He expected you to come home, and you never showed up. Are you sure you'll be OK by yourself?" "Susan, please go and have a good time. You really need to get away from it all." Tom observed the interaction between both sisters and it was very nice to see.

Chapter 65

"Tom, I've been giving Rachel's condition some thought. In my opinion, she appears to be a bit weak. Of course, she thinks otherwise as she wants us to think she's in great shape so we can go back home and leave her all by herself." "I agree; she could use a bit more hand-holding and TLC." "I have a suggestion for you. Maybe you should go back home and leave me here with her for a little bit longer," Susan proposed.

"You are aware that Rachel's not going to take this news lightly." "I know. I'll just let her know it was your idea." "OK, I can handle that. You want me to be the bad guy here I see? No problem. If she comes after me, I'll just let her know it's because we love her dearly and I felt you should stay with her a bit longer."

"Tom, coming from you would probably be better than coming from me. You do know, Tom, it's because you have a special place in her heart," Susan said, while she placed her hand over her heart and tilted her head.

"Are we going to start this charade again?" "Look, Tom, if this is what it's going to take for me to take care of her a little longer, I say, let's go for it." Tom agreed it was a good idea for Susan to stay with Rachel a bit longer to make sure she is 100% to be left on her own.

"Rachel, you got a minute?" "Is this another intervention, guys?" Rachel asked, with her hands by her hips. "Absolutely not!" "I just want to share a suggestion that Tom just came up with. He did say he had your best interest at heart, and you know what that means. Tom, since it was your idea, I feel you should have the honor of letting her know yourself."

Meanwhile, Rachel looked at them wondering what was going on. "Rachel, you do know we both love you very dearly…" "Oh, oh, here it comes," Rachel muttered, as she rolled her eyes. "As I was saying," Tom continued. "Yeah, yeah, because you love me, go on…" Rachel interrupted.

"Your sister and I feel you have made wonderful progress since you've come home from the hospital." "Get out the boots, here it comes," Rachel was on a roll, and she didn't like the direction the conversation was headed. "Susan, would you like to share our suggestion with Rachel."

"Absolutely not, my dear! This was your idea, and I don't want to rain on your parade," Susan tried, but this was Tom's idea to run with it, so to speak. Somehow, Tom was cornered to suggest an idea that originated with Susan.

"OK, Rachel, here it goes. I'm planning to go back home in a couple of days…" Rachel jumped in and interrupted him again. "What do you mean *I'm planning to go back home.* How about my dear sister? Is she going back home as well?"

"In my opinion, I think Susan should stay here a bit longer to keep you company." "Susan, is your boyfriend kidding with me because if he is, I don't see the humor in it." Rachel did not like the direction of Tom's conversation.

"Rachel, he convinced me to stay a bit longer, not because of you, but because I needed some rest." "Sis, this guy's good." "I know, Rachel, but he also convinced me to stay here where it's much warmer—it's much colder in Providence as you know." "I don't miss those winter months in Rhode Island at all either." "Thanks, Rach, for letting me stay here with you; I'll try not to get in your way."

Tom realized the thought of Susan staying longer with her sister was being accepted much easier than they had anticipated. "Isn't it time for you guys to take Harvey for a walk?" Rachel asked. "Good idea, Rachel. Would you like to come with us? You are more than welcomed to join us." "Thanks, Tom. I need my alone time—I have to get used to it again."

"Another brilliant talk-your-way-out of it routine on your part, my love," Susan said, as she grabbed Tom's arm on their walk. "I said the same thing we talked about before, but I just used a different twist." "You're getting good at this. I can see why Rachel loves you." "Are you going to start with me again?" Tom asked, as he looked at her in their special way. "You know I like to kid with you, my love."

"Just remember, while you're with Rachel, you have to let her do her own thing; otherwise, she's going to think you stayed behind to take care of her."

"Before I forget, Tom, we have to go to the bank tomorrow before you leave so we can take out the $20,000 for Rachel's car. We have to put half in your account, and half in my account so we can give her two separate checks—one from each of us for $10,000."

"I almost forgot about that. I guess I'll be away when she picks up her Tesla. Have you given any thought to how long you're planning to stay with your sister?" Tom selfishly asked. "I think a couple of weeks should do it." "Please don't stay too long; just thinking about it is making me miss you already." "I'll miss you, as well, my love."

Chapter 66

As usual, Tom arrived at Starbucks early to reserve their favorite booth. As he sat thinking about Susan and their recent adventures, he looked around and reminisced about all the chats he and Jim have had in this coffee shop. In retrospect, Tom felt that getting Jim to have coffee was a way of getting himself to be with family. Jim and everyone else were aware that Tom had overworked himself — everyone knew but Tom. It had to take a short circuit in his body for him to wake up and realize it.

"Tom, it's so good to see you again. It feels like you've been gone forever." Jim greeted his brother with a big hug. Something was different about his brother — he just couldn't put his finger on it. "I missed you terribly as well, bro. Is everything OK, Jim? You're looking at me strange?" Tom asked, anxiously waiting to find out what Jim noticed differently about him.

"There's something different about you, Tom. I meant to say something the last time we had coffee, but I didn't. I was very excited to see you again. You look younger. Did you lose weight?" "I was only away for a couple of months." "Well, Tommy, you must have gone through a transformation of some sort in those couple of months because you came back looking younger and healthier."

"I guess that's a good thing? Thanks for the compliment." "Most definitely. I sincerely think the trip did you a world of good. I believe your girlfriend must have been a big factor as well. OK, don't leave me guessing. When are you getting married?"

"What is this about getting married? Ya know, in the last couple of months or so, two other people asked about our being married—you happen to be the third." "I guess there is something other people have noticed that neither you nor Susan have seen." "And that would be?"

Jim could see the going back and forth started to weigh on Tom. "Jim, please just come out with it." "Tommy, you look healthier, and you look like you've been to a health spa." "Again, that sounds like a good thing, Jim?"

"Yes, most definitely. Either getting away or falling in love or both has done wonders for you, bro." "You know, I feel better—I feel alive. I can feel the difference from when I left. I don't know if it's being away from work or falling in love with Susan, or, as you said, both."

"Tommy, I'm very happy for you. Getting away was something you needed for a long time—it was way overdue. And, falling in love, was an added bonus. I can't wait to meet her and thank her for what she has done for you."

"Jim, I really miss her, and I've only been away from her for a couple of days." "That's the effect love has on you. I can't recall the last time you were in love. Were you ever? It really is great to see you this way. You look happy and content!"

Jim saw a different side of his brother he had not seen before. He felt as if his brother had grown up overnight, and was more confident than ever before. Tom wanted so much to share some of his experiences while he was away: the men in black, the diamonds, and the intimate relations he had with Susan, but he felt certain things needed to be left unsaid—*let sleeping dogs lie*, as the saying goes.

Jim could readily see Tom beamed from ear to ear whenever Susan's name came up. Ever since high school, this was the first time Jim experienced this reaction from Tom. "Jim, I have decided to put my house up for sale and move to San Diego," Tom got the courage to finally tell his brother his plans to move across the country. "Why San Diego?" Jim asked surprised.

"Well, aside from the weather, Susan has decided to sell her house and move closer to her sister. You might consider that as an option as well," Tom proposed to his brother. Jim gave it some thought. "With Betty's passing and now that you'll be moving there, that certainly could be a possibility," Jim offered, as he was in deep thought with his hand under his chin.

"You know, Jim, you should come down and visit once we've relocated. We'll even introduce you to Susan's sister, Rachel." Jim stepped back and noticed what Tom proposed. "Wait a minute bro, I see a set-up in the making." "Absolutely not, Jim—I wouldn't do that to you." "Why not? You wouldn't after I've tried to set you up for years?" Jim felt this was payback from his brother.

"Rachel's really a very nice person. It won't hurt for you to simply meet her." Tom observed Jim pause to hear what else Tom had to say. "I really haven't dated much since Betty passed away," Jim volunteered, while he sat back in the booth and thought things over.

"I'd like to know what you think of my leaving the northeast and moving to San Diego?" "Tom, it really doesn't matter where you live as long as you're happy.

What are you going to do about your job?" Jim posed, checking to see if Tom had given that any consideration.

"Good question. As you are aware, I've been in the west coast for about two months. While I was there, I kept in touch with my office on a daily basis. More importantly, I made a concerted effort to stay in touch with my clients while I also kept my boss in the loop. So, as far as he and the company were concerned, I've been doing my job. With the use of texts, phones and emails, staying in touch with my clients was as easy as 1-2-3."

"And, where do you see yourself with Susan?" Jim saved the best question for last, as he felt Susan was the pivotal reason for Tom's moving out west. "Jim, in the two months that I've been with Susan, we have gotten very close. We spent one week riding in a train together twenty-four-seven. In addition, we've been doing a lot of things together — even sleeping together." "Tommy, I think you're sharing more information than I need to know."

"I know, Jim, but first, you are my brother, and, second, I had to tell you how I really feel about her." "Does she feel the same way you do?" "I really believe and feel she truly does," Tom said, as he looked directly into Jim's eyes with a genuine look. Jim saw and sensed his brother was very serious and sincere about his feelings for Susan.

"Tom, I can see you are very much in love with Susan, and flying across the country is the least of your concerns. If it means anything at all to you, you have my blessings to pursue your feelings towards Susan. I really hope and pray that you two are very happy together. It may have come later in life for you, but; nevertheless, it came."

"Thanks, Jim. You have no idea how much your support and blessings mean to me. I love you brother," Tom said to Jim, as a tear rolled down his cheeks. The two continued to chat for hours, as they have done in the past.

Chapter 67

After a few months, Tom arrived home from San Diego. He soon realized his house felt emptier than before—an emptiness without having Susan around. He also realized his phone was turned off while he had coffee with Jim at Starbucks. He noticed there were two voice mail messages: one from Susan and the other from his boss, Marcus.

Susan had called to see if Tom had arrived home OK. She must have called shortly before he called her to let her know he had arrived. The second message was from his boss, Marcus, to inform him of a staff meeting that was scheduled in a few days.

Staff meetings at Tom's company had been held on an ad hoc basis. The meetings were usually held to keep everyone apprised of the activities of the company. In the last couple of years, staff meetings were not necessary because of the wide use of emails. Marcus would send one every couple of weeks to keep everyone informed; however, the upcoming one was to be held live, and it was mandatory.

Tom called Marcus and left him a message confirming his attendance. For a split moment, he wondered what the purpose of a live meeting was, but he would soon find out. Tom looked forward to getting together with his old cronies again.

Tom walked around his house and visualized what he had to do to get everything ready to put his house on the market to sell—a form of visual staging. He looked forward to selling his house, and moving to San Diego to be with the love of his life. While thinking of Susan, he looked at the clock on the wall to see if it would be too early to call her. *What would Susan be doing at ten o'clock in the morning?* he asked himself.

"Susan, is this too early to call?" Tom couldn't wait to hear her voice again. "Hello, my love. How are you doing? Rachel and I miss you terribly. No, no, I'm not starting in between you and Rachel—I'm just happy to hear your voice. What have you been up to?" "I'm doing well, and I'm trying to catch up to eastern time again. You know the phrase, *west is best, and east is least.* How is Rachel feeling by the way?"

"Well, you know Rachel. As much as she loves me, she wants her house back, not that I blame her. Her dog, Harvey, on the other hand, is thrilled that I'm here. I take him for walks often to leave Rachel alone to relax and get some rest. She is constantly doing things around the house. As you suggested, I am leaving her alone, but I really think she is pushing herself. I'm sure the pooch is going to miss me after I'm gone. All in all, I think she is doing better. I think she's making me believe she is recuperating at lightning speed for me to leave her alone sooner." "That's great to hear. At least, she's going in the right direction." "What's happening on your side, Tom?"

"Well, Jim and I had coffee at our usual watering hole yesterday and I told him all about you. When I mentioned the possibility of my moving to San Diego, he was very happy for me. He would like to pay us a visit after we're all settled in to see if San Diego is a place where he would like to move to as well. I also lightly mentioned Rachel, but he immediately saw that as a pending set-up."

"Do you think, Tom, there's a match there?" "I don't know. I think Rachel might run circles around him, but who knows, stranger things have happened. We'll see, but at least he seemed open to the idea." "Are you anxious to go back to work?"

"Speaking of work, I received a strange voice mail from Marcus informing me that we have an upcoming staff meeting—a live one at that." "A live one? Is something happening at work that you need to have a live meeting?" "That's what I thought as well. Yes, it's a live in-person meeting in the company conference room. I really have no idea what's on the agenda."

"I thought live staff meetings were a thing of the past?" "Well, this one is live, and it must be a very important meeting. I'll let you know afterwards."

Tom and Susan spoke on the phone for hours. After all, they've only been apart for a couple of days and they felt they had a lot to catch up on. After being together for twenty-four seven, not seeing someone for a day seemed like an eternity and there was a great deal to discuss. Neither Tom nor Susan liked being apart.

Chapter 68

"Good morning, everyone. We'd like to welcome Tom back. We all missed you very much although we practically spoke to you or emailed you every day. It looks like the west coast has been good to you — you look tanned and relaxed," Marcus reported on Tom's return as the first order of business. Everyone in the conference room waved hello to Tom, and gave him a welcomed applause. Tom was very pleased at the reception he received.

"First, we know we haven't had a live meeting in a while, but this one is very important as our company's future depends on it. I'd like to report that we have scheduled an afternoon get-together at the country club with a dozen of very wealthy potential clients. It would be a big plus if they were to join our company. I would like to meet with our sales team after this meeting to develop a strategy on how we are going to approach these potential clients."

Tom was glad he was not part of the sales team as he just consulted with the clients on financial planning once they were on board. As the meeting came to a close, Marcus asked Tom to meet with him in his office privately.

"Tom, first welcome back — glad to have you back," Marcus said, with a very sincere and welcoming smile. Tom felt very welcomed to be back. "I know you service and guide our clients, and I continue to get a lot of positive feedback from them. They especially love how you work very closely with them. I'm also aware you speak various languages." Tom wondered where the conversation was headed.

"If I could split you in half, part of you would be in sales, and the other part in financial consulting." "Thanks, Marcus, for the compliments and for the very warm welcome you all gave me for coming back." "This is why I would very much like you to join our sales team for our afternoon get-together at the country club with these potential clients."

"Thanks, again. I'm flattered, Marcus. Why did you say you were glad I spoke other languages?" "Because we have some out of towners who would be very impressed if you spoke to them in their native language." "OK, I would be more than glad to do that."

Tom paid very close attention to every word Marcus said. "We have about a dozen confirmed guests scheduled to come tomorrow to the country club and I would like you to be there to mingle and chat with them on how beneficial it would be for them to join our firm." Marcus paused, to see if Tom had any reaction to his proposal.

"Looking forward to it, Marcus, and thanks for giving me the opportunity to assist you in any way possible." "Great, Tom. See you tomorrow at the club," Marcus got up and shook Tom's hand, and welcomed him back again.

Tom couldn't wait to call Susan and share his latest developments with the company. "That's great that your boss thinks so highly of you to help the company out. How do you feel about it?" Susan asked. "Well, it definitely breaks up my routine of just working with financial statements — I'm looking forward to it." "Tom, in the short time I've known you, you can schmooze anybody."

"In addition, Susan, he wants me to talk with some of these potential clients in their native language." "You speak other languages?" Susan asked, surprised at this new discovery. "Oh, yes: Spanish, Italian and French." "I did not know that about you. That's another thing I love about you—you are constantly surprising me." "I just never had the opportunity to use them with you around. Remember, we haven't known each other for that long. More importantly, Susan, how's Rachel doing today?"

"She's doing great. She even picked up her new car today." "How is it?" "It looks like the car is from outer space with all the fancy gadgets and screens. It's like learning to drive all over again." "Have you had a chance to drive it yet?" "Yes, Rachel let me drive it and it's like a rocket—faster than anything I've ever driven before. Well, you have to let me know how your meeting goes tomorrow. I hear Rachel, we're supposed to go shopping and go to lunch afterwards."

"Lunch? Sorry, I forgot it's about one there; I keep forgetting about the time difference." "OK, my love, I'll talk to you later." Tom and Susan had a very nice chat. Tom felt very comfortable he had someone to share his life with other than his brother. He was in a very happy place.

Chapter 69

Tom looked forward to attending Marcus' meeting with potential clients. This was a total change for Tom as he typically sat behind a computer and made all sorts of calculations and financial planning with his clients. For the meeting, he put on one of his business suits with a white shirt and a business-like tie. He looked forward to playing a different role in his company. He arrived a little early at the club to see if Marcus needed any help in setting up for the meeting.

"Good afternoon, Marcus. Is there anything I can help you with? Although, I see, you have everything under control?" "Thanks, everything is all set up; however, I'm so glad you came in early. I want you to go over the slides you are going to present." Tom was confused. He was not aware he was going to make a presentation to potential clients, and was a bit concerned Marcus had entrusted him with this responsibility.

"Marcus, I was not aware you wished me to make a presentation," "My apologies, Tom. I thought I did. Is it a problem for you?" "No, not all. I'm very familiar with all the facets of the company. I just need to see the slides you prepared in advance." Tom didn't wish to disappoint the president of the company who had just entrusted him with such a responsibility.

"Great! We have plenty of time, please take my laptop and go over the slides. As you review them, please let me know if you have any questions." Tom found himself in a precarious position, but he felt he was comfortable enough he could handle the task Marcus entrusted him with.

He just needed to familiarize himself with the contents of the presentation material. After having spent time with Susan and falling in love, he felt more confident in himself than he had ever felt before.

The potential clients began to enter the room, and Marcus proceeded with the meeting. "Good afternoon, ladies and gentlemen. Thank you very much for taking time out of your busy schedules to come and spend time with us. We look forward to chatting with you one-on-one after a brief presentation by one of our top representatives, Tom Stevens."

When Marcus made Tom's introduction, his sales staff was surprised that Tom was asked to make the presentation; he was usually the backroom consulting guy, but everyone was confident Marcus knew what he was doing by selecting Tom to make the presentation.

"Good afternoon, everyone. Thank you all for coming this afternoon. We at ABC Financial are proud of the company we have built in the past fifty years. Our focus is to work individually with each and every one of you. We want to see where you currently are with your portfolio and where you would like to go. We have a proven track record of above average rates of returns for our clients. Our philosophy is that in order for us to succeed as a company, we have to ensure that you succeed first." Tom made an exemplary presentation, one that Marcus and his sales staff were extremely proud of. Tom felt proud as well.

After the presentation, Tom mingled with several of the invitees and spoke to some of them in their native language. Marcus noticed that Tom made the rounds with various individuals and handed out his business cards in the process. The meeting ran longer than expected which was a very good sign for Marcus and his team.

After everyone left, Tom decided to stay and help Marcus clean up, take the screen down, and gather all of the promotional material left behind. "Tom, I want to thank you for helping us out in a pinch. I received very good feedback as everyone left." Marcus beamed from ear to ear as he thanked Tom.

"Thanks, Marcus, glad to be of help. Is there anything else I can do for you?" "No, I think we've wrapped everything up. See you at the office, Tom, and thanks again for pitching in."

That night Tom called Susan and shared the impromptu presentation he was requested to make when he arrived at the club. "Marcus must have had a lot of confidence in you for you to pinch hit like that." Tom could hear Susan's smile over the phone.

"Thanks for your vote of confidence, Susan. That means a lot to me. At least I got to practice some of my languages. You should have seen their faces when I spoke to some of them in their native tongue—they totally did not expect it."

"Susan, I really felt good at the meeting this afternoon, and I owe it all to you. I believe you elevated my level of confidence." "I did? I thought you raised mine." "Well, we might have raised each other's like two plus two equals five."

"Excuse me, what did you mean by that?" Susan asked, puzzled at Tom's remark. "The two of us together created something larger; like two plus two equals five." "I see what you mean. Sometimes you say things that are above my head; it takes me a while to see where you are coming from."

"Susan, can you imagine how I felt when I first met you?" "Well, I think we've been good for each other." "I wouldn't want to have it any other way." Susan and Tom spoke for hours when she decided to let him go to bed as, she knew, it was very late on the east coast.

Several days had passed and Marcus called Tom for a meeting at his office. "Thanks for coming, Tom. Would you please close the door?" In all the years Tom has been working with the company, he didn't recall ever being called to the *principal's office,* so to speak.

"Hi Marcus. What can I do for you?" "Tom, please sit down. There are few things I would like to discuss with you. First, you were brilliant the other day at the club. For not giving you any advance notice, you knocked it out of the park." Tom noticed Marcus was very pleased with the way the meeting went at the country club. "Well, thanks, Marcus. That was very nice of you to say; very much appreciated."

Marcus continued, "I want to share the results of that presentation with you. As you know, we had eleven very wealthy participants attend. I believe you had the opportunity to personally chat with five or six of them." Tom wondered when Marcus was going to get to the point of this meeting.

He was starting to lose patience with him, but he made all attempts not to show it—he just sat cool and collected and listened carefully to every word that came out of Marcus' mouth. He was mostly concerned for the need to close the door. *What was so important that Marcus needed to have the door closed?* Tom asked himself.

"Tom, of the eleven who came and listened to your

presentation, four of them have signed with us. Three of them specifically requested for you to service their accounts." Tom sat flabbergasted to hear the news Marcus shared with him. *Why the closed door?* Tom continued to ponder.

"Tom, congratulations. I am very proud of you. I have a proposition I would like to discuss with you." *OK, so is this the reason the door was closed?* Tom asked himself.

"Tom, I intentionally put you in the position I did at the country club. First, I wanted to see how you were going to handle yourself under pressure, and, second, how you were going to interact with our guests. I know I took a gamble with the caliber of individuals who came, but I had the confidence you were going to do a bang-up job. I just had that gut feeling, and my gut feeling has not failed me in the past. As far as I am concerned, Tom, you aced both of them." Tom felt great with the compliments Marcus threw at him. Tom continued to sit patiently to see where the train was going to stop. *Where are on earth is Marcus going with all this?* Tom asked himself again, trying not to lose patience with his boss.

"Tom, for personal reasons, I have opted to retire, but I haven't made it official. I haven't discussed this with anyone other than my wife. I've had the pleasure of knowing you for a long time, and I have valued our friendship and trust tremendously." *OK, enough, Marcus.*

"Tom, I'm offering you the position of president should you decide to accept it." *Now I see why the door was closed.* "Marcus, I don't know what to say. I did not expect this when I woke up this morning." Tom was at a loss for words—this news came from left field.

"The reason I have not made this official is because I wanted to have a replacement in mind before I formally announced it. I don't want to leave the company in limbo plus it would send the wrong signals out there in the market."

Tom sat frozen in his seat at a loss. Marcus noticed Tom was processing everything he said. "I know this is a lot to take in, but I want you to give it serious consideration." Tom realized the impact this decision was going to have on Susan and him. He wanted to discuss it with her before getting back to Marcus.

Chapter 70

Rachel and Susan were having breakfast when Rachel asked, "have you heard from Tom lately? When was the last time you spoke to him?" Susan was used to talking with him on a nightly basis. They were both concerned they hadn't heard from him.

"No, Rachel, I have not heard from him in a couple of days, which is really strange—it's not like him. I know he just got back to work, and he had a big presentation he was asked to make. Do you think I should give him a call to see how he is?" Susan asked worried.

"Susan, give him some space. He probably has a lot on his plate at the moment. Remember, he was away for a couple of months, and he is probably buried in paperwork." Rachel made an attempt to ease Susan's worrying. "Rachel, it's not like him not to take a few minutes before going to bed to say goodnight. He also knows there are three hours difference, and I would still be awake. Maybe something's wrong, or maybe he's hurt?"

"Susan, if you're that concerned, send him a goodnight text," Rachel suggested. "That's a good idea." Susan grabbed her phone and began to type: *Tom, I haven't heard from you in a few days and I miss talking with you. Please let me know you're OK. Love, Susan.*

Tom received Susan's text just before going to bed. When he opened her text, he felt bad he hadn't called nor texted her. With his recent offer of the president's position, he didn't know how to tell her about it. In

Tom's opinion, he felt once Susan heard about the offer, she would readily come to the conclusion he was not going to leave Providence in the near future to move to San Diego. *I'm at a crossroads and I don't know how to tell her*, Tom thought.

Tom had a great deal on his mind: he found the ideal woman in his life whom he loved very much, dealt with a crazy diamond ordeal with Susan, and was offered the position of a lifetime with his company. He could not remain silent with Susan—he had to share his recent promotion with her. He felt it wasn't right to keep all those things bottled up inside.

He also wanted to discuss his new development with Jim, first. Before retiring for the evening, Tom sent a text to Jim to see if they could meet at Starbucks first thing in the morning. Surprisingly, Jim had not gone to bed and he texted Tom back that he would love to meet him for breakfast.

"Tommy, good morning. Good to see you again. You must be very busy at work. Your text last night had a sense of urgency tone to it. What is it?" Jim could see that his brother's body language had a sense of uneasiness.

Tom did not have the vibrant I-have-the-world-in-the-palm-of-my-hands look. With so much on his mind, Tom did not know where to begin, but he knew being with his brother was the best place for him to be at the moment.

"Jim, thank you very much for meeting me this morning. I couldn't sleep a wink last night," Tom said, with a sense of concern. "What in the world has happened to you since we last spoke? Is it Susan? Did you guys have a fight?" Jim was very concerned for

Tom, and he would do whatever it took to get him out of his mood of despair.

"Jim, I cannot believe that I have this fantastic woman whom I can't wait to share my life with, and I also have this fantastic job that I am very fortunate to have." Jim was now totally confused. *What could possibly be wrong with my brother?* Jim asked himself, as he sat dumbfounded and confused on what could be troubling him; nevertheless, here he was—with the world weighing heavily on his shoulders.

"Jim, as you are aware, I would like to sell my house and move to San Diego to be with Susan—she's the most wonderful person I've ever met," Tom paused, and took a sip of his coffee—refills were not too far away. Tom continued, while Jim was riveted to his booth.

"The other day, my boss, Marcus, put me in a precarious position, unbeknownst to me, to make an impromptu presentation to potential wealthy clients. He invited the sales team and me to the country club to meet about a dozen clients to bring over to our company.

I arrived early to the meeting to see if Marcus needed any help setting up. When I inquired if he needed any help, he turned around and threw me a curve ball—he wanted me to make the presentation. I had no idea prior to going to the country club that I was going to make any presentation."

Jim decided to interrupt him—he wanted his brother to take a deep breath. "Hold on to that thought, Tom. I'm going to get two more venti coffees. I think this is going to take a while." Tom sat in his booth while Jim got up to get more coffee—it was going to be one of those get-togethers.

After Jim got back with refills, Tom continued, "as I

was saying, Marcus then gave me his laptop to review the presentation material before everyone else arrived. Jim, I did not know what to say or do at that moment, but look over the slides I was going to present."

"But Tommy, I'm sure you knew the information about your company like the back of your hand." "Jim, it's one thing to service your clients about their financial investments and another is to sell the overall company to total strangers to persuade them to come and join our company." Jim got a clear picture of the position his brother found himself in.

"To make a long story short, I looked over the slides and to my surprise, I made a stellar presentation. Remember, I had just come back from being with the love of my life, and had made up my mind I was going to sell my house and move out west to be with her." Jim stepped in and decided to put everything Tom had outlined into perspective.

"OK, Tom, this all sounds great. You made a bang-up presentation to new clients and you made your boss very happy." "There's more, Jim." "Oh?" "After the presentation, I made the rounds and met with each client—I even chatted with a few in their native language."

"That's great, Tom. You got to practice some of your languages that you rarely used since mom passed away. Is that it?" Jim thought he had heard the end of Tom's trials and tribulations.

"No, I managed to convince four of the people we invited to switch their investments to our company." "That's fantastic! I can only imagine how your boss must have felt. So, you're feeling down after that?" Jim asked, hoping he had heard the end of Tom's woes. "No, there's more."

"What else could there possibly be, Tom? He offered you to run the company?" Jim asked facetiously. "Yes, Jim he did!" "Oh my. Should I congratulate you? Ah, I see where this is going—your plans to move to San Diego might be put on hold?" "Yup!"

"Have you had a chance to share this with Susan?" Jim asked, hoping Tom had informed Susan of everything he had just heard from Tom. "No, I have not and I am torn, Jim. I know I need to discuss all of these things with her."

"Tom, this is big! If Susan means that much to you, and you love her dearly; so much so, that you'd like to live with her for the rest of your life, you need to be honest and up front with her." Tom listened very carefully to Jim's wisdom, and knew Jim hit the nail on the head. *He's totally right on this one. I have to be honest with her and tell her face to face*, he thought.

"Thanks, Jim. I really appreciate your candor and advice. I know that talking to her is the right thing to do." Tom knew what he had to do—he just needed confirmation from Jim.

After several days of Tom remaining incommunicado with Susan, he felt it was very important to finally touch base with her. He did not plan to reveal Marcus' offer to her over the phone, but to inform her he planned to pay her a visit for a few days. The news of the promotion needed to be said in person— it was too big to say over the phone. Susan meant a lot to him, and he needed to communicate all of this in person.

Tom got home, grabbed a bottle of water, and decided to call Susan. "Hi, sweetheart, great to hear from you. Did you forget about me? Don't you love me anymore?" Susan decided to pour it on. "Susan, I hear you loud and clear and I deserve everything you throw at me," Tom informed her apologetically. "Where have you been? I was starting to get concerned. I wanted to call you, but I didn't want to interrupt you."

"As I mentioned a few days ago, there are a lot of things going on at work. We are trying to expand, planning to move our offices, we're changing systems...well, you get the picture," Tom attempted to paint a picture of pandemonium; although, everything he mentioned to Susan was true. "And, you're involved with all that?" Susan asked, with a surprised tone about her. Tom could see Susan was as sharp as a tack.

"In a way, yes. Before it slips my mind, I'd like to pay you guys a visit, if it's not too much of an inconvenience." "That's great. I can't wait to tell Rachel. On second thought, I'm not going to mention it to her. You know how she feels about you — she might make her famous tuna noodle casserole again."

"OK, then tell her pooch I'll be seeing him shortly," Tom threw in a little brevity to clear the tension in his voice. "Tom, I've really missed you since you've been gone. And when I didn't hear from you a few days in a row, I thought you *wrote me off* as you folks say in finance." "Not going to happen, sweetheart. You are stuck with me for as long as you want me." This put a big smile on Susan's face.

"Tom, did you at least have an opportunity to get together with Jim?" "Yes, I did. I met him for coffee the other morning before heading out to work." "How is the old boy?" "You mean my baby brother? He's doing fine. As a matter of fact, Jim mentioned that I looked more relaxed and younger than I have in a long time. I let him know that you have affected me in a very special way. I actually mentioned to him that I would like to spend the rest of my life with you."

"You told him that?" This was great news for Susan to hear at a time where she was very confused and concerned at not hearing from Tom in a few days. "Most definitely. Why not? It's the truth as far as I am concerned. Mind you, I didn't' speak on your behalf. I told him the jury was still out for you." "Tom, really?" Tom enjoyed his tête-à-tête with Susan—their camaraderie couldn't have been more aligned.

"Susan, as I mentioned to you before, after this week it's going to be very hectic at work. If it's OK with you and Rachel, I'd like to visit you guys at the end of the week from Thursday to Sunday. I cleared it with Marcus, and he gave me the green light as he felt I was going to be extremely busy when I got back. All I need is an OK from you and Rachel."

"I think Rachel and I have plans to go out this weekend." Susan attempted to kid with Tom, but she knew it would take more than that. "OK, I'll make it another time. I hope you guys have fun," Tom decided to volley back. "Tom, do you think I'm serious? I was just kidding with you."

"I know you were, I just wanted to play along. OK, when I hang up with you, I'll book my flight for this weekend. Susan, I can't wait to see you and hold you in my arms again," Tom said, in a very serious tone. "Me too, my love." Tom felt more relaxed after chatting with Susan. Somehow, she made it all better. In retrospect, he felt he should have called her sooner.

Chapter 71

As Tom had been working with Marcus for years, he was not only his boss, but he was also a very good friend. Tom decided to pop his head into his office to see if Marcus had a few minutes for him. "Got a minute, Marcus? I don't want to take too much of your time."

"Please, Tom, come on in. After all, this could be your office soon. Have you decided on my offer? Interested?" "Yes, definitely, but since I met Susan, I'd like to pass it by her as a formality. I think this girl is the *one*. That's exactly why I'm planning to visit her this weekend—to go over my position with the company, and to spend some quality time with her. I can't believe I miss her after only being a way for a couple of weeks."

"Tom, that's great you're making her part of the decision. I think she's really going to appreciate your candor and openness. Tom, I wish you the best with Susan; hopefully, I can meet her one day."

Tom set out for San Diego and looked forward to warmer weather and, more importantly, to be with Susan. The little time they've been apart had created a large chasm for him. He looked forward to seeing her again; he couldn't wait to hold her in his arms again. *Where has this woman been all my life?* he thought while on his way to the airport.

How he missed her warm embrace at night, the sweet smell of her perfume, her girlish smile that would light up a room, and the list went on. The effect Susan had on Tom was overwhelming—the effect of his first love—something new and endearing for him.

After going through security, Tom headed to his gate where he anxiously waited to call Susan. "Susan, good morning. I'm at the airport. I should be boarding in half an hour. How are you and Rachel doing? Is she feeling better?" "Tom, please catch your breath. Have you been running?"

"Yes, the traffic to the airport was backed up due to an accident, and when I got to the airport, I ran to security, ran to the gate, and here I am. Phew." "Catch your breath. Hopefully, you can catch a few winks on the plane," Susan suggested for him to get some down time and relax. "That's not a bad idea. It might help me with the time difference when I get to San Diego. How is Rachel?"

"Well, Rachel has been sitting in her car lately playing with her new toy and all the gadgets that came with it. That car has kept her very occupied. In a way, Tom, it's been a great distraction for her. Even little Harvey is feeling it—she's not petting him as much as she used to. I think the little guy is jealous of her Tesla. By the way, she convinced me to let her go to the supermarket on her own."

"And you let her go?" "Sooner or later, she's going to be on her own, and I won't be here to watch her," Susan informed Tom. "I guess you're right, Susan." "Tom, the doctor cleared her, and she's been home for several weeks." "That's great news—our little girl is growing up." "I guess you can say all the babysitting she's had…" Tom had to cut his conversation short as he was ready to board. "Sorry, Susan, I have to run—my row has been called." "Have a good flight sweetheart. I can't wait to snuggle next to you tonight," Susan left

Tom with a comfortable feeling.

Tom sat in a first-class seat for the first time to reward himself for his promotion. The flight attendant came by and offered Tom a drink prior to take-off. He rehearsed in his mind how he was going to approach Susan with the news of the promotion. The last time they chatted, they discussed selling their respective homes in Providence and purchasing a home in San Diego.

Susan and Tom's plans were pretty much set in stone until Marcus upset the apple cart; it created a disruption in Tom's plans whose ripple effects had not yet reached Susan. Tom had known her for a couple of months, and he thought he knew her quite well, but not well enough to know how she was going to react to the big news that still remained in the Genie's bottle.

Tom's mind worked overtime with his new duties and responsibilities which made him very tired. Too much thinking and too much planning had taken its toll on him mentally, as well as physically. He decided to close his eyes and give his mind a rest. For a few hours, he was going to be away from it all and relax.

"Ladies and gentlemen, good afternoon, and welcome to San Diego where the local time is three in the afternoon." Tom faintly heard the news from the flight attendant when they had landed. Tom could not believe five hours had gone by in the blink of an eye.

He turned on his phone and called Susan to let her know his plane had landed. "Hi, Tom, I cannot believe you're already here!" Susan's excitement came over the phone loud and clear. "Can't wait to see you, love. I'll meet you at the baggage area."

Since Tom did not check his bag, he was able to go directly to the baggage area to meet up with Susan. He

did not have the patience for either checking his bag or packing a lot of clothing.

Tom looked for Susan's car, but he was not able to locate it. He finally called her to see where she was. "Tom, Rachel and I are by the median waiting for you; look out for a red Tesla—Rachel will be driving us home." *I guess Rachel's feeling better*, was the immediate thought that crossed Tom's mind.

Tom spotted the shiny candy apple-red Tesla, and ran towards it to meet up with Susan and Rachel. Rachel came out of the car first and ran towards Tom to welcome him with a big hug and a kiss, followed by Susan. "I hope you left me some hugs and kisses," Susan asked her sister, as she approached Tom.

"You see, Tom, my sister has not changed a bit!" Before Susan could say anything else, Tom held her in his arms, and didn't want to let go. He smothered her with kisses. "OK, guys, do you need to get a room?" Rachel commented to Susan and Tom.

Tom knew Rachel well enough for him not to be surprised at anything that came out of her mouth. As a matter of fact, when Rachel was in a coma, it's when she behaved the best. Rachel was Rachel and no one was going to change her, and both Susan and Tom loved her very much for being the person she was.

Chapter 72

"Thanks, Rachel, for picking me up. Your car looks amazing! How do you like it?" Tom asked, while looking at all the gadgets on the dashboard. "I love it! I want to thank you guys again for making it possible." Susan and Tom were very pleased that Rachel was very appreciative for their gift.

Tom was in awe with the car as he looked at the laptop-looking dashboard in the middle of the console. The car had a very futuristic look. This was the first time Tom had been in a Tesla, and he couldn't believe how quiet it was. The doors opened like a spaceship. Thoughts of getting one crossed his mind, but the thought of running out of electricity in the middle of Route 95 scared him.

Rachel explained to Tom that charging stations were very common in California. As a matter of fact, Tesla has a screen that shows you all the charging stations nearest to you. Tom was just in awe; it was like having a new toy.

"Tom, if you like, you and I can go out later and take the car for a spin—you can even drive it, if you like." Susan did not like the sound of that and gave Tom an elbow on his side to signify: *don't even think about it*. Tom got the message loud and clear.

"Thanks, Rachel, maybe tomorrow. I'm exhausted from work and the flight." Susan was very pleased with Tom's response. She was glad they had their own way of communicating.

When they arrived home, Rachel informed Tom dinner would be ready in an hour. "Guess what she's making, Tom?" Susan asked facetiously, knowing full well what it was. "Well, if you are making dinner, Rachel, let me help you set the table," Tom offered, as he opened several cabinets looking for the dishes to set the table.

"Susan, is this guy for real?" "Yes, MY GUY certainly is," Susan stressed certain words to get her point across. "That's not necessary, you're our guest, Tom." "Thanks, Rachel, but I'd like to think that I am part of your family, and this is what families do." "Thanks again, Tom."

Tom needed to find the time to spend with Susan to inform her of the situation he was in at work. He also looked forward to her opinion and input as the promotion would certainly have an impact on the plans they had already discussed and agreed to earlier. *Who would have thought Marcus was going to offer me the position of president?* Crossed Tom's mind over and over.

After dinner, Tom asked Susan if she wanted to take the dog for a walk. "Susan, do you mind if we take Harvey for a walk? I need to stretch my legs from sitting on the plane for so many hours," Tom asked. For the short period of time, she knew Tom, Susan knew him well enough that the request to take the dog for a walk was for more than that.

"I could use a walk as well. Rachel, would you like to join us?" Susan asked to be polite, but she knew Rachel would decline the offer. "Thanks, sis, but I think you guys need to have your alone time as well." "If you change your mind, you are more than welcomed to join us."

"I'm just going to snuggle with a new book I picked up before the accident." "If I may ask, what's it called?" asked Tom. "It's called *Believing in Second Chances*—it had good reviews." "OK, I'll read it after you finish it," Susan said.

"Interesting title, don't you think?" "I suppose there's a lot of truth in that title. How many people go through life and don't get second chances. I was fortunate to have met Tom, and I got a second chance at happiness."

"Susan, I totally agree with you. Had I not taken that train to San Diego, I never would have met you. Just to think, I never would have known what love was all about," Tom informed her, which put a big smile on Susan's face.

Tom and Susan walked the dog under a moonlit night with the temperature in the low seventies. "I wanted to go for a walk with you so we can talk in private—there are several important things I need to discuss with you," Tom informed Susan, in a serious and somber tone.

"Tom, is there something wrong? Was there a reason you couldn't have mentioned it over the phone? Do you have reservations about us?" Susan asked, with a concerned tone of voice.

"Nothing like that, sweetheart. I absolutely have no reservations about us at all. I love you very much, and I would love to spend the rest of my life with you. I believe I've expressed this to you on numerous occasions." Susan listened to every word Tom said, and was worried about the direction the conversation was going. *Maybe he's just very tired*, Susan thought.

"Is this why you came to see me? You didn't want to

give me the bad news over the phone?" Susan asked, as she was beginning to sob. "Susan, I have no bad news for you. It just depends how you will interpret what I'm going to say." Susan grabbed the leash and focused on everything Tom was about to say.

"Do you recall when I told you that Marcus had put me on the spot, and requested that I make a presentation at the last minute before the potential clients at the country club?" Susan nodded, acknowledging Tom's conversation. "Well, it seems Marcus knew in advance and had planned all along to have me make the presentation."

"Why didn't he give you the courtesy to let you know in advance so you could be prepared to make it?" Susan asked a very logical question. "That was the point, Susan. One of his reasons was to see how I would react under pressure." "So, this is what you wanted to share with me in private?" Susan asked, as she stopped for a brief moment and faced him.

"No, not exactly. There's more." Susan was more confused the more Tom spoke. "Another reason was that Marcus wanted to see how I would interact with the potential clients. Not only did I interact well with them, four of them switched their investments over to us, and they specifically requested that I service their accounts."

"Tom, is that it? I don't see why you couldn't have mentioned all of this over the phone, and save you the trip of flying across the country." "Susan, my first purpose for flying across the country was to be with you. I would do that every week because that's what you mean to me," Tom relayed, with a very compassionate tone.

He turned around, held her close, placed both of his

hands next to each side of her neck, and gave her a very endearing and loving kiss. Susan felt his tears of happiness roll down her cheeks. "Tom, I do love you so much." "Susan, I have to share the last part of what I had to tell you." *What else could Tom be holding back*? she thought.

"The reason Marcus put me to a test, for lack of a better word, was that he offered me the position of president of the company." Susan stopped short and asked, "Are you serious?"

"Yes, but I told him that I needed to share this news with you in person first. You are aware this decision could affect both of our lives, and I didn't want to make this decision totally on my own. We are partners in life, and any major decision to be made, I feel, has to be agreed to jointly." Susan stood frozen, and did not know what to say. She felt very important and privileged that Tom made her part of his big decision.

"Tom, you don't need my approval to make this decision." "Susan, I love you dearly, and I wanted to make this decision with you by my side. I want to go through life with you hand in hand." "I don't know what to say—you left me speechless. No one has ever made me part of a big decision like this before." Susan was deeply touched at Tom's feelings for her.

"I am also aware that before I flew back to Providence, we discussed the idea of selling our homes back east and purchasing a new one here in San Diego." "Well, we can still implement part of that plan." "I don't understand, Susan." "I can still sell my home in Providence, and move in with you, if that's OK with you?"

"Of course, it is, but I was under the impression you

wanted to move here to be closer to your sister." "Yes, I wanted that very much, but the timing is not right at the moment. Besides, she could use a break from me for a while."

"So, you'd rather stay in cold Providence for now?" Tom was very pleased to hear Susan's reaction. He had not anticipated hearing this from her. "No, I'd rather be with a very warm-hearted man who loves me very much." *I did not expect Susan to react this way*, he thought, while he looked at her with tear-filled eyes.

Tom was pleasantly surprised how Susan handled his news. "Now, Tom, I'm going to make a decision that I would like your approval on." *What decision could Susan possibly want me to make with her*? Tom wondered. "You know very well I would love to live with you the rest of my life; however, I have a very important question to ask you. I am asking you with all my heart to see if you would like to marry me?"

Tom stood frozen and did not see that one coming either. There was no doubt they were both in love with each other, but he did not expect marriage to be brought up so early in their relationship. This has been a word that has been tossed around by several people in the past month. *I guess they were all trying to tell me something*, he thought.

"Tom, are you here?" Susan tried to get him out of his momentary trance. "Yes, yes, and yes I will definitely marry you." Tom was caught off guard, and had to replay Susan's request over and over in his mind to ascertain if he had heard her correctly.

Who would have thought a train ride from Providence to San Diego took a detour to Nuptial, USA? Neither Tom nor Susan could believe what just happened –a proposal and a promotion in the same week. Susan could not wait to go back to the house and let Rachel know she needed to be fitted for a maid of honor dress.

Similarly, Tom needed to get in touch with Jim so he could be fitted for a best man's tux. Tom also needed to inform Marcus of the acceptance of both the position and the recent marriage proposal.

Susan and Tom arrived back home to tell Rachel the big news. She would be the first to know except for Harvey, but the dog was sworn to secrecy. "Rachel, why are you still awake? Shouldn't you be in bed by now?" Susan asked with both hands on her hips.

"It's only ten o'clock; besides it's not a school night," Rachel said, not surprising Susan with whatever came out of her mouth. "Were you getting ready to go to bed?" "No, sis, I was reading my book and I was waiting for you guys to get back from walking the dog. Did Harvey mark the whole neighborhood?"

"Yes, he did," Susan hesitated, while she knelt down to Harvey to take off his leach. "That is really strange. When I take him for a walk, he sniffs a few bushes, and gets it over with right away. He just wants to go back home and go to bed. I guess he likes to stay out later with you two."

"That's it, Rach. But leaving the dog aside for a moment, we have some news we'd like to share with you." "Oh? OK, let me have it," Rachel caught her breath and was anxious to hear what the lovebirds had to say. Before Susan informed her of the big news, Rachel took a stab, "Are you guys moving in together here in San Diego?"

"No, Rachel. Although that might still be true one

day, but there's more to it. Rachel, we got engaged tonight." Rachel got up from her seat and hugged Susan as though she hadn't seen her in ages. "Really? Can I see your ring?" "No, Rach, we don't have a ring yet; it just happened very suddenly."

"First, we decided to take Harvey for a walk, and as we got talking, well, one thing led to another, and here we are—engaged to get married!" "Tom, did you get down on one knee under the moonlight with violins serenading both of you?" "Tom, do you see what I mean about my sister's imagination? She's really out there." There was no end to Rachel's imagination, and she was at liberty to let the world know about it.

"Guys, are you still selling your houses in Providence and buying one here?" Rachel remembered very well what Tom and Susan had relayed to her not too long ago. "There are a few twists and turns. First, Tom was promoted this week to president of his company." Rachel ran and threw herself to him again. "Congrats, Tom! Congrats sis! I'm so happy for the both of you. Tom, you've made my sister very happy."

Neither Tom nor Susan wished to disclose that it was Susan who had proposed, and not the other way around as it's customary. They just left out that part of the proposal story, but in Rachel's mind, Tom got down on one knee under a moonlit sky and proposed with violins serenading the both of them.

"Rachel, the other news we have is we are not moving to San Diego right away. I will be selling my house in Providence; however, I'll be moving in with Tom. With Tom's promotion, he needs to be in Providence for a while."

For a quick moment, Rachel was a bit disappointed

as she expected both of them to live nearby. "Susan, I am so happy you are moving out of that house—it has too many bad memories for you." Susan nodded and looked down.

"Rachel, I know you wanted us to be here in San Diego with you and we wanted that as well, but his promotion was totally unexpected—a total surprise to Tom and me." "Really, Tom? You had absolutely no idea at all?" "None at all, Rachel. Honest, not a clue." "How about getting engaged to my sister?" Rachel always wanted to know the details of everything.

"As you know, I love your sister very much, and I hoped our relationship would have taken us there one day, but as we said, one thing led to another, and here we are." "Well, guys, I'm truly very happy for you both. Can Harvey be your ring bearer?" Rachel asked, as everyone had a good laugh at her request, which couldn't have come at a better time.

"If you don't mind, guys, I'm going to call my brother and let him know the good news." Tom grabbed the phone, and went outside to give the sisters their privacy to discuss; most likely, wedding preparations. There was a great deal to discuss and plan.

"Hi Jim. I hope I didn't wake you up—it must be late in Providence." "Yes, it's between one and two in the morning here." "What are you doing up so late? Why don't you go back to bed; I'm so sorry for waking you up." "Tommy, you didn't wake me up. I've been watching old movies because I couldn't sleep. That's what happens when you drink coffee later in the day. What's up bro? Why the late call?"

"Jim, can I call you tomorrow to discuss a few things? It's getting very late." "OK, Tom, you're right.

It's already very late here and I should be getting to bed." "I'll call you tomorrow, Jim?" "That sounds great." *Why would Tom call me so late?* Jim's last thought were before he went to sleep.

The following morning, Tom texted Jim if it would be a good time to resume their conversation from the night before. Before providing any background, Tom decided he was going to dive right into the heart of the matter.

"Jim, it happened suddenly. Susan and I got engaged to get married." "Tom, it was only a matter of time the way you had Susan on a pedestal. Congratulations! You really deserve it. Just curious, why the rush?"

"Well, Jim, as we discussed at Starbucks about letting Susan know about the promotion in person, I flew to San Diego to let her know. Well, I asked her to go for a walk, just the two of us, to give her the big news." "That's great, what was her reaction? She must have been very surprised." "I also informed her I wanted to tell her in person of the offer as the decision to accept the job impacted the both of us."

"Jim, she was as surprised as I was when Marcus first offered the position to me. I have to say, she was very mature about it. She felt I needed to be in Providence, and San Diego is, in her own words, *a discussion for another day.*"

"Wow, Tom, she's definitely a keeper. Just curious, how did you propose? On one knee under the stars?" "Have you and Rachel been talking to each other, Jim? No, I didn't propose." "You mean, she did?" "Yup. Bro, she surprised the hell out of me. Two surprises within one week."

"Tom, I am very happy for the both of you." "Thanks. Oh, I almost forgot one very important thing before I let you go, would you be my best man?" "I would be honored, bro." Jim could not believe that not only did his brother start dating, but he also got engaged to get married.

Tom felt he was in a good place after he chatted with Jim. He was fortunate to have a go-to person as Rachel was for Susan. They both felt they had a great deal to do. They also agreed not to be overly consumed with the whole wedding activity, and forget the important things in life — each other.

Tom also had a company to run which was a job he did not have any experience in. At the moment, he was not aware of Marcus' timeline — short or long term. This was one topic of discussion he needed to have when he got back to the office. Fortunately, he knew everyone in the company albeit in a different capacity. In all the years he's been with the company, he's had no one to supervise. Overnight, hundreds of people were to be under his wing.

Chapter 73

The time came when Susan felt very comfortable that Rachel was back to normal. After a few follow-up visits to the doctor, Susan was more convinced and, more importantly, less stressed that Rachel was capable to take care of herself. Needless to say, Rachel looked forward to being left alone with Harvey again. Harvey, on the other hand, did not look forward to Tom's and Susan's leaving, as he was taken for many unexpected walks during the day—a very content dog at that.

"Susan, I don't know how to thank you for all of your time, effort, care and love you have given me after my accident. You literally put your life on hold to take care of me," Rachel said to Susan, with a very warm embrace. Tom knew that tears would soon be flowing. He grabbed a box of tissues and was ready for them. *This is going to be a crying fest*, he thought.

"Rachel, you would have done the same for me, I'm sure," Susan informed her sister, as she pulled back from Rachel's embrace. "With one minor difference, my dear sister," Rachel interjected. Susan was taken aback, and did not know what Rachel meant by that comment. "Oh, how so? Are you inferring that you would have taken better care of me?" Susan asked surprisingly.

"No, silly. I wouldn't have taken any better care of you. I would have just gone home sooner." Tom and Susan just shook their heads in total disbelief expecting to hear nothing less from Rachel. Rachel was her usual self, and no one was going to change her.

After saying their good-byes, both Tom and Susan left to go to the airport. While on their way, Susan shed a few more tears—she hadn't left yet, and she already missed her sister. Tom held her close, and felt a bit sad Susan was going back home rather than staying with her sister in San Diego. He did witness the bond and closeness the two sisters shared.

When Susan and Tom got on the plane, they were shown to the first-class section. "Tom, is this some kind of mistake? Why are we in first-class?" Susan was very surprised, as she had never flown in first class before. "No, Susan, there is no mistake at all. I just feel you should be treated like this once in a while." "But, Tom..." "No ifs, ands, or buts about it. Please sit back and relax." *Wait till Rachel hears about this,* she thought, as she looked around at her large, comfortable seat.

"Tom, you are too good to me," Susan said, as she looked into his eyes. "And, this is a problem, why?" Susan laid her head back on the head rest and closed her eyes. Recollection of her sitting with her eyes closed on the train came to mind. *We both have come a long way since that ride,* Tom thought to himself. He noticed Susan's hand gently held his all the way to Providence.

Tom closed his eyes as well and thoughts of all the things that lay ahead of them, surfaced: planning a wedding, straightening Susan's house after the police turned it upside down, getting her house ready to sell, getting his house ready for Susan to move in, and getting ready for his new job as president of the company. Everything suddenly became overwhelming. *One step at a time,* he lectured himself—*you can't do everything all at once.*

Chapter 74

As they were on their way home from the airport, Tom recommended to Susan for her to stay at his place as her house looked like an unmade bed. They agreed to straighten her house and get it ready to go on the market to sell when they got back. "Tom, I just can't crash at your place. That's your house, not mine." "Susan, that's not my house anymore." "You mean you sold it already?"

"No, the house is *ours*. It now belongs to you and me." Susan was touched by Tom's remark. *What did I do to deserve such a wonderful guy like this one?* she thought. "Thank you, Tom. That's very nice of you. If you don't mind, I would like to stop by my house first, and pack some clothing and things to take to your house."

When Susan and Tom entered her house, she didn't recognize it. *At least they could have straightened the house before leaving,* were one of the many thoughts that came to Susan's mind as she walked through her unkempt home. "Tom, I wonder what the police were looking for when they searched my house."

Tom immediately put his right forefinger on his lips to indicate to Susan not to say anything. Tom took out a pen and wrote on a piece of paper: *the house might be bugged. Watch what you say unless you intentionally want the police to hear something.* Susan had watched enough mystery movies to catch on to Tom's note.

"Didn't you say, Tom, when you came to water my plants, the police had found what they were looking for during their search?" Tom immediately gave her a thumbs up for playing into the possibility the house might be bugged.

As they left Susan's house, Tom and Susan noticed an unusual grey van parked diagonally across from her house. Susan immediately concurred with Tom's theory the house was likely under surveillance.

Susan went into Tom's house for the first time with two bags of clothing while Tom motioned to her where the bedroom was located. "Tom, I see you keep a very neat house for a man," Susan made mention of the condition of the rooms when she entered the house. "Now, what is that supposed to mean? That men in general live in a pigsty?"

"Yes, that is a fact, my love. Go check it out. How is your brother's house?" "Well, Betty always kept a very neat home so Jim was trained early on to live in a neat environment." "What's your excuse, Tom, not that I'm complaining. Has Marie Kondo visited your house lately?" "Susan, I really don't know. I can't give credit to anyone for my neatness. By the way, who is this Marie Kondo lady you referred to?"

"Marie Kondo is this tiny Japanese woman who has a tidying consulting business. She unclutters people's homes; I'm surprised you never heard of her." "Nope, can't say that I have. Anyway, if you give me a few minutes, I'll empty some of the drawers in my dresser so you can put your things in them." "Thanks. If you don't mind, I can empty some of them for you."

"Not a problem, make yourself at home." When Susan approached the dresser and opened the first drawer she pulled out, she was flabbergasted. "Oh my, Tom. I take back that neatness comment I made. Your drawers look like you stuffed your clothes in there. First thing tomorrow, I'm going to call Marie Kondo to come and help you," Susan was in the mood to pick on Tom.

The following day, Tom and Susan went out for breakfast to discuss all the things that needed to be done. "Susan, I'm planning to go to the office on Tuesday to meet with Marcus and develop a transition plan for him to leave the company. As of now, I don't know his sense of urgency to leave the company."

"Tom, it looks like you have a lot on your plate with the wedding, selling my house and your new job. The only way I can help you with your new job is to make it easier for you on my end. I can straighten my house, start throwing things away and call a realtor to list the house. I'll probably get good staging ideas from the realtor."

"Do you have a realtor in mind, Susan?" "No, I don't. I'll go online and check the reviews." "I'll check on my end to see what realtors invest with us. We also need to talk about our wedding. Do you think we need a wedding planner?" Susan and Tom had a great deal to discuss.

"The first thing I would like to do is go shopping." "Shopping for what?" Susan asked. "For an engagement ring for you. I would like to get you something nice. Once we pick a ring, we need to decide on a date. Do you have a date in mind, Susan?" Tom's wheels were already spinning. "No, I don't, Tom."

"The only thing I have on my mind is that I want to marry you." "I, as well, Tom. Did you have any thoughts on how many people you would like to invite? I'm thinking we should have a small wedding—nothing too elaborate. What about you?" "I agree, just a small wedding with family and close friends. It looks like we're making progress. You come up with your list, and I'll come up with mine."

"Sounds like a plan, Tom." "We also have another option we haven't discussed." "And, that is?" "We can always get married by the justice of the peace, and have a nice dinner with close friends and family afterwards. I can go either way. It all depends if you would like to walk down the aisle or go to City Hall?"

"To be honest with you, Tom, I'd rather go to the justice of the peace in a few months, and reserve a fancy restaurant to celebrate our special day with family and friends. I was not aware which way you wanted to go as this is your first wedding, Tom." "OK, settled. Justice of the peace it is."

Tom and Susan felt they had a good breakfast and a few major decisions were made: to get Susan's house on the market, to get married by the justice of the peace, and best of all, to go shopping for an engagement ring for Susan.

"Susan, I have a dinner scheduled with Jim, and I would very much like for you to join us for you to meet him." "That sounds wonderful; I would really like to finally meet him." Tom was pleased Susan looked forward to meeting Jim. "OK, I'll call the restaurant and change the reservations to three." "Tom, I don't want to intrude on your dinner with your brother if you guys had already made plans."

"No, not at all. It was my idea to have dinner with him so I can introduce you if you were going to be available. I also let him know that I was not certain if you were going to make it, so I'm glad that you are. Jim is going to be very excited that he's finally going to meet you."

"Is this place we're going to for dinner fancy?" "Have you heard of Fleming's on Exchange Street?" "Yes, I did. It's a little on the fancy side for me." "Don't worry about it, you'll fit right in—you're a classy lady." "Thanks, but I would like to go shopping for a nice dress. I'll catch up with you later at your house." Susan wanted to make a good impression on Tom's brother.

After Susan agreed to go out to dinner with Tom and his brother, Tom called Jim to confirm they were still on for dinner. "Jim, are we still on for tonight?" "Yes, Tom. I'm in the mood for a steak tonight. Did you ask Susan to join us?" Jim asked, with excitement in his voice that he was finally going to meet Tom's mystery woman. "Yes, I did. She's looking forward to meeting you as well. I have to go; Susan is calling. See you tonight."

"Susan, hi, is everything OK?" "Yes, I called to see if you got in touch with Jim to let him know I was going to join you guys tonight? Also, is there a dress code in that restaurant?" "Yes, Jim is looking forward to meeting you—I just got off the phone with him. As far as the dress code is concerned, the guys usually wear slacks and a sports jacket." "Ties?"

"No, no ties. Today when people go out to dinner, suits and ties have become a thing of the past; people like to dress comfortably when they go out to dinner." "Will you be wearing a tie to our wedding dinner?" "Of course, I will. I decided sweats would not be appropriate." "OK, my love, I'll see you at your house," Susan was never surprised at Tom's sense of humor.

Tom went home to make room for Susan's things in his dresser. They still had to work out the details on how they were going to combine their furniture. As he looked around his house, he found it hard to believe he was going to share his home with someone else for the first time in his life. Every now and then Tom had to stop to get a reality check that he had met someone, fell in love, and was on the threshold of getting married.

For Tom, it was a great deal to absorb that so much has happened in a very short period of time. In the back of his mind, he thought about the plans he and Susan had made about moving west, and how those plans got tabled when he got promoted. He felt he had to make it up to Susan, one way or another.

Tom decided to go to the kitchen and make a pot of coffee when he heard a car door slam. Houses in the neighborhood were close to one another. It could have been from a neighbor so he didn't give it much thought. Suddenly, his doorbell rang. He walked over to the door and noticed it was Susan struggling and trying to balance many shopping bags.

"Susan, great to see you. Please, let me give you a hand with all those packages. Why did you ring the door? This is your house as much as it is mine," Tom asked, as they walked into the house with all the shopping bags.

"First, I don't have a key; and, second, your door was locked." Tom immediately went to his kitchen drawer and pulled out a spare key for her. "Did you buy out the stores, sweetheart?" Tom asked, as he put his arms around her and gave her a big welcome home kiss.

"Tom, do you remember the time when we were on the train and I had to explain to you about *retail therapy*?" "Yes, that's when women who are stressed go shopping to relieve stress." Tom remembered well the lesson Susan had taught him. "Wow, Tom, you were really listening! I am so impressed." "Are you stressed out?"

Tom asked, as he looked at all the packages Susan had brought into the house.

"Tom, do we need to go over everything we've been through since we met?" "No need, my dear—enough said." Susan realized that Tom got the picture very quickly. *Maybe he put all that out of his mind*, she thought.

Susan proceeded down the hall to unpack all the shopping bags she had binged on. "Before I take a shower, what time do we need to leave here to meet up with Jim?" "We should leave here in a couple of hours." "That's great, that gives me plenty of time. I'll join you for a quick cup of coffee before taking a shower," Susan informed Tom to spend a little time with him before leaving for the evening.

Afterwards, Susan went to get ready to go out to dinner. She had gotten a very nice elegant black cocktail dress with high heels. Tom was a half a foot taller so she wanted to add a little height to herself. She was also interested in impressing Tom's younger brother. After all, she's heard so much how Jim tried all of his life to set Tom up with a date.

After a few hours, Tom turned around and noticed how Susan was dressed. "Susan, you look fantastic! I cannot believe my eyes—you look stunning!" Tom's jaw dropped to the floor. She was very pleased that her man reacted like that. "Well, Tom, can I assume you like the dress?" Susan asked, knowing full well from his reaction that Tom went gaga over her. Tom approached her and walked around her to see if she was real.

"Are you OK, Tom?" "Susan, I don't' know what to say. You are the most beautiful woman I've ever seen—your dress, your shoes, your earrings; I mean everything goes very well in perfect harmony," Tom was definitely speechless at the way she looked.

While Tom and Susan drove to the restaurant, Tom occasionally glanced at Susan trying to convince himself she was really going to marry him. He still did not believe that he was about to marry this beautiful woman.

"Jim, I would like to introduce you to my fiancée, Susan," Tom proudly introduced Susan to his brother. "Nice to finally meet you, Susan. Your boyfriend talks about you all the time, and now I can see why." Jim was stunned at the way Susan was dressed. "He didn't tell me how beautiful you looked. Was this intentional, Tom?" Tom was still in awe himself on how beautiful Susan looked. He never had the pleasure of seeing her all dressed up—she looked very elegant.

"Susan, I do have to say my brother is a very lucky guy." "On the contrary, Jim, I am the one who is very lucky to have him in my life." Susan smiled at Tom when she answered Jim. "Tommy, she's definitely a keeper." Tom was very proud of her. They talked for hours. Jim made it very obvious he approved of Susan. Tom was certain he was going to get an earful the following day from his brother.

On the way home, Tom and Susan chatted how nice the restaurant was and how great the food was. She also found Jim to be a very nice guy. "Tom, your brother is very nice and personable. I'm certain Rachel would also approve. Has your brother dated much since his wife passed away?" Susan was very curious to hear how outgoing Tom's brother was after his wife died.

"If I recall correctly, it was pretty rough for him the first year after Betty passed away. His wife was very sick for a while. After the first year, he had casual acquaintances but nothing serious. He found it hard to get into the dating scene again after so many years of being married. Are you thinking what I'm thinking?" "The possibility that Rachel and he might click? How old is your brother?" Susan inquired, to find more information about Jim.

"I believe he and Rachel are about the same age, give or take a few years. We'll see if there's a fit for those two in the next couple of months. That reminds me, Susan, we should decide on a venue soon before time passes us by. What about the place we had dinner tonight?"

"That was very nice. We could have it there, or we can look around to see if there's another place you would prefer." "Let's see if we can reserve a place by the end of next week. Since tomorrow is Sunday, we should sit down and consider other options."

"Tom, I'm going to call you Mr. Planner." "And speaking of next week, I would like to go out with you on Monday and get you a nice engagement ring." "That would be nice, Tom. Do we need to do this right away?" "Absolutely! A beautiful ring for a beautiful woman." "What am I going to do with you, Tom?"

"Also, what do you think about going to Disney World for our honeymoon?" "Tom, I've learned that you really pay close attention to whatever I tell you." "I just want to make your dreams come true." Susan smiled at Tom's recommendation for a honeymoon. *He remembered it was a place that made me happy in my dreams*, she recalled.

Chapter 75

*O*n Sunday, Tom and Susan decided to go to her house and look around to see what needed to be thrown away or donated to charity. As the police had already scattered everything on the floor, it made it a little easier for her to determine what was to be kept, thrown away, or donated. Susan couldn't believe the mess the police had made out of her house. She just wanted to clean it up and move on. Her house continued to hold bad memories for her.

When they approached Susan's house, they noticed the same unidentified van parked in the same place — diagonally from her house. "I know, we have to watch what we say when we get into the house," Susan recalled the possibility her house might be bugged. "Yes, please, let's play it safe. Maybe we are wrong, and we hope we are. I guess I'm guilty of seeing too many mystery movies myself."

"Do you think they are listening to what we say in the house? The van does have three antennas on its roof." "Let's assume they are the police. I don't think we should take any chances after you found a box full of diamonds in it," Tom brought up the diamonds.

Within an hour of packing garbage in large, heavy-duty black plastic bags, the doorbell rang. "I wonder who that could be on a Sunday — I usually don't get any visitors." Susan moved the draperies aside from the living room window to see who it could be. She noticed a well-dressed individual. *I wonder who that is,* she thought.

Susan opened the door. Since it was cold outside, she allowed the visitor to come in to the house to chat. "Good afternoon, Miss, my name is Randall Lapointe; I'm a good friend of Max. My apologies for stopping by on a Sunday, but I have an important matter to discuss with you. Ma'am, did you have an intruder in your house?" Randall asked, as he noticed everything spread out on the floor. "May I please speak with Max?" Susan and Tom looked at each other in total bewilderment. Apparently, this person had not gotten the memo as well.

"I'm sorry sir, if I may ask, how do you know Max?" Susan asked with intense curiosity. "Max and I met at the post office. He was very helpful when I needed assistance." *Something's not right. Max worked in the backroom and had no customer contact*, recollected Susan.

"Ma'am, I came for a package he was holding for me. I had to go out of the country for a while, and your husband was very kind to hold on to it for me until I got back. Is he around?" At this point, Tom hoped the mysterious van parked across the street was the police, and they were listening to their conversation.

"Mr. Lapointe, I'm so sorry you had to make the trip, but my husband is no longer here," Susan informed Randall. "Would you happen to know how I can get a hold of him?" Susan stopped short of saying he was in *hell*, and Tom sensed it, but she behaved and held her tongue. "Mr. Lapointe, my husband died nine months ago." Immediately, they noticed Randall's complexion change. They knew very well the box he was referring to.

"Mr. Lapointe, the mess you see around the house

was not from an intruder, but the police. Last week when my fiancée came to water my plants while I was away, the police came with a search warrant and trashed my place. As you can see, this is the result of their search," Susan pointed out to him, as she moved with the open side of her hand from one side of the room to the other.

"What were they searching for? Do you have any idea?" "I have absolutely no idea, sir. As a matter of fact, my fiancée asked one of the police officers if they had found what they were looking for, and one of them said they had." Tom and Susan could see from Randall's body language, it was something he didn't want to hear.

"Do you think if I were to go to the police, I would be able to claim my box?" Randall asked, anxiously waiting to get a response from either one of them. *Good luck with that*, pondered Tom. "Also, Mr. Lapointe, if it was your box my husband was holding for you, what was in that box, if I may ask? And do you have any idea why the police were looking for it, if in fact that was your box you think the police took?"

"Miss, I truly don't know what the police were looking for," Randall said, as he attempted to give the impression that he didn't have any idea what box Tom and Susan referred to. "Everything from my cabinets and closets are on the floor as you can see. If you would like to walk around and see if you come across the contents of that box, please be my guest. I forgot to ask you, Mr. Lapointe, how big was the box that Max was holding on for you so we can be on the lookout for it?"

Randall proceeded to describe the dimensions of a box similar in size to the box Susan had come across. Susan and Tom were not aware of the size of the box the police claimed they found. The lovebirds hoped the police were across the street and were listening to Randall's conversation.

"Mr. Lapointe, I have a business card one of the policer officers left with me in the event I came across anything unusual in the house." Tom took out a card from his wallet and proceeded to show Randall. "Do you mind if I take a picture of it so I can ask the police officer about the box they claim they found?"

"Sure, I have no problem with that. Also, Mr. Lapointe, please take my number down in case you need anything from us. May we have yours as well?" "Thank you, Tom, I will gladly do that and here's mine." Susan was quiet for a while until she asked,

"Mr. Lapointe, do you mind sharing with me what was in the box you are looking for in the event we come across it? Maybe the police found your box and threw the contents on the floor with everything else." "I assure you, ma'am, the police would not have emptied the contents of the box on the floor."

"From your reaction, Mr. LaPointe, were the contents of the box valuable?" "Ma'am, I want to thank you for all of your time and assistance today, and, please do not hesitate to call me should you come across any unusual box." "Will do, sir." Randall left and Susan and Tom looked at each other perplexed.

Tom took out a piece of paper and wrote: *I wonder if that was a detective asking questions to see what our reaction would be.* Susan shrugged her shoulders and said, "you never know, that certainly is a possibility."

Susan and Tom continued to pack both of their cars with plastic bags to take to Goodwill. The furniture Susan did not plan to take to Tom's house was placed in the garage to be picked up by Habitat for Humanity.

While they packed the cars, Tom turned towards Susan and asked, "what are your thoughts of contacting the police officer who gave me his card and inform him about the visitor we had today?" Susan gave it some thought and offered her opinion.

"First, it can't hurt to let them know we're on their side; and, second, we can inform them there's someone else out there looking for the same thing they are." "It's also possible that Randall may just be the police in disguise." Tom and Susan tossed all possible scenarios of their recent visitor. "Even so, it could demonstrate to the police we have nothing to hide and we have attempted to assist them in their search."

"OK, Susan, I'll call the police in the morning. If you're up to it, we can continue to pack more plastic bags. I have a question that I wish to ask you, and, believe me, I'm no exception. Why do we hold on to so much garbage in our lives?" "Because, Tom, it is easier to hold on to it than to make a decision to throw it away." "I guess you're right, my dear."

Chapter 76

Tuesday morning came quickly enough, and Tom was ready to conquer the world in his new job. Marcus and he decided to have their first breakfast meeting away from the office to talk in private. This was a new venture for Tom which he had never anticipated nor for that matter, considered. If someone had informed him a few months ago he was going to be president of his company, he would have laughed at them.

As usual, Tom arrived early to the restaurant. Marcus had already arrived and waited for him at a corner table requested by Marcus for privacy. "Good morning, Tom. I see your trip to San Diego was a very successful one. You went as a single man, and you came back engaged. Did you have any idea you were going to propose when you left for San Diego?"

"Marcus, here's the funny thing. I had absolutely no idea I was going to come home engaged because I had no immediate intentions of proposing." Marcus, at this point, appeared a bit confused, and Tom noticed there was some confusion in Marcus' face.

"As you know, I went to San Diego to inform Susan about the promotion you so kindly offered me. One thing led to another, and she proposed to me. And, no, she did not get down on one knee. Marcus, she totally caught me off guard. I had no doubt I would propose to her one day, but I had no inkling at all she was going to do it now."

"Well, how do you feel about it?" "I feel great, and

I'm very happy about it. She's a wonderful girl who I would like to spend the rest of my life with." "I'm very happy for you, Tom—you deserve it."

After all the pleasantries were discussed, Marcus decided to get down to business. "First, thank you for accepting the position of president of the company. I have known you for many years, and I have trusted you implicitly. You have always been very honest with me, and your work ethics are second to none." Tom listened very carefully to Marcus and he appreciated his candor and faith in him.

Marcus continued, "I have already sent out a companywide memo informing every one of your promotion to be president of the company. To date, I have received kudos from practically everyone on my choice to succeed me. Needless to say, I did get the approval of the board of directors first before I offered you the position—they voted unanimously. It seems you are in good standing with many of the members because there was hardly any discussion prior to the vote. I'm also very familiar you have counseled many of them with their financial matters."

"Marcus, we have known each other for many years, which brings me to a very important question I would like to ask you…" As Tom was in the midst of finishing his question, Marcus interrupted him. "You are going to ask me why all of a sudden I've decided to step down, aren't you?" "Yes, Marcus, I guess you read my mind."

"Tom, there comes a point in everyone's life whether to take one road or another. Sometimes, there are factors beyond our control that lead us to that point quicker than anticipated. My health has forced me to make this decision. Remember, when one is on his death bed, one doesn't ask to have one more day of work, but for one more day to spend it with one's family. As you will see, your family is the most important thing in life. Material things can be bought and sold, but a family cannot. Once they are gone, they are gone—they cannot be replaced."

"Fortunately, my wife is still with me, but our children and grandchildren are all over the country, and we would like to spend more time with them. Running this company is up to you now. I'll always be here for you. I'm very much aware I put a lot on your shoulders, but deciding who my replacement was going to be was an easy one. You deserve it, my friend."

"Marcus, I don't know what to say, but thank you very much for giving me the opportunity and putting your trust in me. More importantly, I'm so sorry to hear about your illness; Susan and I will pray for you and Michelle." "Thanks, Tom."

"Marcus, with your guidance, I would like to develop a plan to make the transition as seamless as possible. I have big shoes to fill and I would like to do whatever it takes to fill them. First, I would like to meet one-on-one with the staff that reports directly to you, and ensure that I have a team of professionals I can work with. The emphasis, in my opinion, is on the clients who make our company successful—without them we have no company."

"Tom, what did you do with my Tom? How did you just come up with all this?" "I believe this a logical approach to take, isn't it?" "Most definitely, Tom. It looks like you're on your way to becoming an effective executive. Also, as you know, Darlene, my executive assistant, is top shelf. I hope you keep her on as your executive assistant as well."

"Marcus, I have worked with her for many years, and I have the greatest admiration and respect for her. We're going to work very well together as an effective team. If I may ask you another personal question, do you have a date in mind for the transition?"

"Yes, that was the next topic I wanted to discuss with you. I am shooting for a month from today. Does that work for you?" "Marcus, you are a hard act to follow. Please stay as long as you wish—maybe in a consulting capacity, if you like? I'll respect whatever you decide; you've been my mentor for many years, and I will treasure that for many years to come."

"I have also learned in life that you don't overstay your welcome. I've given some thought to your recommendation, but I've decided to cut the cord in one month's time." "I respect your decision, sir. Does anyone else know about your time frame?" "Just my wife and Darlene."

"Marcus, if there's anything I can do for you, I'm here for you." "Believe me, Tom, by accepting the position, you have already done a great deal for me. You have allowed me to leave with a good conscience." Tom smiled and shook his hand along with a small hug when they left. Tom had a great deal of admiration and respect for Marcus.

When they got back to the office, everyone stopped by Tom's desk to congratulate and wish him luck. Tom's first day back with a new title felt different from any other time when he had returned to the office. He now felt a sense of responsibility to both the company and to all the staff who worked there.

More importantly, he wanted to make sure he didn't get himself in the same boat as he had before. He recalled very well how he couldn't get up from the floor in his bedroom from all the stress that had accumulated in his life. Words of wisdom from his doctor/client, Dr. Prescott, continued to resonate in his mind: *to take it easy.*

He also recalled that it was Dr. Prescott who stressed with him to slow down. In so doing, Tom chose to take a train ride across the country to San Diego where he met Susan, the love of his life.

Chapter 77

"Tom, how was your first day at the office as prez?" "Thanks for asking. As you know, I met with Marcus first thing this morning for breakfast away from the office — we felt it was more private. At the office, you never know who was going to barge in and interrupt us. There's always something pressing in an office that requires immediate attention. Overall, it went well. Marcus is a good guy; he felt he needed a change in his life and he made the decision to retire."

"How long is he going to babysit you?" "He said a month from today, but I informed him he could stay as long as he wanted." "Tom, how do you feel about the change after your first day?" Susan was very interested on how Tom's first day as president of the company was.

"The most important thing that I learned from personal experience, is not to let the job get to me and stress me out. I have to be conscious I have the right team in place to coordinate all the activities of the company so we can reach our goals — it has to be a team effort. Susan, I also learned that I cannot do everything by myself." Susan was very impressed with Tom's attitude and approach to his new job.

"Can you imagine if you let this job get to you again?" "Yes, I would probably take a train to San Diego and meet someone in the first car." "You are not getting back on any train — I don't like the odds." "You know, any train I take in the future will have you as a passenger sitting next to me." Susan felt Tom could always make her feel at ease—one of the many things she loved about him.

"Are you hungry after a long hard day at work?" Susan asked, ready to surprise him with a home cooked meal. "A bit, would you like to go out for dinner?" "No, let's stay in tonight, you must have had a very busy day." "Thanks, what is that I'm smelling?" Tom asked, as he took in several deep breaths to see if he could identify the source of the aroma in the air.

"Does it smell good, Tom?" "Yeah, as a matter of fact, it does." "Great, I hope you like it. It's Mrs. Paul's fish sticks." At first, Tom thought Susan was joking, but soon learned she was not when she put the tartar sauce on the table. "Wow, Susan, you went all out. Is this a special occasion?" Tom asked with a smirk on his face.

"Nothing but the best for my future husband." "That's the first time I was referred to by the name *husband*. And that would make you…" "Yes, your future wife." Tom stopped for a moment to take in those names. "Tom, are you here? Where are you?" Susan asked, concerned with Tom's blank stare. "Susan, I went over and over in my mind *future husband*."

"Tom, are you getting cold feet?" "Absolutely not, sweetheart. This was the first time I heard those words, and they caught me off guard—I had not heard them before." "That's understandable." Tom thought this was not the first time Susan had heard the title of *wife* before, but he was not about to inflict any pain on her by bringing it up; it's bad enough she's aware of it. *My goal in life is to always make her happy to drown that pain out of her life*, Tom thought, and made it a life-long mission to accomplish.

"Thanks for dinner—it was very nice of you to cook.

When will you be making Rachel's famous tuna noodle casserole? Did Rachel happen to give you the recipe?" "Tom, are you pulling my leg? You know that I'm saving that dish for a special occasion." Susan knew how to throw it back to Tom. *Two can play the same game*, Susan thought, as she smiled and was happy they had that kind of repartee.

"How was your day, sweetheart?" Tom asked. "Well, I went back to my house and packed more things to be thrown away and donate." "Was that mystery van still parked in the same spot?" Tom curiously asked.

"Yes, it was. And speaking of the mystery van, I called the police officer who was on the business card you had. I informed him there was an individual who stopped by and inquired about a box that my late husband, Max, had kept for him while he was away." "And?"

"Well, he paused for a moment, and then asked me if I remembered the person's name so I provided him with Randall's name. I also informed the officer that Randall planned on calling him to see if he could claim the box the officers found during their search." "He probably laughed his ass off when he heard that," Tom said smiling. "That's exactly what I thought as well." They both shared a good laugh at Randall's expense.

"The officer also wanted me to elaborate about the box they found. I told them I had no idea the box they referred to. I really think sometimes these guys like to play games to see if people are straight with them. Well, I gave the officer Randall's phone number for him to contact him personally. It should be very interesting to see if the police will actually contact him."

Since Tom and Susan were in Tom's house having

dinner, they felt they could speak more freely, and not be concerned that the house they were in was bugged. "I thought all this craziness with the diamonds was behind us, but somehow the diamonds have a way of creeping back into our lives."

"The puzzling fact, according to one of the officers who searched my home and claimed they had found what they were looking for, is whether there's another box hidden in the house." "I don't know, Susan, but it certainly raises doubts whether there is, in fact, a second box. We know for a fact you found one box. Whether the police found another one or not will be a mystery, and we may never find out. If you recall, Jacob only inquired about one box. Do you have an attic in the house or a crawl space underneath the house?"

"Yes, I have both an attic and a crawl space." "I don't know if the police searched those areas. They looked as if they were on a mission, and I didn't want to get in their way." "Did you happen to see any of the officers leave with anything in their hands?"

"No, I didn't. I was overwhelmed with all the activity to notice anything like that. It was only after they were finished and they were on their way out, that I decided to ask one of them if they had found what they were looking for, and one of them, surprisingly, said yes."

After dinner, Susan and Tom decided to go back to Susan's house to pack more plastic bags with clothes to donate to Goodwill. While in the car, they decided to chat more about Randall. "It does appear Randall was looking for Jacob's box." "Do you recall whether Randall's name was on that box?" "No, I don't recall, I just looked for a name and address to return the box back to the sender."

"It is possible Max may not have stolen the box from the post office after all." "Tom, the police told me they had a video surveillance of Max taking the box." "Maybe Max was in the process of transferring the box from one station to another within the post office. We will never know that for sure."

"Maybe there's some truth to Randall's claim that Max looked after the box for him while he was out of the country." "As far as I'm concerned, that claim seems to be farfetched. Why would anyone give a box to Max to keep in safekeeping for such a long period of time?" "Tom, I've come to that same conclusion. If we were to find a second box, if there were to be such a box, I recommend we turn it over to the police." "I don't want to get on that roller coaster ride again."

Tom stopped what he was doing, and just stared at Susan while he packed her house. He found it hard to believe that they were on the threshold of getting married. *How life puts you in different situations that changes your whole life entirely in an instant,* Tom thought.

"Tom, why are you staring at me? Is there something wrong?" Susan asked. Tom dropped what he was doing and slowly walked towards her. "Tom, are you OK?" Susan asked again, concerned what Tom was up to. Tom held her in his arms, and gave her a very passionate kiss.

"Susan, I'm just crazy!" "Like mentally crazy, Tom?" "No, I'm madly in love with you, and I'm so fortunate to have you in my life." "Tom, as am I. I can't believe it was not too long ago…" "Shh," motioned Tom with his forefinger on his lips.

"Susan, isn't it time to go out and pack the cars with

the bags we packed?" Tom asked, as he gave her a wink and moved his head to the right signifying to leave the house. Susan nodded in agreement.

When they got into the car after loading the bags in the trunk, Susan resumed her conversation. "Tom, I forgot that my house may be bugged. As I was saying, it was not too long ago when we were both on a train ride to San Diego, and; somehow, you got into an empty car on the train with only the three of us; myself, Jacob and his partner, Joseph. As you are aware, all the seats had been purchased by Jacob so the three of us could exchange the diamonds. Lucky for me, you purchased a seat just before Jacob bought the entire car out." "Talk about timing, Susan."

"Susan, when you opened the box and saw that it contained diamonds, did it cross your mind to take them to the police?" "Most definitely, but I didn't because of the possible ramifications they would have created. First, I would have been interrogated by the police as to why they were in my possession. Second, do you think the police would have believed me, Tom?"

"But the police had a video of Max taking the box." "I didn't know that at the time I found the box. I only found out about the video when I spoke to the police as they were about to search my house. Tom, we can talk about this until the cows come home, and discuss all different options I could have taken, but nothing is going to change what already has happened."

"I'm very glad you didn't opt to take the diamonds to the police." "Why?" "Had you taken the diamonds to the police, you wouldn't have taken a train ride to San Diego, and we wouldn't be here talking about it." "So, I guess I did the right thing after all? Thanks, Tom." "I have my whole life to thank you for it, Susan." "Were you always a romantic at heart?" "I guess you bring that out in me."

Tom was very comfortable and happy. Who would have thought that love was to be found in the first car of a train headed to San Diego? Neither Susan nor Tom had planned on it, and neither one of them thought, at the time, that the train ride would change their lives forever.

Chapter 78

Marcus and Tom worked together practically every day while Marcus counted down the days for his big departure. Had Marcus not gotten sick, he never would have contemplated leaving a company he had devoted all his life to. Marcus was very pleased and had no reservations about turning the company over to Tom. Marcus had worked with Tom very closely over the years and admired his dedication to the company. More importantly, Marcus admired Tom's dedication to his clients—he always put them first and never lost focus of that.

Tom now came to the office in a suit—a practice he did not have prior to his promotion. Everyone noticed his change in attire, and, according to many, he looked very presidential. Everyone also noticed that Tom's promotion didn't change his personality. He was always pleasant and helpful with everyone. This was a new era for Tom, and he felt comfortable stepping into Marcus' shoes.

On several occasions, Tom and Marcus' personal assistant, Darlene, met privately to discuss Marcus' going away party. Tom was very pleased with Darlene's take-charge attitude; one of the reasons Marcus requested Tom to keep her on staff after he left. In turn, Darlene enjoyed working with Tom over the years, so his promotion did not change the way she felt towards him—they just worked closer together on a daily basis.

Darlene suggested that Tom and his future wife ask

Marcus to have dinner at the club for his surprise retirement party. Tom concurred it would be a great idea on many fronts. First, for Marcus to meet Susan, and, second, to get him to the club for his surprise going-away party.

"Marcus, if you are available for dinner at the country club next week, I would like to introduce you to my future wife, Susan. Are you and Michelle available next Saturday for dinner at the club?" "Tom, that's very nice of you, we look forward to meeting the girl who managed to sweep you off your feet." Tom was very pleased to hear that Marcus and his wife were going to join Susan and him for dinner at the club. The wheels were set in motion to give Marcus a surprise send-off.

Tom couldn't wait to tell Susan about Marcus' going away party, and have her wear the same black cocktail dress she wore when they went out to dinner with Jim—she looked so elegant in it.

Marcus deferred to Tom to make decisions and made it a point to introduce Tom to the large clients he had brought into the company. "Part of the job is to continue to cultivate and bring in large clients to the company—it's our bread and butter. When I put you on the spot at the country club to make the presentation, I was very impressed with your performance. Now it's part of your job to continuously bring in those big clients. And, you have to do this while you're running the operations of the company. This is a big job; however, you have proven to me over the years that you can handle it. I wish you the best, my friend."

"Thanks, Marcus. I really appreciate the support you've given me in the last couple of weeks." Tom was also extremely thankful for Marcus' support over the years; more so now, that he was about to take over the company.

When Tom got home, he shared his day with Susan. "It looks like you're going to fit right in. I have a lot of faith that you'll do well." Tom loved the way Susan supported him in everything he set out to do.

"Thanks, sweetheart. Your support means a lot to me. Who would have thought two months ago that my life was going to go through such a transformation? I remember a movie, the name escapes me at the moment, where the main character in that movie said that *your life is like a box of chocolates; you don't know what you're going to get*." "I vaguely remember that movie, but I do recall that line." "As your life has changed, so has mine — for the better that is."

Both Tom's and Susan's life changed dramatically for the better from the moment they met. Susan had lost her husband and found a box of diamonds. Tom fell out of bed afraid he was not going to walk again. Each took a train across the country in search for something: Tom, to get his life back, and Susan to look for peace and tranquility in her life. Neither had anticipated that they would have found each other the way they did — that was not in the cards for them.

"Tom, how is everyone reacting to the fact you are now his or her boss?" Susan asked, curious to find out how everyone was towards Tom in his new role as president. "Fortunately, everyone has been very supportive. Before I forget, the company is throwing a surprise going away party for Marcus at the club next week."

"That's really nice of you all to do that." "As far as I know, he has no idea we're throwing him a going away party "Am I invited?" Susan asked, assuming it was just for the employees of the company. "Yes, you and I are taking Marcus and his wife to dinner. At least, that's what he thinks. Unbeknownst to him, everyone from the office will be there to send him off. More importantly, Marcus is also looking forward to meeting you."

"Tom, that's fantastic. You mean he doesn't have a clue?" "I don't think so. Darlene and I have kept it to ourselves. We are going to tell everyone personally so there are no emails that will go astray and wind up in the wrong hands."

"Oh my, I just realized I have nothing to wear." "You can wear that great black cocktail dress you wore when we out with Jim." "You think that would be appropriate for this type of occasion?" "Most definitely. I think that would be great, or, if you like, go and get another dress." "That would be wasteful, Tom, if I already have a dress." Tom was surprised to see the frugal side of Susan, not that he minded.

Tom continued, "Susan, you would look fantastic in anything you wear." "Thank you. You're such a darling." "As a matter of fact, everyone is dying to meet the girl who swept me off my feet." "Am I supposed to be your trophy girlfriend, Tom?" "Trophy? What's that? Is that like retail therapy?"

"Where have you been? A trophy wife, as it's usually referred to, is when someone is regarded as a status symbol for the husband." "Susan, you are teaching me so much. Remember, I worked all my life seven days a week, and I didn't get out much as you can see." "Duh, really? That's one of the things I love about you." "That I lived in a cocoon?" "No, my dear. That you are just you and that makes you very special."

Chapter 79

For Marcus' retirement party, Susan decided to wear the same black cocktail dress, high heels, and wore her hair up as she did when Tom and she went out to dinner with Jim. When Tom walked into the bedroom, he was very much taken aback again—similar to the time he did the night they went out with Jim. "Susan, you look ravishing! I can't say it enough times. I can't wait for you to be my trophy wife, as you referred to it."

"Why are you looking at me so strange this time? Is everything OK?" "Wait a moment, I'll be right back." Susan wondered why Tom suddenly left the room. Tom stepped out of the room and came back with a gift he had gotten for Susan. He handed her the box.

"I got you something that I think might go well with your black dress." "What is it?" Susan took the box that Tom handed her, and didn't know what to make of it. She looked at it carefully. "Tom, what is this?" "Go ahead, open it."

Susan opened the box and was very pleasantly surprised to find a pearl collar necklace. "Tom, this is beautiful! Thank you. It's absolutely gorgeous. What did I do to deserve this?" Susan couldn't stop looking at it.

"Just because you are you, and you are very special to me." Susan embraced Tom dearly. "Do you think the necklace goes well with the dress?" "It's perfect, sweetheart! That was very thoughtful of you." Tom made it his mission in life to continuously surprise Susan.

Tom had recommended to Marcus that they pick up him and his wife to go to the country club. He let Marcus know that he wished to be the designated driver for the evening. Marcus agreed wholeheartedly, as he enjoyed his Jim Beam on the rocks. Marcus thought it was a nice touch on Tom's part that he was going to pick him and his wife up at their house.

When Susan and Tom arrived at Marcus' house, Tom got out of the car to open the door for Marcus and Michelle. "Hi Tom, great to see you again. Congratulations on your promotion. You really deserve it." "Thanks, Michelle. I would like to introduce you to my fiancée, Susan." Susan stepped out of the car to meet Michelle and Marcus.

"Good evening, Mrs. Jefferson. It's very nice to finally meet you both." "Please, Susan, call me Michelle. I must say, Tom is a very lucky guy." "Thanks, Michelle. I feel very lucky as well," Susan responded.

Tom noticed the laidback interaction between Michelle and Susan—it was nice to see. Tom pulled the car in front of the club and handed his keys to the valet. As they entered the club, Tom looked for the location of the grand ballroom where Marcus' employees awaited him.

"Tom, isn't the dining room down and to the left?" Marcus motioned to Tom. "Yes, Marcus, but I found a short cut through the grand ballroom." Tom attempted to distract Marcus. "I've eaten here hundreds of times, and I don't recall such a short cut." "Well, Marcus, you're in for a surprise." Little did Marcus know, Tom literally meant what he said.

As soon as Tom shared the short cut with Marcus, he opened the doors to the grand ballroom and it was dark. In a split second, the lights went on, and everyone yelled SURPRISE. Marcus and Michelle were shocked. Marcus did not expect a surprise going-away party. "Michelle, did you have anything to do with this?" Michelle just shrugged her shoulders giving him the impression that she did not know anything about the surprise party.

Darlene had hinted to Marcus that the office planned to have a little going away party for him the following week to throw him off guard. Marcus turned around to Tom, and said, "I guess you got me back, my friend." "Marcus, you know me better than that. I wouldn't do that to you." "Thank you, Tom." "Marcus, please thank Darlene—she had a great deal to do with all the planning," Tom gave credit where credit was due.

Tom and Susan watched Marcus make his way around the room as he shook hands with his staff, board members, and many of his clients who had been with the company for many years. Darlene walked over to Tom, and suggested that he make a speech about Marcus. Tom thought it was a good idea. After all, he was used to making impromptu presentations.

Tom got up to the podium to thank everyone for coming to Marcus' surprise retirement party. As he looked over to Marcus' table, Tom asked, "Marcus, we hope you were pleasantly surprised. The office worked very hard to keep this party from you," Tom noticed Marcus nodded in agreement.

"Well, Marcus, you have been an inspiration to all of us, and we will remember you for a very long time. Our apologies in advance to your wife, Michelle. He's all yours now, Michelle!" Tom noticed a little snicker from Michelle as she held on to Marcus' arm. Tom raised his champagne glass and looked at Marcus and then around the room, motioning for everyone to join in a toast for Marcus.

"Marcus, on behalf of all of us at ABC Financial, we're all better off today because of you and your wisdom. You've been a leader, an inspiration and a company executive that has made this company very successful, and, more importantly, you've been a good friend to all of us. You always made it a point for everyone in this company to call you by your first name. We all have the greatest admiration and respect for you and we wish you the best of luck in your retirement," Tom said, as he noticed a few tears roll down Marcus' face. Tom turned the podium over to Marcus to say a few parting words to which he was surprised to do so as well.

"Tom, Darlene and to all of you who made this party possible, thank you from the bottom of my heart. It's very touching to have so many friends come tonight to say goodbye. Thanks, Tom, I guess this is your way of getting back to me," Marcus said in a very joking matter, but everyone knew exactly what he alluded to.

"Ladies and gentlemen, it is time for me to say goodbye and leave you in Tom's very capable hands..." Marcus paused, as his emotions had caught up to him and they were winning the battle. "By now, you all have met Tom's fiancée, Susan. Tom what on earth did you do to deserve such a wonderful woman? I don't know where you found the time to meet her; you have always been at your desk seven days a week. Did you order her from Amazon?" Everyone laughed at Marcus' comment.

Marcus decided to throw a little brevity into the room at Tom's expense, but Tom was a good sport about it and knew Marcus well enough that he said it with the best of intentions. Marcus spoke for a few more minutes when Tom came back to close the speeches for the evening.

"Marcus, you will probably drive Michelle crazy staying at home all the time. To give you guys a break, the company is giving you and Michelle a two-week vacation in the Hawaiian Islands. In addition, Tom presented Marcus with a plaque of appreciation for his untiring efforts and dedication to the company. Tom could see Marcus was completely surprised and looked at his wife to see if she had anything to do with all the presentations.

As the evening came to a close, everyone stopped by to wish Marcus and Michelle the best of luck in his retirement. Tom witnessed the love and admiration everyone had for Marcus. It was nice to see the culmination of one's business career. You know you've done well in life when all of your friends wish you the best and give you a great send-off.

Susan and Tom drove Marcus and Michelle back home. They got out of the car to wish them both well. "Marcus, I would like to call you from time to time to see how you're doing—maybe have breakfast once in a while." Marcus nodded and gave Tom a goodbye hug. It was a very emotional evening for the both of them. Susan observed them, and she was not surprised at all to see Tom's warmth extend to Marcus and Michelle. She was very proud of him and she couldn't wait to be his wife.

Chapter 80

$\mathcal{I}t$ was time for Tom to attend his first board of directors' meeting. The chair called the meeting to order. The first thing on the agenda was to welcome Tom as the new president. The chair, Frank Marenda, went over the minutes of the previous meeting, and then turned the meeting over to Tom.

"Thank you everyone for your vote of confidence to run this company. I also would like to thank you for coming to the club to send Marcus off on his retirement—he will be missed. The only item I have on the agenda aside from the customary items, is to discuss with you my recommendations for the direction of the company to take."

"First, I propose to bring in more wealthy clients, as well as to focus on the middle-income sector. We have found a percentage of this sector will grow and become very wealthy. I would like to get this group on the ground floor and assist them in reaching their financial goals. Second, I would like to see how we can make this company operate more efficiently—cut out unnecessary expenses."

At this point, one of the directors interrupted Tom to ask him a question. "Speaking of expenses, Tom, how much did it cost the company to send Marcus and Michelle off to Hawaii for a couple of weeks? Not that I have any issue with it in the least—the guy certainly deserves it—it's more of a curiosity." Tom noticed the faces of the other directors turn toward him when that question was asked.

Tom paused, and wished this subject had not come up. Phil, a former accountant, was curious to know the cost as well, as in Phil's opinion, Tom had not requested approval from the board for such a lavish expenditure. The board noticed Tom's hesitation to address this question, and anxiously waited to hear from the newly elected president of the company.

"Gentlemen, with all due respect, I would like to keep this subject within these four walls, if you don't mind." All the directors wondered where Tom was headed. "Gentlemen, it didn't cost the company a dime. I personally absorbed the cost totally on my own." Tom looked around the room to see the reaction of the members of the board. Everyone in the room was silent; they didn't know what to say—even Phil was quiet.

"Tom, why would you have done this?" the chairman asked, and noticed Tom's head was down. He raised his head up and said, "I've worked with Marcus for many years, and I have the greatest admiration for him—I just wanted to do this for him." "Tom, that was very generous of you," the chairman thanked Tom, and asked Phil if he had any more questions on the subject. "No, Mr. Chairman. That will do. Thanks, Tom."

Tom continued with his proposal for the company. "The third item I would like to propose is to have a company-wide effort to help the less fortunate families. For example, when I was in San Diego, my future wife's sister introduced us to working in a soup kitchen. This is not an expense but a company-wide participation to reach out. There are many individuals and families out there who are in dire straits. If the company so chooses, the company can donate food to the soup kitchen."

"Tom, I think this is a noble gesture for the company to do—participate and contribute food to the soup kitchens," the chairman informed the board.

"Tom, do you have any other items you wish to bring to the board?" "Yes, Mr. Chairman. I just want to inform the board that I will be creating teams to come up with recommendations to achieve and track these goals, and I will then report those results back to the board."

"Do I have a motion to approve Tom's recommendations?" The chairman asked the members of the board. Phil made a motion for Tom to pursue this program which was seconded by another director. The chairman congratulated Tom for coming on board. "We look forward to working with you in the future, Tom."

When the meeting was adjourned, each of the board members approached Tom, and personally informed him they looked forward to working with him in the future.

Darlene, who took the minutes of the meeting, also approached Tom and congratulated him on his first board of directors' meeting. "Tom, I see you're going to do just fine. I very much look forward to working with you." "Thank you, Darlene, for your vote of confidence. More importantly, I want to thank you again for all of your hard work in organizing Marcus' party," Tom said, with a very earnest and sincere tone.

Chapter 81

When Tom got home, Susan waited for him with a glass of wine. Even though Tom was not a wine drinker, he was very appreciative of the gesture. "Tom, I would like to congratulate you on your first board of directors' meeting. I want to hear all about it. How was it? Did they attack you from all sides?" Susan asked, anxiously waiting to hear about the day that Tom had.

"The members of the board of directors are nice people. They all knew me as the financial consultant, not the president." "That's all? Nothing exciting—no fireworks?" Susan decided to ask Tom all sorts of questions how his first board of directors' meeting went. "They didn't put you through the mill? No initiation rites?" Tom stepped back to take in all the different questions Susan threw at him.

"Like everything else, Susan, when someone new comes in, they try to see how he or she is able to handle different situations, and to see if they can work with the new president in the future." "And?" "All I can say, Susan, is that I believe we're all going to work very well together," Tom recapped briefly his get-together with the board. He noticed how interested and concerned she was how Tom's first board meeting went.

In Tom's mind, he had already settled prior to his promotion, that he was going to retire and move to San Diego. Being president was just a momentary diversion he agreed to do with Marcus—Tom didn't need the job. He looked forward to moving to San Diego to live with

Susan, and possibly, have Jim move there as well. Somehow, Tom took a U-turn to run the company he had worked very hard for so many years. As far as Tom was concerned, he was not about to get stressed with all of the daily activities of running a company. He already had a taste of stress, and he was not about to swallow that pill again.

"So, Tom, do you think you're going to enjoy your new job?" Susan asked, and decided to stay away from the particulars of the meeting. She asked Tom how he overall liked his new position. "I've given that a great deal of thought, and yes, I'm looking forward to it. One of the areas I brought to the board's attention was for the company to get involved in charitable activities, such as the soup kitchens."

"You did? That's fantastic that you were able to squeeze that in." "I remember very well seeing all those poor people in San Diego and how rewarding it was to help those who needed our help." "Were they receptive to the idea?" Susan asked. "I informed them it was going to be a company-wide effort and everyone was going to get involved."

"Tom, I'm very proud of you." "You didn't know Rachel was going to rub off on me?" "I can't wait to share that with her. She will be very proud of you as well." Susan was very pleased that Tom had not forgotten the experience he had learned at the soup kitchens in San Diego.

"You can't imagine how many people came over to me after the meeting to inform me how nice and pleasant they found you at Marcus' party—you were a big hit," Tom shared with Susan with a very proud smile. "Glad to hear. I found them to be very pleasant as well. It looks like it's a very nice company to work in. I hope you are happy there."

"It also felt very strange not having Marcus around the office. Since I started with the company eighteen years ago, he has always been there, and has always been in the same office. Now, he's not there, and *I'm* sitting in his office. It's really a strange feeling."

"It has to be a real change for you, Tom." "Susan, speaking of change, I've been surrounded by change ever since you came into my life — I wouldn't have it any other way. Now that we're finding ourselves proceeding towards getting married, I'll be your husband, and you'll be my wife."

"I think that's the way it goes. Are you getting cold feet again?" "I don't recall ever getting cold feet except when we're in bed, and you put your cold feet on my warm leg." "Does that bother you, Tom?" "Not in the least. You can put your cold feet on me anytime you want."

Chapter 82

Tom went back to the office early the next morning to develop a strategic plan for the company. He thought it best to meet with the senior management team to develop the plan jointly. When the plan was developed by the group, the group will then have ownership of the plan it developed, and will work hard to ensure its success. Tom felt it was very important that everyone had input.

Darlene sent an email to the senior executives of the company to inform them of a meeting to be held early the following morning at 7:00 AM—the meeting was mandatory. Tom felt he needed to set the discipline in the company. This was something that Marcus did not get around to talk about during their transition meetings.

The following morning, Tom was in the conference room at six-thirty in the morning to prepare for the first senior executive meeting. The meeting included the following personnel: head of human resources, the chief financial officer, head of retail investment, head of commercial investments, head of compliance, and Tom's personal assistant, Darlene. Tom was very anxious to get the team involved to set the direction of the company.

"Good morning, ladies and gentlemen. Thank you all for coming early. Please help yourselves to coffee and pastries before we begin. First, I want to thank you all for the warm welcome you have given me. My management style may be the same or different than

Marcus; however, our goals are the same. We may take different roads to get there, but we get to the same place."

"The other day I met officially with the board of directors, and I recommended several goals and objectives for the company to take — they approved them unanimously. I, myself, cannot take the company from point A to point B without all of you — this has to be a team effort," Tom very carefully observed the body language of everyone in the room. He wanted to gauge their reaction to his direction for the company.

One of the participants, Phyllis, from human resources, raised her hand and asked, "hasn't the company been doing OK so far?" "Thanks, Phyllis, for asking — that's a very good question. When you look at the past five years, our growth has been declining and our expenses have been inching up. The age of internet investments has been chipping away at our customer base. Many have felt very comfortable buying and selling investments from their kitchen table. All they are doing are transactions — buying and selling. It is up to us to lead them in the right direction so they can reach their overall financial objectives. As our base has decreased and our expenses climbed, we need to be proactive before we find ourselves behind the eight ball."

Tom went over various slides to support his response to Phyllis' question. He noticed his management team paid close attention to the slides as this was a new approach they had not seen before.

"Our objective is two-fold: bring in additional clients, and analyze our expenses to come up with cost cutting measures. If we are able to operate our company more efficiently, we will be in a better position to be

more competitive. In the near future, I would like to
meet with you individually to go over how we are going
to reach our goals and run this company more
efficiently. I'm looking forward to hearing your
recommendations."

"For now, I would like to hear some ideas from you
to see what recommendations you have off the top of
your heads. Just remember, for each of us to be
successful, our company has to be successful. And for
our company to be successful, our clients have to be
successful."

"In front of you are a pad and pencil for you to jot
down the first thing that comes to your mind for us to be
more efficient and be more competitive in the
marketplace. For now, we will just brainstorm. Later on,
we will get more formal and develop an overall plan.
Please take fifteen minutes while I get a refill for my
coffee."

Tom noticed that everyone paused to think about
the tasks they were given and, on occasion, noticed some
of them jot something down. Tom felt comfortable in his
new position and was having fun at the same time.
Darlene noticed Tom's leadership abilities come to the
surface, and she felt Marcus had made a wise choice in
selecting Tom as president.

Tom went around the room and requested each of
them to share their recommendations. As everyone
voiced his or her recommendations, Tom made notes on
a white board. Tom was also scouting who in the group
expressed leadership abilities. Although early in his
tenure as president, he observed who in the group could
walk into his shoes one day.

As everyone expressed their opinions, Darlene took

copious notes to prepare the minutes of the meeting to circulate to each one after the meeting was adjourned. "Thanks again for coming so early this morning and for sharing with us your views on serving our company. I have one more assignment before we adjourn which is due one week from today. Please formalize your recommendations on what you would do to reach the goals and objectives you came up with today."

"Within a week of receiving your report, I will sit down with each one of you to go over your recommendations. Within one month, we will have a follow-up meeting to distribute the results of the combined recommendations to your team. Remember, as the top executives of the company, it is our responsibility to grow this company in size and profitability." Before each member of the management team left the conference room, each one thanked Tom and said they looked forward to working together.

One of the members of the senior management team stayed behind to chat with Tom. "Tom, do you need any help with anything before I leave?" "Thanks, Steve, very much appreciated. Thank you for your participation today; you came up with some thought-provoking suggestions."

"Do you mind if we have a word in private?" "No, not at all, Steve. What is it?" "I want to thank you for getting us involved in the planning process of the company. Don't get me wrong, we all loved Marcus, but he was, how should I put this, a one-man show. We all loved him dearly, but he rarely got us involved with developing goals and objectives let alone implementing them. We all went about our jobs on a daily basis in a vacuum." "Thank you, Steve. I appreciate your candor and I look forward to working with you."

Since Tom had not been part of the senior management team before, he never realized the information Steve had brought to his attention. It was very refreshing for Tom to hear that he brought a different perspective to the company which, in turn, reinforced his efforts. He was pleased he was headed in the right direction.

A few months had passed and the senior management of the company worked very effectively together. The team made recommendations to secure more business, and there were many cost-effective measures that were implemented. The board of directors began to see the results of their efforts immediately, and the chairman acknowledged Tom's hard work periodically.

Chapter 83

"Tom, the wedding is less than a couple of weeks away, and I would like Rachel to come and stay with us to help us with our wedding plans." "Susan, that sounds like a great idea. What do you think of getting a round trip ticket for her?"

"I think that's very sweet of you." Tom paused, and gave her that certain look. "Sorry, Tom, very sweet of *us*…Excuse me, my sister is calling."

"Rachel, speaking of the devil. Tom and I were just talking about you. Were your ears ringing?" "Yes, they were. That's why I called you. I'm looking at the calendar, and I noticed how fast time has flown by—your wedding is in two weeks."

"Yes, Rach, that is the reason we were talking about you. Tom and I would like you to come to Providence, and stay a couple of weeks with us to get ready for the wedding."

"Thanks, sis, but I don't know what to do with Harvey. He is a wreck every time I leave him at the kennel." "No problem. Bring him with you on the plane; we'd love to have that little guy here as well." "Thanks, Susan. Harvey has been on my mind for a while and I didn't know how to tell you."

"I forgot to mention, Rach, we're getting the tickets for you to fly here," Susan offered Rachel. "Susan, that won't be necessary. You guys already have helped me with the car." "Rach, what are families for?" "You guys have been great; I don't know what to say."

"Tom, Rachel and Harvey will be here the day after tomorrow," Susan informed Tom, with excitement in her voice." "Oh, Harvey will be joining us as well? I like that little guy. I'm glad Rachel is bringing him. He would be all alone without his mommy around. Susan, it's great to see you all excited. Can we make little Harvey the ring bearer?"

"Since you came into my life, my life has taken a turn for the better. I mean it, Tom. My life at the moment is not what it used to be before I went on that train ride." "It's really great to hear that you are happy. If you are happy, then it makes me very happy as well. After what you've been through in your life, you've been given a second chance at happiness."

"So, when Rachel comes, you guys will be shopping for dresses?" "I can't wait for her to come! Have you and Jim been fitted for tuxes?" "We felt to go to City Hall and then go out to dinner afterwards, it would be more appropriate to get fitted for new suits. Speaking of dinner, we should plan on the four of us going out to dinner before the wedding." "The four of us?" "Yes, you and I and Rachel and Jim." "Tom, are you starting to play match maker again?" "No, not really; we're just going out to dinner—not double dates."

"We should also sit down later and go over how many guests will be celebrating our wedding day dinner." "If I recall correctly, it should be between ten to fifteen who have confirmed, and that includes Marcus, his wife and Darlene from your office." "Then what else do we need to do?" "Aside from our dresses and your suits, we should be in good shape." "I can't believe that our wedding is around the corner."

Tom had already resolved that marriage in his

fifties, albeit middle fifties, was not in the cards a few months ago. He also did not expect to be on the floor of his bedroom and not being able to get up. Many things came to mind, as he stared out of his window: riding across the country, meeting a girl on a train, being part of a diamond crusade, getting married, getting promoted to the president of his company, and the list went on and on. *How blessed and thankful I am*, he thought over and over.

Susan had resolved to get remarried was not in her cards. She had her share of an abusive husband and now she had to get her life back in order; however, she didn't know how to go about doing that. Little did she know when she stumbled onto a box of diamonds hidden in her house, that her life was about to change for the better.

Squire D. Rushnell, American author and inspirational speaker, had coined the word Godwink, meaning an event or personal experience often identified as coincidence, so astonishing that it is seen as a sign of divine intervention when perceived as the answer to a prayer. Anyone can come up with his or her interpretation how things happen in life; however, Tom's and Susan's life had changed dramatically for the better, and they were both very thankful, no matter what beliefs they may have had.

Susan went to the airport to pick up Rachel and Harvey. She looked forward to getting together with her sister again, even though it was only a couple of months since they last saw each other. She liked being with Rachel, and she liked doing things with her. *If only she lived closer*, she pondered. Susan felt one day will come when Tom and she would move to San Diego to fulfill their original plan that had been sidelined by Tom's promotion.

As Susan pulled up to the baggage area, she noticed Harvey pull Rachel towards the curb. Rachel waved to Susan to attract her attention. Susan got out of the car and gave Rachel a big hug and a kiss and then knelt down to give Harvey a pat on his head.

"Rachel, it's so good to see you again. How are you feeling without having your big sister to boss you around?" Susan asked, as they both got into the car. Rachel paused and was careful how she was going to respond to her sister.

"Susan, I really missed you as well. Harvey also missed you as he got used to be taken out more often than usual." Rachel almost blurted that she was happy to have her house back, but she hesitated to do so. "Well, Rach, it's great having you back. Tom missed you very much as well, and he's looking forward to seeing you again."

When they got into the car, Rachel asked Susan how Tom was doing since he was promoted. "Has he found it overwhelming being president of the company?" "On the contrary, Tom's having fun in his new job—as he was neither vying for it nor expecting it."

"How do you feel about it? I'm sure it's taking a lot of his time?" "Yes, it certainly is consuming a lot of his time, but I'm very fortunate to have him in my life, and I do appreciate the time we have together when he comes home."

"I have to honestly say, Susan, it is great to see you happy again. You; unfortunately, went through a roller coaster ride before and after Max died. The train ride to San Diego definitely took you on the ride of your life." *If she only knew what really happened on that train ride,* Susan thought.

The camaraderie between the two sisters was in full swing. It didn't take them long to get back where they left off when they were in San Diego. Susan pulled up to Tom's driveway, unbeknownst to Rachel who's house it was. "Susan, why are we pulling up here? Did you move? Or is this Tom's house?"

"Rachel, my house has been turned upside down — that's a story for another day," Susan informed Rachel. Rachel had no clue what Susan referred to. As they opened the door of the car and got out, Tom came out to greet them. Immediately, Harvey recognized Tom and there was no stopping Harvey's tail — nonstop wagging.

"Harvey, my boy, how are you doing? I really missed you fella," Tom asked, as he knelt to pet Harvey and scratch his back. "I can see who rates here," Rachel noted, while Tom continued to pet the dog. "Come here, sis, it's great to see you again." Tom gave Rachel a very warm hug, and she did not want to let go. Of course, Susan took note of Rachel's heartwarming reaction towards Tom. Tom opted to pull away to prevent war within the family.

"I can see you really missed us," Susan said in jest. "How was your flight, Rachel?" "Great, and thank you again for the airfare — you didn't have to do that." "I know. We did it because we wanted to," Tom responded. Susan took note of *we wanted to.*

"Rachel, Tom lost the recipe for your famous tuna noodle casserole, so he didn't make it tonight." Tom noted Rachel's facial expression regarding Susan's comment about the tuna noodle casserole. "So instead, we're taking you out to dinner. Tom's brother, Jim, has agreed to join us, that is, if you don't mind?" "No, not at all, Tom. Susan has told me a lot about Jim, and we are going to be related soon anyway."

Tom was glad to see Rachel didn't have an issue with Jim joining their night out. "Susan, can you show me where I can wash up? Tom, what time did you plan on going out tonight?" "In about two to three hours, if that works for you?" "Sure, that works. I'm looking forward to meeting Jim. Tom, can I put Harvey in the backyard?"

"Sure, the backyard is fenced in so you can put him out without having a leash." "I can see that my little Harvey is not going to want to go back home." "That's OK, Rachel, you can leave him here with us." "He would love to, so you can spoil him to death."

Rachel went to her room and laid down to rest a bit before going out to dinner. "Susan, your sister looks well since we saw her last—she has recovered nicely." "I know. I didn't know what to expect, but I'm glad she's doing better. I wonder what she's going to think of Jim." "I hope we didn't put her on the spot with my brother." "No, Tom, she's been looking forward to meeting him, and it's good they'll meet before the wedding."

After a couple of hours, Rachel came out dressed to the hilt. Tom and Susan's mouths were agape on how elegant she was dressed. "OK, Tom, put your eyes back in your head. Rachel, what have you done with my sister? You look beautiful!" Rachel succeeded in getting the reaction she got from Susan and Tom. She hoped Jim would react the same.

Tom pulled up to the restaurant to let the girls out while he parked the car. Coincidentally, he noticed Jim looking for a parking space as well. They both parked their cars in close proximity to each other. Tom did not intentionally wish to give Jim heads-up on Rachel; he wanted to see his reaction for himself when they got to the restaurant.

Jim was dressed very nicely as well. When they arrived at the restaurant, Jim opened the door for Tom. Rachel and Susan waited for them before they got seated. Both Tom and Susan were fixated on Jim to see his reaction when he met Rachel.

"Rachel, I would like to introduce you to my brother, Jim." Rachel stuck her hand out to shake Jim's hand. Jim's expression said it all. "Rachel, so nice to meet you. Tom has told me so much about you. So glad you came out of that accident and are doing better. That must have been very scary for you," Jim had totally forgotten that Tom and Susan were present and kept on talking directly to Rachel as if there were no one else around.

The hostess showed them to their table — a secluded spot Tom had requested so they could talk without any interruption. "Rachel, your future brother-in-law did not mention how elegant and beautiful you looked." "Well, thank you, Jim. Tom has had a lot on his mind lately with the wedding and his new job."

The four chatted for hours, and before they left, Jim asked Rachel if she would be available tomorrow for coffee. "Thanks, Jim, we have a lot of things to take care of for the wedding, but we can meet for breakfast, if that's OK with you and Susan? Susan, would you mind picking me up afterwards so we can go shopping?" "Not a problem, Rachel. Just send me a text when you're ready to be picked up."

There was no doubt in either Tom's nor Susan's minds that dinner went well, and Jim and Rachel connected well. When they got into the house, the three chatted for a little while when Tom and Susan noted Rachel got tired all of a sudden.

"Rachel, glad you were able to finally meet my brother." "Me, too, Tom. I did not know what to expect, but your brother exceeded my expectations." "Glad to hear, Rachel. I'm not biased or anything when I say this, but he's a good guy. I've known him all my life if that means anything. Glad you guys hit it off." "I'm looking forward to getting together with him again." Rachel informed Tom with a smile.

When Susan and Tom got ready for bed, Tom informed Susan that the dinner went better than he had anticipated. Susan agreed as well. "I can't believe how beautiful my sister looked tonight. I guess she wanted to make an impression on Jim." "I think she succeeded." "I also noticed how you drooled when you saw her." "Susan, when I saw her last in San Diego she was recovering from a major accident." "Smooth, Tom. No wonder you became president of your company."

The following morning, Jim picked up Rachel at nine and they hugged when Jim came to the house. Susan got the address where Rachel and Jim were going to have breakfast for Susan to pick her up afterwards and go shopping.

Meanwhile, Tom and Susan went out for breakfast as well, to discuss what needed to be done for the wedding. Tom had prepared a checklist and provided Susan with a copy to see if there were anything else that needed to be added. Susan pointed out a few things that Tom had overlooked, like flowers and place settings, to name a few.

Jim and Rachel got together every day till the day of

the wedding—they became an item overnight as far as Susan and Tom were concerned. "Would you believe your sister and my brother are getting married in a few days?" Jim pointed out to Rachel. "Yeah, it's very hard to believe. Susan was so unhappy and miserable the past year before she met Tom. He has lifted her spirits and made her very happy—they're so good together, Jim."

"Although my brother didn't have the past your sister had, he was always working and never made time for life. I've tried to set him up on dates over the years, but he always gave me one excuse after another." "Why do you think Tom kept avoiding you?" "I don't know, Rachel. Maybe he was shy around women."

"I wonder what happened with Susan." "I believe they were both in the same place at the right time, and neither one had the opportunity to avoid each other. They were both on the same train stuck with each other, so to speak, for days until they arrived in San Diego. Something must have happened on that train that brought them together. Rachel, we may never know for sure what that was."

"As far as I'm concerned, it doesn't really matter. Today, they are both very happy and content, and that's what matters," Jim relayed to Rachel, with a very affectionate tone for his brother. He had never seen his brother so happy which, in turn, had made him very happy as well.

"Jim, I can see you really love your brother very much," Rachel pointed out, as she felt every word he relayed about his brother. The sincerity was very real and it came through. At times, Rachel shed a tear or two because she felt the love that Jim had for his brother. Rachel's love for her sister was just as sincere and heartfelt.

"Rachel, do you see what's happening here? The love our siblings have for each other, I believe and hope, is getting passed on to us." Rachel could see that Jim's heart was talking on his behalf. "Rachel, my apologies. I feel the love that Tom and Susan have for each other, may be transferring to us. I've only known you for a short while and I already feel like I'm falling in love with you."

"Jim, what are you saying?" "Again, I did not plan to pour out my heart out to you. You haven't known me that long, and it's not fair to you," Jim said regretfully. "Jim, there's absolutely no reason you need to apologize. I happen to share the same feelings and I've only known you for a short while as well."

Both Rachel and Jim sat back in their booth and took a deep breath—neither one knew what had just happened, but they felt they were falling in love. "Love does not have an instruction guide or a recipe that unites two people," Jim pointed out. They were in the right place at the right time.

"Jim, what are we going to tell Susan and Tom?" "Rachel, that thought had crossed my mind as well. I recommend we keep this quiet for the time being as they are getting married in a couple of days. I don't think we should take the focus away from their wedding. There will be plenty of time afterwards to express our feelings to them. And knowing my brother, he might just suspect where our relationship is headed anyway."

"Let's get together with them tonight and go over what needs to be taken care of in the next couple of days. After all, you're the maid of honor and I'm the best man—we can't be derelict in our duties." Rachel looked at her watch and noticed that Susan should be picking her up shortly to go shopping for the last-minute items. At that moment, Susan sent her a text that she should be arriving in the next five minutes. "Jim, I'm going to wait outside for her." Rachel leaned over and gave him a goodbye kiss. Jim did not see that coming.

"Hello, my dear sister. Where is your lover boy?" "Whatever do you mean, Susan? Are you referring to Jim? He is inside finishing up his coffee." "I noticed you guys have been spending a lot of time together. Is there something going on between the two of you that I should know?" Susan asked coyishly, sensing full well what the answer was going to be. "Is it that obvious, sis?" Rachel asked rhetorically.

"Rachel, you've barely known each other for a couple of days, and you've managed to fall in love with my fiancée's brother?" "You are my sister, and I love you very much, and I can honestly say, we might be headed in the right direction. For now, sis, we should be concentrating on your wedding day."

"So, you want to change the subject?" "Please, can we?" "We have a lot of things we need to take care of in the next couple of days. For example, we have to be fitted for our dresses that have been altered. We also have a lot of other important things to do." "OK, Susan, we'll put this conversation on hold for now, but we will circle back after the wedding if you like?"

Chapter 84

Tom and Susan were up bright and early with their marriage license in hand ready to go to City Hall in Providence. Jim picked up Rachel as they all planned on meeting there. Tom had arranged for a limo to pick them up and offered Jim and Rachel to join them. Jim and Rachel both agreed that their wedding day was a special day and they should be taken in style by themselves. Harvey informed Susan and Tom that he needed more advanced notice to be ring bearer—he had other commitments—so he couldn't make it.

As they sat in the back seat of the limo, they held hands, looked at each other and smiled. "Susan, I can't wait to be your husband." Susan responded accordingly. This is the day they waited for and it had finally come.

As they entered City Hall, they proceeded to meet the court-approved officiant. Jim and Rachel were already there waiting for them. They served as the two required witnesses. One would think by looking at all four that a double wedding was to take place. They met the officiant in one of the chambers and waited anxiously for the ceremony to begin.

"Is this really happening, Tom?" Susan was in a state of euphoria, and she could not believe she was about to marry Tom. Although they knew each other for a short time, the days leading to the wedding were quite full and filled with all sorts of adventures.

Neither Tom nor Susan visualized this day when they first met on the empty train in Providence on their way to San Diego. No one believed the journey they took to get to this point in their lives. Tom and Susan vowed certain activities were to remain between them and were to be kept secret for all eternity.

The officiant continued with the ceremony. "Do you, Susan Anderson, take Tom Stevens to be your husband to have and to hold from this day forward, for better or worse, for richer or poorer, in sickness, and in health, to love and to cherish; from this day forward until death do you part?"

"I, Susan Anderson, take you, Tom Stevens, to be my husband to have and to hold from this day forward, for better or worse, for richer or poorer, in sickness and in health, to love and to cherish; from this day forward until death do us part."

The officiant turned towards Tom: "Do you, Tom Stevens, take Susan Anderson to be your wife to have and to hold from this day forward, for better or worse, for richer or poorer, in sickness and in health, to love and to cherish; from this day forward until death do you part."

"I, Tom Stevens, take you, Susan Anderson, to be my wife to have and to hold from this day forward, for better or worse, for richer or poorer, in sickness and in health, to love and to cherish; from this day forward until death do us part."

"In addition, Tom and Susan would like to share their individual vows. Tom you may begin:"

"My darling Susan, I have known you for a short while, and in that time, you have shown me the loving and caring heart you have for me and for others. We rode together across the country on a train where we took long walks at every stop. We walked through small towns hand in hand, and I quickly got to know how caring and special you were. We worked together in soup kitchens feeding those who were less fortunate. You showed me the path to happiness when I thought my life had been derailed. I pray to God that He allows me enough time in my life to show you how much you mean to me. I look forward to walking through life with you. I love you so much; there aren't enough words that can describe the love I have for you." Tom did not have anything written; the vows he read flowed with ease from his heart.

"Susan Anderson, you may begin your vows:

"Tom, I stand before you today to declare my love for you. You have pulled me out of the abyss of unhappiness, and you have shown me that I can love again. You have been the beacon that has led me through the densest of fogs. The train may have gone to San Diego, but I was standing still and I was not going anywhere. You took my hand and showed me the way. Through thick and thin, you have stood by my side as we walk through the threshold of life together. I love you, my darling; you have made me the luckiest woman in the world. I take you as you are, loving you today and for all our days to come. From this day forward, I will be thankful for our adventures as one. To love and to cherish every moment, to give generously in our life together. I will always put us first every day for the rest of our lives." Similarly, Susan did not have anything written.

"By the power vested in me by the Commonwealth of Rhode Island, I now pronounce you husband and wife. You may kiss the bride. Congratulations to you both!"

Rachel and Jim congratulated their respective siblings with heartfelt emotions. Jim and Rachel stood by their side disappointed they had not brought enough tissues. Even the officiant had a tear or two that made their way out. Tom and Susan went back to their limousine to head to their wedding reception. They were each in a temporary state of shock. *Was this a dream?* they each thought.

Chapter 85

$\mathscr{R}$achel and Jim made it a point to go directly to the restaurant immediately after the ceremony. They took it upon themselves to ensure everyone was settled at the restaurant before Susan and Tom arrived—a quasi-surprise so to speak. Rachel and Jim also decided to make the chairs a bit more elegant by covering them with banquet chair covers.

The limo pulled up to the restaurant where everyone awaited the newly married couple. As they entered the restaurant, everyone stood up and gave Susan and Tom a round of applause. They did not expect everyone to arrive early. Also, Susan took note of the seat covers and glanced at Rachel sensing she had something to do with them.

Susan and Tom made the rounds and greeted everyone. Those who knew of Susan's past greeted her with tears of happiness in their eyes—they knew the life she had led with her late husband. This was a special day for both Tom and Susan—a day they will long remember.

Tom especially knew what the day meant for Susan. He was very happy that he played a role towards her happiness. He loved her very much, and made it one of his life's goals to make her smile and make her happy every day of her life.

Tom and Susan noted that Jim and Rachel were together all evening during the reception. Their affection towards each other was very obvious to everyone at dinner. As Tom's best man, Jim stood up to make the customary toast to the groom.

Everyone could see that Jim was very proud of his brother who had remained secluded most of his adult life until Susan walked in and opened the door to set him free.

"Tom, thank you very much for being an amazing brother. I am so proud of you. You have stood by my side all of my life growing up—especially when Betty passed away. Those Starbucks' get-togethers were priceless to me. I'm sure you will recall all the blind dates I organized for you when we were growing up, but you insisted that homework was more important and declined them all. You didn't even give the girls a chance to meet you. After a while, they didn't believe me that you existed." Jim noted a little laugh come from Tom before he continued.

"Not too long ago I was very worried about you when you couldn't get up from the floor. Per your doctor's orders, he prescribed for you much needed rest, so you took time off from work and decided to take a train ride across the country. You surprised us all, not only for coming back looking healthy and tanned, but you came back as an engaged man to get married to the most wonderful person in the world. More importantly, that wonderful person is here today as your lovely wife. Congratulations big brother, I wish you both all the luck and happiness in the world." Tom approached his brother and gave him a very warm heartfelt hug.

As Jim sat down, Rachel got up with her champagne glass in hand, and began to give the customary maid of honor toast. "Sis, I am so proud to stand beside you today to wish you and Tom the very best of luck and happiness. It is truly great to see you happy again. It was not too long ago when you were very unhappy and miserable. You called me one day to inform me you were coming for a visit. Instead of flying which would have taken a few hours, you decided to take a long train ride that took days because you wanted some alone time to think. As much as I tried to convince you to fly, I am so happy you didn't listen to me. Had you listened to your sister for once, you would not have met Tom who is your husband today. In turn, I would not have had the opportunity to meet Jim." Rachel quickly decided not to dwell on Jim as this was Susan's day, not hers.

Rachel continued, "when you introduced me to Tom, I introduced him to one of my favorite recipes, tuna noodle casserole. I have to say, Tom, you really loved the casserole and I haven't shared the recipe with you as of yet." Everyone around the table found this a bit humorous, as everyone knew the recipe was on the back of every cream of mushroom soup can.

"Tom, anytime you are in the mood for it, I would be more than happy to make it for you. Enough about the casserole, I don't want to make everyone hungry for it!" Rachel joked. "Lastly, I don't know what I would have done without the support and care Susan gave me after I had the accident. You both took very good care of me and I will never forget it as long as I live." Tears began to flow from Rachel's eyes. "Would you please all raise your glasses and wish Susan and Tom the best of luck and happiness. I love you both very much." Susan got up and gave her sister a very big hug and a kiss.

Before dessert was brought out, Marcus got up and paid Tom a visit. He did not have an opportunity to chat with him before dinner had started. "Tom, congratulations, my friend. I want to personally wish you the best. I also wanted to share a few business-related words as I don't know when I'll be able to talk with you again. As you know, my Hawaiian cruise is around the corner, and I want to personally thank you for it."

"Marcus, that trip was on behalf of the company." Marcus did not want to make Tom aware that he knew for a fact that it was he who had purchased the tickets for him and his wife. "I also wanted to let you know that the board of directors is extremely pleased with your performance. Thank you for making me proud."

"Marcus, it is I who should be thanking you for giving me the opportunity that you did; I will always remember it for as long as I live," Tom graciously thanked Marcus with a warm embrace. "I very much would like to keep in touch with you when you come back from the islands." "Tom, I look forward to getting together with you as well."

Unbeknownst to Susan, Tom added a separate dessert from the wedding cake they had ordered for themselves. When the server brought out a large pecan pie and put it in front of Susan, she was very pleasantly surprised. It reminded her of when they shared pecan pie on one of the train stops along their way to San Diego. *He remembered that I loved pecan pies*, Susan thought.

As everyone left the restaurant, they each stopped by to give their well wishes to both Susan and Tom. Some even asked if there was any significance to the pecan pie that was brought out.

Tom and Susan went back to their limousine to head home and offered Jim and Rachel a ride if they wanted to join them. "Thanks, Susan, I brought my car, and I already offered Rachel a ride to your house." *Of course, you did*, both Tom and Susan thought the same thing. "OK, Jim, we'll see you at our house," Tom said. *Our house. That has a nice ring to it*, Susan stopped to think what Tom said.

"Thanks, you guys for your help in making our wedding day very special," Susan thanked both Rachel and Jim. Rachel almost commented to Susan on how many times did someone get married in life, but she held back. Rachel was very happy for her sister — she was due for some happiness. Jim, in addition to being very happy for his brother and sister-in-law, was also very happy to have met Rachel.

Chapter 86

While Tom and Susan acted like children in Disney World, Rachel decided to stay in Providence and house sit until they got back. While in Providence, Rachel and Jim became very close, so there was no hurry for Rachel to get back to San Diego. She was in Providence and Jim was here. Harvey was at Susan's house. Life was good!

Thoughts of moving back to Providence had crossed Rachel's mind as Tom and Susan already lived there. Wouldn't this be an about face? Not too long ago, plans were made for Tom and Susan to sell their homes and move to San Diego. *God does have a sense of humor*, Rachel thought.

"Rachel, have you given any thought to moving to Providence? I'm fully aware that you guys have great weather in San Diego which is definitely much better than what we have here, but your family is here," Jim asked, as he decided to plant a few seeds in Rachel's mind.

"I don't know if you are aware, but, at one time, Tom and Susan had planned to sell their houses in Providence and move down to San Diego." "Yeah, I know. I'm fully aware of that—Tom had made me aware of it. Then Tom had to get that promotion. Can you imagine that—the nerve of that guy!" Rachel knew that Jim was kidding with her; he wanted nothing but the best for his brother.

"Jim, would you like me to move to Providence?" Rachel asked, while holding on to his hand. Jim felt she was putting him to the test; he wanted to be careful how he answered. "Rachel, I would love to move to wherever you are, but since you asked, yes, I would love for you to move to Providence. Then the four of us would be closer to each other. As a matter of fact, I know of a house that will be coming on the market pretty soon. I believe it's owned by one of your relatives."

"I also have to consider the job I have in San Diego. I work for a national company and I have to see if there's an office in Rhode Island."

For the short time Jim and Rachel have known each other, they had gotten to know each other quite well and have gotten very close. It was apparent from discussions Jim had with Rachel, they wanted to follow in their siblings' footsteps. Suddenly, Rachel noticed she had received a text from Susan. *She's on her honeymoon, why did she need to send me a text?* Rachel asked herself, as she was about to open Susan's text: *Rachel when you get a chance, would you please stop by my house to see if everything's OK? Thanks! Love, Sis.*

Rachel found it strange that Susan texted her about her house when she was away. "Jim, you're not going to believe this, I just received a text from Susan requesting for us to go to her house to see if everything's OK," Rachel read Susan's text to Jim. "While she's on her honeymoon?" Jim reacted. "Yes, that's what I thought." "OK, she must have a reason. We'll just hop over to her place and check it out," continued Jim.

The thought of going to Susan's house puzzled both Jim and Rachel. When they arrived at the house, they noticed a man coming out of the backyard, and he immediately increased his pace when he took note of Jim and Rachel walking towards the house.

"Excuse me, sir, can I help you? What are you doing

at my sister's house?" Rachel asked, while Jim snapped a picture of him with his phone. Jim ran after him and stopped the individual from walking any further. "Sir, I'm going to ask you again. What you were doing in my sister's backyard?" Rachel queried again.

The man hemmed and hawed and responded, "I'm your sister's neighbor, and I came to water her plants." Jim decided to speed dial Tom much to his discontent. While he dialed Tom, he sent his brother the picture of the alleged intruder. Tom received the picture while he answered Jim's call.

"Sorry, Tommy, for disturbing you on your honeymoon, but Rachel and I felt it was important to contact you. The picture I sent you was from an individual we just caught leaving Susan's house. Tom, are you there? Did I lose you?" "Yeah, Jim, I'm still here. I've seen that person before, and he is not Susan's neighbor. He looks like someone Susan and I met once before. I think his name was Randall, Randall Lapointe, or something like that."

"Again, my apologies for bothering you. We'll take it from here. Regards to Susan, and sorry again. We'll chat later." Jim turned towards the intruder and proceeded to ask him, "Is your name Randall Lapointe?" Jim asked, and he could see from the intruder's reaction, he was indeed Randall. "What's it to you?" Randall snapped at him.

"Look sir, we have a picture of you leaving my sister-in-law's house. I just sent her your picture and she knew exactly who you were." "I'm done here. I have to go." "You're not going anywhere. We just got off the phone with the police, and they're on their way here. If you wish to run, go ahead run. I have both your name and your picture. You still want to run?" Jim asked, while Randall looked at Jim straight in the eye. This was a confrontation that neither Rachel nor Jim expected.

The police came faster than expected as they might have been in the area when Jim called. One of the officers came out of the car and proceeded towards Jim and Rachel. "What seems to be the problem folks?" the officer asked Jim. "Officer, we found this individual leaving my sister-in-law's backyard." "And, who are you?" the officer asked Jim.

"Officer, my name is Jim Stevens, and I'm Tom's brother and Susan's brother-in-law. Sir, this is Susan's sister, Rachel, and she's the homeowner's sister." "What makes you think this individual left your sister's house?" the officer asked Rachel, while Randall had a smug look about him. "Officer, as soon as we spotted him, I immediately took his picture," Tom informed the police while he turned the phone to the officer to show him Randall's picture."

"Mr. Lapointe, what were you doing leaving someone else's house?" "Officer, I'm Susan's neighbor, and I came to water her plants," Randall informed the officer, as he attempted to make up a story to protect his innocence. "Officer, I can call the owner right now, and she can confirm that she neither requested this individual to water her plants nor that he is her neighbor," Jim informed the officer, while he called Susan on the phone.

Jim handed the phone to the officer after he informed Susan of the situation at hand. "Officer, this is Susan Stevens and I'm the owner of the house, and this person, Randall Lapointe, is neither my neighbor nor did I request him to water my plants. Incidentally officer, he came to my house once before a few weeks ago inquiring to see my late husband. Mr. Lapointe claimed my late husband held a box for him. Coincidentally, the officer recalled talking with Susan a few weeks ago about Randall. The officer approached Randall and informed him he was under arrest for trespassing.

"Officer, I can explain. Her late husband had a box that he held for me while I was away." The police officer stepped back and proceeded to return to his patrol car, and was seen scanning his laptop. He shortly came back and informed Randall, "so the homeowner's late husband held a box for you while you were in prison?" the officer asked.

The look in Randall's face said it all. The officer put handcuffs on Randall and walked him over to the patrol car. The officer then requested Jim and Rachel to go to the back of the house to see if there was any forced entry into the house. Sure enough, the window in the back door had been broken and the back door was ajar. The officer took various pictures of the broken window and proceeded to search the house.

After the police left with Randall, Rachel texted Susan to give her a call when she had time. Susan called her back immediately. Rachel relayed everything to Susan and apologized again for disturbing them while on their honeymoon. Susan then relayed Rachel's called to Tom. They were both puzzled about Randall's breaking into Susan's house. Both Tom and Susan knew exactly the purpose of Randall's search, but they wished to continue to keep that a secret to themselves.

Chapter 87

$\mathcal{T}$om and Susan were like two children in an amusement park—away from it all and having a great time. They went to Magic Kingdom and Epcot, going back and forth on the monorail frolicking through the rides. "Tom, I think we need to do this more often. Life will still be there in Providence when we get back." "And speaking of when we get back, Randall will also be there." "But, isn't he in jail now?"

"How long do you think he's going to be in jail for a possible misdemeanor?" "Misdemeanor? Tom, he trespassed and broke into my home." "I don't know, they might just give him community service and let him go."

"Tom, we have to deal with him one way or another. He's not going to stop until he finds a box that doesn't exist. Could there be another box we don't know about, Tom?"

"It's very possible there's another box unless we create one." "Create one?" "Yes, we're just going to get a box and put something in it and hide it…" Susan stopped and realized Tom had suggested to set up a decoy to throw Randall off his tracks.

"Susan, we can go and get very creative and realistic in what we put in that box. Get costume jewelry or Zircon diamonds, put Jacob's return address, and hide it in the shed. What do you think?" Tom noticed Susan gave it some thought and found it to be a very plausible possibility.

"Tom, are you seriously giving this ruse a scintilla of consideration?" Susan asked, with total disbelief in her voice. "If we make this very realistic and hide it in the shed, Randall might find it and go away once and for all, or…" Tom stopped, and gave it some more thought.

"We can let Randall know that we found a box." Both Tom and Susan acted as if though they found a new game: *How to Fool Randall.* "Yes, I do recall letting him know that we would call him if we were to find a box." "Great, we'll call him and let him know that."

"Do you think he's going to trust us after we just put him in jail?" "I really don't believe Randall is going to stop pursuing his search for that box—he knows it could be very valuable."

Susan and Tom looked online and found various websites that carried costume jewelry. They had a game plan to throw Randall off course. Now they had to get a box similar in size to the one Susan had found, and create a realistic label from Jacob's jewelry company—it had to look realistic and authentic enough for Randall to take the bait.

While Susan and Tom were in Disney World, they ordered various supplies online to attempt to fool Mr. Lapointe. The supplies should be delivered to their house by the time they got back from Disney World. They had more fun creating a box of goodies for Randall than they had in Disney. *Thanks, Randall, you've helped us in reaching our goals of getting away and having fun*, Susan thought.

The week in Disney World went by faster than Susan and Tom had anticipated. It was now time to go back to the real world. They both looked forward to seeing Rachel and Jim, and, of course, they couldn't forget Harvey—Rachel's little pug who had his own personality.

Chapter 88

Rachel and Jim went out to Starbucks to cool off after their confrontation with Randall and the police. They were both puzzled and confused with Randall's situation. "Rachel, there has to be more to this than we have been led to believe. It can't be a coincidence between Susan calling you from her honeymoon and running into Randall after leaving your sister's house."

"Jim, that's been on my mind as well; maybe we should bring it up to her when she comes back." "Is it possible there are reasons why Susan and Tom haven't brought it up? They must have known about it before they left on their honeymoon. Since we were involved with Randall and the police, we can bring it up when we see them to see if they can shed some light on the subject," Jim suggested to Rachel, as he looked at his watch.

"Rachel, what time is their plane landing? We should be leaving soon to go to the airport to pick them up." "The plane should be landing at four-thirty," Rachel informed Jim, as she checked her phone for confirmation.

"I have an idea, Rachel. Why don't we take them out to dinner after we pick them up?" "That sounds like a great idea, Jim. They've only been away for a week and I miss them both already." "Me too, Rachel."

Rachel and Jim waited for Susan and Tom outside of the baggage area. According to the schedule they found online, their flight was on time. Within fifteen minutes they both came out of the baggage area, and Rachel and Jim got out of the car to help them with their luggage.

"You guys should go away more often; you both look so relaxed and tan," Rachel said, as she gave each of them hugs and kisses. "Are you guys hungry? I know the airlines don't feed you on the plane anymore," Jim asked. "We can go for a bite and a drink," Tom suggested.

"Since when do you drink, Tom?" "I think it was when I took the train ride across the country to San Diego." "Ah, did that train ride drive you to drink?" Jim asked. Tom turned towards Susan who knew the many reasons that led Tom to drink, but that was to be their little secret.

At the restaurant, they all ordered drinks to celebrate Susan's and Tom's return. "Did you guys have a relaxing week with Mickey and Donald?" asked Rachel. "It definitely was entertaining to be around the Disney characters. The light show at the lagoon was spectacular."

"Not to change the subject, but what made you text us to check on your house while you were on your honeymoon? Were you bored?" "No, while we were at Disney, Tom and I were talking about an incident we had while we were getting my house ready to put on the market. In the process, this guy, Randall, whom you've had the pleasure of meeting, rang the doorbell on a Sunday afternoon. At the time, he was very well dressed and asked if Max was home..."

"Oh, that's a bit weird," Rachel interjected. Susan continued, "you can say that again. He led us to believe he was not aware that Max had died. He also said that Max held a box for him while he was away..." "Did he happen to tell you where he went?" Rachel interrupted.

"No, he didn't say where he had gone." Rachel continued, "when we called you, the police officer had informed us he had previously been in jail." *That explains a few things*, Tom thought.

Tom informed Rachel and Jim that Randall was looking for a box, the contents of which he did not divulge. "We informed him we had not located such a box. I guess he wanted to look for it for himself when you saw him leave my backyard. Was he carrying anything when you saw him leave my house?" Susan asked.

"No, as a matter of fact, he started walking away at a fast pace when he saw us approach your house. He also broke the window to your backdoor." "So, I guess he didn't find anything?" "My guess is, that he might try again to see if he can locate this mysterious box," Tom professed.

"Tom, do you know if there's a connection between Max and this Randall character?" Jim asked, while he attempted to connect the dots, so to speak. "According to Randall, Max helped him while he was at the post office. He had asked Max to hold on to this box while he was away. We all know now that he was in prison." Susan jumped in, "for your information, Max did not have any customer contact while he worked at the post office—he worked in the backroom operations of the post office."

"Is it possible that both Max and Randall worked in the backroom of the post office and smuggled the box out?" Susan continued to share the information she had. "The police officer also made us aware that they had a video surveillance of Max taking that box." "Is it possible both Max and Randall were part of the surveillance, and the police only mentioned Max. Furthermore, they did not make us aware that Randall was part of it?" "Yep, that makes sense." All four spent hours speculating what could have happened between Max and Randall and the infamous box; all the makings of an Agatha Christie mystery novel.

Jim asked Susan, "is it possible that box is still in your house?" Susan almost denied the box was still in the house, but held back responding to that question. She, as well as Tom, did not wish to let that cat out of the bag.

The remainder of the dinner was spent talking about the different rides and exhibits Tom and Susan visited while at Disney World. Jim and Rachel enjoyed Disney World vicariously through Tom's and Susan's eyes; they were as excited as Tom and Susan were.

Before they all left the restaurant, Tom offered, "we should all go to Disney World one day." Susan recalled having a similar dream to Tom's recommendation while on the train ride across the country. She recalled the dream very vividly—she was very happy and content when she dreamt about it, and now she was very happy living it.

Chapter 89

Randall Lapointe paid a visit to a very good friend of his, officer Andy Fitzpatrick. "You know, Andy, you had me convinced you were one of the good guys when you arrested me at that lady's house, Susan something or other. How well did you search that lady's house?" "Randall, we searched it with a fine-toothed comb." "Did you search the attic and crawl space?" "Definitely, Randall. This is not our first search in our line of work. I even sent Jack underneath the house to search the crawl space." "And?" "And what? There was no sign of a box anywhere."

"I noticed when I searched myself, there was a shed in the backyard. Did you gentlemen search that as well?" "We opened the doors and looked inside." "And? Did you go through the shed to see if there was a box inside?" "Randall, the shed was full of crap. There was nothing there but cans of paint, ladders, a lawn mower, garden tools, and crap like that."

"Damn it, Andy. Did you take everything out to see if there was a box hidden?" Randall asked, while his face turned red with anger. "No, I did not." "Then, Andy, you need to go back with another search warrant and tear that shed apart—there just might be a few million dollars there waiting for us," Randall demanded, getting upset and angry that Andy had overlooked the shed.

Andy was terrified of Randall. He's worked with Randall for years, and he has made Andy a very rich person. Andy had a lot of faith and confidence that

Randall was going to make him even richer, so whatever Randall requested, Andy was there for him.

Back at home, Susan and Tom unpacked their bags and resumed with their daily lives. The boxes of costume jewelry were at their front door waiting for them. They couldn't wait to begin to create a box of make-believe jewelry from Jacob's diamond company. Susan worked on a label and made it so authentic looking, Jacob would have sworn it had come from his office. The wrapping paper was even crumbled and soiled to give the box a look of authenticity.

In rethinking their strategy, Tom and Susan agreed not to contact Randall as it would have appeared to be very suspicious, considering they were responsible for putting him in jail, or so it appeared. The alternative, as they had discussed in Disney World, was to hide it in Susan's shed very inconspicuously. They wanted to ensure it was very well hidden behind all the cans of paint. In order for someone to find it, everything had to be taken out of the shed — item by item.

Sure enough, four days later, officer Andy Fitzpatrick paid them a visit with another search warrant while Tom and Susan continued to throw things away to get the house ready for sale. Suddenly, the doorbell rang and Tom proceeded to answer it.

"Haven't I seen you before?" Tom asked, as he stared at officer Andy to see where he had seen him before. "Yes, sir, you have. I was here once before with a search warrant." "Oh, did you come back to straighten out the mess you guys left behind the first time?" "My apologies, sir, but we are not required to put things back just in case we have to come back to photograph what we searched."

"What do I owe the pleasure of your presence again, officer? Did you forget to search something when you were here last?" asked Tom. "As a matter of fact, sir, we did. We need to search your backyard; specifically, your shed. When we came the last time, we did not have an opportunity to search the shed as it got late and it was very dark inside."

"Look officer, I don't know what you are looking for. My wife's late husband passed away many months ago, and my wife has no knowledge of anything her late husband had. We've either thrown all of his things away or given them to charity." "I understand, sir. I'm just following orders—just trying to do my job, sir. We apologize for any inconvenience we may have caused, sir."

"Do you at least promise to put everything back in the shed in the same way you found it—before you leave?" Andy paused for a moment, and reluctantly agreed to put everything back in the shed in the order he found it.

From the window, Tom and Susan observed officer Andy and his partner carefully remove every item from the shed. After forty-five minutes, Andy stumbled on the box he'd been looking for. They observed him shake the box. Upon locating the box, Andy took out his cell phone and made a call.

Susan and Tom concluded he had called Randall as they observed his lips mention his name. "I don't believe this, Tom. Randall and officer Andy are in this caper together. I wonder if officer Andy is even a police officer."

As soon as Andy got a hold of the box, he stopped by the front door to inform Tom he would come back later to put everything back in the shed. For the moment, he had to answer a call that came in from the station. Susan and Tom both felt he did not plan to come back. In fact, officer Andy did them a big favor by taking everything out of the shed for Tom and Susan to either dispose or donate.

After the patrol car left, Susan and Tom looked at each other, slapped their hands together, and gave each other high fives. "Susan, do you think we've seen the last of those guys and Randall?" Tom asked, as they looked pleased their subterfuge had worked. "I certainly hope so. They found what they were looking for, and their job, for all practical purposes, was done."

Chapter 90

The evening after officer Andy made the big discovery, Randall contacted one of his buyers to purchase the diamonds in the box. Randall and Andy were to meet the buyers at their usual secluded place outside of town. This dynamic duo had been stealing from the post office for years. They had this system down to a science.

"Randall, how many more times are we going to do this? I just feel we are going to get caught soon and end our streak of robberies," Andy asked Randall, with a very concerned look about him.

"Look, Andy, any time you would like to break loose from our foolproof system, please do not hesitate to do so. I'm sure I will have no problem finding another low paid police officer who is more than happy to build a nice nest egg for himself and his family," Randall attempted to paint a very lucrative arrangement to lure Andy from taking the high road.

"Let's get through this and see where it takes us." Andy concurred with Randall, as the box of diamonds was already in their possession, and all that was needed was to cash the diamonds in. After all, the hard work had already been done.

Randall and Andy sat in the car waiting for the buyer to show up. "Andy, why would you want to leave a good thing we have going for us? Also, I still don't know why you gave the box to Max in the first place. Remember, the other cop put me in jail, and I was not able to get a hold of you for one reason or another. I think you were away on vacation or in some conference, but I had to give the box to someone, and Max was the only one available. Leave that as it may, we have the box now in our possession, and the buyer is going to make us wealthier than we already are."

"Randall, what are we going to do now that our inside man is no longer around?" Andy asked, hoping Randall would want to end all of the robberies. "That's too bad about Max. He was definitely a keeper. I think his last gig was the biggest one," as Randall pointed to the box.

"You can't go back to work for the post office anymore." "Why the hell not? I can have a different identity created. The post office would never know the difference. It's such an archaic institution."

"There's no end to your creativity, is there Randall?" "The trick, my boy, is to always stay one step ahead." "That's why you make the big bucks, Randall. By the way, where is this buyer? Is he always this late?" "No, he isn't. He's usually pretty punctual. I wonder if he forgot?"

"Do you have a number you can call to check in on him?" "Let's give him fifteen more minutes. If we don't hear from him, I'll give him a call." "OK, fifteen minutes it is."

After ten minutes, two cars approached their meeting place. *Why two cars? This doesn't make sense*, Randall thought, and he couldn't figure out the need for two cars. One car stopped about one hundred feet from where Randall's car was parked; the other car approached Randall and Andy.

"Jason, good evening. I was starting to worry about you," Randall commented as he got out of his car.

"What's with the second car? Is this something new?" Randall inquired, while he looked at the second car. "He is my buyer. I buy from you and I sell to him." "A quick turnaround for you?" "I decided to change my methods—streamlined my operations," Jason said jokingly.

"You need a website like eBay to sell your merchandise." "You're a funny man, Randall. Look, I don't have all night. Let's see the diamonds that you recently got; my guy's very anxious to see them and get back on the road."

Andy went back to the car to retrieve the box. "What's with you guys? You didn't even open the box to see what you got?" "We've never seen anything bad come from Jacob's diamonds in the past, Jason. He's always had high caliber stones," Randall informed Jason, as he began to open the box.

The contents were neatly wrapped in bubble wrap. Jason held up the diamonds towards the headlights to get a better look at the diamonds. He looked at them oddly. He has seen more diamonds in his life than the average jeweler has.

"Something don't make sense, Randall. These rocks have too much color to be D grade diamonds and they don't feel as heavy," Jason pointed out, as he took one of the diamonds and approached Randall's car. *I wonder what he's going to do*, Andy asked himself.

Jason approached Randall's windshield and attempted to scratch his windshield with the stone—test #1. The diamonds scratched the surface of the windshield. Test #2: Jason took out his loupe and studied one of the diamonds carefully. Test #3: Jason put water in a paper cup and dropped one of the diamonds in it to see if the diamond would sink to the bottom—it did not. He raised his head and showed his disappointment—the diamonds were not real. Jason immediately walked over to the other car to explain the situation to his buyer.

After a few minutes, they noticed the other vehicle approach them with no signs of Jason. The vehicle stopped in front of them, and they saw a huge man who could pass for a football player. "Which one of yous is Randall?" Randall immediately identified himself.

No sooner than he did, he was shot twice with a gun that had a silencer. Instantly, Andy went for his service revolver, and the other person in the vehicle shot him dead as well. The football player-like individual took the rest of the diamonds from the box and poured them on both of the dead bodies. He got back into his car and left the scene.

Two days later, Randall and Andy made the front page of the local newspaper. While having coffee at home, Tom went out for the daily paper and noticed Randall's and Andy's name on the front page: *TWO DIAMOND THIEVES ASSASSINATED*. Susan and Tom were speechless. They stared at each other for a while. Tom just stared into oblivion not knowing what to say or think.

"Susan, can you imagine? We could have wound up like them eventually." "I know, Tom, but I think it was our make-believe diamonds that got them killed." They were both flabbergasted—speechless at that. "Can you imagine how many people have died from stolen diamonds like these." "Let's just pray that they were the last to die from them."

Rachel, Jim, Susan and Tom met for breakfast at

Starbucks. All four had contact with the infamous individuals who appeared on the front page. "Can you believe we all knew both Randall and officer Andy? One day you see them, the next day they're gone," Tom said, as he slowly shook his head back and forth in disbelief.

Susan and Tom glanced at each other thinking back to when they met Jacob and Joseph one day, and the next day *they* both had died in an airplane crash. Was this the end of the dying duos?

"Not that I'm looking forward to your leaving, Rachel, but do you have a date in mind when you have to get back to work?" Susan asked, as she attempted to find out what Rachel's schedule was. "Since you brought it up, sis, there's something I would like to share with you."

Now Rachel had Susan's and Tom's undivided attention. Rachel continued, "while you were away, I did some research on the company I work for. As you are aware, my company is a multinational company and they have an office here in Providence." Susan and Tom had an idea where Rachel's conversation was headed.

"As I was saying, my company has an office here in Providence, and I have requested a transfer from the San Diego office to here. In addition to physically moving from San Diego, I will also be moving into a new position with the company—a number two position in a satellite location." This totally took Tom and Susan by surprise.

"Rach, how long have you been planning this?" "Actually, not long. I met Jim, we fell in love, and you guys are here—a *perfect storm* to move back." The surprises just kept on coming for Tom and Susan—they did not see this one coming at all.

"What a pleasant surprise you've given us, Rachel! That's fantastic! Not too long-ago Tom and I were going to sell our homes and move to San Diego. Now we've all done an about face from our original plans."

Tom decided to get in on the conversation. "Had I not taken a train ride to San Diego, we wouldn't be sitting here talking about this." Jim also decided to jump on the bandwagon. "Tom, Susan, thanks for taking that train ride to San Diego; otherwise, I wouldn't have met my sweetheart," Jim said, as he reached across the booth to hold Rachel's hands.

Tom and Susan were sad to hear that Randall and Andy had perished because of the box of fake diamonds they had packed. On the other hand, they were ecstatic Rachel planned to move to Providence from San Diego. Who knows what lay ahead for Rachel and Jim?

Chapter 91

"Good morning, Tom. How was your weekend?" Darlene asked, as Tom passed her desk. "Fine, thank you, and yours?" "Fine, thanks. You have a visitor waiting in your office."

"What a pleasant surprise. Good morning, Marcus. To what do I owe this pleasant surprise? How was your trip to the islands?" Marcus got right to the point of his visit.

"I'm sure you've seen the front-page reporting on the two guys that were murdered in town the other night. Real tragic! Who would kill a police officer and an outstanding citizen?" Tom was puzzled at Marcus' series of queries. "Marcus, you knew these guys?"

"Yes, Tom. Randall Lapointe did a lot for this community for years; I believe he was one of our clients." *Was there another Randall Lapointe*? Tom asked himself, trying to understand Marcus' comment about an outstanding citizen. Tom was really confused at this moment.

"Marcus, didn't this Randall Lapointe serve time in jail?" Tom began to question Marcus to verify if they were talking about the same individual. "He, in fact did serve time, but we think he was falsely accused of robbery. He had worked in the post office for a while until he got mixed up with this other guy, and he was just in the wrong place at the wrong time."

Marcus sat back in his chair and pontificated all the good things Randall had done. *There had to be another*

Randall; he can't be talking about the same person, Tom continued to think in his mind and was totally confused.

"Marcus, did you know Randall? You seem to be bringing him up a lot." "He was my wife's brother." Tom sat back in his black executive chair and felt his body sink in disbelief.

"Oh my, she must be a wreck. I'm so sorry to hear. My condolences to Michelle. By the way, Marcus, what brings you here? It's great to see you again—you look well and relaxed."

"Tom, my wife is driving me crazy at home, and I really miss this place." Tom looked at Marcus and felt sorry for him. After many years of heading a company, Marcus found himself at home with his wife twenty-four-seven and, to top it off, he was not in the best of health.

"Tom, I'm very proud of you since you've taken over so successfully. The board cannot say enough good things about you. I guess you didn't know you had it in you," Marcus informed Tom, with a very pleasant smile of pride in his face.

"Sometimes, Marcus, we are put in different situations in life to see what we are capable of doing—tested, so to speak," Tom informed Marcus, as he decided to philosophize to a very good friend who understood every word Tom had said.

"I recall distinctively, Tom, when I asked you at the last minute at the country club to make a presentation, and you surprised the shit out of me. I knew then you were the right person for the job." Tom continued to sit back in his seat and listen to an old friend who did not have a hidden agenda—he meant every word he said.

Chapter 92

"During the week Tom and Susan worked in Susan's house to get it ready to sell. On occasion, Rachel and Jim added a helping hand. The police who turned Susan's house upside down by emptying everything in sight, aided in the process of cleaning by taking everything out from all the drawers and closets. Needless to say, Susan encountered many things she thought were lost. Daily trips to the dump and Goodwill were as common as having their daily coffees.

"Tom, what do you think about putting a coat of paint on the walls to freshen the house a bit before we put it on the market?" Susan asked, while looking at a room that was screaming to be painted. The walls and ceilings looked like they hadn't been painted since the day the house was built twenty years ago.

"Well, Susan, we found a lot of paint in the backyard thanks to Randall and Andy. Let's see if the paint can be salvaged and put to good use. We might as well use it if we have it. It really doesn't matter if the color is not to your liking since you won't be living here anymore. If it's still good, we'll put it on — why waste good paint? It will definitely make the room look cleaner."

Susan and Tom asked Rachel and Jim out to dinner to catch up, as they hadn't seen each other much lately. Rachel decided to stay in Jim's house as they might as well have been married for all practical purposes. Susan and Tom took side bets when *their* big day was to come.

"Hi guys, how's married life?" Jim asked, as he and

Rachel laughed a little at Tom. "May I ask you guys what is so funny?" Tom asked, wondering how he provided entertainment to his brother and sister-in-law. "Tommy, do you realize you have paint on your nose? Is this part of your new job—adding color to your company?" Jim pointed out to his brother. Tom turned towards Susan to confirm Jim's allegation.

"Yes, hon, you do, and I apologize for not catching it before we left the house." Tom took out his handkerchief, dipped it in his glass of water, and was ready to wipe the paint off when Susan grabbed his handkerchief and wiped the paint off his nose herself.

"See what happens when you're married Rachel? Your wife gets to wipe paint off your nose. Isn't that romantic?" Jim asked, as he added more entertainment at his brother's expense.

Susan and Tom noted how comfortable Rachel and Jim were with each other for only knowing each other about a month. Susan already visualized going shopping with Rachel for a wedding gown, although this was a subject she did not wish to ask—tempted as she was on many occasions. Similarly, Tom wanted to ask his brother when he was going to ask him to be his best man. Both Tom and Susan felt this was a sensitive question to ask.

Even though Jim and Rachel were already living together, they didn't want to put any more undue pressure on them. They had enough pressure put on them when they had to deal with Randall and officer Andy. *Can you imagine if Rachel and Jim knew about the adventures of Jacob, Joseph and the diamonds*? Tom thought at times.

Susan and Tom had accomplished a great deal of

painting on their own. Tom recalled the many times when his assistant, Darlene, had made comments about Tom's painting after seeing paint on his hands. He was now very conscious of wearing gloves, and double checking his hands before going to the office.

Tom realized his life was turned completely around after meeting Susan on that train. Now they became painting partners. They had set up three sections in the garage: one for the dump, one for Goodwill, and the last one for Habitat for Humanity. They researched how to get rid of the boxes of paints that were still outside of the shed.

They were both very thankful to Randall and Andy for having taken everything out. The shed appeared totally empty and cleaned. All the shelves were empty and the shed floor was now visible to any potential buyer coming into the shed to inspect. He couldn't wait to show Susan the extremely clean shed.

Susan came out to see what Tom's excitement was all about. As she approached the shed, Tom kept the doors closed until she was by the entrance—he wanted to surprise her. Tom immediately opened the doors and beckoned her to walk in to check it out.

"What do you think, Susan?" Susan stood at the doorway of the shed, peeked in and was pleasantly surprised how clean everything was. Tom even wiped the shelves of all the dust that had accumulated over the years. "What about that top shelf?" Tom looked up and noticed it was empty.

"Did you wipe the dust of that shelf as well?" "No, as a matter of fact, I did not, but I'll get the ladder from the Habitat for Humanity pile we have in the garage, and I'll wipe it down. The shed is immaculate, Susan.

Who is going to notice the dust up there anyway?"

"It doesn't take any effort to get a ladder, climb up and wipe it down. After all, you did such a nice job with the rest of the shed — that will put the finishing touch to all the hard work you did. Anyone would be proud to put all their gardening tools in it."

Tom knew she made a good point. "Suit yourself, it's not worth the effort, but, for you sweetheart, I'll clean it anyway." Tom walked to the garage to get the ladder.

Tom brought the ladder into the shed to wipe down the top shelf. He looked around the shed and mentally thanked Randall and Andy for emptying it. He straddled the ladder inside the shed and climbed up to clean the dust from the top shelf. When his head went over the edge of the shelf, he noticed one dirty box of Sherwin-William's paint covered in a thick layer of dust.

He brought the box down to wipe off the dust as he didn't want dust to fly all over his sparkling clean shed. He then noticed the box did not weigh much — probably filled with half full cans of paint.

Susan brought Tom a bottle of water to take a break, as he put the box down on the grass. "Thanks, Susan. Almost done." "What's that?" Susan asked, as she pointed to the box of paint Tom had brought down. "That, my dear, is the last piece of garbage that occupied the shed. We can put it on the pile to go to the dump."

"What's in it? Just curious. Is it more cans of used paint?" "I suppose old cans of paint that will likely go to the recycle bin at the dump." Tom knelt down to take the cans out to see if the paint could still be used in the house. Susan and Tom opened the box as the dust flew all over the place.

"I can't believe what I'm seeing, Tom. Is that what I

think it is?" Susan asked in total disbelief, locating a small box inside from a jewelry company in Chicago.

Chapter 93

Tom and Susan stared in disbelief at the contents inside the dusty Sherwin-Williams paint box that was before them. A box similar in size had plagued their relationship from the moment they met on the train. In thinking back, Tom recollected that Susan was on the same train as he was but for different reasons: he was on the train for rest and relaxation; Susan was on the train to relinquish the diamonds to Jacob.

Tom bent over to retrieve the box from inside the dirty paint box except, this time, the address label did not have Jacob's diamond company as the return address. This box was from Silverstein Jewelers in Chicago. *Is this another box of diamonds? Did Max hide this box as well? How did Randall and Andy not find it?* These were questions that Tom and Susan asked themselves over and over. They could not believe they were back to square one.

"Susan, we can contact Silverstein Jewelers in Chicago, and inform them we came across their box." "Or we can pack this box in another box, and mail it to them," suggested Susan. "I think I like your idea better. Let's not get involved with any conversations with these guys. Had Randall and Andy found this box in the shed, they might still be alive today."

Tom went online to confirm Silverstein's address, and was informed it had gone out of business. He immediately shared the news with Susan. "Do you have any other recommendations what to do next?" Tom asked. Susan, in jest, replied, "We can always call Marlene to see if she's interested in another box of diamonds." "That may be a great idea; however, I don't know if I would like to get mixed up with her and her clan again. Who knows what may happen this time?"

"Susan, would you like to open another Pandora's box again?" "We don't even know what's in that box in the first place. We've just been staring at it, and neither one of us has volunteered to open it." "Susan, all along we've discussed how to return the box to the sender without considering whom it was meant for."

"Let's see if we can find a number for the person the box was addressed to." Susan went online and located the contact information of the owner of the box. "Mr. Jenkins, we just received a box addressed to you, which we believe was sent to us in error," Susan informed the owner of the box. "Thanks, Miss, but we were told the box was lost in transit. Silverstein Jewelers already sent me a replacement shipment, as they had been reimbursed by their insurance company."

"Mr. Jenkins, what would you like me to do with the box?" "Miss, I'm sorry, I didn't get your name." "My name is Vanessa Fillipelli." Susan created the name out of thin air; she didn't need to get involved with more than she had to. "Miss Fillipelli, I can't believe the box just turned up—it's been missing for over a year."

Since Susan had put him on speakerphone, Tom heard the whole conversation. "Thank you for your assistance, Mr. Jenkins. Have a good day, sir, and my apologies for disturbing you." "Not a problem, Miss Fillipelli, you have a good day as well."

Susan and Tom were now in a quandary, and they did not know what to do. The jewelry company had gone out of business, and the owner of the box had received a replacement for the box that was lost in the mail. The only solution was to find out the name of the insurance company who paid the claim to Silverstein Jewelers.

Tom made a recommendation to search for the names of different insurance companies that insure jewelry firms. "When you finally find the name of the insurance company that paid the claim, are you going to tell them you have the lost diamonds, if in fact, that's what's in the box?"

"Isn't it illegal to open someone else's mail?" "Yes, it is, but aside from contacting the insurance company, what other options do we have? I can see them interrogating us why we were in possession of stolen goods."

Susan and Tom decided to open the box as they saw no other possible avenue at the moment to determine its contents. The thought of taking the box to the police was an option that was discussed; however, it was immediately disregarded. That option would have opened many uncomfortable avenues for them which they did not wish to pursue.

"Susan, would you like to do the honors and open the box?" "Absolutely not. One box in my lifetime is enough. You can have the pleasure of opening it this time." "I just thought if the label were missing, we wouldn't be opening someone else's mail."

"Tom, I have no idea what you are referring to. I don't see a label on that box, do you?" Suddenly, the label that was half peeled off, mysteriously disappeared. Tom opened the box, and the brilliance of the diamonds inside blinded them both. "Tom, what are we going to do with these diamonds?" "Sell them and give the money to charity?" "Great idea, Tom!"

Chapter 94

Tom, Susan, Jim and Rachel found themselves getting together more often. Susan found it very therapeutic to have family around. At times, she had to ask herself if all this were real, and not just a dream. She had a husband who loved her very much, a sister who was always near to her and not across the country anymore, and Tom's brother whom she felt was going to be part of her family soon. She no longer had to dream she was in Disney World in order to be happy. She was there on her honeymoon which made her dreams come true. It had been years since she remembered being so happy. For her, it felt like life was too good to be true.

"Susan, are you OK? You look like you spaced out on us," Rachel looked at her to see if she were feeling OK. "No, sis, I'm fine. It's just great to have all of you here and for us to be one happy family," Susan said, with a sincere and genuine happy smile. Her warmth radiated with love. Rachel knew all too well what Susan felt; she was there with her in the gloomiest of times. It was very special to see her this way and she hoped and prayed this feeling would last for many years to come.

To add to Susan's euphoric state of mind, Jim and Rachel took Tom and Susan out to dinner to a very special restaurant where Dom Perignon champagne was served as soon as they sat down. "Mr. Stevens, how are you and your guests doing tonight?" asked the sommelier with a slight French accent, looking at Jim.

"Very well, Francois, thanks for asking. Hope you

are doing well. I would like to introduce you to my sister-in-law, Susan Stevens, my fiancée, Rachel, and my brother, Tom." "Very nice to meet you all. I'll have the menus out shortly; enjoy your champagne." Susan and Tom honed in on Jim's introduction of Rachel as his *fiancée*.

As soon as the sommelier left, both Susan and Tom turned towards Jim, and almost asked in unison, "Is there something you forgot to tell us?" They looked at Jim, and he pretended he didn't know what Tom and Susan were referring to. Suddenly, it hit him. "Oh sh-t...Sorry guys, I slipped. My apologies—I usually don't curse," defended Jim. "Honestly, this is the first time I've heard Jim cuss," Rachel informed them, as she attempted to protect Jim.

Jim continued, "Rachel and I invited you both tonight to give you the good news..." Jim turned to Rachel to finish his sentence. "Jim and I got engaged last night at dinner. I guess my future husband couldn't hold it back," Rachel added. "Sorry, darling, it just came out on its own—I couldn't stop it," Jim turned towards Rachel and apologized.

"We noticed, Jim. It just means you are very happy and it became part of your normal conversation." "Good come back, sis." Susan interjected. "You almost sounded like Tom. Are you sure you two are not related?"

Tom got up from his seat, and gave his brother a congratulatory hug. "I'm very happy for you guys, bro," Tom said, as he hugged his brother. Similarly, Susan mirrored Tom's hug to Rachel. "I'm so happy for you both. This was fast!" "Excuse me, Tom. I didn't hear that. Would you mind repeating that again?" Tom realized he had spoken too soon, as it didn't take him and Susan long, as well, to get engaged.

Tom sat in his chair as he shook his head in disbelief that his brother got engaged. He was very happy for Jim. He realized Jim and Susan had both gone through turbulent times themselves—it was definitely a time for celebration for them.

"Rachel, have you guys picked a date? In City Hall or in a church?" Susan rifled one question after another; although, it was very early for them to have the answers to the many questions that lay in the queue.

"We picked a date six months from now, and definitely a church wedding. Of course, I would like you to be my matron of honor…" Jim jumped in before Susan responded, "Tom, would you like to be my best man?" The evening was full of surprises—pleasant ones at that. Susan and Tom both agreed to their respective nuptial roles requested from their siblings.

No sooner than Rachel and Susan had planned one wedding, another wedding surfaced on the planning board. "We have to go shopping for a wedding dress, look for a venue, get flowers…" "Rachel, Rachel, hold on, my dear. This is what I'm here for. When you get out of work, we can meet somewhere and go over every little detail—it's too overwhelming when you try to think about them all at once." "You're right, sis. I have to slow down." It was very obvious both sisters were very excited and happy about the upcoming wedding.

Wedding conversations dominated Rachel and Susan's time. Tom and Jim discussed the recent Patriots game. They were not going to interrupt the two sisters who had no interest whatsoever in football.

Chapter 95

"Conductor, I'm looking for my sister, Susan Anderson. Is this the train from Providence, Rhode Island, number 7625? Would you happen to know if she disembarked? I was supposed to meet her here at the station, and I can't seem to find her anywhere. She told me over the phone she had a great seat in the front car of the train."

"Yes, ma'am, this is train number 7625 that initiated from Providence. Let me go check to see if she got off. Most of the passengers got off ten minutes ago." "Thank you, conductor, very much appreciated." The conductor returned shortly to give Rachel an update.

"Miss, I believe, she's still sleeping—she must be having a nice dream, cause she's sitting nicely with her eyes closed and a smile on her face." Usually, I don't like to wake anybody from their sleep; especially, if they are having a nice dream. I'm afraid to wake her up. Again, she looks like she's having a nice dream. Ma'am, this train is scheduled to be here for another couple of hours. I figured I would give her another fifteen minutes, and then I would have to wake her up to clean this train for the return trip."

Rachel decided to wait for a few minutes. She then decided that Susan would be very happy to see her even if she was woken up. "Conductor, do you mind if I go in and wake her up?" "No, by all means, be my guest. You would be doing me a big favor."

Rachel walked up the steps of the train, and noticed

her sister sleeping very peacefully with the smile spread across her face as the conductor mentioned. She, as well, did not wish to wake her up as her sister did appear to be having a nice dream, but it was time to wake her up and go home.

"Susan, Susan, we have to go. Please wake up," Rachel shook her hand gently so as to not startle her. She noticed her hands were ice cold. She ran back off the train and found the conductor. "Conductor, did you have the air conditioning on for a while?" "No, ma'am. As a matter of fact, some of the passengers complained it was getting cold so we turned up the heat."

Rachel went back inside the train and tried again to wake her up. In doing so, Susan fell to the side—she had died in her sleep. Rachel stood in front of her with tears rolling down her cheeks. *My poor sister. I was hoping she was going to have a new life in San Diego, and possibly meet someone who was going to make her happy again*, she thought, while watching her be in such a peaceful state. "Sweet dreams, my dear sister. I hope you are in a happy place at the moment." She kissed her on her head and left the train with tears of sadness.

After the coroner had taken Susan, Rachel stayed behind in total shock. She could not believe her sister had died at such a young age. As Rachel was ready to leave the train, she noticed that Susan's handbag and small carrying case were left behind. With her eyes filled with tears and barely being able to see, she bent down and grabbed her bags to take with her.

Susan's handbag and case remained in the same place for a couple of weeks in the kitchen as Rachel wasn't able to get rid of her sister's things just yet. Her emotions did not allow her to do so. One morning as she sat and had a cup of coffee, she decided she was going to donate all of her sister's clothing to charity—even her bags. Before doing so, she opened the carrying case from the train and piled all of Susan's clothing to donate to Goodwill.

She proceeded with her handbag and turned it upside down on her kitchen table. Coins and loose change rolled off the table in the process. She found the usual things one would find in a handbag: wallet, brush, train ticket, lipstick, and a few other sundry items with one exception—there was a small purple velvet bag tied with a string. Rachel pulled at the string and emptied its contents into an empty bowl. "Oh my, Susan, what on earth were you doing with these?" The purple velvet bag was filled with brilliant diamonds!

About the Author

E.R. Bendrihem (aka "Rocky"), was born in the Rock of Gibraltar, a British colony in southern Europe and grew up in New York. He received an MBA from Pace University in Finance in New York. He currently resides in South Carolina with his wife Elaine, where he retired from a banking and consulting career. Today, he is a full-time Certified Tax Professional with clients nationwide.

His hobbies include: flying, boating, writing, gardening, carpentry, and barbecuing. He is an avid sports enthusiast following his favorite New York teams.

Last Train to Happiness is his third novel; *In Pursuit of Happiness* was the second novel; and *Believing in Second Chances* was the first novel